THE WORLD IN SHADOW

Books by Theodore Beale

The War in Heaven
The World in Shadow
The Wrath of Angels*

forthcoming

Published by Pocket Books

THE WORLD IN SHADOW

THEODORE BEALE

POCKET BOOKS
New York London Toronto Sydney Singapore

An *Original* Publication of POCKET BOOKS

 POCKET BOOKS, a division of Simon & Schuster, Inc.
1230 Avenue of the Americas, New York, NY 10020

ISBN: 0-671-02454-X

First Pocket Books trade paperback printing September 2002

10 9 8 7 6 5 4 3 2 1

For information regarding special discounts for bulk purchases, please contact Simon & Schuster Special Sales at 1-800-456-6798 or business@simonandschuster.com

Printed in the U.S.A.

This book is for Dr. Greg Boyd,
whose commitment, passion, and faith
are an inspiration and an unforgettable example
to all who encounter him. 16:8.

ACKNOWLEDGMENTS

Special thanks to Frederick R. Dawe and Sgt. Gary Rivet of the St. Paul Police, for their willingness to share their technical expertise with me. Thanks to Scott Shannon and Carol Greenberg of Pocket Books, without whom this series would not exist. And thanks, as always, to Heather.

Contents

THE WORLD IN SHADOW

PROLOGUE

The white-haired pastor lifted the purple stole from around his neck, folded it carefully, and gently placed it in the cabinet drawer. He drew his robe over his head, and as he did so, he noticed that its thick cloth looked faded and yellow beneath the overhead lights. It was time to get a new robe; how long had it been since he'd bought this one, six years ago, maybe even seven?

He glanced at the clock on the corner of his desk. Nine thirty-six, and he'd missed dinner again. Ah well, it wouldn't hurt him to miss a meal, he thought as he ruefully patted the round curve of his paunch. Vanity, my goodness, but everything is vanity. He stared at his reflection in the dark window that looked out over the parking lot. Even past the promised three-score and ten, a man might cling to the tattered shards of his vanity, to the sagging, wrinkled remnants of his youth.

He might, but it would be foolish of him. The pastor frowned at his reflected image and picked up the telephone. There was a single ring, and an answer.

"Hello?"

"Marjorie, it's me."

"Gerald, where have you been?" His wife's voice was neither accusing nor concerned, only mildly curious. "I thought the board meeting was going to be over at eight-thirty."

"So did I." He manfully resisted the temptation to share the uncharitable thoughts that were still flowing rancorously through his mind. "Ed and Linda are concerned about the associate pastorship. They didn't come right out and say it, of course, but they may as well have. It seems that the general view of the congregation is that I'm liable to drop dead at any moment!"

1

His outrage was apparent to his wife of fifty-one years, but she betrayed no hint of the knowing smile that crossed her lips to the other side of the telephone line.

"I'm sorry, dear," she told him sincerely. She listened patiently as he vented his wounded feelings before weighing in with her own opinion. He paused to take a breath, and she seized her opportunity. "But they do have a point, you know."

"A point?" Pastor Woodhouse stopped his pacing at this attack from an unexpected front. "You think . . . I mean, you agree with them? You think I'm too old?"

His wife chuckled. "Not for me, Gerald. And surely not for God. But I always knew the day would come when it would be time for you to step down from the pulpit, and I knew it would be hard for you. Now, maybe that day isn't here yet, but it is something you need to think about. And pray about."

Gerald was silent for a long time. Then his wounded sense of pride abruptly disappeared, like a balloon popping before the pinprick of his wife's gentle wisdom. He laughed suddenly, the same hearty, rolling laugh that had won her heart so many years ago.

"Of course, you're right, Marjorie. What was I thinking? This church needs new blood, a young man with spirit and energy, not a tired old Methuselah like me."

He heard Marjorie make a clucking noise over the phone line.

"Now, don't you be writing your resignation tonight, either, Gerald Woodhouse!" She knew her husband very well, and his thoughts were transparent to her. "Come home, I'll put a log on the fire, and we'll talk about it over a nice hot cup of tea."

"Okay," he agreed ruefully. "I'll be home in ten minutes."

"Drive carefully, my love. That nice young woman on Channel Nine says the roads are rather slippery tonight."

"I will," he promised her. "Be home in a bit, honey."

"Bye, dear." There was a click and the line went dead.

In like a lion, out like a lamb. Those words sounded nice enough, but whoever wrote them never lived through a March in

Minnesota, Gerald thought critically as he fumbled for his keys under the parking lot lights. It had been fifty-six degrees only two days ago, but the temperature had dropped below freezing again, and the misty rain of the early evening had hardened into pellets of ice that now pummeled his exposed face and hands. It felt as if he were being bombarded by a barrage of invisible needles, tiny jabs that stung but did not penetrate.

A sudden tightness gripped his chest, like a massive hand grabbing him over the left shoulder, and he dropped his keys. As they struck the pavement with a jangling sound, the invisible hand squeezed, and Gerald grunted, first in surprise, and then in pain. He clutched the roof rack of his Oldsmobile to steady himself, and he tried to inhale, but found that he couldn't, for the pressure on his chest prevented him from taking any but the shortest of breaths.

"Heavenly Father, be with me!" he gasped aloud, and the cold, and the wind, and the pain abruptly disappeared. A peaceful warmth enveloped him, as if a pair of strong arms were holding him from behind, offering gentle support and strength. He closed his eyes, leaning back into those restful arms, and then he smiled.

Ah, how great thou art, he silently praised the God he had served for so many years. How great thou art!

CHAPTER 1

THE IDES OF MARCH

IN MY EYES, INDISPOSED
IN DISGUISE AS NO ONE KNOWS
HIDES THE FACE, LIES THE SNAKE . . .
—Soundgarden ("Black Hole Sun")

Jami stared intently at her Bible, but she was not reading any of the words on the tissue-thin paper. She was instead trying to keep a surreptitious eye on her brother, who was sitting on a couch two people over and looking as if he were just about ready to explode. Christopher's social skills had improved a lot over the past few months, but he still forgot to keep his mouth closed sometimes, especially when he was running out of patience.

She winced as she saw that his eyes were closed, and his head was slowly moving from side to side. This was not a good sign. Christopher did that whenever he was trying not to listen to something, and she knew tonight's aimless discussion must be driving him up the wall. It was hard enough for her to sit through it all, and she could listen to one of Holli's endless lectures on the importance of eyeliner without even blinking.

". . . so that your faith might not rest on men's wisdom, but on God's power."

Asako finished reading the verse. She was a cheerful Asian girl with long raven-black hair. "I don't know, I just think that's really neat!"

Christopher's eyes snapped open suddenly. Oh, please help him keep his temper, Jami whispered under her breath.

"You think . . . what?"

Her brother's voice was low and controlled. Too controlled, Jami thought to herself. She could hear the venom lurking beneath his polite tone.

"Well, I just think it's really neat. You know. What the verse says, and all."

Jami had to bite her lip to keep from laughing when she heard Christopher groan, and saw him put his head in his hands. She could understand if he was feeling frustrated tonight, because she was, too. The last hour had been nothing but a repetitive circle of readings followed by agreeable but meaningless responses. It would have been almost funny, if it wasn't so painfully boring. Christopher smiled briefly, and for a second Jami thought they were past the danger zone, but she was wrong.

"I mean, don't you think so?" Asako looked to the rest of the group for support.

There were several nodded heads, and a few voices mumbled assent in one form or another. Jami desperately shook her head at her brother, but he ignored her as he closed his leather-bound Bible with an audible snap and rose to his feet.

"Yeah, it's really neat," Christopher echoed sarcastically. "It is the eternal Word of the Creator Lord of the Universe, and it's neat, you say? Well, that's tremendously insightful. We can all agree on that, can't we? The Bible is neat! It's really, really neat!"

Now it was Jami's turn to put her head in her hands. She didn't have to look up to know there were ten horrified sophomores, juniors, and seniors all staring at her brother with open mouths. This wasn't the first time he'd gone off like this in public.

Mr. Maples, the youth pastor who led the study group and was the only adult there, tried to defend poor Asako, whose cheeks were bright red.

"Really, Christopher, it's important that everyone shares their feelings—"

"No, it's not!" her brother interrupted impatiently, his brown eyes blazing. "How many times do we need to repeat this nonsense? Look, we're all Christians here, right? And this is a Bible study, right? So can we just, once and for all, agree that everything in the Bible is really, really neat? Then no one has to mention it ever again! Yes, it's all neat and it's all good and it's all important—so what? Can't we just forget about how it makes us feel, and for once talk about what it says we should do?"

"Sure we can," Mr. Maples assured him. "That's what we're here for, after all."

"Then why don't we ever do that?" Christopher asked, his voice suddenly soft. He pointed toward one muscular senior, a football player. "Blaine, you were asking why our prayers don't get answered, like when we prayed for Jim's shoulder and it didn't get better. Well, maybe it's because we don't do what we're told, or maybe it's because we really don't have enough faith. That could be all it is, you know? Either we have enough faith or we don't, and the evidence would seem to suggest that we don't!"

The youth leader frowned. He was a friendly, good-looking red-haired man, whose only flaw, as far as Jami was concerned, was the cheesy mustache which appeared to be some sort of occupational hazard. But, she realized, he wasn't really equipped to deal with her brother, at least not in this argument.

"I don't know, Christopher, I think you're treading on dangerous ground there. I mean, the last thing you want to do is question someone else's faith. Suppose there's a person who had a car accident, and they're in a wheelchair now. Is it fair to blame them for being in that wheelchair, to tell them that if they had enough faith, they could be healed? That's being pretty judgmental, and I don't think you'd want to go there."

Christopher smiled thinly. "Is it judgmental or is that just how it goes? Tell me, how many times in the Gospels does Jesus come right out and tell people that they had too little faith, Bob?"

Mr. Maples frowned and scratched at his mustache. Jami sighed, knowing Christopher wouldn't have asked the question if he didn't know the answer already.

"Why, I don't know."

"Twelve times, Bob. Twelve times. And he said, according to your faith will it be done to you. And he also said that nothing was impossible for us. Nothing. So I don't understand where the problem is. If the mountain moves, you've got enough faith. If it doesn't, you don't, end of story."

No one responded right away, not even Mr. Maples, to Jami's surprise. Christopher shook his head, in sheer frustration, Jami thought, not without sympathy.

"Look, I'm sorry, everybody, but I just don't see any point in what we're doing here tonight." He reached behind the couch and retrieved his blue jacket. "I should probably go. I'll see you all later."

Most of the girls were too surprised and upset to say anything, but Jami saw that Scott and Blaine, the Bible study's two seniors, were more amused than offended. Mr. Maples, though, looked worried as he walked her brother to the door and softly told him to take care.

"Well," the youth leader said as he returned to the living room. "That was certainly interesting! Does anyone want a can of pop or anything before we go on to verse six?"

Jami thanked Mrs. Maples for having them over, then walked out into the darkness as the door closed behind her. It was cold, and she could see her breath floating before her. The night sky was dull and dark as the clouds lingered overhead, threatening more snow, and she could not see the moon or the stars. But she was not afraid of the night anymore, not as she'd once been. Although she couldn't see her guardian angel any better than she could see the moon right now, she knew that Paulus was just as real and that he was somewhere nearby, watching over her and keeping her safe from evil.

Sometimes, she thought, it was easier to remember you were a Christian than others. It wasn't that she didn't believe in Jesus anymore or forgot who He was when she was at school or with her friends. It was just that it was so easy to fall into the flow of things, to go to school, hang out with everybody, and just live your life.

Sometimes that was really all you did. And was that such a bad thing, when you were fifteen years old? What was she supposed to do anyhow? She was a freshman, after all, not a superhero. What was she supposed to do, like, save the world from itself?

Her boots made squeaky, crunching noises as she walked over the remnants of the icy snow that had fallen the day before, and as she passed the last of the study group's parked cars, she saw her brother standing under the pale yellow glow of a lamppost on the other side of the street. His back was to her, and despite the cold, he was still holding his jacket in his folded arms. She knew he could hear her approaching, but she didn't call out to him. Instead, she stopped a few feet behind him and waited for him to break the silence.

"I know what you're going to say," he told her. "And I will go back and apologize to everyone. But not now. Not tonight. I need to think first, and I can't think around those people."

Okay, she nodded thoughtfully, feeling a little relieved at his relaxed tone. That was fair enough. Except that he was wrong about what she was thinking.

"That wasn't what I was going to say at all," she told him.

He turned around, and she saw a brief flash of amusement in his eyes. "Well, thanks for not getting on my back and all, but you're still telling me I'm wrong, right?"

"No!" she said, just to be difficult, and he rolled his eyes.

"Hey, I understand why you're so frustrated," she told him honestly as she leaned over and punched his shoulder. "At least, I understand some of it. But what I don't understand is why you, of all people, expect them to be any different than they are?"

And she didn't understand. What they both knew to be true, beyond any shadow of a doubt, was mostly hypothetical to everybody else. How could you blame people for doubting what, to them, was mostly poetic-sounding words on a thin piece of paper? Sure, most of them knew the truth, but they just couldn't believe in it the same way that she and Christopher could. They hadn't seen it in action, hadn't had it slap them in the face. She knew her brother probably understood this on an intellectual level, but he still seemed to hold something against their newly made friends anyhow.

"But they should believe," he argued. "I know they say they do, but it's just words, that's all. What bugs me is that even if you haven't seen Jesus face to face, or haven't personally stuck a flaming sword into an angel, any reasonable reading of the Bible makes it quite clear that there's a heavenly war going on, right? But you'd never know it by what was going on back there!"

"But they fight in their own way, you know that. They pray. They sing and praise God. The war isn't the same as it was on Ahura Azdha, Christopher, it's different here."

She thought Christopher was shaking his head, disagreeing with her, until she realized he was only shivering. A light, icy rain had begun to fall, and she'd been too absorbed in their conversation to notice. Christopher hadn't, either, and she was willing to bet he'd forgotten he had a jacket draped over his arm.

"Oh, put your coat on, you idiot! You'll freeze!"

"Oh, yeah, thanks," he said lamely as he slipped it on and quickly zipped it up. "Man, it's cold out here! Wasn't it about fifty degrees warmer, like, two days ago?"

"I hate March. It's the worst."

Christopher made a face and stuck his hands in his pockets. "I know you're right, but here's the thing that gets me. There was this movie on the other night; it was pretty bad, but it made me think about us."

"What movie?"

"You wouldn't know it. It was a remake of an old Heinlein novel, *Starship Troopers,* but that's not the point—"

"Wasn't Denise Richards in that?" Jami interrupted him.

"Who?"

"Dark hair, pretty, big chest, can't act."

"Oh, her. Yeah, that's the one. Anyhow, the movie wasn't very good, and I think the costume designer had some kind of fascist thing going on, but one thing was perfect. Everybody, from the highest general all the way down to the kids, knew that there was a war going on, and that the war was something to take seriously.

And then here we are in this war that's got eternal implications, I mean, we're talking about people losing their souls forever, not just their lives, and yet it barely affects us at all! We act like nothing's happening! Not most of the time, anyhow."

Jami nodded, but inwardly she was cringing a little. A similar line of thought had crossed her mind uncomfortably from time to time, but she'd always been able to distract herself and avoid thinking about it. Maybe they were supposed to be Warriors now, but except for going to church once or twice a week, their lives hadn't really changed all that much from before.

Her face must have been showing her chagrin, because her brother patted her on the shoulder.

"Look, I really didn't mean to go off on anyone tonight. It's just that I was sitting there listening to everyone spin their wheels, and I suddenly realized, hey, that's exactly what I'm doing, which is basically nothing. But the worst thing is that they've got an excuse. I don't."

Jami studied Christopher's face. It was the same as it always was, thin and winter-pale, marred by a reddish band of acne that crossed the bridge of his nose. But his brown eyes, half-hidden behind his long bangs, looked older than they should. It was as if someone had stolen his own eyes from him and replaced them with those of a haunted stranger. Despite their past differences, it made her feel sad.

"You know, Christopher, one of these days we've really got to talk about what happened to you back there."

"Back then," he corrected her, then pushed her toward their green Explorer, which was parked three cars down. "I know, we probably should, but there's some things I don't want to think about right now, okay? Much less talk about."

The lights flashed and there was a loud clicking noise as the doors unlocked themselves at their approach. Christopher pulled the keys from his pocket and they each opened their own door.

"So what do you think we should be doing?" she asked as she clambered up onto the seat on the passenger's side.

Christopher started the engine, then leaned back in his seat and ran a hand through his hair. "I don't know, sis, I don't know. But I know one thing." He waggled his Bible as he reached back and tossed it gently onto the backseat. "I know where to look."

Melusine watched nervously as the white-haired old man breathed his last in front of her. The freezing temperature did not bother her in the least, although her meager attire would have been more suitable for Maui than Minnesota at this time of year, at least if she'd been human. But she wasn't human, and her black-feathered wings and slender, snaky tail would surely have attracted a good deal of attention on the beaches of Hawaii. Or anywhere, for that matter.

But right now, attention was the last thing Melusine sought. In fact, she was doing her best to keep the large, horned mass of Ar-Balazel between her and the giant black-skinned archangel who was holding the dying man in his muscular arms. Tears of grief streaked the Guardian's face as he whispered reassuring words of comfort to the man. The old man did not speak, and his lips did not move, but Melusine felt the silent echo of his final praise to Heaven's King rip through her spirit like an electric shock.

The unpleasant sensation was only momentary, and as it faded, she saw the Guardian laying his mortal charge's lifeless, empty vessel down gently onto the cold asphalt of the parking lot. Melusine cringed as the archangel dashed away tears from his dark face with one hand and reached for the giant sword he'd dropped with the other. That sword had already cut down Gezerael, the Mordrim who'd instigated the old man's heart attack, and judging by the fire in the Divine angel's grief-stricken eyes, he wasn't the only Fallen who was going to feel its bite tonight.

"You have won no victory here!" the big Guardian shouted, pointing his sword at Balazel. "You thought to destroy him, but already he stands in glory before the Lord Most High!"

The powerful archdemon did not trouble to argue with the angry angel; instead, he spread his hands in open defeat and ducked his horned head in a gesture of submission.

"It was within my authority to pursue him, Ar-Shakael, you

must admit that. This is within the Prince Bloodwinter's demesne. But his soul has escaped me, and the victory is yours."

"The victory is not mine, it belongs to Him who sits on the throne." The Divine angel sheathed his weapon, but his grieving rage was undimmed. "And to the Lamb!"

"Yes, yes, of course," Balazel conceded easily. "Whatever you say. But this battle is over now, isn't it? Go find some of your white-winged friends, and you can all sing praises for the safety of your blessed mortal's soul all night long."

Melusine quietly breathed a sigh of relief as Shakael nodded slowly.

"I will do just that, Balazel. And though you are graceless and defeated, I will say a prayer for your spirit as well." He started to turn away, then stopped and turned back to face the two Fallen angels. "When you next see Gezerael, tell him I have forgiven him, but I have not forgotten."

And with those ominous words, the archangel leaped into the sky, arcing heavenward like a shooting star in reverse.

Balazel shook his head as they watched the Divine angel depart. "I thought he'd never leave."

"Yeah, well, I thought he'd take us out," Melusine hissed, more than a little irritated at the other demon. Balazel had risked much by taunting the archangel, and for all his great power, his style was far too risky for her liking. Still, the way he'd choreographed the mortal's end had been rather amusing, she admitted to herself—at least it was now that they were safe. "Oh, did you see the look in his eyes when he realized what Gezerael had done?"

"I did indeed," Balazel snorted. "His agony was exquisite. Sheer poetry! I didn't think poor Shaka would be quite so upset, but those Divine fools never see the whole picture."

Melusine nodded. "They always get wrapped up with their little trees and forget about the forest. How many more lives are you hunting here, Baron?"

"Four, but only two of them are of real import."

Balazel sounded relaxed, so Melusine was taken by surprise

when he suddenly reached out and seized her face with one horny hand. She gasped and tried to pull away, but it was no use; the demonic baron's grasp was far too strong. He squeezed her cheeks uncomfortably hard, grinding them painfully against her teeth as he leaned toward her, whispering softly and deliberately into her ear.

"And you, my lovely temptress, must keep your little boy out of my way, understand? If he interferes just once, I'll add him to the list. Do you understand? And if that costs you his soul, I'll be sure you pay the price!"

Chapter 2

Those Who Stalk the Night

The great purpose of school can be realized better in dark, airless, ugly places. . . . It is to master the physical self, to transcend the beauty of nature. School should develop the power to withdraw from the external world.
—William Torrey Harris, *The Philosophy of Education*

The last bell rang, and Brien Martin slipped his heavy economics textbook into his backpack with some relief. Econ was mostly for brain-dead idiots who couldn't figure out how to balance a checkbook, but it was required for graduation, so he was forced to suffer through it. It wasn't always that bad, though; the fantasy stock-market game had been fun and he'd found some pleasure in trouncing his classmates, turning his five thousand dollars of fake money into nine thousand three hundred by the end of the month. Even Miss Beverly had been impressed, since the second-place contestant had only managed to make an additional two thousand dollars on her investments.

Also, Econ was the only class he had with Tessa Fenchurch. She wasn't one of the in-crowd, her sandy-brown hair was straight and unremarkable, and her features were too sharp to be what most guys considered pretty, but Brien had secretly harbored a crush on her since she'd transferred to Mounds Park two years ago. Her father was into some kind of international business, and her family had been living in England for a while before they'd moved back to North Oaks. Tessa lived less than four miles from him, and they'd even ridden the same school bus in tenth grade, but in three years he hadn't said much more than hi to her. But every day he surreptitiously admired her and planned what he might say to her after class, plotting a hundred different ways to ask her out.

And this Friday was just like every other day, for as the bell rang, his courage deserted him and he shuffled out of the classroom with only four people in between them. Instead of heading straight for his locker, which was on the north side of Senior Hall, he followed her down the stairs that led to the cafeteria. Her locker was on the south side, but this longer route was quicker since it avoided the crush of people filling the hall, and she took it almost every day.

Brien walked slowly, allowing Tessa to pull away from him. He stopped at the soda machine, inserted his money, and pushed the Sprite button. He popped the top on the ice-cold can and sipped at it, enjoying the sweet, crackling taste of the clear soda as it trickled down his throat, then continued on through the cafeteria. Making his way past the small lockers belonging to the sophomores who crowded the stairs was no problem, and he saw that his timing had been perfect again as he reached the top step. Tessa had already opened her locker and was facing him as she returned her Econ book to the neat, light blue-papered shelves that organized her storage space.

Their eyes met briefly. Tessa's were hazel, a little on the narrow side and undecorated by any makeup, but they opened a bit wider as recognition sparked in them. Brien smiled, nodded slightly, and was rewarded with a friendly greeting.

"Oh, hi, Brien."

Her voice was kind of flat and high-pitched, but to Brien, hearing his name on her lips magically transformed her voice into that of an angel. He found that he couldn't speak, he only nodded again, and, in sudden embarrassment, looked down. For one stricken moment, he felt trapped, as if his beating heart was exposed for everyone around them to see. Then he was past her, and the awful feeling was gone, replaced by a wonderful sense of exhilaration. Not only had she said hi to him, but she'd said his name, too! Ten minutes ago, Brien wouldn't have bet a whole lot on her even knowing what it was.

He took a deep breath and stood up straighter as he walked past the clusters of girls in excited conversation about the inevitable Friday night parties and groups of guys plotting to buy beer for the weekend.

"No, seriously, I know this dude," he heard one boy say. "His brother will . . ."

He never learned what the brother would do as his path took him next past a loud, annoying black-haired girl with a vicious look on her face.

"Don't you dare tell Kathy about it!"

He idly wondered what it was that Kathy could not know. Probably a party, or maybe the black-haired girl had been messing around with Kathy's boyfriend. He froze for a second, and the heady, happy feeling abruptly deserted him when he saw Kent Petersen laughing at a joke someone was telling. His avid tormentor since the ninth grade, Kent wasn't very big, but what he lacked in height, he more than made up for in meanness. He was close now, too close, less than ten feet away from Brien. Alarmed, Brien looked down to avoid meeting the other boy's eyes and slipped behind the steroid-built bulk of a football player, then shoved his way past two girls stuffing their homework into backpacks. He felt his backpack bump into one of them, but he did not dare to stop and apologize.

"Hey!" the girl protested.

"Sorry," Brien muttered under his breath, and then he was past her, out of Kent's sight and out of danger. He breathed a sigh of relief when he reached his locker and rapidly spun the combination dial: 34-16-35. It was an easy combo, and he could do it quickly, thank goodness. He didn't want to linger too long at his locker, just in case Kent and his posse of soccer buddies were looking for someone to beat on.

But even as he hurried, the fear of being bullied passed quickly from his mind. Even the thought of Kent couldn't keep him down for long, as his imagination spun a romantic fantasy of how he would drop by Tessa's house tonight, and invite her out to a fancy restaurant for dinner on Friday. Tessa would be surprised and flattered, and then, when he confessed over candlelight that he'd been in love with her since their sophomore year, she would blush, smile shyly, and then admit that she, too, had been harboring feelings for him. . . .

"Hey, Bry, whas'sup?"

Derek Wallace's reedy voice intruded on his romantic daydream, and he turned around reluctantly.

"What?" he demanded.

"What do you mean, what. As of today, it's officially six weeks to graduation. Twenty-eight working days, dude!"

Derek was a tall, skinny boy with white skin, long black hair, and a thin, sensitive face cursed with a bad complexion. He was Brien's only real friend at Mounds Park. He raised his hand expectantly and Brien dutifully slapped it.

"And then we're out of this hole. College will be so much cooler than this! At least we won't be surrounded by losers and idiots all the time."

And jocks, Brien added mentally. Let them be damned to their community colleges and vo-tech schools forever! They could keep their stupid memories of their glory days here, because once he got off the waiting list at Northwestern, he had it made. The guidance counselor had assured him that with his SAT scores, it was only a matter of time before he was accepted. It's all right, it's okay, he thought savagely, you can work for me someday!

"So what are you doing tonight?" Derek asked him, placing his hands together in an odd manner.

Brien looked around to see if anyone was watching, then inverted his right hand and placed his fingertips against his left palm, as he held up his pinky and index finger. It was the secret sign of La Nottambuli, Derek's fantastic guild of darkness to which they both belonged. The gesture was an invitation, and Brien had signaled his acceptance by returning it. Derek didn't have to tell him where the gathering would take place; it wasn't necessary. There was only one meeting place for those who stalked the night. His dream date with Tessa would have to wait for another time.

Jami sneaked a peek at the back of her textbook, and groaned when she realized her answer was wrong again. According to the answer key, the mysterious X, for no good reason that she could see, was four, not three. I hate math! It's so stupid! And quadratic equations were the absolute worst, that was for sure. Chewing with frustration on the end of her pencil, she sank back into the cushy corner of the couch and glared at the book from a safe distance.

It didn't help that Christopher was walking through the room every five minutes as if he was in a hurry to go somewhere. But he never left, he just kept marching in and out of the family room, until she was about ready to sharpen her pencil and stick it in his ear. Holli had been sitting in the kitchen talking on the phone for the last twenty minutes, with someone from school, from what Jami had overheard, but she was used to hearing her twin's voice and so it didn't bother her as much as Christopher's annoying interruptions.

Christopher marched in again, and Jami had finally had enough of it.

"Knock it off!" she cried, leaping off the couch and brandishing her pencil at him.

Her brother blinked and stepped back. He didn't look deep in thought anymore, now he just looked surprised. Surprised and a little alarmed. She and Holli had finally managed to talk him into cleaning himself up a bit over the last three months, and his hair no longer hid his eyes like a sheepdog with split ends, but there were times like this when she was convinced they'd taken on a hopeless task. Sometimes, she thought, he was just weird, and there wasn't anything they could do about it.

"Huh?" he said finally, like an idiot.

"What do you mean, huh?" she replied angrily. "I'm trying to get my homework done, and you've been walking in and out of here all night like some kind of psycho cuckoo clock that can't tell time! Don't you have anything better to do?"

Christopher nodded in apparent understanding. "Oh, yeah, sorry 'bout that." He rubbed at his eyes. "That's exactly what I was thinking."

Huh? Okay, now she was the confused one. "I don't get it."

"That's just the point. Remember what we were talking about after Bible study last Tuesday? We're supposed to be warriors." Christopher punched his palm. "So we should be doing something, not just sitting around the house like three kids in high school!"

"Hello, we are three kids in high school, just in case you forgot." Jami pointed to the math book. "Do you think I'd be doing this stupid algebra if we weren't?"

Her brother rolled his eyes. "That's not the point, James. The point is, I think we should be doing something worthwhile, something that would help make a difference. We can't do that by sitting around inside here!"

Jami looked out the window to the backyard. It was snowing again, sort of, and even though it was supposed to be spring in a few weeks, there was still plenty of unmelted gray ice bordering the walk and the driveway. The mounds of snow that had been heaped up on the deck over the last four months had shrunk noticeably, but they were still there, dingy and hardened by the icy rain of the last few days. And it was dark, too. The sun had disappeared hours ago, and the night sky was about as close to pitch black as it got this close to the Cities this time of year.

"What do you want to do, go out and patrol the neighborhood, looking for fallen angels to mess with? You've been watching too much Buffy, Christopher. It doesn't work like that in real life."

"I know a lot more about the Fallen than you do." His voice was starting to rise and she could tell he was getting irritated with her. "So, yeah, maybe that's exactly what I'm going to do!"

Okay, whatever. She shook her head and fell back onto the couch, reaching for her textbook. She still had ten problems left, and this was not a conversation she was going to waste any more time on.

"Don't forget your stake, then," she said mockingly.

"What?" He looked puzzled, then understanding dawned in his eyes. "Oh, shut up!"

She laughed at him as he spun around and stomped into the front hallway. Still amused, she listened intently as he took a coat and something that sounded like a dog leash from the hall closet, then slammed the front door as he left the house. I wonder if he's got a paper he's trying to avoid or something like that, she thought to herself.

"What was that all about?" Holli asked as she came out of the kitchen.

"Oh, nothing. Christopher's taking Duke for a walk, that's all. Who're you talking to?"

"Paul Johnson. You know him."

Jami stared at her twin, puzzled.

"Of course I know him, he's on my indoor team. The senior." What was up with this? She was surprised Holli even knew the guy. She usually only noticed the football studs and the pretty boys. "What were you talking to him for so long for? Was he calling me?"

Her twin shrugged innocently. "Yeah, he said to tell you that Jason somebody—"

"Jason Case?"

"Yeah, that's what it was. Anyhow, he can't come on Saturday, so bring someone to play for him if you know anybody."

"Um, okay. Thanks." Jami filed a mental note to think about it later and started to return to her algebra, but the equations and numbers now seemed strangely out of focus on the pages in front of her. She closed her eyes hard and blinked, but it didn't do any good. 2X this, 4Y that, whatever! What little sense the math had been making to her abruptly disappeared in a swirling cloud of cryptic variables.

A thought struck her. "Holli?" she called after her sister, who'd vanished into the kitchen again.

"Yeah?" Holli stuck her head around the corner. "What?"

"Did Christopher ever tell you much about what happened to him? You know, about what happened when he was on Ahura Azdha? I mean, like, the stuff that happened before we found him."

Holli twirled a delicate white curl around her finger and shook her head thoughtfully. "No, not really," she said. "I asked him if he wanted to talk about it once, and he said no, so I kind of left it alone."

Jami nodded. She'd tried prying the story out of Christopher more than once herself, but hadn't managed to get anything out of him, either. She sighed and slumped back on the couch with her arms crossed, thinking about the three times she'd seen him on that ancient world that God's angel had destroyed. No, it was twice, she corrected herself, because the last time, the time he'd saved them, had been right here on Earth, at the elementary school, of all places.

An unwanted vision entered her mind, and she shuddered at the frightening memory of a rage-filled face of gold, the face of a demonic killer of angels, the face of her brother. Then a disturbing thought occurred to her. Christopher had been an angel-killer himself, and even if Khasar, for one, hadn't stayed dead, that didn't mean Christopher didn't know what he was talking about. He probably did know a lot more about the Fallen than she did, and why, who knew what he might have gotten himself into already? All thoughts of algebra disappeared from her mind.

A moment later Holli was yelling at her from the kitchen. "What's going on? What are you doing?"

"I'm, ah, just going out for a run!" Jami shouted back as she rifled through the coat closet in the front hall. Well, that was true, after all, she was going to run. She didn't feel like telling Holli anything more, because her sudden worries sounded stupid, even to herself. Maybe it's nothing, after all. No sense in freaking both of us out for no good reason. Finally! She found the nylon Adidas pullover she'd been searching for and slipped it over her head, then jammed her feet into her old Nike crosstrainers.

"Back in a few!" she yelled as she ran out the door. Holli might have responded, but outside, the night wind was much louder, and Jami could barely even hear the glass storm door as it banged violently shut behind her. It was cold, bitterly cold, and for a second Jami wondered if she should go back into the house and put on something warmer. But there was something urgent about this sudden compulsion to find Christopher, so she decided to fight the cold by running instead.

She headed down the cul-de-sac at a quick but easy pace. It was dark, as there weren't any streetlights on their dead end street, but she'd run this route dozens of times, training for one sport or another, and she knew where she was going. The only question was if Christopher had crossed the boulevard into Sims Court, or followed it down to the park at the lake. Well, they lived at the very end of their street, so she had a little while before she had to make up her mind.

The big oak trees for which the avenue had been named didn't look so friendly now by night. Their twisted branches arched high over her head, creaking weirdly like an alien life-form muttering threats she couldn't quite understand. They were like a moaning army of giants, surrounding her on every side. They were giving her the creeps, and she increased her pace in nervous anticipation. The ice-rain stung her face a little bit, but that was okay. At least it gave her something else to think about and kept her imagination from running away with itself. Trees! She snorted, irritated with herself for being so jumpy. What was a tree going to do to her anyhow, fall on her?

CHAPTER 3

AN EVENING RUN

YET GOD HATH PLACED BY THE SIDE OF EACH A MAN'S OWN GUARDIAN SPIRIT, WHO IS CHARGED TO WATCH OVER HIM—A GUARDIAN WHO SLEEPS NOT NOR IS DECEIVED. . . . SO WHEN YOU HAVE SHUT THE DOORS AND MADE A DARKNESS WITHIN, REMEMBER NEVER TO SAY THAT YOU ARE ALONE; FOR YOU ARE NOT ALONE, BUT GOD IS WITHIN, AND YOUR GUARDIAN SPIRIT, AND WHAT LIGHT DO THEY NEED TO BEHOLD WHAT YOU DO?

—Epictetus

Melusine was not in the mood for all this activity tonight. She'd done her best to distract Christopher from his sudden onset of conscience, but Paulus, Mariel, and Aliel had ganged up on her and kept her away from the boy. It wasn't her fault, though, because if Shaeloba and Pandaema had been where they were supposed to be, namely, here with her and keeping an eye on their twins, the cursed Guardians wouldn't have been able to push her around.

And now, since Pandaema was still trailing along after Shaeloba like a boy with a crush on his baby-sitter, Melusine was stuck following Jami. She hoped the little rat would trip and break her neck; after all, it wouldn't cost her anything if the girl went straight to Heaven, and a little grief and loss might help strengthen Christopher's fading spirit of bitterness. She sighed as she spread her black wings and coasted on the powerful night winds high above the running girl. It would never work, of course, but it was a pleasant thought.

And what was Shaeloba up to now? Melusine was pretty sure

that the demoness wasn't going to interfere with Balazel's plans, since the archdemon wasn't one of the local Fallen Lords. Despite his rank, Balazel's favor meant next to nothing here in the Cities. She knew Shaeloba was rather closer to a certain captain of Mordrim than she liked to let on, and she wondered if that nasty band of brutes was plotting against Prince Bloodwinter again. It wouldn't surprise her if that was the case; it had been three years since the last major brouhaha, and the Principality was almost overdue for another wave of angelic rebellion.

Poor Pandaema. She wasn't the brightest of angels, in more ways than one, and she still found it thrilling to get involved in Shaeloba's secret plots. But plots like that were for fools, and it's a good thing you've finally learned better, Melusine grimly told herself. Her lessons had come the hardest way; before the Black Throne of Judgment. She could almost laugh about her naïveté now, almost, but not quite. Five hundred years was a long time to suffer at the hands of the Sons of Sorrow.

She shivered, not due to the coldness of the night air, but at the remembered feel of her tormentor's soft, misleadingly gentle touch. Of all the dark spirits she had encountered, Those Who Bring Remorse were the most twisted, the farthest fallen of all. Surely they had been angels of Raphael's order, for how could they know to cause such pain, if they had not once known how to heal. They were soft of voice, soft of manner; indeed, softness of one kind or another was nearly all she could remember of them now. That, and the pain. Always, there was the pain. How very polite they were, and yet so cruel. She barely remembered what had happened to cause her to fall into their terrifyingly gentle hands.

But she remembered Provence. That summer land, she would never forget. It was the place of her first and only true possession. How exhilarating it had been, to live and taste and feel life as a mortal, to know the passion of the woman for her lover, to savor, to exult, in the hatred of a father for his son. Ah, those had been heady times indeed, intoxicating enough to leave her drunk with ecstasy and power, and wholly devoid of judgment.

Never again, she vowed for the thousandth, the ten thousandth time, never again would she dare to tread the left-hand path. Two rebellions were quite enough for any angel, and now she would be the loyal warrior, the cunning temptress, the artful seducer; whatever was required, and if Lord Balazel saw fit to reward her, then so much the better. If a safe and easy opportunity presented itself, she would not hesitate to seize it, of course. But that was something altogether different, and she was done with intrigue, that much she knew.

"It's just not worth it!" she shouted down at the running girl.

Jami didn't hear her, of course. What did this girl know about power and treachery, of betrayal and punishment? Nothing, and yet the silly mortal might hope to defeat her simply by calling on The Name. It galled her! It was so wrong! It was unfair! Why did Heaven's King care so much for these petty beings, who dried up and died like the autumn leaves of this cold and ugly land? Even this little girl knew less about beauty than the lowliest angel. Really, she thought contemptuously, the King of Heaven must lack any sense of aesthetics.

"Christopher!" Jami kept shouting for her brother as she ran, even though she knew he was probably out of earshot. "Duke? Christopher!"

As she turned the last corner, she caught sight of the streetlight marking the intersection with the boulevard below, and the warm glow of the light made her feel a little less twitchy. But now she had to decide, straight or go right? She could go left, too, but she knew he'd never have gone that way; it led right into the collection of strip malls that passed for the town center.

"Show me which way to go, Lord," she whispered toward the heavens. Then she stopped to catch her breath, and touched the yellow-and-black Dead End sign that was her talisman for a run finished, her personal punctuation mark for completing yet another four-mile circuit of Lake Johanna.

She'd run a little harder than she'd meant to, and it was hard to hear anything but the wind over the sound of her own breathing. For a second, she thought she might have heard something in the distance, and she held her breath, listening intently. But there was nothing but silence, and she exhaled deeply, then started to cough. Running in the cold always made her cough; she didn't know why, but she hated it. At least it wasn't cold enough to freeze her eyelashes the way it did in January.

Just as she stopped coughing, she heard a dog bark somewhere ahead of her. Another dog answered it, and then a third, but as Jami listened to the three dogs, she realized that the first dog sounded angry, or maybe scared. The other two were just yapping, she was pretty sure, but there was something different about the way the first dog was barking.

"That's Duke," she told herself. "Maybe it's Duke. Only one way to find out."

She couldn't help feeling annoyed, though, as she ran up the hill in the center of the road. The boulevard was nicely and brightly lit, while Sims Court was even darker and woodier and scarier than her own street. She remembered her first Halloween, and how they'd been forbidden to cross the boulevard to trick-or-treat on the other side. The houses were older there, and smaller, and she remembered Christopher telling her once that the older boys who lived in that neighborhood liked to hide in the bushes and leap out shrieking at little kids passing by, scaring them half to death.

The barking grew louder as she approached the top of the hill, and just as the road flattened out, she spotted the barking dog despite the darkness. It wasn't much more than a white blob, and she couldn't see it very well, but she was pretty sure it was their Brittany.

"Duke?" she called, and the dog wheeled around, continuing to bark as he ran toward her. He jumped up on her, and his claws raked her hands as she tried to push him off her.

"Off! Get off me, you dumb dog! Off!"

Cheerfully unrepentant, he stopped jumping on her and slobbered on her hand instead.

"Jami, is that you?"

Christopher startled her as he stood up suddenly, not far from where Duke had been. He was standing under a tree, looking at something that she couldn't quite make out, and his dark blue jacket had hidden him from her sight. But as she waved at him and stepped cautiously onto the crusty, rain-slicked snow toward him, she saw he had a worried look on his face.

"Yeah, it's me. What are you doing?"

He pointed to the object on the ground. "I think something's wrong with this guy; Duke was barking, and when I went to check it out, I saw this guy just lying here on the side of the road. I got here right before you did."

It was a man, Jami realized. He was a black man, an older guy about her dad's age, and he was lying on his side. His face was twisted and his arms were cradled around his chest, but his eyes were closed. He didn't seem to be moving.

"Is he dead?" Jami asked as she stared uneasily at the man.

"I don't know. I tried to see if he was breathing, but I couldn't tell. I couldn't wake him up, though.

"So what should we do?"

"Get help—" Jami started to say, but a loud crack interrupted her. It sounded almost like thunder, but without the boom. There was a thud, and she blinked with surprise as Christopher fell to the ground almost at her feet. She froze, and looked around wildly, wondering what had knocked him down.

"Christopher?" she asked slowly, then again, with more urgency. "Chris, what's wrong? Are you okay?"

But her brother didn't answer, he just lay there in an oddly crumpled position right on top of the unconscious black man.

"Christopher . . . Christopher! Come on, don't do this to me!" she hissed at him as she felt about his neck for a pulse. It was there, nice and strong, and if it wasn't for the fact that he'd just been talking to her a second ago, she could have sworn he was sleeping. Okay, sleeping a little soundly, perhaps, but sleeping was alive, so that was good. He was breathing, too, she assured herself when she felt a faint kiss of warm air on her cheek.

He was all right, thank God. That made her feel a little better. But what happened? Had the Fallen struck him down, too? She was tempted to run, but she couldn't just leave him there, could she?

She rolled him gently off the stranger and onto his back, then leaned over the other guy to take a closer look at him. But when she pushed him onto his back, she saw that his chest, unlike her brother's, wasn't moving. She could hear Christopher breathing steadily, but this man, whoever he was, didn't seem to be.

"Oh . . . son of a beaver!" Jami tried very hard not to panic.

She fell to her knees next to the man and placed her hand on his throat, and then his chest. She couldn't feel anything, but he was still warm, so she wasn't sure if that meant he was dead already or not. Was he having a heart attack, or was it already too late to do anything for him? She glanced up at the closest house and, seeing the flickering blue light of a live television screen through a window, thought for a second about running there to call 911. This man needed help, there was no question about that.

But there wasn't time for that, she realized. The hospital was about fifteen minutes from here, and while she was no doctor, she was pretty sure this guy wasn't going to last that long, if he wasn't dead already. The only help he was going to get would have to come from her.

Now she bitterly regretted that day in September when she, Angie, and Ann Marie skipped out of health class on the day the paramedics came in to teach CPR. Why shouldn't we blow it off, she remembered thinking at the time. It's not like I'm ever going to use it, after all. She shook her head, furious with herself at the thought of how she'd laughed as Angie had dismissed Ann Marie's objections.

"But what if I, like, run into someone who's, I don't know, drowning or something like that?" the curly-haired girl had asked, actually sounding a little concerned about the possibility.

"I don't know, I guess they'll, like, die!" Angie said, grinning wickedly. What were the chances, after all? They'd all laughed at Angie's callous indifference, then spent the afternoon wandering along the paths that meandered through the hills behind their school.

Looking down at the dark face of the man, Jami suddenly didn't find the whole thing so hilarious anymore. It wasn't just unfair, it was stupid; this poor guy might actually die because she was a selfish idiot who blew off class one day.

"I'm sorry, sir," she told the man. "I really am. If I knew what to do, I'd do it. I swear!"

Well, she knew one thing, at least. She'd seen enough *ER* to know that the first thing they did when someone was having a heart attack was to rip off their shirt. Jami took a deep breath and straddled the man's body, then quickly unbuttoned the wool overcoat and the button-down shirt underneath it. His chest was smooth and more muscular than she'd thought it would be—he must lift weights or something, she guessed—but his heart was definitely not beating.

Okay, so far, so good. Now what? She closed her eyes and tried to remember something, anything, from the TV show. But the shock machine was the only thing that popped into her mind, and she sure didn't have one of those with her. That left just one thing.

"God?" If it was his will for this guy to live, then he'd live. She had no doubts on that score; she'd seen way too much of his power in Heaven and on Rahab even to worry about that. The question was, was it his will? How was she supposed to know? "I have no idea what I'm doing, but if you sent me here for a reason, then you're going to have to help me out here!"

She shrugged. Not much of a prayer, maybe, but she was sure he got the point. He was God, wasn't he? All right, then. What had happened before could happen again, couldn't it? She took a deep breath and placed her hands on the man's dark skin.

"Wake up, in Jesus' name."

There was a crackling sound, and then her hands were tingling as the man jerked once underneath her. The sensation was strange; her hands seemed to have fallen asleep all of a sudden, but she could still feel a burning heat in her palms. She stared at them, wondering what, exactly, had just happened. Then she looked down and shrieked, alarmed, when she saw that a pair of very confused brown eyes were staring up at her.

"You're a very nice young lady, I'm sure. . . ."

Jami stared down at the dead man under her, who was showing every sign of not being dead after all. He was breathing, his heart was beating, and then, of course, he was talking to her now as well. His voice was rich and deep; it sounded a little bit southern and and kind of smoky. It made her think of barbecue sauce.

". . . but I think my wife might have a few questions about this, you see."

What? Oh, yeah. She scrambled off his chest, her face warming with embarrassment as she glanced around to see if anyone had seen her. What with his shirt being unbuttoned and all, it must have looked bad. Even worse, Jami didn't know what she should say to him. How were you supposed to tell someone that you might have just raised him from the dead?

"I'm sorry," she told him. "You just . . . you just . . . Well, I thought you maybe needed help."

The black man nodded soberly, and brushed the snow off his coat and trousers as he rose to his feet. He was tall, with broad shoulders that made her think he must have played football when he was younger. He wasn't exactly handsome, but his face was kind, and despite the awkward situation, he was very polite.

"I see," he said slowly as he buttoned his shirt, leaving his dark wool coat hanging open. He coughed twice into a leather-gloved hand, then shrugged. "That is entirely possible, since I don't remember anything. . . . One minute I was leaving my house to go for a little stroll around the block, and the next thing I saw was you sitting on my chest!"

"I'm sorry," she said. "I really don't know what happened to you."

He frowned and looked down at the ground. "I don't suppose you have any idea about who this young man might be?"

Young man? What young man? Oh, no! In the shock of seeing

the man come back to life, she'd forgotten about Christopher. How could she do that?

"He's my brother," she told him as she kneeled at Christopher's side, pushing Duke away. "I think he's all right, but I don't know what happened to him, either."

The man bent down beside her and, after taking off his gloves, carefully cradled Christopher's head in his hands. He checked Christopher's pulse twice, then shrugged off his coat and slipped it under Christopher's body. Shifting his position to get more light, he examined one of his hands before reaching back under Christopher's unmoving head.

"Look at this," he said a moment later, holding two fingertips out toward her.

There wasn't enough light for Jami to see anything, though, on the man's dark hands.

"It's blood," he told her. "Not much, but it looks as if he was struck in the back of the head by something heavy enough to knock him out. . . . In fact, I think I even know what it was!"

He stood up gracefully, then reached over and picked up a large tree branch that was lying a few feet away from Christopher. He glanced at it, then held it out toward her. She could see that one side, the thicker one, was jagged and uneven, and had several large pieces splintered off the end.

"See, look there. See that dark patch there, almost on the edge. That's blood, too. That's where it hit him." He pointed up at the oak tree that towered over them. "And right there you can see where the branch broke off the tree. It's strange, though. That tree is healthy, it's not very old, and the wind doesn't seem to be all that strong. . . ."

Oh, man, she thought. Not again. It couldn't be happening again, could it? Well, if it was, then she only wanted one thing— her guardian angel! Paulus, where the heck are you?

The man looked at her, and he must have realized that she was about to freak out, because he smiled kindly and reached out to touch her shoulder.

"What's your name, honey?"

"Jami," she said. "Jami Lewis. My brother's name is Christopher. We live on the next street over."

"Well, I'm Charles Walters, and I thank you for helping me, Miss Lewis. I just wish I knew why you had to. Now, my wife and I live just down the street, so let's get your brother inside where it's warm, and I'll have Lowell come take a look at him. He's a good doctor, and while he's checking out your brother, perhaps we can call your parents and get some hot chocolate inside you. You're shivering."

CHAPTER 4

THE GEEK SQUAD

I CAME INTO THIS WORLD AS A REJECT
—Limp Bizkit ("Nookie")

Giovanni di Verde watched from the rooftop as the vampire struck, like a flash of ebon lightning. Its victim was a curvaceous young woman, a waitress by trade, who'd chosen a very bad time to retreat into the back alleyway for a smoke break. Giovanni wasn't sure why the vampire preyed on the employees of this particular restaurant, but this was the third time he'd seen it lurking here in as many nights. This kind of repetition was highly unusual, and he wondered if a power struggle among the undead might be the reason behind these strange, reoccurring attacks.

The monster fed quickly, and Giovanni took in the details of its appearance. Its face was that of a beautiful man, but white and hard, as if carved out of the same stone as the marble statues standing before the nearby Duomo. It wore a well-cut gray suit, and a pair of black leather shoes that Giovanni recognized as Ferragamo. The expensive clothing indicated that the vampire surely belonged to the Mostrare clan, the elegant Florentine pretenders who stubbornly refused to submit to the Black Crown of Avignon.

The vampire looked up in shock, blood spilling from its open mouth, as Giovanni caused himself to appear immediately in front of it.

"What . . . who are you?" it stammered. "Where did you come from?"

Giovanni smiled, unconcerned, even as the monster aban-

doned its kill, standing erect and glaring angrily at him with the
eerie red eyes of the undead. "I could ask you the same thing," he
remarked blithely. "Aren't you taking quite a risk, returning to
this place night after night to feed on the unfortunates working
here?"

"My prince sends a message," the vampire told him. "This is
Mostrare ground. The owner is a human who does not understand yet that it is only the mortal mafiosi that Justice has broken,
not us. Soon, he will understand and pay the necessary price for
doing business in our dominion."

It smiled, baring two long canines that looked very white in its
blood-stained mouth. "And what business is it of yours, that you
should spy on me? Aren't you the one taking a stupid risk, magician, in confronting me? Your dark spells will not save you here.
Tell me why I shall not drain your blood"—it gestured at the lifeless body beside it—"as well."

Giovanni laughed, genuinely amused, and made a sign with
his hands. The vampire stepped back with a startled look on its
flawless, petrified face.

"I will tell you why, mosquito of the Mostrare. My prince
also sends a message, a message to your master. The Mostrare
may claim this ground, but the night belongs to us. Your master
will bow before the Black Crown, or be destroyed with all his
spawn."

"Brave words, magician," the vampire spat, and struck.

Its long-nailed hand arced out like a blade, slashing through
Giovanni's neck. The blow was struck so fast and well that Giovanni felt no pain as his head was severed from his body.
Moments later there was a mild sensation of discomfort as the
massive wound healed instantly, and he was again whole. He
blinked, once, and saw the vampire cringing before him with terror, daunted by this miraculous display of immortal power.

"You are no mortal, no mage," the undead monster snarled
fearfully, cringing before him.

"No, I am not," Giovanni agreed as a pair of great charcoal-
gray wings spread out over his shoulders.

"I will bear your message to my prince."

The proud, handsome monster was humble, its voice wheedling.

But Giovanni was unyielding.

"No, you will not," he refused it coldly, and the vampire took fright.

It transformed itself into a cloud of black smoke that was almost invisible in the dim light of the alley, but Giovanni, correctly anticipating the monster's response, caused a small bottle to appear. He chanted a brief spell, and the cloud that was the essence of the vampire began to flow slowly into the bottle. When every wisp of smoke was trapped within the bottle, he sealed the mouth with a twist-cap, then reached into his pocket and withdrew a label, which he pressed onto the bottle. The label bore the address of a residence located in one of the better parts of Florence.

Inside the bottle he could just make out two amber dots of light glowering at him.

"You are the message," Giovanni informed the vampire, and he smiled cruelly.

"Hey, that's not fair," one of the new guys complained. "I didn't know he was a demon!"

Brien glanced at Derek and rolled his eyes. The three new players were Rob's friends, and except for the freshman, who was new to role-playing games altogether, they were old-school Vampire gamers who found it hard to get used to the idea that they weren't so high and mighty anymore. Demon: The Unseen was a new game that Derek had devised himself, combining some of the best elements of Vampire, Werewolf, and Mage, with Brien's old favorite, The Call of Cthulhu. As often as they could, Rob, Jeremy, Derek, and Brien gathered together in the dimly lit basement of Rob's house to play the role of evil spirits wandering the six hundred sixty-six realms of Hell.

"Well, you didn't stop to find out, did you?" Derek pointed out correctly. Tonight, he was dungeon master, the referee in complete control of the game. Aside from some of the super-geeks at GenCon, Derek DM'd a game better than anyone Brien knew. He was fair, but flexible, and always laced his storytelling with dark and mythic color. He had little patience, though, for foolish gamers. "Next time take the time to see what you're up against before you pick a fight."

"Geez, Todd, don't you ever learn?" Rob complained. He shook his head and reached out for the half-empty bowl of Doritos. "This isn't a hack-and-slash like some of those other games, I told you that!"

Rob was their backup dungeon master, a fat junior with long, greasy hair and glasses. He was a great host for their gaming sessions, and always kept them well-supplied with snacks and soda. He seldom saw the sun, and his skin was white enough that he might have passed for one of the undead himself, except for a faint greenish tinge that came from spending hours in front of the computer screen.

"Yeah, well, this whole thing is lame," Todd said in a petulant voice. "What's with this homemade stuff anyhow?"

Brien glanced at Derek, half-expecting an explosion, but Derek only pursed his lips contemptuously and shook his head.

"Just because you have no creativity doesn't mean nobody else does." Derek yawned. "You don't like it, go back to playing Hunt the Wumpus."

Everyone laughed, except for Todd and the freshman.

"Hunt the Wumpus?" The freshman looked confused. He had a mouthful of braces that made him look like he was about twelve years old. "What's that? I've never heard of that."

"It's what we call Dungeons and Dragons," Brien explained helpfully. "In all its myriad editions."

"Oh, okay, I get it." The freshman nodded his head. "I get it. I think."

"So what do you guys want to do next?" Jeremy covered his mouth with his fist and burped loudly. The freshman laughed, a little too hard, and Brien grinned as he saw Derek roll his eyes.

"Anybody want to see my thirty-second level mage on Ever-crack?" Rob asked. "I've got some pretty cool new spells this guy in Brazil traded me."

"Brazil?" The freshman whistled. "That is just so cool! I bet he's got some major voodoo mojo, right?"

The five older boys ignored him as they contemplated Rob's suggestion. It was just after midnight, and Brien knew they weren't going to be able to finish whatever they started. Brien wasn't a huge fan of online role-playing himself, but he was a little curious about Rob's new spells.

"I say we forget this and go blow something up."

Derek was leaning back against a couch with his hands folded behind his head. There was a stunned moment of silence, broken finally by the freshman. Besides Brien, only Rob appeared to be unsurprised.

"Blow stuff up? Do you mean, like, with a pipebomb or something?"

"No, with a freaking ICBM, what do you think, jerky?"

Brien laughed, as did everyone else but Derek and the freshman. Derek and Rob had been engaging in a friendly pyrotechnics competition for years, ever since Rob's father bought him his first package of bottle rockets in eighth grade. It hadn't been long, though, before they'd gone from taping the fireworks to their bike handles and "strafing" the neighborhood garage doors while playing Luftwaffe, to assembling homemade explosives of ever-growing "bang power."

Rob always used the same simple model, just packing more gunpowder into bigger pipes when he sought a bigger bang. Derek, on the other hand, liked to experiment with what he called "delivery packages," and in tenth grade had briefly achieved hero status at school when he detonated a smoke bomb in the principal's car by remote control. He'd been suspended for two weeks when word of the culprit finally made its way around to the authorities, but even Brien's dad admitted that the prank had been pretty impressive.

"That Wallace kid," he remembered Dad chuckling upon hearing about Brien's escapade. Mr. Van Nuys, their old neighbor, had filled Dad in on the latest over beers in the backyard. "He's a handful, I tell you. Too clever for his own good, if you ask me."

"So what do you got?" Rob asked Derek. "I haven't built nothing since we took out the tree stump with Fat Boy Three."

Derek arched an eyebrow mysteriously. "I've got a new delivery package," he told them. "Last weekend I was trying out some stuff from the Cookbook. There's some weird recipes in there, you know. Like, how to make smokables out of banana skins, stuff like that. But there's some interesting packages, too."

Brien was enjoying the half-appalled, half-enraptured look on the freshman's face. Derek could be very convincing when he wanted to be, but Brien knew he was putting the younger boy on. The thing with the bananas didn't work, at least not the two times they'd tried it. You could probably get a better high from shredding a brown paper bag and smoking that instead.

"Okay, so what're you gonna blow up?" Rob asked.

"Oh, shut up!" Todd broke into the conversation. "You guys are so full of it! You're not going to blow up anything!"

Derek stared at the junior for a long, silent moment. When he spoke, he spoke very slowly, as if Todd might have trouble understanding him otherwise. "Yes," he said carefully, enunciating each word. "Yes, Todd, we are."

"I, um, I don't think that's such a good idea," stammered the freshman. "I mean, you know, you can get in trouble for that, don't you think? It's against the law, I'm pretty sure."

"Oh, no—is it?" Derek drawled, and Brien started laughing.

"It's . . . against . . . the law!" He couldn't help it. The wild look in the kid's eyes made him look like a panicked horse trapped in a barn fire. "Jimmy, we're not going to blow up the doggone school! We're talking about, like, a mailbox or something."

"Actually, I'm pretty sure bombing a mailbox is a federal offense," Rob pointed out, as he brushed Doritos crumbs off his chest. Brien noticed that the bowl was empty now. "Not that I care, just FYI, you know?"

"Fed-dead-erals." Derek bobbed his head to an imaginary beat and pushed himself up to his feet. "Look, you losers can do whatever you want. Come along, or not, I don't care. Brien, you're in, right?"

It wasn't really a question. Brien nodded. "Ya."

"All right, well, if you'll excuse us, gentlemen, we have some very important business to attend to, which may or may not involve the reduction of a United States Postal box to its component elements. Meet us outside in about ten minutes if you want to come along; there's something Brien and I have to do first." He paused and made a mock bow to his little audience. "You'll notice I haven't actually told you what we're going to do, thus allowing you to maintain plausible deniability in the extremely unlikely event that anyone happens to harbor a serious interest in the potentially altered state of said mailbox."

He headed for the stairs, and with a quick wave to the others, Brien, grinning, hurried to follow him. They quietly made their way out of the house, being careful not to wake Rob's sleeping parents. But when they reached the Jeep, Derek turned to face Brien with a strange look on his face.

"What is it?" Brien asked him.

Derek shook his head and pulled a rolled-up plastic sandwich bag out of his jacket.

"Were we ever that clueless and geeky? Did we ever need to fit in so bad?"

He didn't have to tell Brien to whom he was referring. Brien nodded slowly, reached into his pocket, then flicked his lighter to fire up the half-smoked fattie in Derek's mouth.

"Yeah, I'm afraid we were."

Derek inhaled thoughtfully. The glare from the house lights passing through the tree branches cast a strangely patterned shadow over his face, as if he were a Maori warrior or maybe a Dark Lord of the Sith. Brien couldn't see his eyes, lost as they were in the darkness.

"I think you're right," Derek said at last, although his voice was too tightly suppressed for Brien to tell if his friend was feeling sad or just reminiscing. Then a cloud of smoke exploded in his face as Derek laughed and was himself again.

"So do you think we should just kill him now and spare him the misery?"

Brien grinned wryly. "That might be kinder."

The Walterses' house was a cozy, unpretentious rambler across the street from the lakeside homes. Mrs. Walters was a tall, attractive woman with a southern drawl who didn't seem at all put out by her surprise guests. She made a comfortable bed for Christopher on her living room couch, then hurried off to the kitchen to heat up some hot chocolate for Jami and coffee for her husband. Mr. Walters called the doctor, who promised to come right over, and he must have lived quite close because his car pulled into the driveway less than five minutes later. Christopher had woken up before they reached the house, but the Walterses refused to let him off the couch until the doctor checked him out.

Jami was impressed by how smoothly Mrs. Walters steered her into the kitchen and away from Christopher when the doctor arrived. She didn't protest, though, she just felt grateful to be able to sit down with her mug of hot chocolate and small plate of cookies. For some reason, she'd felt that everything was going to be okay from the moment she walked into the Walterses' modest house. Everything about them felt safe, and friendly, and good. In fact, she felt so comfortable that for a moment, she almost forgot what had brought her here.

It made her curious, and before she thought about it, the question had slipped out of her mouth.

"Has your husband ever had any problems with his heart, Mrs. Walters?"

The older woman raised her eyebrows.

"My goodness, no. Why would you say that, honey?"

Jami wished she'd bitten her tongue instead of opening her big fat mouth, but as she looked into the concerned brown eyes of the other woman, she knew she wasn't going to lie to her now.

"Well, because when I found my brother, he was lying right by your husband. He was unconscious, too. I guess, I'm pretty sure, um, that he had a heart attack or something."

She winced as Mrs. Walters raised a hand to her mouth in shock. That was stupid, she accused herself. Why worry her about it, since her husband was obviously okay? He'd carried Christopher all the way to his house without any problem, after all.

"Charles? Oh, no. . . ." The woman shook her head. "That doesn't seem possible. Charles has always been very healthy. He keeps himself quite active. He used to be quite an athlete in his day, before he went to seminary."

"Yeah, I was thinking maybe he played football," Jami said. "Wait a minute, did you say seminary?"

The black woman nodded. "Oh, yes. My husband is the pastor at Elim Baptist Church, in Roseville. You didn't know that?"

Jami shook her head. "I had no idea."

But now she had another idea in her head, and it wasn't one she enjoyed at all. That nice warm feeling inside her was gone now, as goose bumps made their prickly way up both her arms. Those . . . those Fallen jerks had tried to kill Pastor Walters tonight, and probably her brother, too! She was sure of it. Whatever doubts she'd had about the weirdness being a Warriors thing disappeared now, and although she knew she was among friends, she couldn't help but feel frightened and dismayed. It was as if she'd suddenly found herself standing at the edge of a big black hole that was just waiting to suck her in and chew her up.

"It's okay now, honey."

As the pleasant drawl broke into her nightmarish thoughts, Jami was amazed to find that Mrs. Walters, despite hearing the frightening news of her husband's collapse, was the one comforting her. The pastor's wife stroked her hand soothingly.

"It must have been terrible for you, finding him like that. And then to have that branch fall on your poor brother, what were the chances of that, I'd like to know! But don't you be afraid, because everything is going to be fine." She smiled gently at Jami. "This is one house that trusts in the Good Lord. And even though I surely hope there's nothing wrong with Charles's heart, the main thing is he's got the Lord Jesus Himself inside it."

Jami was awed, and a little humbled, by the woman's fearless faith. Here she was, just about ready to burst into tears because the stupid Fallen were scaring her again, while this pastor's wife was barely fazed by the news of her husband having a heart attack.

I wish I could be like her, Jami was thinking to herself when the sound of a familiar voice in the next room interrupted her. She grinned to herself. Christopher was arguing with the doctor, surprise, surprise.

"There you go." Mrs. Walters squeezed her hand again and rose from the table. "The Lord looks after his sheep, honey, and I can tell you're one of them. Now, you go bring some cookies to your brother, and I'll see if I can get that husband of mine to tell me what happened."

CHAPTER 5

BULLET THE BLACK SKY

It was dark, but even so, Melusine preferred to stand in the shadows cast by the outside lights of a nearby house. She waited in the darkness, her anger building with every passing moment. Christopher hadn't interfered with Lord Balazel's planned slaying of the preacher, but Jami had, and in the worst possible way. Not only that, but a squalid fool of a tree-demon had panicked at the sight of the Divine accompanying Christopher and tried to kill him by dropping a branch on his head!

What a disaster! The cursed preacher was going to live, and the Lewis children were not only back in action, but were even performing miracles. Lord Balazel was not going to be in the least bit pleased about all this, and she would have been in all kinds of additional trouble if the dryad had actually managed to kill the boy. The twins could die and rot in Heaven for all she cared, but the loss of Christopher's soul would fall squarely on her shoulders and she preferred to put off the payment for as long as possible. He was young, and there was plenty of time for him to see the light and turn his back on Heaven.

In her irritation, she must have been thinking too loudly,

because Mariel chose just that moment to turn around and smile at her. It was a sweet, cheerful smile, full of triumphant contempt, and Melusine was filled with the sudden urge to rush out from the trees and throttle the infuriating angel. Everything about her, her white wings, her long, red-golden hair, and her round, insipid little nose, filled Melusine with hatred.

"Anytime, Melusine darling, anytime at all."

Mariel was still smiling, but her green eyes were hard and her hand was resting lightly on the scabbard of her sword. Melusine had experienced its burning flames before, and she had no desire to feel them again now.

"Just wait, Blondie. One of these days, I'm going to claw out those teary little eyes of yours and really give you something to cry about."

Those eyes, which were not teary at the moment, narrowed even more as Mariel took a step forward, but Paulus grabbed her arm.

"Not now, Mariel. This is not the time or the place."

"Let me go, Paulus. . . ." Mariel protested, but she could not break free of the big angel's grasp.

"Oh, my hero," Melusine jeered, clasping her hands and provocatively thrusting her chest out at the handsome Guardian. "You saved me . . . how can I ever reward you?"

Paulus pushed Mariel behind him, then folded his arms and stared at her.

"Your charms, such as they are, Melusine, hold no interest for me. I am a servant of the Most High God, not a corrupted spirit driven by petty fallen lusts."

Melusine grinned evilly.

"Why, Paulus, I had no idea. You don't like your own kind? You prefer the little mortals, I suppose. And here I'd thought your King rather frowned on such . . . abomination."

Paulus's face darkened, and he clenched his fists before he remembered his self-appointed role as the peacemaker.

Melusine laughed at the Guardian as he turned his back on her and angrily followed his Divine companions. It was only a

minuscule victory after an evening of defeats, but it was a satisfying one all the same. Now she had another small matter to
which she must attend, and her momentary amusement turned
into anger as she thought about what one foolish demon's mistake might have cost her.

She marched into the middle of the yard just as the revived
preacher man was carrying Christopher into a small house some
two hundred cubits away. The guilty tree stood on the edge of the
snow-covered lawn, not far from the street, its missing branch an
open confession of its crime. She grabbed the tree with one hand,
seizing its large trunk as if it were the throat of a living being.

"Get out of there right now, whatever your name is!" she
screamed, digging her long black nails into the rough, icy bark
until a dark green liquid began oozing out from under her hand.
"You heard me! Don't make me come in after you!"

She squeezed harder, and a stream of the green stuff abruptly
squirted out of a knothole above her head. It coalesced first into a
mist, and then, reluctantly, into a solid form. It was a demon, if
one chose to call it that, but fallen so far from its former angelic
state that Melusine almost felt tempted to destroy it out of sheer
disgust, if not pity.

"Please, please, great Mistress, I did not know." The dryad fell
to its knees, pleading for mercy. It was a small, pathetic being,
with brown, lumpy skin that looked more like toad warts than
tree bark. "I was just trying to help!"

"Help who, that prissy blonde?" Melusine shrieked at him.
"What were you trying to do, send him straight to Heaven? What
about me, did you ever think about what would happen to me?"

"Yes!" the dryad screamed, then he cringed as she raised her
fist. "I mean, n-no, no, no! I'm sorry, I didn't think at all. I was just
scared with all those white angels and their terrible swords. Their
swords are fire!"

Melusine rolled her eyes. "What do you think they're made of,
aluminum? They're angels, for Lucere's sake. So are you, or did
you forget that while you sat here holding up bird nests and getting peed on by dogs."

"You don't understand, Mistress. This tree is all I have!" The dryad was crying now, spilling green tears that smoked as they fell upon the icy snow. "A Great Lady like yourself cannot imagine what it's like, I know, but this tree is all I have left to me. I know you are angry, and you are right to be angry, but please do not take it away from me. Have mercy, Great Lady!"

Melusine was disgusted by the little demon's sniveling, but she found her anger draining from her nonetheless. The dryad may have thought she couldn't understand his position, but she did, really. How long had it taken her to work her way back to where she was now, only a lowly Temptress? A Temptress with an important charge, to be sure, but she was no Great One. She frowned at the little spirit quaking in front of her. She could destroy him so easily, but what would be the point? She liked how he addressed her, too—Great Lady. There had once been a time when many had addressed her so.

"What's your name?" she asked him.

"Bogspittle, Mistress," he whispered, not daring to look up at her.

"Well, Boggie"—she couldn't quite bring herself to utter his ridiculous name—"from now on you will serve me, do you understand? No one else!"

The dryad nodded fervently.

"Yes, yes, Great Lady, I understand, I understand! Your word alone shall be my law, Mistress!"

"Very well."

Melusine peered more closely at her new subject and shook her head. His tree was not unattractive; it was actually a handsome, healthy oak with thick, muscular branches that stood in stark contrast to Boggie's own spindly little limbs.

"And do something about yourself. You should be strong and tall, and handsome, like your tree. And do something about that skin, you look like some kind of swamp spirit, not a proper dryad at all. All of my servants must be beautiful, like me."

Boggie lifted his head and met her gaze for the first time. He was obviously beginning to believe he just might survive this encounter after all. "I hear you, Mistress. I will try my best to please you."

Melusine nodded and forced herself to tousle his lank, greenish hair. She hid her distaste, even though it felt like grimy bean sprouts. "You do that, or I'll shred your spirit, Boggie. You've already made your one mistake, and I won't permit another." She pointed at his tree. "Now go back and stay there until I call for you."

She didn't wait for his response; instead she spread her wings and leaped theatrically into the sky. Boggie was nothing, less than nothing, but a retinue of one was better than no retinue at all. The encounter made her feel just a little more confident as she flew to find Lord Balazel to deliver her bad news. None of it had been her fault, but that didn't always matter and she knew that the archdemon was not going to be happy. It had been a bad night already, and, she feared, it was about to get worse.

The suburban neighborhoods all seemed the same from the windows of the car. Little clumps of trees flashed by, indistinct, devoid of all character except for the occasional birch tree standing out in thin white contrast to the dark evergreens and thickly towering oaks. Once, there had been elms lining the avenues, their massive branches reaching out to form a canopy of leaves over the street, but the image was only a dim one in Brien's memory. They'd been gone for years, cut down in a desperate attempt to save the few that had not yet contracted the dreaded Dutch elm disease.

He frowned as he drove, remembering how hard Mom had cried when Dad told her that the big elm in their front yard had to go; the tree crews had already marked it with the yellow paint of doom. It had seemed strange to him at the time, that Mom would shed tears for a tree. But now he understood, at least a little. The white oak that they'd planted the next spring had reached a respectable size now, eleven years later. But the oaks, massive as they were, just couldn't shade a street like the giant, sheltering elms. They populated a neighborhood, instead of defining it.

The neighborhoods at night seemed to be missing people as well as elms. There were plenty of lights on, of course, both inside and out, and every driveway had an extra car or two parked outside the two-car garages, but the only active sign of life was the eerie blue glow that flickered out through the ground-floor windows of nearly every home. Some of the bigger houses boasted two glows, and a few even had three. To Brien, driving here at night felt almost like an out-of-body experience, as if alien life-forms from some spectral planet had somehow caused all the people living here to vanish. He imagined strange beings of blue light squatting triumphantly in the empty living rooms of their victims, performing ghastly, ghostly rituals of unspeakable evil, and shivered.

An unexpectedly cool breeze brushed the back of his neck and made him jump, jerking him rudely back to the real world. One of the guys in the backseat had rolled a window down, and although it was spring, the night air still had a shiveringly cold edge to it.

"Hey, put that up!" he yelled back at them.

He had to shout to make himself heard over the crushing roar of the speakers. He was already getting sick of the Rage CD, but Derek had insisted on it, and Zack the Ripper was shrieking something about guns and bullets and heads when a real gun boomed about two feet behind his own head. It sounded like a bomb going off in his ear, and in shock, Brien just about ran the Taurus into a telephone pole.

"Holy Cthulhu, what was that!" he shouted as he struggled to keep the car from swerving out of control.

Peals of hysterical laughter were the only response he received from the backseat, so Brien slammed on the brakes and pulled over to the side of the road in a towering rage. He punched the Off button on the stereo, then twisted around and glared at Derek and Rob, who were slumped against each other, laughing uncontrollably. In Derek's hand was a sleek-looking black handgun, and from the smell of gunpowder filling the car, it was clearly the one that had just been fired.

"Look at him," Rob gasped, pointing at him. "I think he's gonna kill you!"

"Ooh, I'm scared." Derek giggled, waving the pistol in Brien's face.

"You stupid freakazoid!" Brien spat at his friend. "Give me that before you shoot somebody in the freaking head!"

He grabbed the barrel of the gun and jerked it out of Derek's hand. It was a Glock, one of the nine millimeter models. The gun felt lighter than it looked; he remembered hearing that Glocks were made out of plastic or something like that. It had to be Mr. Wallace's; Derek had said something once about his dad liking Glocks. Shaking his head, he popped the magazine out, then eased back the action and carefully popped the last round out of the chamber. He slipped the ammunition in the plastic side-pocket of the car door before tossing the Glock back into Derek's lap.

"What the hell are you doing, man? You could have killed somebody out there!"

Derek rolled his eyes. "Oh, come on, relax, dude. There isn't anyone within miles of here. Besides, I was trying to hit that Deer Crossing sign."

"Trying, that's right." Rob chuckled. "I bet you missed that sucker by twenty feet."

"Yeah, well, if you hadn't bumped my arm—"

"Hey, you missed, didn't you? So pay up, where's that dime bag—"

Brien saw red for a moment. "Shut up, you idiots! What's the matter with you, Derek? What if someone was out walking or jogging, and you hit him? I mean, what if a cop pulls us over now?"

"Then we'll make the front page: Armed Drug Gang Arrested in Mounds Park! Dude, we are the criminal element!" He grinned and high-fived Rob. "Seriously, they had this headline in the *Strib*, like, two years ago, when they busted these guys in this house who had, like, two shotguns, a pistol, and four plants in the basement. Four! I mean, we've probably got more weed than that between the three of us!"

Brien put his head in his hands, but he couldn't help seeing the humor in spite of everything. He couldn't believe the things Derek did sometimes, but his friend's reckless insanity was part of the fun of hanging out with him. It was kind of like making a deal with the devil, he supposed—it was always a lot of fun, but sometimes you got a little more than you bargained for.

"Way to go, Bry. You just had to say the word, didn't you!"

As Rob launched into an inspired avalanche of four-letter words, Brien looked up and his heart sank.

In the rearview mirror he could see a white-and-green police car approaching from behind them. Please, please, keep going, he thought desperately. It's only six weeks until graduation. I do not need this right now! He held his breath as the squad car came closer, dreading that heart-stopping explosion of blue light that always signified trouble.

He could almost hear his heart thumping, and it was hard to swallow. Derek and Rob were silent and motionless, like two fawns holding stock-still in the hopes that the wolf stalking them would somehow fail to see them lying helplessly by the side of the road. Thank you, thank you, he thought, relieved beyond measure, as the white car marked MOUNDS PARK POLICE did not slow down as it passed them by, seemingly without notice.

"Man, that was too close," he said, turning back to the others with a sigh of relief. "Son of a gun, the weed would be bad enough, but with your stupid pistol and that pipe bomb, we'd be drinking age by the time they let us out!"

"No doubt," Rob agreed heartily, but Derek didn't say anything. He was staring past Brien with a strange look on his face, and his dark eyebrows were drawn together in focused concentration.

"Um, Brien, I hope you got a good arm," he said finally.

"Why's that?" Rob asked, but Brien understood even before

he turned around to see the red glow of the cop's brake lights. His knees suddenly felt weak, and his stomach hurt.

"Because possession is just a misdemeanor," Derek explained softly, his eyes still locked on the police car as it came to a halt about forty feet in front of them. "A gun, on the other hand, we're talking felony."

CHAPTER 6

ABOMINATIONS AND ALTERCATIONS

YOU WILL LIVE IN CONSTANT SUSPENSE, FILLED WITH DREAD BOTH
NIGHT AND DAY, NEVER SURE OF YOUR LIFE. IN THE MORNING YOU WILL
SAY, "IF ONLY IT WERE EVENING!" AND IN THE EVENING, "IF ONLY IT
WERE MORNING!"—BECAUSE OF THE TERROR THAT WILL FILL YOUR
HEARTS AND THE SIGHTS THAT YOUR EYES WILL SEE.

—Deuteronomy 28:66–67

Jami looked down at the hard plastic tray in front of her brother
with dismay and more than a little disgust. The food from the
school cafeteria was always questionable at best, but looking at
today's pizza, she felt the hairnet ladies had managed to outdo
themselves again. The presumed pizza was a concoction of what
appeared to be slugbelly-white and schoolbus-yellow plastic
melted over a browned doughy substance which bore only a
passing resemblance to real pizza crust.

"Looks pretty nasty, huh?" commented her brother.

Jami didn't bother to reply. The nastiness of the pizza, she
thought, was beyond words. She held her tongue and winced as
he picked up his slice and bit into it. This should be good, she
thought as she waited to hear Christopher pronounce his judgment. They'd been having lunch together once a week since
school had started again after the New Year's break, usually on
Fridays, and she'd learned that his little rants could be pretty
funny as long as they weren't aimed at her.

Christopher chewed, made a face, and wiped a drop of yellow

oil off his chin. Then he glanced at her plate and saw that in place of pizza she had two apples and a banana sitting in her plate's largest rectangle.

"Hey, where'd you get the fruit?"

Jami grinned and slapped away his hand that was reaching out for an apple.

"Get away, you!" She pointed the banana at him as if it were a pistol. "Don't even think about it. I'll shoot, I swear I will!"

"Ha ha." He made a face. "Seriously, where'd you get it?"

Jami indicated an overweight boy with glasses sitting three tables away from them. A brown paper bag in front of him was marked with a large grease stain which was the only remnant of her pizza slice.

"I traded Greg Lundeen for it. He brought a bag lunch, but he loves this cafeteria slop. I don't know why. I mean, pizza I can understand, kind of, but they even screw up the hamburgers here. Hamburgers! How do you screw that up?"

"Jami!" Christopher was appalled. "All that fruit—he's probably on a diet!"

"So?" Jami shrugged indifferently and peeled back the banana skin. "It's not like there's anything real in that stuff, it's mostly plastic anyhow. Can't be too many calories in it."

She laughed as Christopher shook his head and returned to his lunch. Her brother didn't seem to be feeling any ill effects from the knock on the head he'd taken the night before; fortunately, his hair covered the spot where the branch had cut his scalp. They hadn't been able to keep the Walterses from calling Mom and Dad, but thanks to a mild rearrangement of the facts, they'd managed to leave their parents with the impression that Christopher had simply slipped on the ice while the two of them were out jogging together.

Something familiar caught the corner of her vision, and she looked up. Her twin sister, Holli, was entering the cafeteria at the side of a tall senior who walked with the easy grace of the natural athlete. She recognized Paul Johnson at once; he was the guy from her team who had called the other night. He also happened to be the star of Mounds Park's varsity squad. But what was his arm doing draped around her sister like that?

"What's up with Paul?" she asked Christopher as she polished off the last bite of her banana. She pointed in Holli's general direction. "Did I miss something?"

She dropped the empty banana peel onto the hard plastic of her lunchtray, and it landed with an unpleasant splat.

"What's up with what?" Christopher looked back at her blankly.

"That!" Jami pointed again, rolling her eyes. Guys were so clueless! "He's, like, all over Holli. Did I miss something here?"

"Oh, that." Christopher nodded. "I forgot, you crashed before she got home last night. Anyhow, I guess Paul asked her out after the basketball game. He's taking her to a party on Saturday or something like that."

Oh. "A party, huh?" Jami shrugged. She wasn't sure what she thought about Holli going out with Paul. It wasn't as if she had a crush on the guy, or anything like that, but she always thought of Paul as one of her people. He was her teammate, after all, and so it was just a little strange, no biggie. "It's probably that one at Jill's I heard about. Gina told me her parents are in Europe again."

"Cool." Christopher nodded approvingly, although they both knew he wouldn't be going, either.

"Don't worry about it." She winked at him, knowing what he was thinking. "There'll be others."

For the last three months, following the strange experience with the supernatural they'd shared, Jami and Holli had worked hard at helping Christopher fit in better with the in crowd at Mounds Park. He'd made quite a bit of progress, thanks to them, and he'd even had two dates, but there was still a lot of work left to be done within the rigid social circles of the high school.

Jill Mondale was only a freshman, but she was at the very center of Mounds Park's social elite thanks to her boyfriend, the all-state tennis star, and her parents' frequent habit of vacating their large house in North Oaks in favor of Italy or some other exotic destination. Only the jocks and the cool people were allowed at her parties.

"I'm not going, either, so don't give me that hurt-puppy look. Jill thinks Dan has the hots for Holli, so she hates both of us, of course. She's such a dimwit, I'm not even sure she realizes there's two of us. I don't need to deal with that."

"But Holli's going to go?" Christopher was puzzled. "I thought you said Jill doesn't like her."

"Paul asked her out, dummyhead!" Jami couldn't help but laugh at her brother's inability to grasp the obvious. "She's not going to blow him off just because that little Mondale brat is jealous. I'd almost like to go, just to see Jill's face when Holli shows up with the super soccer stud. Serves her right."

"Serves who right?" Holli asked, as she joined them, followed closely by the super soccer stud himself, who was carrying a tray in either hand. "Paul, do you know my brother, Christopher?"

The tall senior grinned absently down at Christopher, passed one tray to Holli, and extended his free hand to her brother.

"I guess I do now. How ya doin', Chris," he said, in a friendly but superior manner as he shook Christopher's hand. He nodded at Jami, too. "What's up, James?"

"Hey, Paul," Jami returned the greeting. "What's up is his name is Christopher, not Chris."

"Sorry, my bad. So, Christopher, then." The tall boy smiled easily. "Mind if we join you for lunch?"

The request was more of a formality than anything. Holli was already pulling the cheese off her pizza.

"Go ahead," Jami said. "But what's this I hear about you hitting on my sister?" She glanced at Holli, who glared back at her.

Paul laughed, completely unfazed. He'd never struck Jami as a particularly interesting guy, but his laid-back, easygoing attitude was hard to dislike. She'd known of him for years; everybody in the local soccer world had, but he was a senior and she hadn't gotten to know him personally until Beth Carlsson asked her to play on their coed indoor team this fall. He was an okay-looking guy, but only in that boy-next-door sort of way that lots of the soccer players had. It surprised her that Holli was up for going out with him; he wasn't really her usual type.

"We're just going to Jill's party," Holli said, sounding exasperated. "Don't have a cow. When did you turn into Mom and Dad?"

"Yeah, you can even come with, if you want," Paul told her, ignoring Holli's worried glance at him. "I mean, we've got a game that afternoon anyhow."

Jami stifled a grin, and mischief tempted her. Holli wouldn't mind her going to the party, of course, but there was no way she wanted Jami to ride along with her and Paul. Her sister's blue eyes pleaded with her to turn down the invitation, but for a moment she pretended not to notice.

"That sounds great!" she said slyly, enjoying Holli's obvious discomfort. She paused for a long moment, then laughed and stopped tormenting her sister. "But sorry, I can't. Angie and Rachel wanted to go to the Megamall on Saturday night, and I told them I'd go."

She stole a glance at Christopher, and predictably, his ears perked up. He had an awful crush on Rachel Jensen, which he thought he had kept secret. But, of course, he hadn't. Fortunately, he wasn't about to do anything about it. Rachel was nice enough, so she wouldn't shoot him down too hard, but it was unlikely that she'd be interested in him, even if Jami pushed the idea. At least, not now. It just took more than a few months to lose the L from your forehead.

"Well, if you guys need a ride down there . . ." Christopher suggested. "I was thinking about going down to Peter's house, in west Bloomington. So I could take you."

"Really?" Jami pretended to be surprised. Holli's lips twitched, and they exchanged a glance. Guys were just too easy sometimes. Even her brother wasn't hard to figure out, now that she had a handle on what made him tick. "Hey, the mall would be right on your way, then."

"Wait a minute!" Paul exclaimed suddenly. He was staring at Christopher, his brows knit together in concentration. "You play soccer, too, don't you? You played B-squad this year, right? I thought you looked familiar, from tryouts."

"Yep." Christopher nodded. He wasn't very talkative, all of a sudden, but Jami knew that was only because he was in awe of the senior. They played the same position, but whereas Paul was a scoring machine, her brother had a terrible habit of kicking field goals instead of putting the ball on net.

"He's a forward, just like you," Holli informed Paul.

"Only I'm not quite as good in the air," Christopher admitted. "Or on the ground, for that matter."

"Can you play defense?"

Not really, Jami almost said, but she managed to keep her mouth shut. She hadn't gone to many of his games last year, but she'd seen enough of them to know that her brother was a one-dimensional player. He was fast, but that was about it. He didn't finish well, which kept him from scoring very much, and he had the typical forward's dislike for getting back to help the midfield. When her varsity team had scrimmaged the B-squad boys, she noticed that he only came back on corner kicks, and once, when she found him defending her, she'd dogged him badly with an easy nutmeg. But that was last year; she didn't want to embarrass him in front of Paul now. He'd already had enough trouble with the seniors on the team.

"Not really," Christopher said. "I mean, I can play it, I'm just not very good at it."

"I get that. I'm a disaster on defense myself," Paul assured him. "Illinois was trying to recruit me as a midfielder, but there's no way I'm going to spend half my time making runs down the sideline and the other half trying to cover the other guy making his runs into our end. That's just too much work!"

"Admit it," Jami teased him. "You're just not man enough for the midfield!"

"Nope." Paul didn't seem to mind admitting his limitations. "And you are?"

"Rrrr!" Jami pretended to flex her arms, and both the boys laughed.

"Is that why you decided to go to Santa Clara?" Holli placed her hand on Paul's arm, a little possessively, Jami thought. "Because you didn't want to go to Illinois?"

"Yeah, pretty much," Paul replied, and then, to Jami's surprise, he blushed a little. "The winters are a lot nicer than here in the Midwest. That, and I didn't get into Duke. My grades were okay, but . . ."

Paul started to say something about his SATs, but the buzzer signifying the end of fifth hour drowned out the rest of his sentence. Jami sighed and pushed away from the table, thinking that if the school divided the day into hours, then she should have a whole hour for lunch, not just forty minutes. She glanced inquisitively at Holli, but her sister shook her head, and Jami nodded, understanding immediately. This wasn't the time to quiz her about what was going on with Paul. So she said goodbye to the others, then gathered up her books and headed toward the stairs that led to her geometry class. Friday afternoons were always the worst; they seemed to last forever.

Oh, well, she thought, at least Holli had given her something to occupy her mind now. Paul Johnson. She shook her head. Who would have guessed?

Brien closed his eyes and leaned against the open door of his locker. The hated, boisterous voices of the jocks were growing louder as they came closer, heading for their first-hour classes, and he put his head down, desperately hoping that for once they would decide to pass him by. He didn't dare to look and see how many of them there were, but he could hear at least three different voices, one of which was Kent Petersen's.

Too late, he realized that his locker door was open, exposing the color scans of CD covers and clipped-out magazine pictures that decorated the interior. If he'd learned anything in three and a half years of high school, it was to give them nothing. Anything, a picture, a word, a piece of clothing, or just a simple meeting of the eyes might set them off. And it would end the way it always did, in pain and humiliation.

He started to quietly close the locker, but suddenly a hand shot past his shoulder and held it open. He cursed under his breath and turned around slowly, steeling himself for the imminent confrontation.

"Ooooh, nice locker, Brain."

As he'd feared, the hand belonged to Kent Petersen. Kent was small, but was much stronger than he looked, good-looking in a stocky way, with curly brown hair and small, mischievous eyes. But now those eyes were hard and full of cruel anticipation.

"KMFDM, Rammstein." He peered past Brien and read the names on the CD covers. "Wow, I guess you got the complete collection of eurofag buttmonkeys. What a big surprise."

"What a big thurprithe!" Jim Shumacher repeated while affecting a lisp. "A real big surprise, you fat homo!"

Jim's voice crescendoed on the last word, and he shoved Brien with both hands, slamming him hard into the locker with a loud metal bang. Brien felt a sharp stab of pain exploding in his back, just as Kent's foot adroitly pulled his own feet out from under him. Before he'd even realized what they were doing, he found himself writhing on the ground with a painfully bruised tailbone as Kent, Jim, and the third guy, Jay, leaned over him and playfully ripped down the pictures he'd painstakingly scanned from his CD collection, printed out, trimmed, and taped up in his locker. What had been the work of hours was destroyed in less than ten seconds. When they were finished, the three boys laughed triumphantly, exchanged high fives, and walked away without looking back at him.

There were more than thirty kids in the hallway, but only a few even bothered to look up at the sound of the commotion. Brien could feel the familiar sting of tears threatening to appear in his eyes, but he gritted his teeth, straightened his glasses, and gingerly pushed himself upright. No one offered him any help, although a pretty blond girl passing by bent over to pick up one of the torn pictures. She smiled sympathetically as she handed it to him, then continued on her way to class, or the cafeteria, or the library, or any of the hundred circles of this hateful place that Brien knew as Hell.

He looked down at the ripped paper in his hand. It was a picture of a yellow sunflower on a psychedelic blue background. The name of the CD was torn away, but the band name remained: My Life With the Thrill Kill Kult. He read the name twice, and stared down the hallway where the three jocks had disappeared into the crowd. Someday, he vowed to them silently, I'll get you for this, I swear. I will get you back!

He heard someone approaching behind him and spun around, holding his fists up. Rob, surprised, put his hands up.

"Relax, dude. Hey, what happened to your locker?"

"What do you think?"

"Oh, yeah." The large boy nodded sympathically. "Petersen, I'll bet."

"And Shumacher," Brien added. "What is with this place? I thought it was supposed to be the football players who were evolutionally challenged!"

"They're all jocks. What's the difference?" Rob peeled off one torn strip of paper still attached to the locker. "Too bad, this was looking pretty cool, you know? But I suppose you've still got the j-pegs if you want to do it again."

"Yeah, but I don't know if I'll bother."

"I can understand that." Rob nodded. "Hey, Derek left a message on my cell phone. He had to go down to the police station at eight this morning, but he wanted you to meet him at Caribou at one o'clock. Can you do it?"

"Sure." Brien shrugged. "I can skip gym, no problem. Is he in a lot of trouble?"

"I don't know. He didn't sound too worried."

"All right. Do you want to drive? We can take my car if you don't want to."

Rob shook his head. "That's sixth hour. I've got a test I can't blow off. You'll have to go by yourself. He said the one you worked at, by the way. The Caribou, that is."

"Yeah, that's what I figured," Brien said as he closed his locker.

He rearranged his history books in his arms. "I hope he's all right. It's not really fair that he got stuck with the blame for everything."

"He'll be all right." Rob nodded seriously and patted Brien on the shoulder. "Don't worry about Derek, Brien. He's cool. He knows how to take care of himself."

The Caribou was a little more crowded than it normally was at this time of day. They got a lunch rush, but it was usually over by now. It was pretty small for a coffee shop, but the manager had some kind of deal worked out with the bagel shop next door, and as he waited for Derek and sipped at the chocolate-sprinkled whipped cream that topped his Turtle Mocha, he saw several people walking between the two shops, carrying bags of bagels in one direction and paper cups of coffee the other way. He worked here part-time; eight hours a week wasn't much, but it paid enough to keep his car running.

He gave a halfhearted thought to getting a turkey bagel sandwich, but the notion of food deserted his mind as two pretty girls walked in and sat down two tables away from him. He tried not to stare too much, but one of them, a petite Asian girl he'd seen in there before, was wearing a tight sweater, and he found it almost impossible to look away from her.

"Close your mouth, Brien. I don't think they like it when you drool."

Embarrassed at being caught with his eyes locked on the girl's chest, Brien nearly spilled his mocha all over the circular little table. He managed to steady it before it toppled over completely, but the sweetened coffee was hot and burned his fingers as it ran down the sides of the tall paper cup.

"Ouch!" he cried, and he quickly put the cup down on the table amidst a small pool of light brown liquid. "Doggone it, Derek, don't do that!"

He looked up and saw his friend was smirking apologetically to the two girls.

"It's okay, folks, nothing to see here, everything is now under control."

The Asian girl rolled her eyes, and whispered something behind her hand to her blond friend, who giggled at them.

Brien felt his cheeks burning and he stood up quickly. "I'll be right back," he told Derek. "I've got to wash my hands off; the caramel makes it sticky."

Three minutes later he returned to the table and saw that the two girls were gone. He glanced over toward the bagel shop and saw that they had relocated there to join two boys wearing red-and-yellow Irondale jackets. He shook his head, still a little embarrassed, but even more irritated at the unfairness of it all. What did those two rockheads know about anything? Nothing, probably, except how to catch a football or something like that. I'm sure that made for really interesting conversations, he thought bitterly, not that pretty girls like that Asian chick probably cared.

Oh, well, so life wasn't fair, what else was new? He looked down at the table and saw that the mess he'd created was gone, but so was his mocha. He glared suspiciously at Derek.

"Did you drink that?"

"Yeah," Derek answered, making a face and pretending to brush his tongue. "Those suckers are so sweet, I don't know how you can even stand them."

Brien looked up at the ceiling, trying not to lose his temper. This had not been an easy week, and Derek wasn't on his short list of favorite people at the moment.

"Hey, relax." Derek held up his hand, then pointed toward the counter. "Half of it was already on the table anyhow, and, besides, I ordered you another one. I had to get a real coffee for myself, straight-up, none of this girly-girl stuff."

"You mean, chocolate? Or caramel?"

"Yeah, whatever." Derek widened his eyes and pretended to look curious. "So, Derek, how did it go at the police station today?"

"Oh, I'm sorry, dude," Brien apologized. How self-centered could he be? He was worrying about girls and coffee spills, while his friend had actual problems. Especially considering that Derek had been cool enough to take the rap, letting him and Rob off the hook. "What'd they do to you, how'd it go?"

To his surprise, Derek smiled broadly and bobbed his head with satisfaction.

"Most excellent. The cops aren't even pressing charges or anything. The sergeant chewed Dad out about the gun, but since it was empty, it really wasn't that big a deal. They kept the pot, though, and I'll bet you some of those cops are going to smoke it. You know that spot where they speed-trap by the hockey rink? There's about five ditchweed plants totally growing right there, probably from a joint one of those cops tossed out the window!"

"Well, they do have to sit there for a long time," Brien offered. "It's not like they have anything better to do."

"Yeah, that's true. Anyhow, the sergeant told Dad that I should see a psychiatrist about my 'potential drug-abuse problem,' so Dad made me go talk to Mom's shrink today."

"What, this morning?"

"Yeah, I thought I might as well get it over with." Derek grinned. "I guess we get a family discount or something. So check this out!"

Brien watched as Derek reached into his black backpack and triumphantly pulled out a bottle. It was clear, and he could see there were pills inside it, but the label was on the other side.

"Dah duh dah!" Derek twisted the bottle around. "Listening to Prozac, baby!"

Brien raised his eyebrows as he read the label. He didn't understand why Derek was so cheerful.

"Xanax? Isn't that, like, an anti-depressant or something?"

"Anxiety, depression, who cares?" Derek's laughter was full of glee. "Apparently there's nothing wrong with me that a few pills won't fix. The shrink was a complete moron, I mean, she kept asking me questions about whether I'd ever been abused, or if Dad had ever hit me, you know, stuff like that. It took me, like, about ten seconds to figure how to play her, so I made up this story about how I always feel like everybody hates me, because I don't have a girlfriend, and I'm no good at sports, yada, yada."

He indicated the bottle.

"So half an hour later she diagnoses me with an official Anxiety Disorder and sets me up with a prescription. The final score is, no fine, no jail, and a legal prescription for mood-altering drugs. Derek three, society zero!"

"That's awesome! I thought you'd at least, I don't know, get a fine or something."

"I probably would have if you hadn't chucked those bullets so quick." Derek slipped the bottle back into his backpack. "Dad was pretty pissed that I took his gun, but I told him I was just trying to impress you guys and he bought it. It was a good thing the cops gave it back to him, or I don't know what he would have done. Boy, he was mad! I went back and looked for the magazine before coming here, but I couldn't find it. But what does he care, I mean, I'm sure he's got extras."

Brien stared at his friend, then laughed. "That is awesome. But I thought the whole reason you had to see the shrink was because of the weed. Didn't that come up at all before the shrink decided to put you on more drugs?"

"Brien, Brien, you really don't get it, do you?" Derek leaned back in his chair and folded his hands behind his head. "I was self-medicating, see?"

"I cannot believe that! No wonder the whole world is such a freaking madhouse."

"Yeah, they let people like us run around loose." Derek looked past Brien and pointed a finger at the counter. "Hey, I think those are ours."

Brien got up and went to the counter, grabbing extra napkins this time in case he managed to spill again. He carefully handed Derek a white mug that was perilously close to overflowing. His friend set it down cautiously on their little round wooden table, then rubbed his hands and grinned mischievously at Brien.

"Remember in junior high, when we used to sell our Ritalin to Mike and that burnout kid, what was his name?"

"Alex. Yeah, I remember. What did we get for it, like, a dollar a pop?"

"Something like that." He jerked a thumb at his bag. "I wonder what the going rate is for this stuff?"

Brien rolled his eyes and glanced out the window. The Asian girl was walking through the parking lot, hand-in-hand with one of the Irondale jocks. They were probably headed for Blockbuster, he guessed, looking for a movie to provide cover for their make-out session in her parents' basement tonight. He sighed regretfully as he watched the traffic start up again on the busy street that lay beyond the lot filled with BMWs, Mercedes, and about a million different sports-utility vehicles. What a waste. What a freaking waste!

CHAPTER 7

GANGBANG OFT AGLEY

NOT EVERYONE WHO SAYS TO ME, "LORD, LORD," WILL ENTER THE KINGDOM OF HEAVEN, BUT ONLY HE WHO DOES THE WILL OF MY FATHER WHO IS IN HEAVEN.

—Matthew 7:21

Jami sat on the edge of her bed, flipping through the latest Soccer Express catalog and wondering if the new pair of kangaroo-skin Pumas that Dad promised to buy her next season would give her enough Express points to get the Arsenal jersey she'd been saving up for. It was going to be close, she thought, so maybe she should ask Dad for the red ones. They cost a little more, but the extra two points would definitely push her over the edge. No, she decided, wearing red boots was just asking for trouble, and unless you were, like, All-State or something, they weren't worth the stick you'd end up taking. If she made All-Conference next year, maybe she'd dare to wear them for her junior season.

She lay back on her pillow and stared up at her poster of Dennis Bergkamp. He was such a cutie, with that intense glare and the little blond curl in the front. A lot of the Dutch internationals were so totally cute, why was that? *Internationals*—she liked the word. The best of the best. It was her goal to someday hear people announcing her name on TV—Jami Lewis, the American international. A few of the English soccer clubs had started to pay their women's teams, so maybe after playing for North Carolina in college she could move to England and play professionally for

Arsenal herself. Forget the WUSA, she was going Premiership all the way. She'd wear number ten, just like Dennis. That would be all right!

"Jami, Christopher, it's time for dinner," Mom called.

She rolled off the bed with a sigh. It had been a long day, and now, to top it all off, Mom had made pasta again. The sickening scent of tomatoes cooking had filled the house all evening. She hated spaghetti, but Christopher loved it, so they ate it all the time. Okay, they didn't really, but it seemed that way to her.

She was walking toward the stairs when Christopher opened his bedroom door. He had an excited look on his face, and he punched her arm as he joined her in the hallway.

"Spaghetti tonight, mmmm!"

"Great." Jami faked a smile, but Christopher was too interested in the thought of dinner to notice her sarcasm. His appetite clearly hadn't been affected by that knock on the head the night before. No surprise there; she'd always known he had a thick skull. She stepped out of the way and he practically ran down the rest of the stairs.

"Smells great, Mom," he announced happily as Jami followed him into the kitchen to join the rest of the family already sitting at the table.

"Yes, it smells wonderful, honey," Dad said, winking sympathetically at Jami. He knew she wasn't crazy about Italian food.

"Jami, dear, there's a plate for you on the counter. Just the way you like it. No sauce on the noodles, only butter and a little oregano, okay?"

That wasn't so bad, Jami decided. It wasn't the noodles that she hated so much as the marinara sauce. It usually had chunks of tomatoes in it . . . yuck! Pizza sauce was all right, but spaghetti sauce even looked gross. The only thing that was worse was chili, with those huge gobs of smushed tomatoes that glopped into your bowl with that nasty plopping sound.

She returned to the table and grinned when she saw that Holli had served herself her usual bird's portion, about one-tenth the size of the heaping mass piled up on Christopher's plate.

"Hey, Jami, Paul called this afternoon and wanted to know if you'd found anyone for tomorrow's game," Holli told her. "I said I didn't think so, but you know what? He said Christopher could play because he couldn't find anyone, either."

"Really?" Christopher's voice was partially muffled by the forkful of pasta in his mouth. "Awesome!"

"Christopher, you can speak or you can eat, but you can't do both at once." Mom waved her fork at him. "And you can forget about playing after taking that fall you had last night."

Jami winced, recalling their not-exactly-true explanation of Christopher's injury. But it was sort of true, well, not really, but then, lying to your parents wasn't really lying. Okay, maybe it was, but it was necessary sometimes. Like telling someone they don't look fat when they really do.

"Mom!" Christopher protested.

"I don't see why he shouldn't," Jami added. "It's not like he's going to head the ball!"

She smiled mischievously as her brother glanced back at her with uncertainty, not sure if she'd supported him or slammed him. The answer, of course, was both. Christopher wasn't a bad player, but he'd been afraid of heading the ball since junior high, when he'd broken a pair of glasses by using his face instead of his forehead. He was pretty much useless in the air despite his height.

"Did the doctor say anything specific about sports when you saw him today?" Dad asked.

"I didn't ask about soccer because I didn't know I'd have a chance to play," Christopher confessed. "But he did say I was fine, no concussion or anything. Come on, Mom, I never get to play with these guys. They're varsity! This might help me make the team next year."

Mom looked like she was almost ready to relent, but she was still frowning.

"Honey, if the doctor says he's okay, then I'm sure he's okay," Dad said. I don't see what would be the point of forcing him to miss the game. It's not like he's playing hockey or football. It's not a contact sport."

Mom sighed and reluctantly nodded her head.

"I'm sure you're right, Jim." She pointed a finger at Christopher. "But you be careful. If you hit your head in any way, I want you to come out of the game immediately, understand? And Jami, you'd better make sure he does."

Jami nodded dutifully. She wasn't all that keen on him playing anyhow, since he wasn't an adequate replacement for Jason Case, but he would do for one game. It was better than playing down a man.

"All right!" Christopher punched both fists in the air. "I'll be careful, Mom, I promise."

"Well," Holli added casually. "Since it's going to be a family affair, I might as well go, too. Especially since I'm going out with Paul after."

Jami felt a sudden surge of jealousy despite herself. That was weird, she thought, disturbed by her own reaction. It wasn't like this was news to her. She'd never even been interested in Paul. If she was going to go out with anyone on the team, Jason Case was probably the only one she'd be willing to consider. He kept to himself more than the others, and she kind of liked his shyness. It made him seem a little mysterious, or something.

But still, the whole situation just made her feel uncomfortable.

"Excuse me. I believe you meant to ask if it was all right if you go to a party with this Paul," Dad said firmly, but with a touch of humor.

"Provided he comes here to pick you up so we can meet him." Mom added her two cents.

Holli rolled her eyes and pushed herself away from the table.

"We're going to a party after the game tomorrow night at Jill Mondale's. And Mom, you know who Paul is. He's on Jami's team, the tall guy with the light brown hair. He's the captain."

Mom looked thoughtful. "You're right, I have met him and he does seem to be a nice boy. He never gets those yellow cards that the referees are always giving you, Jami. He's very well-behaved, and I've even seen him shake the referee's hand after the game."

Jami groaned. Mom was always going on about her cards. But you had to be aggressive to play center-mid. And besides, she hadn't gotten a red since outdoor ended last fall.

"Maybe that's why he never gets carded," Dad said dryly. "Butter up the ref, that's what I always say."

"You could try flirting with him." Holli batted her long eyelashes and smiled a dreamy smile. "The guy who reffed your last game against Irondale was pretty hot."

Christopher snorted. "I remember that guy. He plays for Arden Hills, their D-one team. I think he's, like, thirty, though."

"Just because he's old doesn't mean he can't be cute," Holli said loftily.

Dad groaned theatrically. "Thirty, and he's old?" He laid his fork and knife across his empty plate. "Darling, what do you say that you and I totter off to the living room and leave the dishes to these heartless children?"

Jami laughed out loud as Dad got up slowly from the table and pretended to walk like a decrepit old man toward the couch in front of the TV. Dad was handsome in his own way. His hair was receding and he'd put on a little bit of a tummy lately, but he was tall and dignified, and his sense of humor always made her think of the cool kind of teacher who lets you have class outside when it's nice and sunny in the spring.

"You don't think I hurt Daddy's feelings, do you?" Holli asked her, genuinely concerned, as Mom walked out of the kitchen with two glasses of wine in her hands and an amused half-smile on her face.

"No, of course not," Christopher quickly assured her, and he was probably right, Jami thought.

Getting old wasn't a big deal, she thought, unless you were a professional athlete and you couldn't play anymore. But Dad was a professor, with full tenure at the U, so Jami figured he had nothing to worry about. Mom didn't, either; she was a babe, not just for-her-age pretty, but overall pretty. Mom watched her weight and played tennis three times a week, and men still whipped their heads around to look at her at the mall when they didn't think anyone was looking. Holli took after her, in some ways. Jami was proud of both her parents, but it worried her that Dad, at least, wasn't saved yet.

But if God could use her to wake up a dead man, then he could save Dad, too. It was something to pray about, she knew, and wished she'd actually spent more time praying for him. Why was it always so hard to remember to pray for things, even the really important things?

"What are you thinking about, Jami?" Holli asked her as she took her plate from in front of her. "Aren't you going to help with the dishes?"

"Oh, sure, nothing really," Jami told her, not wanting to get into it. "So tell me, what's going on with you and Paul . . . ?"

Archdemons were seldom known for their patience, and Lord Balazel was no exception. Less than a day passed before his emissaries had summoned all of the Fallen spirits that were to be held responsible for the failed attack on the black preacher. Melusine, much to her dismay, learned that her presence was demanded as well. The fact that the arrogant imp who delivered Balazel's imperious message to her dared to molest her with his greedy hands did not bode well for her, she knew, but she took a certain satisfaction in knowing that no matter what happened to her, that wretched imp wouldn't bother anyone else for quite some time.

It was hard to feel up a demoness if you were missing your hands, after all. And your eyes.

Melusine shrugged as she flew toward the meeting place. They'd grow back eventually. She wasn't going to waste her time thinking about an overfriendly imp when she had an angry archdemon to worry about. Last night's fiasco wasn't her fault, but that didn't mean she wouldn't be held responsible for it. She had no doubts as to where the responsibility really lay, but avoiding the consequences of her actions had always been Shaeloba's primary talent. Melusine consoled herself with the thought that one of these days the demoness's sneaky ways would finally catch up with her, the cursed little conniver.

She spread her wings and lighted softly on the stone walkway of the old Methodist church where she had been summoned. Lord Balazel was there, his huge frame darkening the doorway, but to her surprise, he was unaccompanied.

The archdemon smiled at her; at least, she thought he did. It was hard to tell, with all those tusks protruding from his thick-lipped mouth.

"Don't be afraid, Melusine," he growled at her. "This is no Inquisition. The interference of the Counselor was an unpleasant surprise, but Reverend Walters's survival is a nuisance, nothing more."

"But the imp you sent to me—"

"Overstepped himself." The archdemon's yellow eyes sparkled with cruel humor. "I would have punished him for his impertinent disobedience, but you seem to have taken care of that already."

Melusine curtsied gracefully.

"I am glad to have been of service, Baron."

"Spanking an imp is sport, not service, as far as I'm concerned." The archdemon shrugged dismissively. "And poor enough sport, at that. But there is more interesting game to be found, and I have need of you tonight. Walters, you see, was a mistake. Kaeli-Thugal thought to anticipate my desires, and in doing so, she struck down the wrong man."

"A mistake?" She laughed ironically. Some mistake! No doubt the demoness would pay. "So, what would you have me do, Lord Balazel?"

The Baron placed his hands together and cracked his knuckles. He seemed pleased with himself.

"Tonight, we will strike in the open. I intend to convince the Divine that tonight is the culmination of all our recent activities in this area. You know the church named after Saint Cecilia? Many slaves of Heaven gather there tonight, and it is my intention for them to witness their leader fall before their very eyes."

"Father Keane?" Melusine gasped, surprised at the Baron's boldness. This sort of thing was rarely permitted, and even more rarely dared. "You're really going to act against him?"

The archdemon shook his powerful head.

"The good Father is more vulnerable than you might think. A score of Dubbiosi have done excellent work over the last several months, and the Father's faith is in decline. He has turned his church into a place of esoterics, not warriors, and of that crowd, hardly a one has called for his protection in years!"

Lord Balazel smiled and shook a black-clawed finger at her. "Don't confuse size with vitality, Melusine. The whole world could call itself Christian and I would not care, so long as they did not have faith. Let them wave their palms. It's meaningless."

Melusine nodded obediently. The archdemon was unusually thoughtful tonight. She found that she was actually enjoying his tangential ruminations.

"But you still haven't told me what you want me to do, Lord Balazel."

"Yes, yes, of course. I have had a long, shall we say, conversation with Kaeli-Thugal, and I am assured that this time she has clearly understood my purpose. But I want more than the one death, I want to strike fear into the hearts of the mortals who witness it. What I need is an angel who has tasted of the flesh before, who will not be overcome by the excitement of the carnal. I know your history, and I have chosen you. So just before Kaeli slays Father Keane, you will take possession of someone in the congregation and predict his fall."

Melusine felt her whole spirit thrill with the thought of taking mortal form again, even if it would just be for a short time. Forget last night, this was going to be fun! "So I'm guessing you want a pretty dramatic show here, right?"

"Exactly," the archdemon confirmed. "I knew you would understand. This must be seen to be the culmination of our work here, and so you must leave the stamp of your essence with the one you choose. As to the moment, it must be precise. The Kesh'Adae will provide the appropriate fireworks, and that will be your cue. But don't overdo it. I don't want any Hollywood theatrics overshadowing the Father's death."

"All right." She sighed regretfully. What a waste of a perfect opportunity! She had all kinds of fantastic ideas for a truly wild night. Then a potential problem struck her. "How am I going to get into the congregation? There's going to be a lot of Guardians surrounding the church, don't you think?"

"Leave that to me, my dear." Lord Balazel's armor creaked as he flexed his awesome muscles.

He stepped forward, and his Aspect shifted into that of a four-armed battledemon, with razor-sharp horns sprouting from his shoulders all the way down to his wrists. A helmet of fire blazed into existence over his head, leaving only his eyes and jaws visible to her.

"One more thing, Melusine."

"Yes, Baron?"

"You won't be staying in that mortal body," he commanded over the crackle and hiss of his helm. "Linger there one second longer than is necessary, and I'll rip you out of it myself!"

Melusine nodded quickly. One of these days, she vowed, she was going to learn how to keep her thoughts to herself.

CHAPTER 8

THE BEAUTIFUL GAME

I LOOKED FOR A MAN AMONG THEM WHO WOULD BUILD UP THE WALL AND STAND BEFORE ME IN THE GAP ON BEHALF OF THE LAND SO I WOULD NOT HAVE TO DESTROY IT, BUT I FOUND NONE.

—Ezekiel 22:30

Jami interrupted her stretching and rolled her left sock down, then adjusted the Velcro strap on her shin pad. As much as she enjoyed playing with the boys, she knew she had to be ready for their more physical style of play. She ran her hand over the rough surface of the tough green carpet and grimaced, knowing she was going to add a few more rugburns to her knees before the game was over. The smaller indoor field kept the number of big collisions down, but when you hit the artificial turf, you paid for it with skin.

"Watch out!" somebody yelled, and she ducked instinctively as a black-and-white Umbro ball bounced over her head. From behind her, there was a thump as the ball was expertly returned to the field, and Jami heard someone talking to her.

"Hey, you ready, James?" Paul was asking as he extended a hand to help her up.

"Yep," she said, reaching out. Once she was on her feet, she pulled her ponytail tight one last time, then smoothed out her gold-and-black jersey. "Where do you want me today?"

Paul didn't reply right away. Instead he looked out at their six teammates who were already on the tiny field. Their opponents, wearing white, outnumbered them with two extra players. The tall senior's brow wrinkled a little as he decided on their lineup.

"Let's keep you at center-mid. You're too short to win any balls in the air against their forwards, so I'm gonna move Adam back and let you direct traffic. Adam can help your brother if he gets in trouble when he's in. Hey, and don't forget to look for crosses."

"Yeah, of course, but why?"

"See that girl with the black hair, and the guy she's warming up with?" Paul pointed to the pair of white-shirted players. "That's their starting dee, and they're not bad, but I've got six inches on him, and Melanie has two or three on the girl. If you take the ball outside and serve it in high, we should get lots of chances."

Jami nodded. It made sense. The St. Paul Blackhawks were always one of the state's top soccer clubs, but this particular team didn't look so tough. She took a deep breath, then jogged out onto the field to join her teammates.

"What were you thinking, you idiot?" Jami snapped at Christopher. "He was your man!"

She glared at her brother, then at the ball lying enmeshed in the back of the net. Their goalkeeper was retrieving it slowly, with a look on his face that was equal parts chagrin and irritation, as the Blackhawk who'd scored on him celebrated with his teammates. It really wasn't the keeper's fault, though, because Christopher had come off his man to help Jami mark the ball handler. When Christopher made his dumb move, the Blackhawk simply passed the ball past him to the open forward, who sent a low shot rocketing past the Sting keeper. The score tied the game, three to three.

"I, uh, thought you needed help," Christopher protested lamely, his face flushed darkly red.

"Well, I didn't! I've been marking him all day without your help, so just stay on your own guy, for Pete's sake. There's only, like, a minute left!"

"Hey, hey, hey," Paul broke in. He'd scored all three of their goals, one of them on an assist from Jami, and despite his sweat-dampened hair and the heightened color on his cheeks, he still looked fresh and confident of victory. "What is this, *Family Feud?* We got time to get another one. Christopher, I know you're out of position today, but just relax, right? You gotta trust your half-back. If she gets beat, she gets beat, okay? That's her business. When you drop your guy, you just create bigger problems for everybody. Got it?"

"Yeah, I got it." Christopher nodded, obviously chagrined. "Sorry, Jami. My bad."

Jami didn't directly acknowledge his apology, as she was still angry about the goal, but she slapped his shoulder to let him know she wouldn't hold it against him before jogging to take her place at the top of the white circle. Beth looked winded, so Paul sent her to the sidelines and replaced her with Melanie. Greg, the defender who'd started for them, had twisted his ankle early in the second half, so they had no choice but to leave her brother in at left back.

The whistle blew, and Melanie passed the ball back to Jami. She dribbled outside, then sent the ball back to their right defender, Adam, as the Blackhawk midfielder rushed her. She got the pass off just as the tall, red-haired boy crashed into her, knocking her onto her hands and knees. The carpet took a layer of skin off of her palms, and she waited expectantly for a whistle, but when it didn't come, she growled angrily and pushed herself to her feet.

Was the ref blind, or what? A late tackle like that deserved a yellow, or at least a free kick.

She shook her head, then looked back and saw that Adam had already passed off to Christopher, and the midfielder who'd leveled her was still chasing after the ball, leaving her unmarked. Jami's eyes lit up, and she ignored her burning lungs and aching side, hoping she had the energy for one last sprint up the little field.

"Christopher!" she yelled, waving one arm high above her head. "Cross! Cross it!"

Two Blackhawks were converging on her brother when he looked up from his feet and met her eyes. Seeing she was open, he sent a hard ground ball skittering across the green carpet just ahead of her. She was all alone, giving the Sting a three-on-two advantage, but the nearest Blackhawk, the stocky girl, immediately came off Melanie and challenged her.

Expecting this, Jami chipped the ball, intending to lift it just over the girl's head so it would land in the box at Melanie's feet. But she was leaning back too far, and in her excitement, she hit the ball too hard.

"No!" she shouted at herself as she pulled up and watched the ball sail well over Melanie's head, arcing wide left of the goal.

But Paul had been watching, like a good ballhawk, and was already racing past his man. He leaped into the air as he coiled his tall body like a spring. The ball appeared to be far too high for him to reach it, but when he snapped his full height forward, his forehead met the ball with a loud *thwack*. The Blackhawk keeper dived backward and punched desperately at the flying ball, but his fist fell inches short, and the ball sailed past him. Jami screamed in triumph, sure that it was heading for the back of the net.

Unfortunately, the ball never made it to the mesh. Instead, it struck the center bar with a sickening metallic *bong* and rebounded in a high, soft arc. The ball seemed to be moving in slow motion, Jami thought, and it was floating right in her direction. She had what felt like an eternity to look beyond it, and saw that on the far side of the goal, the Blackhawk keeper was slow getting up, leaving the near side open. The defender at her side saw this, too, and a look of panic crossed her face as she lunged for Jami, trying desperately to get in between her and the incoming ball.

Jami pushed her away blindly, seeing nothing but the wide-open goal fifteen yards in front of her. She could see every yellow cord of the netting, lying in wait behind the goal line to receive the ball. She never felt her right leg moving forward, never felt her foot strike the ball just as it came off the ground in a furious half-volley. Her entire focus was on one thing and one thing only. *Lean forward!* her mind screamed at her body. *Lean forward! Don't you dare put it over!*

She didn't. The ball flew off the much-polished kangaroo-skin of her boot and hammered into the upper right corner of the net. She punched the air victoriously as Paul shouted and ran toward her. When he reached her, he swept her off her feet and whirled her in a sweeping circle.

"Yes! Oh, baby!" he shouted. "That was beautiful! That was spectacular!"

Her teammates gathered around her, enthusiastically thumping her on the back.

"Way to go, Jami." Melanie embraced her. "You rule, girl!"

She felt someone tugging on her ponytail and turned around to see her brother grinning broadly. "Hey, are you, like, Mia Hamm or what?" he asked her playfully. She laughed and stuck out her tongue at him, then held up a hand, which he slapped enthusiastically.

And that was the game. The Blackhawks had no sooner touched the ball when the referee blew the final whistle, with the score in the Sting's favor, four to three. Jami's hands and knees were skinned, her chest hurt, and her side still hurt where the redheaded guy had bruised her, but she could not have been happier.

Kerchunk! Brien winced as the clutch on his ancient Ford slipped again as he tried to shift into gear. It sounded bad, as if the whole transmission had fallen out of the bottom of the engine, and he just hoped the old car would somehow hold together until graduation time. A new clutch wasn't the most exciting present to look forward to, but it was one he'd be happy with. He'd already dropped a few hints that way; he hoped Dad had been paying attention.

A car behind him honked, and Brien glared at the driver's reflection in his rearview mirror. Hang on, jerky, he thought irritably as he shifted into gear again, a little more carefully this time. The light just turned, anyhow. He eased his foot gently off the clutch and was relieved as the car shifted into first without difficulty. As he pulled away from the intersection, the strip mall to the left caught his eye, and he was tempted to stop in at the Caribou for a mocha-to-go, until he remembered that he had less than ten dollars in his pocket. Better save it for gas, he decided, even though the needle was at three-quarters; it was two days until his next paycheck.

Where did the last one go anyhow? It was amazing how forty-eight dollars could just disappear in twelve days. He couldn't even remember spending any of it. Well, Derek would have plenty of cash; his parents were both rich and generous. Even so, Brien didn't envy him. At least his own parents noticed him every now and then. Derek wasn't so lucky.

In less than five minutes he was pulling up to the Wallaces' long driveway. It wasn't paved, but was covered with a strange pinkish gravel, which was probably really fashionable or something, but in his opinion, just looked weird. Their house was nice and big, with the fancy tiered roofs that were practically required in this neighborhood, but it always felt kind of empty to him. Mrs. Wallace was pretty hot for a woman with a kid in high school, but she was too busy being a vice president of a bank or something to really make the house a home, and Mr. Wallace was usually gone, off flying his plane or killing animals whose only crime was to wear horns.

Derek's RAV4 was parked in front of the three-car garage, so Brien parked behind it and turned off the ignition. He spun his keys around his finger as he walked toward the front door and rang the doorbell. The bell chimed some kind of classical melody that he knew he should probably recognize, but he couldn't properly place it. Mozart, maybe. Or it could be Bach, he wasn't sure. Something like that, anyhow.

"Hey," Derek answered the door. He reached out and pushed the glass storm door open, too. "I didn't think you'd be here for another half an hour."

"I got bored," Brien admitted as he walked into the white-marbled entryway. "I was just surfing around, and I figured I might as well come over now. So what's this computer weirdness you were talking about?"

Derek closed the door and ran his hands through his hair. Then he grinned and shook his head. "I could tell you, but you wouldn't believe me. Come see for yourself."

Brien followed his friend through the high-ceilinged hallway, then down the stairs into the basement. By the time he was halfway down them, he could hear noise coming from the direction of Derek's room, busy and staccatoed, like the radio broadcast of a ballgame with a dial that wasn't quite set on the right frequency. As he followed Derek toward the bedroom, though, he realized it wasn't a ballgame. Now it sounded more like a monologue.

But as he walked into Derek's room, which was cluttered with miscellaneous pieces of computer hardware of varying degrees of obsolescence interspersed with hardcover role-playing books from White Wolf and TSR, he decided that whoever was doing the monologue made Andrew Dice Clay sound like . . . he couldn't actually think of anyone. . . . Like someone who didn't swear quite as much, anyhow.

The voice coming out of the tall, white computer speakers was venomous, filled with hatred and contempt. It spat furious, rage-filled curses that were too serious, too intensely vicious, to be very funny. Brien, taken aback, blinked and looked over at Derek, whose expression clearly indicated the same kind of cluelessness he was feeling.

"So what happened?"

Derek pointed at his twenty-one-inch computer screen. Brien leaned forward and saw a Web page that consisted of nothing but a horned skull sitting between two candles. The candles flickered with a little three-frame animation, and the skull had a red pentagram painted on the forehead, but that was pretty much it.

"Dubyu-dubyu-dubyu dot darkspellz dot com," he read the text from the status bar out loud. "What kind of name is that?

Darkspellz . . . sounds kind of Orky. What were you doing there?"

"I don't know, I was just looking around for some spells, you know?" Derek shrugged. "There's a lot of online grimoires, spell books and stuff. I thought maybe I'd find some cool stuff that the Nottambuli could incorporate before we meet up with those vampire pussies again."

"Well, I don't see what the problem is. Can't you just click back, or is it one of those stupid sites that trap you in? Man, I hate those."

Derek made a twisted face at him. "Yeah, like I'm a complete idiot, Brien. Of course I tried to click back! It didn't work, but so what, that's no big deal, there's lots of pages like that. That's not what's interesting, though. Here, move over."

He pushed past Brien and placed his left hand on the mouse. Brien watched as his friend moved the pointer, which Derek had changed from the usual white arrowhead to a vulgar one-finger salute, across the screen to his pull-down menus. The white finger entered Favorites, then flashed red as Derek double-clicked on ESPN. Nothing happened. The candles continued to flicker, and the obscene stream of invective continued without pause.

"So maybe you're just hung. Once a program is in memory, it can keep running like this after a crash, you know. Did you try a soft boot?"

"Nope, not yet. But check it out. Did you see what's really strange about all this?"

"The candle animation's only three frames?" Brien suggested. Okay, that was a lame guess, maybe, but he couldn't see anything else particulary unusual.

He was pretty sure that the cheesy animation wasn't what Derek was getting at, but he didn't see anything mysterious in all this, either. It was probably just a bug in somebody's Java code or something. But then, as Derek pointed to something on the screen, his eyes widened.

"Hey, your sounds are turned off!"

Derek had brought up the Windows Volume Control, and

Brien could see that the Mute All box was clearly checked. That meant that they shouldn't have been able to hear anything coming out of the computer at all.

"Right." Derek nodded. "So tell me then, why are we still hearing anything?"

"Turn the speakers off," Brien suggested, ignoring the question.

"They are off!"

"No, they're just muted." Brien pointed to the little white cable running from the back of the speakers to somewhere behind the desktop. "Unplug them."

A creepy feeling started to come over him as he watched Derek reach behind his machine for the stereo jack. The creepiness threatened to graduate into a full-fledged freak-out when he saw Derek jerk the jack out of the sound card and hold it up with a dubious look on his face. Amazingly, impossibly, the obscene ranting continued unabated. It wasn't possible, and yet there was no denying the fact that he was still hearing what he was hearing.

"What's going on?" he almost shouted. It was too creepy. "Just turn it off! The whole bloody machine!"

Derek, who was starting to look a little alarmed himself, didn't argue this time. Disdaining a soft boot, he jabbed his finger into the On-Off button to shut the computer down entirely. The screen went blank, and for one blessed moment, there was silence.

"Kerchunk-whirr-whirr-whirr!"

Both of them jumped, literally, as Derek's inkjet printer came unexpectedly to life, its green online light flashing and its jets whirring madly back and forth as first one, then two, then three sheets of paper were drawn from the paper feed and spit out, covered by lines and lines of simple black text, into the paper tray.

This was like *Poltergeist*, only worse, Brien thought, feeling like the world was spinning around him. He stared fixedly at the sheets being rapidly ejected from the DeskJet, counting about fifteen sheets in all printed out and piled up before the green light faded and the printer ceased its frenzied activity. The room was abruptly quiet, and Brien found that he was holding his breath and hunching his shoulders, as if he'd been expecting something to leap up and punch him. He waited before daring to open his mouth, afraid that his voice might spark more of this weird ghost-in-the-machine thing.

"What . . . the . . . what was that?" he said at last. He felt drained, as if the fright had sucked all the energy right out of him.

"I have no idea," Derek said absently as he picked up the printed pages and began to shuffle eagerly through them. "That was cool! I wonder if someone is trying to tell us something?"

CHAPTER 9

SWEET TASTE OF A SOUL

I WOULD BE THE ONE
TO HOLD YOU DOWN
KISS YOU SO HARD
I'LL TAKE YOUR BREATH AWAY
—Sarah McLachlan ("Possession")

Jami slouched in the passenger side, almost totally relaxed, and the rocking motion of the truck as it sped over the highway through the darkness made her eyelids feel as if they were being drawn slowly, but inexorably, downward. At her side Christopher drove silently down the highway toward their home, but there was something about him, a certain inner tension, that prevented her from drifting off into sleep.

Is he mad at me for not inviting him to the mall? Angie had blown them off for Jill's party, so it had just been her and Rachel shopping tonight. Neither one of them had bought much; all she'd picked up was a bag of ponytail holders and a dance mix CD. But Christopher hadn't said much after picking them up in front of Nordstrom's. Actually, now that she thought about it, he hadn't said more than ten words to Rachel on the way there or on the way back, although he'd stolen plenty of sneaky glances at her in the rearview mirror before dropping her off at her house. Jami, of course, had pretended not to notice.

"Hey," she said finally.

Well, that was what she meant to say. It was too much of an

effort to really open her mouth, so it came out as more of an wordless grunt.

Christopher glanced over at her. His eyes were open and alert, and he had an inquisitive look on his face.

"What?"

Jami smiled lazily at her brother. It was kind of nice having someone to drive you around, she thought. As she looked at him, she realized that whatever was bothering him probably didn't have anything to do with Rachel. He didn't look confused and pathetic enough for it to be girl trouble.

"You're so serious," she told him. "What are you thinking about?"

He was, too. She didn't remember him being this way so much before. It made him seem older. She knew whatever had happened to him last winter had been very different than her own experiences on Ahura Azhda, and he still wasn't talking about it.

Not that that was going to stop her from bringing it up. He was her brother, after all, and she had the right to know what was going on with him. She rubbed at her eyes with the palms of her hands, grinding the itch out of them, then remembered, too late, that Rachel had done her makeup before they went out. Oh well, it was dark and they were going home anyhow.

"You look like a raccoon," Christopher told her instead of answering her as they came to a stop at the ninety-six light, and the red glare lit up the interior of the vehicle like a school gymnasium decorated for a cheesy dance.

"Oh, shut up, I do not."

"Okay," he agreed mildly, in a superior, whatever-you-say tone of voice.

She yawned and rubbed her eyes again, too tired to argue or even care what she looked like. Did raccoons hibernate? That's what she needed right now, about six months of sleep. She was still sore from the game, and they had church in the morning.

Forget it, she decided wearily. If Christopher wanted to tell her anything, he'd tell her. There wasn't any point in trying to drag it out of him. She sighed deeply and relaxed, letting her whole body melt into the leather seats. She felt like a puddle, spreading out into nothingness. . . .

The screech of the brakes woke her, and her arms shot out automatically, as she braced for the inevitable collision. Her eyes snapped open, but incredibly, she saw nothing at first but an explosion of red, gold, and white. She shook her head, thinking she was seeing things, until she recognized an angelic form pointing a sword of flame toward the side of the road.

Christopher reacted before she found her voice, and wrenched the wheel hard to the right. The SUV shuddered, and for one awful moment Jami thought they were out of control and heading straight for the ditch. She put her feet up on the dashboard and swallowed a scream, but Christopher, snarling unintelligibly under his breath, managed to control the Explorer's skid and finally wrestled the truck to a stop on the gravel of the road shoulder.

"What was that!" Jami exclaimed breathlessly. Her heart was pounding so hard that it almost hurt.

"I'm not sure. . . ." Christopher's voice trailed off. "I think it was Mariel!"

"That's what I thought, too! But what, I mean—"

She never finished the sentence because as she turned to look at her brother, she saw him raise his hand to his eyes as a bright light began to wash over them. The light sped toward them, like a dragon leaping out of the darkness, with a deep sound like an onrushing wind. It took her a moment to realize just what it was.

"Wheeeeeeeaaaaaaaaarrrrrrrrrhhhhh!"

The Explorer swayed back and forth as a giant pickup rocketed past them, missing them by inches as it roared down the wrong side of the road. It was so close that she didn't really see the truck itself, just the three numbers on the side flashing by and branding their silver image into her brain—one fifty. As in F-150, the Ford. It was going at least a hundred miles an hour, judging by the violence of its passing.

"Oh . . . my . . . God," Jami slumped back in her seat.

"Holy cats!" Christopher was breathing hard himself. "He

must be smashed! How could you not know you're on the wrong side of the road? I mean, if he'd hit us, we'd be in freaking orbit right now!"

Jami felt sick. It was starting all over again. Angels, and demons, and dragons, and blood and magic and death. She didn't think she could handle this sort of thing anymore, not now that she knew it all was real. But maybe it was just a coincidence? Accidents happened all the time. Maybe it wasn't Mariel they'd seen. But then, why had Christopher chosen that very moment to pull over? The thought that someone might be after her again was almost more than she could bear.

"Oh, just shut up. I don't even want to think about it."

Christopher put his head in his hands. She wondered what he was doing, then realized he was praying. But she was far too shaken to follow his example.

When he finished, Christopher ran his hands through his hair and pressed the button that rolled the driver's side window down. The night breeze was cool, but it felt good on her sweat-damped brow.

"Hey, I know you're out there somewhere, Mariel," she heard her brother shout out into the darkness. "Thanks! Thanks for watching out for us, and keeping us from harm!"

Christopher pressed the button again, and the window rolled up. He turned and gave Jami an almost defiant look. He wanted her to join him in the prayer of thanks, she realized; she should. She knew she should. But she just couldn't, at least not right now.

"Well, you know she just saved our lives," he said defensively, as if he was afraid she was going to get on his case. "We were toast there, you know."

Jami started to laugh, but it came out as more of a hysterical sob. She bit her lip, and the pain helped avert the tears that were pressing at her eyes.

"I know she did, I know she did," she repeated, trying to erase from her mind the terrible image of the deadly accident that had been intended for them. "But Christopher . . ."

"Yes?"

"I don't want to talk about it now. I don't even want to think about it. Just take me home. Please."

She closed her eyes, desperately hoping he wouldn't argue with her. There was a moment's silence, and then she heard his seat creak and felt his finger gently wiping away an errant tear that had escaped her eyelids. His surprising gesture comforted her, a little. Before long the motor revved, and there was a bump as the vehicle climbed over the shoulder and returned to the smooth asphalt of the road.

The truck resumed its smooth rocking motion, but Jami found no relaxation in it now. She took comfort in only one thing. As they flew through the night, she hugged her knees tightly and listened to her brother's voice softly reciting that most comforting of Psalms.

". . . though I walk through the valley of the Shadow of Death, I will fear no evil. . . ."

Melusine floated, her wings outstretched, on the periphery of the small Fallen army soaring high above the parking lot of the suburban Catholic church. It was a big parish, an affluent one, and the parking lot was filled with Audis, Acuras, BMWs, Ford Explorers, and more than a few Mercedes. The churchgoers were still filing in to the large brick building, which was virtually indisinguishable in its architectural blandness from the big public high school just down the road, but the constant flow of people had slowed to a trickle as it approached the time for the evening Mass to begin.

There were a lot of Guardians there, too, and by the looks of it, they were alert to the large gathering of Fallen circling above them. They were positioned at both of the main entrances, and most of them had drawn their swords, which from her vantage point made the church look like a wide landing strip lined with orange-red beacons. There were almost enough Divine to make up two full cohorts, which was nowhere near enough to stand against the four cohorts of Mordrim and eight-score malakim that the Baron had summoned. In the midst of all these demons were also seven huge Kesh'Adae. They were purple-skinned archdemons with great skeletal wings three times the spanning length of Melusine's own. Their enchanted armor was constructed of human bones, and they carried evil-looking maces adorned liberally with animal horns.

As she sailed comfortably on the cool night breeze, Melusine spied the Assassin, who bore the painful signs of her "conversation" with Lord Balazel. Melusine winced, for Kaeli-Thugal's back was a truly nauseating sight. From her shoulders to her waist, every vestige of skin had been flayed from her, and Melusine could see exposed muscles moving whenever the tortured angel stroked her wings. She was an object lesson to every Fallen spirit who saw her: Don't screw up tonight! Archdemons could be many things, but subtle they were not. Melusine got the point. She knew what she was supposed to do, and she would do exactly that. This was no time for improvisation.

The last mortal finally finished her trek from car to church door, and at a wave of Balazel's hand, an imp sounded three blasts on a horn. Melusine flew to Kaeli's side as the Malakim lined up in two long rows above the others, while the Mordrim positioned themselves behind their captains in three downward-pointing triangles. She exchanged a grim nod with the Assassin when, below them, more flames flickered into life as the remaining Guardians drew their swords, knowing that the Fallen attack was imminent.

The horn sounded again, but this time the imp gave it a single sustained blast. Immediately the Malakim began hurling their darts down at the enemy, small but deadly bolts of darkly burning flame. Dart after dart plunged downward, but mostly they just bounced off the armor hidden under the angels' white robes or were slashed to harmless pieces by the fiery Divine swords. Melusine saw two or three unlucky Guardians fall and disappear, struck down as their armor failed them, but for the most part, the rain of missiles didn't accomplish much.

It did, however, spark a response flung up at the Fallen by a score of Romakhim slingers who had somehow escaped detection in their position behind the church. The small group of angels braved the darts of the Malakim to leap onto the rooftop and began to hurl their balls of fire skyward. The incendiary missiles worked pretty well, considering that there weren't a lot of them, and several Malakim burst into flames and perished. But the Baron quickly ordered the Malakim to concentrate their darts onto the rooftop, and the heavy hail of descending darts soon sent the Divine slingers running off in all directions.

"Now!" Balazel shouted and the three troops of Mordrim obediently launched themselves toward the ground. With their dark wings furled behind them, they looked just like the Malakim's darts, only bigger and redder. More lethal, too.

"Follow me!" the Assassin cried as she began her descent.

Melusine tucked her own wings behind her back and plunged headfirst in a rapid dive. She saw that Kaeli was following the middle group, which was descending slower than the other two. She felt a tightness in her stomach that she had not known for quite some time; she might be immortal, but there were some things even an immortal didn't want to experience and one of them was the Beyond. Besides, she was a Temptress, not a war demon. She'd been around for a long, long time, and this was the closest she'd been to a real angelic battle since she'd ridden Leviathan so very long ago.

The large group of Mordrim in front of her abruptly peeled off in two directions, apparently intending to encircle the church. She had no idea what they were doing, but she didn't have time to think about it, because she suddenly realized that a Guardian was standing directly beneath her. He jabbed his sword upward, and its flames licked at her arms as she violently twisted her body and narrowly avoided skewering herself on the weapon.

"Help!" she cried as he lashed out at her. "Somebody, help!"

Where did all those blasted Mordrim go? she wondered as he slashed at her head and she ducked under the blow. Wasn't that the whole point, for them to do the fighting so she wouldn't have to?

The Guardian's face was pale, but intense, and he glared at her as if his eyes could run her through. Not that it was necessary, of course, since he was already doing his best to stab her with his sword. She stumbled backward, baring her fangs in futile defiance as he closed in on her.

Then something slammed into her back, and she found herself sprawled facedown on the ground. She rolled sideways and looked up to see Kaeli slipping past a violent thrust from the Guardian's sword. Then, as the Divine angel lurched forward, she slashed one of her curved daggers across his unprotected face and buried the other one in his stomach. Melusine laughed, relieved, as her assailant shrieked and scrabbled at his face, then exploded in a blinding flash of white.

"Thanks," Melusine said as the Assassin helped her to her feet.

"Hurry, we've got to get inside," Kaeli replied urgently. "The Baron doesn't know how long the Mordrim can secure the perimeter if those Divine return in force."

Oh, fabulous, Melusine thought bitterly as she leaped through the bricks of the church wall and into the half-filled sanctuary. First that Guardian tries to stab me, and the next thing is we're getting trapped inside a cursed church, of all places! And I thought last night was bad?

"I got him." Kaeli patted her back reassuringly, then sauntered confidently toward the middle-aged man in the cassock who was speaking at the lectern.

How could she be so calm now? Of course, considering that the poor Assassin had spent the afternoon getting literally torn apart by Balazel, knocking off a priest in the middle of an enemy stronghold was probably a pleasure by comparison. Why, oh why, she lamented, couldn't she have just spent this evening trying to seduce Christopher into surfing porn sites?

Well, time to get to work. She glanced around the people sitting in the pews, looking to see if anyone obvious caught her eye. But no one stuck out; they all appeared to be nice, normal people, the kind of folks you'd expect to show up for Mass on a Saturday night. She sighed and opened her senses, allowing the flow of casual thoughts to sweep over her. . . .

"... *that's an interesting point* ..."

"... *wonder who the Vikes will draft this year.* .."

"... *who's she, she's kinda cute.* .."

"... *and I just pray, Lord Jesus—*"

Ouch! Not that one! Melusine felt as if her brain had been singed.

"... *could I be more bored if* ..."

"... *I hate that little witch, always thinks she's better* ..."

Now there was someone with promise! A little bitterness, a touch of envy, and a veritable cornucopia of raw, spiteful hate. She would do nicely. Melusine easily located the woman she was looking for: She was an attractive, middle-aged woman with brown hair in a navy blue suit, sitting quite properly next to a man who was probably her husband. Her face was calm and impassive, revealing no sign of the malevolent thoughts she harbored inside her head.

Melusine entered fully into the immaterial and relaxed, even as she seized upon the seething hatred that roared like a torrent around the woman's spirit. It was a beaten, scrawny thing, its fire sucked dry by the bile of its surroundings, and offered no resistance to Melusine as she immersed herself in the raging river. She flowed with the hatred, adding to it, letting it engulf her. How this woman could hate! And yet she had so little cause for it, the irony made Melusine laugh. She had food, clothing, shelter, and a husband who doted on her, all of her needs were met and more, and yet she was desperately, almost violently, unhappy.

This would not be a difficult possession, not at all. Melusine simply wrapped herself around the wan little spirit and seized it ... so!

She moaned as suddenly the world changed around her. The river, the spirit, her vision itself was altered. All at once, she could feel, and taste, and smell, and hear. It was exhilarating! It was a rush that simply would not stop! Yes! Yes! Oh, yes! She glanced up and saw the stained-glass windows high on either side of her, and it seemed to her that the lovely hues of the leaded glass were pure light jeweled gloriously in radiance.

Next to her she could hear someone breathing heavily, loudly, and it was the most wonderful thing she'd ever heard. The carnality of it all took her breath away, and she could feel the woman's body, her body, responding to her excitement. She closed her eyes and ran her hands over this exquisite thing, and the feel of the mortal flesh sent shivers up and down her spine. She was overcome with lust for herself, for the babbling priest, for the people sitting next to her, for the flesh of all mankind.

Swept away by pure carnal intoxication, she reached blindly out for the person on her right. There was a shocked gasp, and the deeply offended glare of the elderly gray-haired woman she'd inadvertently touched hurled Melusine out of her blissful state just in time to hear the howl of onrushing wind that marked the arrival of the Kesh'Adai.

All twelve stained-glass windows exploded inward simultaneously, raining sharp shards of leaded glass down on the congregation in a colorful but razor-sharp cascade. People screamed in pain and fear, but mostly in bewilderment, as the evil wind spiraled down inside the sanctuary itself, and swirled around them in a riot of sound and fury. Melusine nodded, pleased by the archdemons' awe-inspiring display.

That, no doubt, was her cue. Showtime!

She leaped to her feet and raised both her hands, shrieking loudly. The winds abruptly died, and she let her arms fall limply to her sides as she dropped her head on her chest like a ragdoll. Then, as people nearby started to point at her, she stumbled awkwardly out into the central aisle. She stood there for a short moment, moaning and drooling, then rolled her eyes back so only the whites would show and lifted her head.

Father Keane was staring at her, she saw, as was most of his congregation. He was a pudgy man, on the short side, with a florid complexion and a full dark head of hair. He seemed more perplexed than fearful, even when she slowly raised one arm and pointed a nicely manicured finger at him.

"You asked, where is my victory, good Father," she mocked him in her deepest, scariest voice. "You asked, where is my sting?

It is in you even now, Father, and there is nothing your Nazarene can do about that!"

It was hard, so very hard, but Melusine steeled herself to relinquish the woman's body. Remembering Balazel's instructions as well as his baleful threat, she stamped an indelible word into the woman's mind, then hurled herself so violently out of the mortal's frame that the body collapsed with the shock, falling unconscious to the red-carpeted floor. Now safely back in the spirit world, she saw Kaeli-Thugal strike. It was a perfect blow. Father Keane raised both hands to his head, then slumped forward, knocking over the wooden lectern and smashing it under the weight of his body as he struck the floor two feet below the elevated platform on which he had been standing.

There were screams of fear and cries of horror, and Melusine felt giddy with delight. She felt revived, renewed, and she shouted triumphantly as she leaped up from the floor of the chaos-filled sanctuary to follow the killer angel out one of the shattered windows. Behind her, the shrieks and cries grew louder and more panicked as the churchgoers discovered that the Father had indeed gone the way of all flesh.

Flanked by the Kesh'Adai, Balazel was waiting for them on the rooftop, grinning from one bestial ear to the other.

"Well done, both of you," he praised them. "Perfect! This was a great victory tonight!"

But was it really? Melusine wondered about that. They hadn't gained the Father's soul; in fact, by killing him they'd lost it forever, and it wasn't as if his mealy, doubt-filled preaching had been doing them any real harm. The whole thing had been fun, to be sure, but how was it a win? Of course, the Baron had hinted that he had something else going on. Well, even if Balazel didn't know what he was doing, she wasn't about to argue with him. Especially since she could see the Mordrim surrounding the church were starting to look pretty nervous.

Just as she noticed this, one of the Mordrim's captains approached and bowed before the archdemon.

"Baron, we've received a report of a Divine force heading this way, led by a pair of Thrones," he informed Lord Balazel. "It's very large, possibly more than a dozen cohorts. I don't think we can fight them."

Balazel was unconcerned. "I have no intention of fighting them," he told the captain. "Go, all of you, return to whatever it is you normally do. Go now, and quickly!"

He turned to Melusine and nodded, a surprisingly graceful gesture in a being so large and powerful.

"You have done well," he repeated. "But don't forget to keep your charge out of my way. That remains paramount!"

Melusine scratched her head and watched as the big archdemon flew away, followed by his seven powerful companions. One of these days she was going to have to learn what the Baron was doing here in the Cities. She smiled as her savior, Kaeli-Thugal, gave her a little wave, and then she, too, was gone, disappearing into the dark night sky. Melusine wondered if she'd ever see the demoness again. She seemed pretty decent, for an angel of death, and the Temptress hoped her back would heal soon.

The Mordrim scattered every which way, reminding her that it was time to vacate the premises unless she felt up to taking on a legion of infuriated Divine by herself. Already she could see the glowing light of their approach appearing on the horizon like a false dawn as they flew from the east. Yes, it was definitely time to go.

CHAPTER 10

IMMORTAL KOMBAT

SINCE THE FIRST DAY THAT YOU SET YOUR MIND TO GAIN UNDERSTAND-
ING AND TO HUMBLE YOURSELF BEFORE YOUR GOD, YOUR WORDS WERE
HEARD, AND I HAVE COME IN RESPONSE TO THEM. BUT THE PRINCE OF
THE PERSIAN KINGDOM RESISTED ME TWENTY-ONE DAYS. THEN
MICHAEL, ONE OF THE CHIEF PRINCES, CAME TO HELP ME, BECAUSE I WAS
DETAINED THERE WITH THE KING OF PERSIA.

—Daniel 10:12–13

The Lewis house appeared to be quiet. The windows were dark, and the mortal family slumbered peacefully. Melusine hoped it had been an uneventful evening for everyone, mortals and angels alike, as she didn't feel up to invading Christopher's dreams tonight. Humans were beasts, as far as she was concerned; they were simply animals endowed with the merest spark of angelic fire, but sometimes she envied them their ability to sleep. How nice it would be to simply shut the world out for a time and not have to worry about anything, anything at all.

She alighted softly on the rooftop. The suburban neighborhood didn't provide for a very interesting view, mostly trees, rooftops, and then more trees, but the night's activities had left her edgy and restless. Below her, she could sense the household angels, Divine and Fallen both, as they kept watch on their charges and each other.

There were three almost directly beneath her, that would be Aliel and Pandaema in Holli's room, joined, no doubt, by Lucrezia, the mother's Temptress, who could always be found almost anywhere except where she was supposed to be. An angel in the next room had to be Paulus, Jami's handsome Guardian, and Melusine amused herself with the thought of slipping down and trying to seduce him. She didn't harbor any hopes of success, but he was so very yummy despite his stuck-up, priggish manner. There were two more Divine on the far side of the house, but she didn't give them much thought. Betty, the mother, was lost, but harmless, and Incandazael appeared to have the father's arrogantly intellectual soul quite firmly in his grasp.

That left only one angel unaccounted for, Mariel. Melusine reached behind her head and twisted her long mane of hair into a loosely knotted bundle. How she'd like to get her hands around Mariel's cursed chicken neck! It was strange how quickly the tables had turned in the last three months, as Melusine had always been able to push her rival around effortlessly in the past. She shrugged. That was how the Great Game was played. Until she could get Christopher to abandon his faith, or at least steep himself deeply enough in sin to provide her with more leverage, she'd be dependent upon her wits to defeat the Divine angel.

Right now the rules were stacked against her, but Christopher was young yet, and there was plenty of time. He was a smart boy, and she still had high hopes for his college experience. College was always a wonderful place to shatter a young man's faith, especially those older sanctuaries that had been personally defiled by the most cunning of the Dark Sefiroth, the Archduke Baal Anath himself.

Then the slightest breeze seemed to brush her cheek, and she looked back just in time to see flames sailing toward her eyes. She leaped back instinctively, and the angelic blade flashed past her face and through the nearby chimney.

"You broke the Concordat!" Mariel screamed at her, her green eyes wild and feral. "You tried to kill him! Both of them!"

What? Melusine might have laughed if the situation hadn't been so dire. Mariel wasn't very big, but she was really looking pissed, and then there was that sword, too. Flames crackled dangerously as the Guardian advanced toward her, sword in hand, holding her white wings arched high over her head like a hawk about to strike. Fortunately, as Mariel approached, she could feel a surge of energy below as the other angels in the house became aware of the confrontation.

Melusine put up her hands and dropped into a crouch, spreading her own wings in preparation for flight. But Mariel was faster than she expected, and struck before she could leap away from the rooftop. Although the angel's thrust missed her body, Melusine couldn't help shrieking as the flames seared her left wing.

Curse the King, that hurt! But the sword had gotten stuck in her feathers, and when Mariel tried to pull it back, Melusine grabbed the angel's outstretched arm. "Drop it!" she screamed as she tugged with one hand and slammed her fist up against Mariel's elbow. There was a satisfying crack, and now it was the Guardian's turn to shriek with pain. Melusine shook her blazing wing, and the searing sensation receded just a little as she felt the weight of the sword fall away from her and toward the ground below. The flames died out a moment later, but the awful stench of her burned feathers was tremendous.

Furious, Melusine lashed out with one clawed hand and managed to score the blonde's insipidly pretty face. Mariel cried out again, and Melusine took advantage of the angel's distress to leap at her, smashing her violently against the chimney. She leaned forward, throwing all her weight into the angel, and kept Mariel pinned with a hand across her face as she drew back her other hand. She was really starting to enjoy herself as she waved long fingernails before Mariel's helplessly raging eyes.

"I told you I'd rip those out someday!" she snarled triumphantly. "Owwww!"

Melusine shrieked and stumbled backward, clutching at her left hand.

"You bit me!" She couldn't believe how much it hurt. Son of Gog and Magog! "You bit me—I can't believe you bit me!"

"And I'll bite you again, Hellwhore!"

"Ooh, watch your language, Blondie!" Melusine laughed at her rival.

Mariel's right arm was hanging at an awkward angle, but she looked more than ready to continue the battle. Fine, Melusine thought, just fine! Let's bring it on, if that's how you want it. You're going down! But then the Divine angel stepped back unexpectedly, just as she heard the sound of someone behind her clapping slowly.

" 'See, I will send venomous snakes among you,' " a familiar voice declaimed theatrically. " 'Vipers that cannot be charmed, and they will bite you,' declares the Lord."

"Shut up, Incanno," Mariel said angrily as Melusine whirled around, plenty mad herself about the unwanted interruption. "She's the snake!"

As she turned around, Melusine saw that Incandazael, the sarcastic, blue-skinned Tempter of Christopher's father, was standing behind her. Paulus was at his side, and both angels, Divine and Fallen, appeared to be amused with the situation they'd discovered. Aliel was there too, and Holli's short-haired Guardian shot her a nasty look before shoving past her to protectively embrace Mariel.

"I love a good catfight, don't you?" Incandazael nudged Paulus. "Give you two-to-one on Mel."

"I don't gamble," the Guardian replied seriously, but he was smiling, the jerk. "Though I have confidence that Mariel would have triumphed in the end."

What-ever!

"Tell Aliel to get out of the way and you can find out, haloboy," Melusine shot back. "I'll finish this right now!"

"No one's finishing anything," Paulus told her imperiously, and to her surprise, Incandazael nodded in agreement. "Melusine, why were you attacking Mariel? You know that's not allowed."

Melusine stared at him disbelievingly. He was blaming her! How unfair was that! She wrinkled her lip and threw her hands up in exasperation.

"Attacking her? What do you mean? I was just up here minding my own business when she tried to take my head off!"

Paulus exchanged a surprised look with Incandazael, but

before either angel said anything, Mariel freed herself from Aliel and tried to get in her face.

"Because she tried to kill him! She broke the Concordat!" The Divine angel was angrier than Melusine had ever seen her before. "You possessed that poor man and you used him to try and kill them. I had every right to go after you, and I still do!"

What in the secret seventh name of the sun, moon, and stars was she jabbering about? Melusine had always been of the opinion that Mariel wasn't quite all together upstairs. Now, the little cow appeared to have sailed completely off the deep end.

"I didn't kill anyone," she corrected her rival. "That Slayer did, and she didn't just try, either. I think she blew out half his brain with the stroke she laid on him."

For some reason, her words seemed to astonish Mariel. She stared blankly at Melusine, her green eyes even more clueless than usual.

"Ah, Melusine, Christopher's sleeping in his room," Aliel said. "He's not dead."

"Of course he's not dead," Incandazael said, sounding irritated. "And why would Melusine try to kill him anyhow? She's not completely stupid."

"Gee, thanks," Melusine told the Tempter dryly. "And who said anything about Christopher? I was talking about Father Keane."

"Father Keane?" All four angels chorused in surprised unison.

"They took him out?" added Incandazael. "Tonight?"

"Yeah, there was quite the fireworks show going on at St. Cecilia's tonight," Melusine explained, enjoying the stunned expression on the others' faces, and most particularly the confused worry she saw now dawning on Mariel's. "You'll hear all about it soon enough. The point is, I was quite occupied with watching the good Father buy the farm, and I'm starting to suspect that I've been falsely accused of something, although I'm not quite sure what."

She cocked an eyebrow at Mariel. "So, what is it, exactly, that you think I did?"

"Well, someone did it," the angel protested defensively. "Don't pretend you don't know! Someone sicced a Nihil on a drunk man and tried to make him smash into Christopher when he was driving home tonight. Jami was in the car with him, and they both would have died if I hadn't warned him to pull off the road and get out of the way!"

Still harboring her suspicions of Melusine, the angel's green eyes narrowed again. "And you weren't here, so I knew it had to be you."

Melusine laughed in the angel's face, which was still marked by her claws, she was pleased to note. "Mariel, could you be more clueless?" She ticked off points on her fingers. "First of all, and unlike you, I'm not an idiot. Second, I don't want Christopher dead, as you, of all angels, should know. Third, I was at St. Cecilia's tonight, like I said, and fourth, there's about, what, five million Fallen in this principality alone, and any one of them might have taken a crack at him."

But even as she spoke, she was worrying about what she'd just learned. Even Balazel, the outsider, knew Christopher was off the death list. She'd lied about the other Fallen, most of whom wouldn't even think of daring to raise a hand against the boy. He was shielded against them, blooded and hedged, so who would be crazy enough to go after him now? Prince Bloodwinter would be furious, not to mention other, even more dangerous spirits whose powerful names she didn't like to even think to herself.

"Well, isn't this interesting?" Incandazael smiled, his teeth gleaming whitely against his indigo face. "Mariel, I really think you should tell Melusine you're sorry. Don't you agree, Paulus?"

Mariel's eyes blazed at the Tempter's provocative words, but Melusine waved him off before her rival could open her mouth and say something that would make her lose her train of thought. Mariel was right about one thing. Someone had tried to kill Christopher and Jami, but who? As she thought about the possibilities, her mind kept returning to one eminently probable suspect.

"Like I care what she has to say." It wasn't as if she was going to accept an apology anyhow. "But tell me one thing. Was Pan-daema here earlier tonight?"

Aliel, the Tempter's longtime foe, nodded her confirmation. Good, that made things a little easier to sort out.

"And Shaeloba?"

"No, she wasn't." Paulus shook his head, then looked at her curiously. "You can't think that she'd try to harm Jami now. That makes no sense!"

Melusine shrugged. She didn't think so, either, but then again, she'd been wrong before. People did things that weren't in their best interests all the time, and strangely enough, so did angels. Of course, unlike their charges, it was unusual for a Tempter to do anything this blatantly stupid. What was going on here? First the attacks, then the deal with Jami, and now this. Events appeared to be spiraling out of control, but was it possible that someone was just arranging things to look that way? It was impossible for her to tell, but she was starting to suspect that Lord Balazel was somehow involved in all this, considering that the chaos had only begun after the archdemon had arrived in the Cities, mysterious and alone.

"I didn't say it did, Paulus." She raised her wings, which had healed and were once again whole, and allowed the wind to ruf-fle her black feathers. The night breeze felt lovely and cool, eras-ing any lingering feeling of their recent scalding.

"Oh, and Mariel?"

"What?"

Melusine swung her arm as hard and as fast as she could, tak-ing Mariel completely by surprise as she slapped her across the face with an open hand. The Divine angel cried out and stumbled sideways, almost losing her balance as she staggered into the hard brick of the chimney. She raised her hands to her face, but not before Melusine saw a satisfyingly red handprint marking the Guardian's white skin.

The other two Guardians hissed, but neither Paulus nor Aliel made any move to intervene, and Melusine had no intention of waiting around to listen to their outraged protests. She leaped off the rooftop in a graceful backflip, then stroked her wings and flew upside-down toward the south, toward the lights of the city, grinning triumphantly as the throaty sound of Incandazael's laughter floated behind her on the dark winds of the night.

First Avenue was crowded, especially considering that it was a Sunday night. The mortal crowd seemed younger than usual, and she wondered if it was an all-ages night or if the steroid-enhanced humans checking ID at the door were simply more lax than usual this evening. The music was frenetic and full of energy, accompanied by a blinding array of colored lights that strobed and flashed madly across the crowded dance floor.

"Hey, Melusine." A cloud of red mist that had been swirling amidst the dancers coalesced in front of her, and a tall, attractive angel stepped out of it. He was clothed only in a charming smile, and his violet eyes were glazed over with vacant hunger. "I found this little girl who's wacked out of her mind on something or other. Utterly zonked! Come on, let's ride her and see if we can make her do anything fun!"

Melusine laughed. Sessarael was one of her favorite lust demons. His specialty was young women, and he preyed on them with the single-minded focus of a starving dog.

"Thanks, Sessa, but I'm looking for someone. Have you seen an archangel called Balazel anywhere around? He's an outsider, and he's big, with kind of a grayish-blue aura."

The lust demon blinked, surprised, and his vacuous eyes almost managed to focus on her for a second. "Lord Balazel? You'd better stay away from that bad boy. They say he tore up a couple of death-angels last night!"

Melusine rolled her eyes. By next week she had no doubts that a story would be going around that the archdemon had single-handedly foiled a major insurrection against Prince Bloodwinter. That, or he'd started one. Gossip was not only a human failing. "That's him."

Sessarael threw up his hands. "Okay, but I don't see what you want with him. He doesn't sound like a good time to me. Sure you don't want to come party instead?"

"Yes, I'm sure." Melusine folded her arms. Sessarael was starting to annoy her. "Now, where is he?"

The lustful demon pointed upstairs. "He's upstairs, over in the corner. Everybody's afraid to go near him. I don't blame them."

"Me neither!" Melusine agreed. Instead of thanking him, she ran one finger slowly down his bare chest. "And have fun. Maybe next time."

The demon's eyes flared hungrily, and he smiled even as his body began to fade back into translucence. Moments later there was only a red cloud in front of her, swaying and swirling provocatively to the rhythm of the furious beat. Then Sessarael disappeared amidst the crowd of mortals, avidly seeking his unsuspecting victim.

The stairs were dark and empty, except for a depressed-looking girl smoking a cigarette on the bottom step and a young couple exchanging furiously quiet words on the landing in the middle of the staircase. As Melusine approached them, she saw that the heavily pierced young man appeared to be trying to kiss the girl, who also sported copious facial metal, but to no avail.

Oh, come on, honey. Get with the program! Melusine lashed the girl with a vivid jolt of sensual desire as she walked past her. The girl responded with an audible sigh and began to stare at the boy with eyes suddenly grown dreamy and heavy-lidded. By the time she reached the top of the stairs, the two were locked in a clench that would have required a bolt of lightning to separate them. Or two big magnets, she thought wryly.

Once upstairs, it wasn't hard to find Lord Balazel. He sat by himself in the far corner of the room, sipping lightly at a half-filled wineglass that appeared to be at great risk in his thick-knuckled, unwieldy hands. Both the nearby angels and mortals were doing their best to ignore him, as in the material world, he looked like nothing so much as an oversize serial killer. His head was bald, three chins sagged around the base of his neck like a terraced hill, and his dark, beady eyes looked mean and petty.

Melusine had to resist the urge to giggle at him as she bowed respectfully before him. The archdemon was a brute, there was no question about that, but she knew he was far more intelligent than his appearance suggested tonight. Perhaps he was slumming and looking for amusement? Melusine reflected on the hideous image of Kaeli-Thugal's back and wondered if she'd made a mistake in coming here. You never knew what might pass for an archdemon's amusement.

"No, you don't," Balazel told her, reading her mind again. "But you didn't make a mistake. I came because I knew you'd show up here eventually. Maybe you'd be more comfortable if I took a different form?"

In an instant the scene before her changed. In the place of the big man-mountain sat a slender, well-groomed man in a high-buttoned Italian suit with a very thin mustache. The shirt collar was fashionably broad, and spread to expose a silk tie of outrageously vivid colors. Only the wineglass, and the beady eyes that now lurked behind a pair of round wire spectacles, remained the same.

"Is this better?"

Melusine shrugged. "The Saloon is down the street and around the corner. I think the raving flamer look might go over a little better down there."

"Indeed?" The delicate man arched his plucked eyebrows. "Very well."

And once again the massive serial killer sat before her. The archdemon waved a thick, stubby-fingered hand toward a nearby chair, and it slid across the floor, coming to a rest immediately behind her. She nodded her thanks and sat, leaning back to keep her nose a healthy distance from the sour, sweaty odor that was emanating all too pungently from his being.

"Do you have to do that?" she complained.

"I believe in a holistic approach to an Aspect. I derive a certain aesthetic pleasure from the artistry involved in the construction of the whole."

Aesthetic? Melusine winced. The acrid smell was making her eyes tear up. Anesthetic was more like it.

"Well, okay." She gave in resignedly. It wasn't wise to argue with a demonic baron. "But how did you know I'd come here?"

"Because I assumed you'd want to find me after you learned that Shaeloba tried to kill Christopher and Jami Lewis."

Melusine started. "You know that? I mean, do you think so, too?" She paused and thought for a moment. "You're sure it was Shaeloba? I thought it was possible, but then, why would she want Jami dead? That doesn't make any sense. She's the one on the hook for the stupid girl, after all."

"You're not much for intrigue, are you, little Melusine." The Baron smiled, exposing several missing teeth. "Can't you see that Shaeloba blames you for the loss of Jami to the Enemy? I imagine that after last night's disaster, she's been trying to figure out how to make you take the fall for the loss of the girl's soul as well as Christopher's. I wouldn't be surprised to learn that she's been planning this for some time now."

"How do you know so much about her?" she protested. "You're not even from around here!"

The archdemon was making a lot of sense, though, now that she thought about it. Shaeloba had been acting strangely of late, but Melusine hadn't paid much attention to her comings and goings. But the demoness had been more than a little secretive, and even unfriendly at times. Still, it didn't seem possible that the Baron could be so well-informed. She wished she could read his mind, for a change.

"I make it my business to know everything about that household. You know that I have plans here, and I do not wish anything to interrupt them, least of all a minor squabble among Temptresses."

"Hey, I'm not trying to cause you any trouble." Melusine couldn't quite keep the thought of flayed skin from entering her mind. Yeouch! She tried to direct the conversation toward safer subjects. "But how could Shaeloba think she'd get away with it, then?"

Lord Balazel raised an eyebrow and waved a knobby finger at her. "A good question. Why don't you ask her yourself?"

He placed his hands together, muttered a spell that Melusine recognized as a summoning, then rapidly pulled them apart. There was a tearing sound, a bright flash of light, and then Shaeloba herself was standing at Melusine's left side.

She was shorter than was usual for an angel, with a broad face and spiky red hair. Shaeloba wasn't beautiful, but, Melusine had to admit, she carried herself well, and her dark eyes were fantastic. The Temptress wore a sleeveless black dress that was cut high to show off her athletic legs, and her wings were an unusual shade of red that complimented her vivid hair.

She also looked uncertain, which was quite natural considering how abruptly Balazel had snatched her from wherever she'd been. Melusine noted that the Temptress glanced at her with what almost appeared to be relief, then eyed the archdemon with a dubious suspicion that was, in Melusine's opinion, quite justified. She grinned despite herself as Shaeloba wrinkled her nose. Apparently she was with Melusine on the whole holistic thing.

"I know her," Shaeloba told the Baron with a note of bravado in her voice. "So who are you?"

"I am the archangel Balazel," the huge demon explained, leering at the Temptress's legs. "You may address me as 'Baron.' "

Shaeloba's mouth formed the shape of an *O*, and she quickly bowed before the Baron. When she straightened up, her dark eyes were calculating, and when she glanced at Melusine again, there was no sign of her previous relief. "To what do I owe the honor of this summoning, Baron?"

"I'm interested in you, Little One. I'm trying to understand why you thought you could kill your charge, lose her soul, and somehow escape suffering the consequences."

Shaeloba held herself very still, as Balazel licked his lips with a grotesquely swollen tongue that closely resembled a spotted sausage. It was not a pleasant sight. Melusine shivered, but she didn't dare to look away. There were dangerous vibes in the air now, and she wasn't the only one to notice them. Several of the lesser angels mingling around the bar began to edge their way toward the stairs.

"I'm also wondering how you'll taste when I devour your spirit!"

Incredibly Shaeloba didn't even blink at the archdemon's open threat. Melusine herself was almost ready to shift into the immaterial and fly right through the walls of the building, but the diminutive Temptress, to her surprise, showed no signs of fear. She simply folded her arms and grinned contemptuously at Balazel.

"You'll never know, you massive pig." Her voice was sharp and confident. "You'd better not even think about touching me!"

The Baron's three chins quivered as he chuckled. "And why not, Little One?"

"Because." Shaeloba clapped her hands three times. "My lord will not allow you!"

There was a roar of wind and an explosion of red light that hurled Melusine to the ground. She didn't look back to see who Shaeloba had summoned, but rolled blindly toward the center of the room, away from the action in the corner. She was just about to crawl after the fallen angels who were fleeing downstairs en masse when Balazel's commanding voice arrested her.

"Melusine, stay!"

She froze, wishing she could simply fly back to the Lewis house, wishing she'd never come to this cursed nightclub tonight, of all evenings. She hadn't even gotten the chance to ask Balazel half of her questions, and it appeared she was going to find herself in the middle of what could be a very deadly angelic duel. Reluctantly she pushed herself to her feet and turned around. What she saw was exactly what she feared, because at Shaeloba's side, towering possessively over her, was a powerful fallen angel whose red-lined robes marked him as an archon.

For an archon, he wasn't particularly handsome, Melusine couldn't help observing with a critical eye, despite her imminent danger. His slack jaw and vacant brown eyes gave her a clue as to Shaeloba's apparent influence over him; while the short Temptress was far too interested in angelic intrigues ever to do much actual tempting, Melusine had always considered her on the clever side. Seeing the two angels together, it wasn't hard to tell which of them called the shots, despite the difference in their rank.

"Baron, allow me to present the archon Bruciaphirael, Lord of the Southwest Suburbs and vassal to Prince Bloodwinter himself!" Despite her polite formality, Shaeloba's voice was filled with cocksure triumph. "Archon, the archangel Balazel."

The archon nodded stiffly, and, Melusine thought, without much going on in the comprehension department. "Greetings, Balazel."

He was civil, though. Give him credit for that, anyhow.

"Greetings, Archon," the obese archdemon replied in kind. "Since I bear you no ill will, I must warn you that this is no affair of yours. You have my permission to leave this place before you come to harm."

"Come to any harm!" Shaeloba snorted in disbelief. "In case you didn't notice, Balazel, darling Brucio is an archon. Get it? I don't know where you come from, but you'd better get your fat buttocks back there in a hurry before he starts smacking you around!"

"Oh, is that so?" Balazel smiled. "You tell me, Brucio. Speak for yourself."

Lord Bruciaphirael glanced at Shaeloba. When the little Temptress nodded, he dutifully turned back to Balazel and confirmed her threats.

"Yes," he said simply.

The archon began to change as he spoke. His head thickened and grew wider, as his nose and jaw stretched forward. His shoulders swelled, and his robes fell away as white fur began to sprout all over his body, except for his belly, which transformed into scaled silver armor. In a matter of seconds, his Aspect had changed completely, into an imposing six-armed lionman. His eyes still lacked intelligence, but there was an alertness that had not been there before, the raw cunning of the killer.

Melusine began to edge slowly backward, hoping to reach the

stairs before the inevitable fight broke out. But Balazel still didn't react, despite his danger; he simply sat in his chair like a massive slug. It was as if the archdemon was too stupid or too filled with fear even to speak, much less move.

Finally he lifted his glass and emptied its contents down his throat.

"Very well," he said, and he began to roll back his sleeves, exposing a colorful tattoo on each of his obesely swollen forearms. "I did warn you, archon. Remember that as you make your way back from the Beyond."

Balazel raised his arms, and without warning, iridescent lightning leaped from his hands. No, not from his hands, but his wrists, Melusine realized, seeing that his arms were suddenly bare. The two tattoos had come to life, and they weren't tattoos after all, but snakes, rainbow-colored dragons, whose venomous fangs were now buried in the throats of both Shaeloba and her archon.

Shaeloba screamed and was gone at once in a feeble puff of green smoke. The archon, far more powerful than the Temptress, fought the dragon longer, roaring with agony as he stumbled violently away from Lord Balazel. Melusine had to leap sideways to avoid being run over as the archon lurched past her, his Aspect dissipating as he desperately tried to pry the lethal snake from his throat. His strength failed him at last, and he collapsed to his knees with a deep, moaning wail before disappearing into the void himself.

Melusine fell to her knees, placing her forehead on the sticky floor of the bar without hesitation. She didn't understand everything that was happening, not yet, but things were starting to make a lot more sense to her now.

"Lord Kaym, I did not know you," she confessed to the demonlord. "Forgive your humble servant, Great Lord!"

She dared to look up, and saw Kaym had abandoned his unfamiliar Aspect in favor of a form that she knew well. As the deadly snakes returned to his exposed arms, he leaned back in his chair, as coldly handsome and arrogant as ever. He winked at her and slipped on his Ray-Bans, then tugged at the sleeves of his leather jacket, pulling them down so they covered all but the heads of the dragon tattoos.

"You can't say I didn't warn that archon," he told her, running a slender hand through his black hair. "And as for you, my dear, there is nothing to forgive, as long as you keep silent about me. There will be others arriving, some of whom are known to you, but no one else, Divine or Fallen, may know of their true nature."

"Yes, Great Lord," Melusine assured him.

"I told Christopher he would see me again," the fallen angel mused aloud. "But I would have him know nothing until the time and place of my choosing."

Kaym's disdainful lips twisted sideways in what was either a sneer or a sardonic grin. Melusine couldn't tell which it was because the fallen angel's eyes were impossible to read, hidden as usual behind their casing of black plastic.

Chapter 11

Where Is Father Brown?

I TELL YOU NAUGHT FOR YOUR COMFORT,
YEA, NAUGHT FOR YOUR DESIRE,
SAVE THAT THE SKY GROWS DARKER YET
AND THE SEA RISES HIGHER.
　　　　　—G. K. Chesterton, *Ballad of the White Horse*

Jami made sure she had a firm grasp on the handrail as she stumbled sleepily down the stairs. The blinding rays of light coming in the window that arced over the front door caught her squarely in the eyes as she turned the corner of the landing, and she raised a hand to her face in a feeble attempt to block out the fierce morning sun. It had taken her ages to fall asleep last night; even when she had, her dreams were haunted by images of cars and trucks and other monstrous vehicles, all flashing past her as she stood, naked, helpless, and alone, on the centerline of a dark, featureless highway.

More than once she'd woken with a violent start and found herself damp with sweat, with a scream threatening to erupt from her throat. Then she would lie motionless in the darkness, clutching her pillow tightly, desperately willing her exhausted body to please just relax and fall asleep. After fitful hours of drifting in and out of consciousness, she'd dozed off at last, and the haunting nightmares, their evil work accomplished, finally left her in peace.

Oh, man. Jami groaned out loud when she saw the green-numbered time on the microwave. It couldn't be twelve-thirty already, could it? There was no way, her mind protested, but then she remembered how the sun had caught her eyes coming down the stairs. It was pretty high in the sky. She glanced at her watch, which confirmed the microwave's implacable statement. Twelve-thirty, Sunday. She'd just missed church, darn it!

So why didn't Holli or Christopher wake her up? It wasn't her fault she'd slept in; after all, she'd dragged Christopher's lazy behind out of bed before. Her righteous indignation quickly washed away any momentary sense of guilt nibbling at her conscience, and she marched through the foyer with a strong feeling that if anyone deserved a nice, leisurely breakfast on Sunday morning, it was her.

But she was surprised when she walked into the kitchen and discovered she wasn't alone after all. Holli was sitting at the table, drinking a glass of orange juice and staring out at the backyard. She was dressed, although far too casually for church, and her blond curls were tied back in a loose ponytail.

"It's funny," Holli told her without turning around. "One day everything is brown, and it's cold and yucky. Then all of a sudden it's just, like, green! Whoever named it spring was right. It kind of sneaks up on you, you know?"

Jami groaned again and rubbed her eyes. She didn't know if she could handle this kind of discussion so early in the morning. Not that it actually was morning, but as far as her body was concerned, it was.

Holli abruptly put her glass down and reached out to squeeze Jami's left hand. "That was awful, what happened last night. I'm so glad you're okay! Christopher said not to wake you—he thought you might need the sleep today."

Jami nodded, and tried to stifle a yawn, but failed.

"Rrrrrraaaahhh." She arched her back and stretched her arms out, then yawned again. "Yeah, I guess I did. I swear, I could go back to bed right now! And hey, what are you still doing here? Did you stay out too late with Paul?"

She peered closely at Holli's face, looking for a clue as to how her sister's date had gone. But there was nothing except mild concern and sympathy in her sister's eyes, until she mentioned Paul's name. Then Holli looked away, and Jami wondered if she might actually be blushing.

"No!" Holli insisted. "That's not it at all. It's just that I told Mrs. Bennett I'd help her with the costumes tonight. She's coming to pick me up any minute now. The children are practicing for the Easter play, so I just thought I'd go to the evening service after we finish making the banners and stuff since I'll be there anyhow." She clapped her hands. "You should come with! I found this design for a bunny outfit, and there's a little duck one too, oh, it's going to be so cute if we can only find the right felt!"

Jami recoiled with horror from her sister's avalanche of enthusiasm. It was just too much, too early. She wasn't going anywhere today if she could help it. Opening the refrigerator, she poured herself a tall glass of orange juice, but instead of drinking it, she closed her eyes and held it to her forehead. The cool touch of the glass felt wonderful against her skin. It was just like a little kiss of winter.

"Bunnies and ducks? No, thanks!" she declared fervently. "Where's Mom and Dad?"

"I think they're having brunch at the club."

Hmmm, brunch actually sounded pretty good. Chef-made waffles would hit the spot. Whipped cream! Maple syrup! Too bad she couldn't drive yet, or she'd join them. Then a thought occurred to her and she opened one eye.

"This is the Church's Easter play, right?"

Holli stared blankly at her. "Yeah?"

"So what's with the ducks and bunnies? What happened to the Passion play?"

"That's the whole point of the play, you see, how Easter egg hunts and that sort of thing aren't the important part of Easter. Jesus is!" Holli grinned and her blue eyes sparkled with delight. "But those costumes are really going to be soooo cute on the children! Annika Lunstad's going to be a duck, and you should see her, she's such a little cutie!"

Well, she would make for a cute duck, Jami admitted as she drained half her OJ in a single long swig. The citrus tang jolted her to a slightly higher level of consciousness, and she felt almost ready to deal with the cereal boxes in the pantry. Almost, but not quite.

Ding-dong ding-dong, ding-dong, ding-dong. The grandfather clock in the front entryway chimed its familiar melody, and Holli was up and racing for the front door.

"Mrs. Bennett," she explained unnecessarily. "Gotta go . . . bye!"

"Bye." Jami waved at her sister's back. Even that small effort made her feel worn out.

She listened as the closet door creaked open and closed, as Holli searched for her purse, then heard the front door jerk open. It was slammed shut with a deep wooden thud, echoed by two noisy bangs as the storm door bounced once before finally finding its latch.

Thankful for the silence of solitude, Jami took a deep breath and found the energy to open the pantry door. The pickings were slim, as they usually were on weekends. Mom always went to Rainbow on Mondays; they had specials then or something. This morning her options were down to Raisin Bran, Rice Krispies, or Dad's weird granola-ish stuff that came in a brown box.

Müeslix, it was, according to the label. She shook the box, wondering if she dared to give it a try. It rattled, making a sound that made her think of twigs and crushed leaves. Ish! She decided to go the safe route with Snap! Krackle! and Pop! only to discover, when she picked up the box, that it was empty except for a few stray pieces that had found their way between the cardboard and the plastic liner.

"Christopher, you lazy bum, you did it again. . . ," she said, glaring at the blue box.

She knew it was him. How many times had she told him? How hard could it possibly be to throw the stupid box away when it's empty? She briefly considered holding on to it and using it as evidence to confront him, but finally just threw it away. What was the point? He'd just shrug and apologize, and do the same thing again next week. Grrrr!

Oh, well, Raisin Bran it was. It took a while to pick out all the raisins, but once you did that and added a heaping spoonful of sugar, Raisin Bran wasn't half-bad. It was basically labor-intensive Bran Flakes. She poured herself a good-sized bowl, carefully sorted out the raisins, then sat down to read the Sunday comics while she ate.

Jami was just finishing her cereal when the telephone rang. She wearily pushed herself away from the table and took the white portable off its little stand.

"Hello?"

"Hey, James, you're up!" It was Christopher. "Look, come meet us at the Caribou."

"Why would I want to do that?"

She had a whole boatload of reasons why she wasn't about to go meet her brother there, and one of the better ones was that she didn't drink coffee, or any of the multitude of beverages they served at the coffeehouse which contained the poisonous stuff.

"And who's us?" she demanded.

"I'm with Pastor Ladd, and one of the guys from the council of elders, Mr. Powell. Come on, it's important!"

"Powell? Who's that?"

"Ed Powell, you know who he is." Christopher's voice crackled on the line; it wasn't a very good connection. "Tall skinny guy, mustache, he's like an expert on angelic warfare and that kind of thing."

Okay. Jami nodded. She knew who her brother was talking about now.

"Where are you?" she said. "There's a lot of static or something. I can barely hear you."

"No, that's just the traffic on ninety-six. I'm on the pay phone in the parking lot by the cleaners."

"So you're already there?"

"Yeah, so you'll have to bike up and meet us."

"I don't know. . . ."

"Come on, I'll buy you a smoothie!" Christopher promised her. "And I've got the bike rack on the back of the truck, so you don't have to bike back."

Jami frowned. Her brother didn't often try to talk her into things, and even though the Caribou wasn't too far from their house, biking in the hot spring sun was pretty much the last thing she wanted to do. Still, if Pastor Ladd was involved, it was probably important.

"I'll try to be there in fifteen minutes," she said. "But I'm not even dressed yet—"

"Cool," Christopher interjected, and he hung up.

"Bye," she told the humming phone. She pressed the button to disconnect the line. "Oh, and remind me to compliment you on your phone etiquette, big brother."

She put her hands to her forehead and sighed. All she wanted was a quiet, lazy day, and now she had to leave the house already. Which led her to her next problem. Were pastors cool with spandex tank tops?

To her surprise, she actually enjoyed her ten-minute ride up to the little mall. The sun wasn't quite as hot as she'd expected it to be, and there was a nice cool breeze that kept her from sweating like a pig. The mall wasn't a bad place, considering that it was pretty much your basic strip mall. It had all the necessities of modern life; a movie rental place, a cleaners, an Italian restaurant with white plastic chairs on the sidewalk, and a bakery. Since it catered to the la-di-da ladies of North Oaks, there was also a jewelry store that somehow managed to stay open despite the fact that she'd never seen anyone go in there, as well as a fancy butcher shop.

Jami leaned her bike against the front window of Bruegger's, the bagel shop next to the coffeehouse, and ran her forearm across her forehead. She wasn't too sweaty, but she still needed to run some cold water over her face to be presentable. She pushed the glass door open and immediately spotted her brother sitting next to Pastor Ladd. His youthful face lit up with recognition as she walked toward them, and he stood up and extended his hand.

"Hi, Jami, I'm Pastor Mark. Your brother told me about you, and at first I couldn't place the name, but I recognize you now! We met this winter, didn't we? I think it was during one of our Saturday night services."

"Um, yeah," Jami said, shaking his hand uncertainly. "Nice to see you again. Would you excuse me for a moment?"

She walked past the line of people waiting to pick up their coffees and knocked on the bathroom door at the far end of the shop. No one answered, so she opened the door and turned the water on. She waited for a second, then splashed several handfuls on her face. There, that was much better. She stared at her dripping face in the mirror and found herself wishing she'd worn more than the tank top and biker shorts.

Well, what do you do. She splashed one more handful of water on her face, then dried herself as best she could with the little brown paper towels that absorbed water about as well as the ceramic tile on the floor. By the time she returned to the table, Mr. Powell had joined the others, and a covered white paper cup was sitting in front of the only unclaimed chair.

"Is that mine?" she asked.

"It is indeed," Mr. Powell said in a surprisingly rich voice. He was a tall, gaunt man with reddish-brown hair and a mustache. "Have a seat. I'm Ed, and you must be Jami."

"Yeah, nice to meet you," she said, and sat down quickly, folding her arms over her chest. "So what's up?"

"This," Christopher said, waving the *Star Tribune*'s Metro section in her face. "Did you see this?" he practically shouted at her. "Did you see it?"

"Settle down, Beavis," she snapped back as she slapped away the paper. "See what?"

Christopher bobbed his head back and forth in excitement, and placed his own smoothie on a nearby table so he could spread out the newspaper in front of everyone.

"There!" he jabbed at a small story at the bottom of the third page. "Read that!"

" 'Fridley man killed in single-car accident,' " Ed Powell read out loud. " 'Jeremy Drummond, twenty-three, was pronounced dead at the scene of the accident late Saturday night in Mounds View. His pickup truck was driving north on Highway 10 before it left the road and struck the 35-W overpass. A toxicology report will be conducted by the local examiner over the weekend. . . .' "

There wasn't a picture; the accident had happened too late for that. But even without a picture to identify the truck, the location made it obvious. Jami looked up at her brother. "This was the guy who almost hit us?"

Christopher nodded slowly and turned toward Pastor Mark. "I know it looks like an accident, but I can tell you, it wasn't. It was intentional. The thing is, I believe there were evil spirits leading that man to do what he did."

The two older men looked at each other. Pastor Ladd's eyebrows were raised, and he seemed to be asking his friend a silent question, when, to Jami's surprise, Ed Powell nodded affirmatively.

"It sounds, well, unusual, of course, but it's quite possible. Here's why. Mark, will you look at this?"

There was a moment of quiet broken only by the crackling of the paper as Mr. Powell turned the pages. When he stopped, Jami looked up at him, startled.

"The obituaries? Why? Did somebody die? I mean, someone you know?"

The red-haired man shook his head, his thin eyebrows drawn close together as he peered down at the page. "Here," he said, jabbing at one name with his finger. ". . . and here."

The names he indicated were unknown to her. Both names were accompanied by a picture, but Jami still didn't recognize either of the dead men. Boone and Woodhouse . . . they were old, which you'd expect, naturally, but when she glanced at the ages of some of the other people on the page, she realized that the two men weren't nearly as old as the eighty- and ninety-year-olds who were listed there.

"Notice anything about them?" Mr. Powell asked them all as he stroked his mustache.

"Mmm-hmmm," Pastor Mark said, closing his eyes with a pained expression on his face. His lips moved silently, and Jami wondered if he was praying.

"They're kind of young," Christopher said hesitantly. "Well, not all that young, but I mean, compared to everybody else who died."

"Right, but look again," Mr. Powell told him. "And have a look at their occupations."

Jami checked the first obituary. Before getting killed in a car accident, Ron Boone had been a pastor, at Calvary Heights Baptist. Hey, she knew that church! It was in Roseville, right across the street from the old Bridgeman's ice cream parlor. Mom used to take them there when they were little. Jami had always wanted to order the big Lollapalooza by herself, but Mom never let her try. These days, of course, she wouldn't dare. A moment on the lips, a lifetime on the hips—no, thanks!

She looked at the man's picture more closely and shook her head. Poor Pastor Boone must have been a very handsome man when he was younger. Earl Woodhouse was the second listing. She pursed her lips as she read more about him, and learned that he'd died of a heart attack. She thought back to last week's incident. Another heart attack. It seemed that these particular Fallen weren't terribly imaginative, or at least they didn't mind repeating themselves.

"They're pastors," she answered. "A Baptist and a Lutheran. Sounds kind of like the start of a joke, doesn't it?"

"I'm afraid that there's one more death which the newspaper hasn't published yet," Pastor Mark broke in. "Father Keane, from Saint Cecilia's. He died in the middle of a sermon he was giving last night. The doctors say it was a brain aneurysm, but . . ."

"You don't think so?" Mr. Powell asked.

"No. One of his parishioners called me from the parking lot.

There were definite indicators of demonic activity—polter-geism, apparently, as there were a lot of broken windows, and there was a suggestion of direct involvement by people caught up in the occult as well. To me, it sounded more like a case of spiritual possession. The man was a little shaken by what he'd seen, so it was a little hard to follow him, but he said something to the effect of a woman in the congregation standing up and cursing the father to his face immediately before he collapsed and died."

"God bless!" Mr. Porter replied, appalled, and Jami knew he wasn't swearing. "This is much worse than I'd imagined! What's going on?"

"It doesn't seem possible, does it?" replied the pastor, staring out at the bright rays of light glinting off the expensive cars and sport-utility vehicles filling the parking lot. "Not now, and cer-tainly not here. And yet, we are told there is evil everywhere under the sun."

"So, do you think the local Fallen are up to something, then?"

"Fallen?" Pastor Ladd stared at Christopher. "What does that . . . oh, as in fallen angels, I see. Well, I think it is extremely odd for three ministers to die in a single week."

"Why is that so strange?" Jami wanted to know. Maybe the men weren't totally, like, elderly, but they were pretty old, after all.

Ed Powell chuckled mirthlessly. "Three pastors don't usually die in an entire year, around here. There are only fifty-nine churches on this side of town in all."

"Is that all?" Jami was surprised. "I guess I thought there were more."

"I don't know, sixty is quite a few when you consider the area. Shoreview, North Oaks, Arden Hills, Roseville, Vadnais Heights . . ." Mr. Powell counted on his fingers. "You're probably looking at a population of less than fifty thousand people in the whole area. Three out of sixty is significant, that's what, five per-cent of the total, particularly in just four days."

"I think there were supposed to be four deaths," Christopher said, glancing at Jami. "There's Pastor Walters, too, from Elim Baptist. He had a heart attack last week, but he lived."

"Not Charlie Walters!" Pastor Mark exclaimed.

"Christopher was with him," Jami said. She was reluctant to mention her part in what had happened that night. "It wasn't normal, either."

"You're sure of that?"

"Totally," Christopher assured him.

Pastor Mark glanced at his friend, then looked back at Jami and her brother. He tapped his fingers on the fake wood of the table.

"Look, it's very clear that you seem to know a lot more about all this than you're telling us. Maybe it would help if you would just begin at the beginning."

Jami looked doubtfully at Christopher. "Are you sure about this? There's no way they're going to believe us."

Her brother nodded. "Just give them a chance. They might surprise you."

"We might," Pastor Mark agreed with a smile. "You never know."

"Well, okay then," Jami said dubiously. "But what would you say, Pastor Mark, if I told you that after you prayed for us the night we met, we spoke to a group of angels? Divine angels, just like those in the Bible."

Pastor Mark and Ed Powell were both staring at her with incredulous expressions. Ed Powell was the first to reply. He sounded more amused than skeptical.

"Well," he said softly, "the first thought that crosses my mind is that you are in dire need of a psychiatrist, to be honest. That, or you have an unusually active imagination. Then again, you don't strike me as silly, or in desperate need of attention. And I have spoken to your brother once or twice, and he seems to be unusually attuned to the realities of the spiritual world as I understand them."

He turned to her brother. "Do you believe what she's saying? Did you see any of this yourself?"

Christopher made a thoughtful face and made a popping

sound with his lips. "Yeah, I believe her. She's leaving most of it out, actually. I didn't see exactly the same things she saw, but then, I was on the other side at the time."

"What do you mean by that?" Pastor Mark asked, frowning. "I don't understand."

"I was with a group of angels, too, but not the ones with the white wings." Her brother shrugged and smiled ruefully. "I got better."

"Are you saying you have been involved with the occult in the past?"

The curly-haired pastor's eyes narrowed with suspicion, and Ed Powell looked troubled.

"Sort of," Christopher admitted. "But not like you're thinking. I was taken away in the same way Jami was taken away, to another world in another time, only it wasn't an angel that took me, it was a fallen angel. That happened first, and it's why Jami and our other sister, Holli, were sent after me, to save me."

He nodded toward her. "And basically, they did. I even accepted Jesus Christ as my Lord and Savior, but not until after . . . well, when we were back here, basically. The experience seemed to last for months, but it was only a couple hours here, on this planet. Very Narnia, in a way."

"But this is fascinating!" Pastor Mark declared. Clearly he was inclined to accept Christopher's fantastic story at face value. "It sounds absolutely incredible!"

Jami glanced at Ed Powell, but the other man didn't say anything, he just sat and thoughtfully stroked his chin. He seemed quite a bit more doubtful than his enthusiastic friend, but Christopher didn't appear to notice that.

"I know it sounds incredible. Look, I wouldn't believe me, either, if I hadn't been there. And I wouldn't blame you for thinking we're trying to pull some kind of practical joke or something, but you have to admit that there does seem to be something very dark going on around here."

"There surely is," said Ed Powell slowly. "But isn't it possible that you are somehow allied with those who are perpetrating the evil? By your own admission, you've got a past history with the occult, and your attitude about it is . . . disturbingly blasé, I must say. Even your knowledge of the spiritual world could well reflect a demonic involvement rather than spiritual maturity. Although not necessarily, since the implantation of false memories is not unheard of in modern psychology."

Oh, this is just great, Jami thought. Mr. Powell thought they might be possessed? Nightmarish visions of the Spanish Inquisition popped into her head. They didn't really do that sort of thing anymore, did they? She sure hoped not.

Christopher was less perturbed. "Don't you have anyone gifted with discernment at the church? Are you really picking up occultic vibes from us?"

Ed Powell sighed. "No, I'm not. And that's the problem. It's just that what you're saying is very, very difficult to absorb, much less accept."

"Well, I think it's absolutely amazing!" Pastor Mark slapped his palm against the table. "You must tell me everything, everything! Both of you! I have so many questions. . . . If your visions or your experiences, whatever, if they turn out to be true, then this could be the most significant revelation about the spiritual world since, well, since the Revelation of St. John!"

Jami had to stifle a giggle at the hilarious notion of either of them as a saint, and even Christopher rolled his eyes.

"I don't know about that," he protested.

"I think we're perhaps getting ahead of ourselves here." Ed Powell still had his doubts. "Your story sounds very . . . well, very unlikely, to say the least. I can't help but feel extremely skeptical about all of it. And yet, I don't get the sense that either one of you is lying."

Pastor Mark shrugged indifferently, while eyeing the two of them in a way that made Jami think he was about to leap across the table to try to shake more information out of her. The guy had so much energy, he made her feel almost nervous.

"Well, even if we put aside the question of their veracity for now, it's clear that there are events of overt spiritual dimensions occuring in this town today. It will obviously require prayer and careful discernment, but I don't see any harm in giving the children the benefit of the doubt at the moment."

Gee, thanks, Jami thought sarcastically. The children? She glared at the man, offended.

"That's good enough for me," Christopher said, kicking her shin under the table. "If we're crazy or just trying to cause trouble, you can always tell our parents later. If we're demon-possessed, you'll probably figure that out soon enough. But if we're telling the truth, and we are, then you should probably help us figure out what the Fallen are up to around here, so we can try to stop them."

"Out of the mouths of babes, wisdom." Pastor Mark nodded appreciatively. "I think that's a reasonable suggestion, at any rate. Ed, what do you say we simply give them the benefit of the doubt for the time being?"

"I . . . oh, I don't know." The scholarly man groaned and threw up his hands. "I suppose I can't see it doing too much harm. It's just . . . the implications are staggering!"

"Well, that's that, then." The pastor turned his attention back to Jami and Christopher. "So, then, seeing as you're the experts, what do you recommend we do about these . . . what do you call them, Fallen?"

Jami was very glad to see that the question of inquisitors had been put aside for the time being, but she personally had no ideas, so she sipped at her smoothie and watched as Christopher thought for a moment. He seemed to be having an internal debate over something.

"Well, for one thing," he finally said, "I think it would be good if we could get ten or twelve people to start praying for protection for all the pastors and preachers in this town. I mean specifically, by name. It looks like they're trying to wipe out the spiritual leaders, which makes a little sense, although I find it hard to believe they can get away with wiping out every pastor in town without waking up the whole world to their existence. . . ." His voice trailed off, and he shook his head. "Unless this is some kind of end-times thing, which I doubt. There's just too many signs that are still missing."

"You said, 'for one thing,' Ed Powell pointed out. "Is that the second? Because I agree, I personally don't see any connection to the events described in the Revelations here.".

"No," Christopher answered slowly. "I just got off on a tangent. The one thing we really have to do is go talk to that woman who was at Saint Cecilia's today. Maybe she's a witch of some kind or another, but maybe she isn't. If she was possessed last night, then I'm thinking the demon is probably still there inside her."

Jami put her face in her hands. Oh, this day was just getting better and better. It had been hard enough just to get out of bed and drag herself here. Watching an exorcism was about as close to the bottom of her list as she could possibly imagine. Visions of spinning heads and projectile vomiting filled her mind, and she shook her head. Man oh man, bunnies and ducks were looking better all the time.

CHAPTER 12

BROKEN WINGS

BUT THE EYES OF THE WICKED WILL FAIL, AND ESCAPE WILL ELUDE
THEM; THEIR HOPE WILL BECOME A DYING GASP.

—Job 11:20

Melusine stood with her arms folded under her breasts, chewing her bottom lip as she wondered where she might find a crack in the Lewis family that she could exploit. She watched from the rooftop of a nearby school as the two children emerged from the coffee shop, accompanied by two older men. Her spiked tail lashed back and forth, reflecting her irritation. This shouldn't be so hard, especially for a temptress who'd once set three mortal kingdoms at each other's throats using just a single child. And still, the key eluded her.

It was obvious that the direct approach wasn't going to work. The one good thing about Shaeloba's foolish attempt on Christopher and Jami was that it was now clear to everyone that the Divine were not about to stand for any slaying of their so-called warriors. While Shaeloba's replacement, an intense, overmuscled Tempter named Maligor, wasn't exactly brilliant, at least he did understand that. Melusine tapped her long fingernails on the brick chimney as she considered the two remaining options, co-option or corruption. Considering that she'd been working on the latter for the last three months without getting anywhere, corruption obviously wasn't going to do the trick. That left co-option.

Christopher's green Explorer pulled out of the parking lot, and Melusine couldn't help smiling sarcastically.

"Have a nice time, Baal Phaoton."

It was too bad the boy wasn't going to find what he was looking for. She had no intention of allowing herself to be subjected to
an exorcism, from all the tales she'd heard, the process was an
extraordinarily unpleasant one. She didn't understand those
angels who had to be dragged kicking and screaming out of the
flesh. Cursed believers! It was so much easier dealing with people who didn't really believe in the supernatural; these days you
just had to use a little restraint and you could pretty much possess anyone you wanted, any time you felt like it.

She sighed. It was wonderful to see what the Prince had
wrought. Look about you anywhere, and you could easily find a
pathetic, rootless soul dangling over the edge, and with just one
tiny push, send them hurtling into the abyss. You could lead
them on the most vicious spree of murder and mayhem and not a
single mortal would ever take it in his head to look for you. Not
that she'd ever done it herself, since carnage wasn't really her
thing, but still, it was amazing what you could get away with
these days. Of course, the times weren't exactly difficult for an
angel of her particular proclivities, either; in fact, until Christopher had unexpectedly switched sides, she hadn't needed to
exert herself much in three mortal decades.

Now she had a problem, though. Her situation would be a
lot easier if Lord Kaym had chosen someone else's charge to
drag through time. And as she thought about him, she wondered how Kaym had managed to conceal himself so well. Until
he'd revealed himself to her, she'd had no idea that Balazel was
anything but what he seemed to be, an archangel on a mission.
The Great Lord seemed to have taken his failure with Christopher quite personally, and she considered the many ways the
fallen angel might seek his revenge. He'd given her more
instructions again last night, but like those he'd given previ-
ously, they were far too specific for her to discern any larger
intent behind them.

She heard a disturbance in the air above her, and looked up to
see Maligor and Boggie flying down towards her, their faces

strained with the effort of restraining the angel they were holding between them. Boggie, in particular, was having a terrible time just keeping the prisoner's left hand pinned to her side. As they came closer, Melusine winced as she saw the captive angel slash at the dryad and rip several shards of bark off his face.

The odd threesome landed, none too gracefully, right in front of her, and it was an irritated Maligor who hurled the captive at Melusine's feet. It was Pandaema, and the dark bruise on Maligor's cheek explained his lack of consideration for the fair-haired temptress. Interesting, Melusine mused. I wouldn't have thought she'd be much of a fighter.

"How dare you!" Pandaema shrieked.

Melusine wasn't quite sure who the blond temptress was yelling at, and she didn't really care. Pandaema hadn't carried her own weight for years, and with Shaeloba out of the picture now, the moment was ripe to rid herself of the useless angel once and for all.

"Do you even know where Holli is right now?" she demanded.

Pandaema drew herself upright and tried to affect an imperious pose. "How is that any of your business, Melusine?" She sneered.

Melusine replied by smashing her fist into Pandaema's face. The temptress cried out and dropped to her knees, and Melusine followed up her advantage by seizing a handful of butter-colored hair and using it to jerk the angel's head back into a painful position.

"Where is Holli?" she repeated.

"I don't know!" Pandaema wailed. "Let me go, Melusine, you're hurting me! I don't know!"

What a surprise. Pandaema never knew what was going on with her wretched charge, she never had. But there was one more thing Melusine needed to know before she decided what to do with her.

"Did you know about Shaeloba?" she asked harshly. "Did you know she was trying to kill Christopher and Jami?"

Tears began to appear in Pandaema's eyes, but she didn't say anything.

"Tell me, or I'll drain you dry right now!"

Melusine relented a little as the Temptress started crying, and when she released her hold on the other's hair, the frightened angel collapsed in a sobbing heap.

"I . . . I didn't know what to do! Shaeloba wanted to try for all three of them, but I was afraid of Aliel. She's so mean! And I was afraid that if the Guardians stopped us, we'd get in trouble." She paused and looked up at Melusine with reddened eyes. "Actually, I was afraid if they didn't stop us, we'd get in trouble that way, too."

She raised her hands imploringly. "I just told her to leave me out of it. So that's all I know."

Melusine nodded thoughtfully. "But you didn't bother to tell me what she was up to?"

"Why should I? You didn't ask. And Shaeloba told me not to. Besides, I didn't actually know she was going to try anything. Sometimes she's so full of it, you know that!"

Melusine nodded again and looked up at the white-golden brightness of the sun. It had no mercy, and neither would Lord Kaym if the children fouled up his plans again. Melusine didn't really have much against Pandaema, but in this particular instance, the lazy Temptress could be a real danger to her. She couldn't afford to leave Holli unwatched; the girl might be shallow, but she had a childlike faith that was sometimes the most dangerous of all.

She reached her decision, and extended a hand to wipe away Pandaema's tears. "It's not your fault, Panda. It's just that you're too stupid to live."

The blond angel's vacant eyes widened as Melusine's black talons tore open her throat, exposing the green fire of her spirit. She screamed hoarsely, almost like a doomed mortal soul at the moment of its damnation, but her shrieks were soon cut off as Melusine stepped back and pointed at Boggie. "Drain her," she commanded.

"Me?" The little dryad gawked at her. He glanced over at Maligor, who only shrugged.

"Just do it," Melusine told him. "Suck her dry. Now!"

She didn't have to tell him again. The dryad's eyes lit up and he leaped upon the convulsing body of the stricken angel. He latched onto Pandaema's throat, and inhaled the escaping green flames, growling and snarling as he ingested her meager power. It was only a matter of seconds before there was a soft bang, and Pandaema's once-lovely form disappeared altogether.

Melusine grinned as Boggie lurched backward and fell awkwardly on his backside, his eyes closed in dreamy satiation. Then his eyes popped open and green sparks flared out of them. The startled dryad's body swelled rapidly, and for a moment Melusine feared that even Pandaema's scanty spirit had been too much for the little demon. Then, as he mastered the fire, his features changed, and he stood before her, tall and well-formed. His skin was still bark-brown, and both his hair and his wings were leafy green, but he was beautiful now, a veritable god of the forest.

She smiled. Now that's better, she thought approvingly.

He bowed to her, and she leaned forward and kissed him on both cheeks.

"You need a new name," she told him. "I don't think Boggie quite cuts it anymore."

He smiled, revealing perfect white teeth. "Call me Boghorael," he said. "If that's all right with you."

"Oh, it's quite all right," Melusine said with a thoughtful smile, running her hand over his powerful chest. "So tell me, Boghorael dear, is it possible that you might be partial to young blondes?"

I guess that wasn't so bad, Jami thought to herself as they drove past the tree-covered houses on Lake Owasso. Most of the homes here had been built a long time ago, and although a few had been knocked down and replaced by bigger houses with twelve-foot ceilings, three-car garages, and funky barn-style roofs, there was still a faded sixties feeling to the neighborhood. Even the trees looked shaggy and a bit run-down.

Alice Taylor was the name of the woman, who, according to Mr. Powell, really had been possessed, although, thank goodness, the demon had left her long before they arrived. No head-spinning, no vomit, just bad, brightly colored modern art. Mrs. Taylor lived with her husband in one of the new houses on the lake; the inside was all modern and stark, and so empty that it didn't feel like anyone actually lived there. Jami didn't like the house, or the woman. She got the feeling that Mrs. Taylor was normally a total wench, although it was hard not to feel sorry for her today.

The woman was completely embarrassed by what had happened to her the night before, and after learning that she'd been possessed, she really freaked out. That was understandable, of course, although when she started going on and on about how responsible for Father Keane's death she felt, Jami started to get the feeling Mrs. Taylor was enjoying the spotlight.

But she seemed to feel a lot better after Mr. Powell talked to her for a while and Pastor Mark prayed over her. Before they all left, Jami helped Mrs. Taylor make coffee for the men in the Taylor's huge Corian-countered kitchen and learned that the woman had two daughters not much older than she, both of whom were off at some college named Saint something-or-other somewhere on the East Coast. Mrs. Taylor seemed to think Jami should know the name of the school, but she didn't. Saint Jennifer, maybe? No, that wasn't it.

Listening to the woman talk about her daughters made the whole possession thing feel even stranger to Jami. Did it just happen like that? How could it happen to someone who was, if not exactly nice, pretty much on the normal side? Mrs. Taylor wasn't a devil-worshipper or a closet Satanist; heck, she'd been at church that night after all. Was it possible that Mr. Powell was wrong, and that Mrs. Taylor hadn't been possessed at all? Couldn't she have just had, like, a nervous breakdown or something?

Jami turned to Christopher, who hadn't said much during the three hours they'd spent at the Taylor house, and hadn't spoken at all since they'd left. He was driving with his eyes locked on the road ahead of him, totally focused on the winding curves in a way that made Jami think he wasn't seeing anything at all.

"So, what do you think?" she asked him. "Do you think Mr. Powell is right?"

"Hmmm?" Christopher made a noise without even opening his mouth.

"I said, did you think Mr. Powell is right?"

"Who?" Christopher glanced at her and raised his eyebrows. "Right?"

Jami groaned. What was with him. He never listened. She'd gotten used to him zoning out, but it still irritated her every now and then, like a blister on the side of your foot you'd forgotten you had.

"Mr. Powell," she repeated loudly and slowly. "Do you think that he is right in saying that Mrs. Taylor was possessed last night?"

"Oh, definitely," Christopher told her, coming to a stop and flicking on his turn signal. "No question about it."

How could he be so sure? Was that kind of self-assuredness just a guy thing, or what?

"I don't see how you can say that." Jami looked out the window, and the cars passing on the other side of the road reaffirmed her sense of the real world. "I mean, you weren't there, after all, and even if everything she says is true, there's got to be an explanation for all of it. I mean, yeah, there's maybe some weird coincidences, but that could be all it is, a coincidence."

"There are no coincidences," Christopher replied lightly.

He grinned at her, and his grin faded when he saw she didn't get his joke.

"No coincidences . . . Call of Cthulhu . . . never mind."

"Thool? Oh, geek humor, right, always very funny—*not!*"

Christopher snorted. " 'Not'? I think that went out about, what, twenty years ago?"

"Oh, and you're going to tell me about what's in and what's not, Mister I-don't-like-girls-as-much-as-geekazoid-freak-toys?"

She accused him in a nasty tone of voice, but then pinched him to show she didn't really mean it. He responded by pretending she'd seriously hurt him and swerved the Explorer to make her scream.

"Knock it off, Chris! I'll tell Dad if you don't cut it out!"

"You will not," he argued, although he stopped messing with the steering wheel and straightened the vehicle out. "Who would drive you everywhere?"

"I'll have my permit in five months," she shot back. Then she realized he still hadn't answered her question. "And anyhow, you still haven't told me why you're so sure she was possessed."

"Oh, that." Christopher nodded thoughtfully, and he bit his upper lip. "Well, it's pretty simple, but I guess there's no reason you would have caught it. I know Ed and Pastor Mark didn't. They couldn't have understood the significance."

"What?"

"Well, did you notice when Ed was asking her if there was anything she could remember, and she said she had the sense that she was only watching what was happening, that her body was being controlled, kind of like a puppet?"

"Oh, yeah." Jami wrinkled her nose and shivered. Mrs. Taylor's description of the experience was pretty creepy. "He asked her if she'd picked up any feeling of a name or, like, a person at the time."

Her brother nodded, and guided the Explorer onto Highway 96. "*Persona* was what he said, but yeah—"

"And she said Melissa, or Millicent, something like that. She said that was the only thing she could remember."

"Yep, and she remembered it because someone wanted her to." Christopher gave her a serious look. "The name isn't Melissa, it's Melusine. I know her."

Jami didn't know how to respond to her brother's statement. You *know* her? Not her, as in Mrs. Taylor, but her, as in the demon? She replayed the sentence in her mind, then once more to be sure. Yeah, that was where the pronouns went.

"Let me get this straight," she asked for confirmation, just to make sure she hadn't misunderstood anything. "You're saying it was some kind of girl-demon that possessed Mrs. Taylor, and that you know her?"

"Yep," Christopher said, biting his lip again. "That's why I think their job here is probably done for now, the Fallen, that is. If they wanted to kill more preachers, attack more Christians, they'd never have let her leave her name with Mrs. Taylor. Melusine is still mad at me, I'll bet, so she told Mrs. Taylor in order to rub it in my face. God used you to save Pastor Walters, but they still managed to knock off three people, and we couldn't do anything about it. I'll bet they were never seriously after us, so what happened last night was probably an accident after all. Or maybe it was just like I said, to rub it in our faces. She knows Mariel would never let her get away with using that pickup driver to wipe us out."

Jami stared out the window, as a bizarre thought captured her imagination. She, Christopher had said, she. She. He said it in the same way that her friends talked about their ex-boyfriends, with capital letters you could distinctly hear. And there was another thing, seemingly insignificant, until now. She and Holli had set Christopher up with April Evenson a few weeks ago, and although the relationship hadn't gone anywhere, they'd both been amused when April reported that their brother was quite the respectable kisser. Natural talent, must run in the family, they'd joked, since Christopher wasn't exactly known for being the Don Juan of the tenth grade. April had been his first girlfriend, as far as she had known. Now, she wondered, just who had been giving him lessons? Or what?

"Christopher?" she asked suspiciously. "There's a lot you haven't told us about what happened to you on Ahura Azdha, isn't there?"

"Mm-hmm."

"Do you want to talk about it?"

"Not really."

There was a long silence which hung uncomfortably between the two of them. Finally Jami could resist no longer, and she gave in to the temptation. She had to know.

"Christopher?"

"Yeah?"

"Was she pretty?"

Jami watched him closely. He was obviously taken off guard by the question, and Jami was surprised at the emotions suddenly flashing across his face. She saw guilt, hatred, and desire, all inextricably intertwined, and despite her burning curiosity about the she-demon, she almost started to wish she hadn't asked the question. It had upset him, clearly, which made her feel guilty, and it worried her to think that her brother could be harboring feelings for what was, after all, a force of incarnate evil.

"You have no idea," he admitted finally, confirming her fears.

Chapter 13

Akkadian Psycho

Ninety-nine out of a hundred are automata, careful to walk in the prescribed paths, careful to follow the prescribed custom. This is not an accident but the result of substantial education, which, scientifically defined, is the subsumption of the individual.

—William Torrey Harris, *The Philosophy of Education*

Rousseau was a moron, Brien concluded as he finally gave up trying to make any sense of the dead French dude's philosophy. What was up with this whole "children as noble savages" thing anyhow? The guy had clearly never had kids of his own, and he'd certainly never seen what life was like in an American high school. Lord of the freaking flies! The question was, why was it necessary to write a report on anything written by such an obvious idiot?

Brien shook his head, watching from the safety of an out-of-the-way beanbag chair as one oversize sophomore wearing a letter jacket adorned with one lousy patch on the sleeve, football, naturally, shoved a scrawny little ninth grader into the big wooden card catalog. The ninth grader's shoulder struck the corner squarely, and hard, and his spectacled face screwed up with pain. The kid was learning, though, because he didn't cry out, or worse, try to say anything back to his attacker. He simply gathered himself together and walked away, rubbing at his injured shoulder.

Okay, Jean-Jacques had the savage part right, it was just the nobility that was missing. Beelzebub was definitely more like it, that, or maybe Darwin with his survival of the fittest. But if intelligence was what made man superior to the other animals, why was it that physical strength was the primary factor in determining who was the fittest here? That wasn't quite right, he corrected himself, you can't forget looks and popularity. Unfortunately, he'd pretty much missed out on all three, thanks to his lousy luck.

Speaking of looks, where was Tessa right now? he wondered. It was fifth hour, so she must be in gym class. He'd thought of changing his schedule around at the beginning of the year, in order to get into that class, but that would have meant losing two straight lunch periods in a row, and besides, Derek wouldn't have liked it, either. It would have been nice to see her running around in shorts every day, but then again, considering how he managed to embarrass himself there about once a week, it was probably for the best that he hadn't made the switch.

He saw Derek enter the library from the far side of the room, and even from here, he could sense his friend's excitement. I wonder what's up with him? He took the opportunity to stretch as he stood up, and waved his hands to draw Derek's attention. The black-haired boy's eyes lighted up as he recognized Brien, and he half-walked, half-ran across the large room, drawing a nasty glare from one of the elderly librarians.

"Dude, you've got to see this!" he whispered excitedly as he pushed an orange paper folder into Brien's hands. "I can't believe it—it's so cool!"

Brien looked down at the unmarked folder, then back at Derek.

"Does this have anything to do with that stuff that came out of your printer? I thought it was just random gibberish. It didn't make any sense, you said so yourself!"

Derek's dark eyes danced as he smiled mysteriously.

"Maybe, maybe. Just look at it and see for yourself. Then tell me what you think."

To the cities of the country . . . I went down. The city of Perria and the city of Sitivarya, its strongholds, together with twenty-two cities

which depended upon it, I threw down, dug up and burned with fire.
Exceeding fear over them I cast. To the cities of the Parthians he went.
The cities of Bustu, Sala-khamanu and Cini-khamanu, fortified towns,
together with twenty-three cities which depended upon them I captured.
Their fighting-men I slew. Their spoil I carried off. To the country of
Zimri I went down. Exceeding fear . . . overwhelmed them. Their cities
they abandoned. To inaccessible mountains they ascended. Two hundred
and fifty of their cities I threw down, dug up and burned with fire.

Brien looked up from the page of what he assumed had to be
some kind of translation.

"Well, it's always nice to hear that somebody enjoys his job.
Who is this guy? Attila the Hun?"

Derek yawned and rubbed at his face, and for the first time
today, Brien realized that his friend was short on sleep. His eyes
were bloodshot, his hair didn't appear to have been washed, and
under his Georgetown sweatshirt was the light blue Astrosmash
T-shirt he'd been wearing the day before.

"No, he's a little earlier than that." He yawned again. "Akkadian psycho, you might say."

"Ha ha, very funny," Brien said, recognizing the reference to
one of Derek's all-time favorite books. Personally, he thought
Ellis was way overrated.

"Dude, I'm serious. Well, okay, it was a stupid pun, but that
stuff that printed out, it wasn't gibberish, it was Akkadian."

"Shut up, it was not!"

Brien wasn't exactly sure what Akkadian was, some old
African or Arabic language, he thought, but whatever it was, it
was impossible for it to have been on those pages yesterday
because any ancient language would have been around for centuries before the modern alphabet appeared.

"No way, it can't be that old! I saw it, and it used our alphabet."

"No, no, it's just that the text was romanized," Derek insisted.
"Updated so we could read it. Trust me, I know what I'm talking
about."

"You? How would you know, you don't know jack about languages. You practically failed Spanish!"

"Yeah, well, last night I was looking at it, and I was thinking it reminded me of the Sumerian in the Necronomicon—"

Brien held up his hand.

"Wait up. The Necronomicon? As in Lovecraft? It's fiction, dude."

"Maybe, although it could be that someone made one up later, you know, inspired by the stories, or maybe Lovecraft didn't invent it after all. Either way, I've seen spells on the Web that are supposed to be taken out of it. That doesn't matter, though, it's beside the point. What I'm trying to say is the words looked familiar, okay, so I checked out this Sumerian language site that's run by the University of Chicago. It turns out, there's this, like, family of languages which includes Babylonian and Akkadian, as well as Sumerian. They're all from the Mideast, in the area that used to be Assyria and Babylon."

Brien looked down at the words. They were harsh and intense, and, he had to admit, full of an implacable attitude that was kind of scary, even when seen from the safety of a couple of thousand years later.

"It was pretty obvious that the language was Akkadian once I compared them all," Derek continued. "And the Web site had a link to this professor at the U, so I blew off everything this morning and called the guy, then drove down to Dinkytown to meet him."

Derek grinned. "He was really curious where I'd gotten this from, but I didn't tell him because he wouldn't have believed me anyways. But the thing is, I was right, and it was Akkadian. Not only that, but he even told me where the text came from!"

Brien wanted to be skeptical, but he was finding it hard in the face of Derek's enthusiasm and what appeared to be actual evidence.

"Yeah?"

"The Black Obelisk," Derek informed him proudly. "It's this huge piece of marble that archeologists found in Iraq and took to the British Museum. And somebody carved these words in stone almost three thousand years ago to record the deeds of this King Shalmaneser. Shalmaneser the second, to be exact. He was kind of like a prehistoric Hitler, or something. Bad to the bone, in a big way."

"Yeah, he sounds like he kicked some butt all right." Brien assumed a theatrical pose. "And then I threw down this city and I burned that one—"

"Punk monkey!" Derek punched his palm emphatically. "He was pretty harsh, from what the professor had to say. Used to leave mondo piles of skulls piled up outside the cities he'd sack and stuff. But here's what's really interesting. According to the professor, the first eight pages were taken right from the Obelisk, but the last four pages weren't. He didn't recognize what other source they were from right away, so he couldn't give me a translation, but he said he'd translate it today himself if he couldn't find a matching source. He said he'd e-mail it to me as soon as he had it."

Hmmm. That was pretty interesting. Brien wondered if where he could get a copy of this Obelisk thing. Certainly not in the school library, which didn't carry much besides Stephen King and *Harry Potter*. It looked as if the Obelisk was a little on the monotonous side to make for good reading, but the historical connection was fascinating and he was extremely curious about anything that might provide a clue to yesterday's computer weirdness. Could this have been some new kind of fancy virus put together by a hacker on an Assyrian kick? Maybe, but if that was the case, then how had the guy programmed that trick with the speakers? A printout could be delayed, that was no mystery, but was it really possible for a computer shutdown to trigger the printer like that? Brien didn't know.

"Can I get a copy of this?" Brien raised the orange folder. "I'm thinking maybe your machine's got a virus, and reading this might help me figure out what the guy who wrote it was thinking." Brien had written a few viruses himself, but he'd never let them loose from his machine. He'd never had the chance to practice safe sex, but safe computing was a mantra for him. His viruses all been very basic, though, and this, if it was really a virus, was really something else!

"It's yours." Derek patted his backpack. "I've got another copy in here, and I'll e-mail you whatever that professor sends me when I get it. So, anyhow, where do you want to get lunch?"

Jami followed Angie and Rachel to an empty table toward the back of the cafeteria. It offered some degree of privacy, as well as an excellent view from where Angie could provide running commentary on the lunchroom's inhabitants if the mood struck her. Her friend reminded Jami of a shark sometimes; if her mouth didn't keep moving, Jami wondered if the girl would just shut down altogether. She had a vicious tongue and a nose for gossip, which was one reason to stay on her good side. The other was that she was Holli's best friend, and had been since they were little kids. Jami still couldn't figure that one out.

The lunch ladies had decided to take it easy on them today. Despite questionable origins of the meat in the hamburgers, there was enough ketchup and mustard to drown out any funny nonburger tastes. It wasn't Burger King, or even White Castle, but at least they were edible.

"Doesn't look so good, does it," Angie complained, removing the top half of her bun and staring at the patterns pressed into the hamburger patty. "I swear, I think I can see something that looks like suckers in there! You know what I mean, like on octopus tentacles?"

Rachel stuck out her tongue and pushed her tray away.

"I think I'll take up smoking," she said. "It can't be any worse for you than eating this."

"Good idea." Jami nodded in pretend agreement, knowing her friend wasn't serious. "I think I will, too, just as soon as they shorten our games to fifteen minutes. I don't think I can run the full ninety if I'm coughing up a lung."

Rachel laughed. She was a tall, slender girl whom no one seemed to notice very much, although she had very nice features which she tended to hide behind her long, straight, brown hair. No one seemed to think she was pretty except for Holli, who predicted Rachel would someday be a runway model. Rachel's height made her awkward and self-conscious, and she tended to slouch a lot in order to avoid towering over the boys in their class. She was really nice, though, much nicer, Jami felt, than most of their friends.

"Didn't your season end last fall?" Angie asked with her mouth full.

"We're playing indoor now," Jami reminded her. "The field's small, but you still have to run a lot. In some ways it's even worse, because you can't rest when the ball's at the other end the way you can on the big field."

"Oh," Angie said, clearly uninterested in the subject. Then she perked up. "Hey, doesn't Jason Case play with you guys?"

"Yeah, he's our midfielder."

"I think he's hot," Holli's friend confessed dreamily. "That game I went to last fall, all I did was watch him run. He's got nice legs."

"He's all right," Jami admitted. "Rache, what do you think about Christopher?"

"Your brother?" She looked genuinely surprised by the question. "I don't know. I don't think he likes me."

"Why do you say that?"

"He didn't talk to me at all when he drove us down to the Megamall last weekend. He was just so quiet, I thought maybe he was mad because you made him pick me up or something."

"You're so clueless, Rachel." Angie rolled her eyes. "He didn't talk? So what. That doesn't mean anything. If a guy likes you, he's either going to pester you to death, you know, showing up at your locker every day and asking if you have notes for English, or he never says a word. He just sits there and stares at you, with this blank look and his mouth hanging half-open like he's about to start drooling. And then they wonder why we don't want to go out with them!"

"At least they're not pulling our hair, or hitting us like they used to," Jami pointed out, feeling Angie had somehow put her in the position of defending the boys.

"Sure, but you have to admit it was easier then." Angie patted Rachel's hand. "If your brother would just slug her one and run away, we'd all know where he stood. Now, if he does have the hots for her, we're all going to have to sit around and wait three months for him to find the guts to ask her out!"

"Gee, how inconsiderate of him," Rachel murmured. "How dare he deprive you of someone to talk about."

"Deprive me? I don't think so. As long as there's beer and parties, someone's going to do something stupid that everyone has to hear about. Besides, I was telling people he was ga-ga over you two weeks ago. I knew he wouldn't stick with April Evenson. She's pretty, but she's too much of a corn-stuffed farm girl for him. She's got those big dopey eyes, just like a cow."

"That's what I said," Jami agreed. "Okay, I didn't say it quite like that, but she is a little . . . placid. But, you know, Holli thought she was nice, and she didn't want to set Christopher up with someone who would hurt his feelings. He's kind of sensitive, you know."

"Do you think he's, like, artistic, maybe?" Rachel asked shyly, glancing cautiously at Angie.

"I don't know," Jami answered. "He likes to read, does that count? Oh, and he likes to paint his little army guys."

Angie nearly choked to death on the milk she was drinking.

"That's not artistic, that's just being a geek." She shrugged her shoulders. "You and Holli have done a nice job cleaning him up and all, and he's kind of a cutie now, but face it, deep down he's still a nerd. You just can't change that."

"I don't think so," Rachel objected softly. "He's changed a lot this semester. He's, I don't know, more confident, I guess."

"So go out with him then, already." Angie sighed theatrically. "Look, enough about your brother, Jami. I have to tell you guys what I heard about Jill's party. You're never going to guess who hooked up. . . ."

As Angie happily launched into a detailed discussion of the

weekend's events, Jami wondered if Rachel really might be interested in Christopher. She wasn't all that keen on her brother going out with any of her friends, since everybody knew that was a good way to lose a friend. Still, it gave her a sense of accomplishment to know that it wouldn't be a joke anymore to suggest one of the girls going out with him.

Jami started when she heard Angie saying something about Holli. "What's that?" she interjected.

Angie wrinkled her nose at her.

"Weren't you listening? I just said that everybody knows Paul is going to ask Holli to the prom."

"Isn't it a little soon to be thinking about that?" Jami asked.

Dumb question. It was never too soon, especially since there were never more than a few freshmen who were lucky enough to get asked by the juniors and seniors. Even Rachel gave her a look.

"It's only five weeks away," the tall girl pointed out. "Not that I'll be going."

"I wouldn't think so," Angie agreed carelessly. "Me neither, unless maybe I put on a thong and hide myself in Jimmy Gertz's locker. Think he'd be surprised?"

"I know I would be," Rachel said acidly, miffed with Angie. "Jami, you keep Jim busy while I get the lock changed. We'll save the poor guy from being struck blind."

Jami grinned. "Yeah, you should get to the tanning booth or something, girl."

"Hey, I said I wasn't going, either," Angie retorted. "Sensitive much? It's not like it's up to me or anything, I'm just telling you what I heard. And it's no big deal if we don't go. We're only freshmen, we've got three more years to get all fluffed up and spend the night watching football players yak in the parking lot."

"Gee, and we're not going? You make it sound like so much fun!" Sometimes Jami didn't like Angie all that much, but she was always amused by her eternal cynicism.

"Oh, I never said you weren't," Angie corrected her. "Heidi Thompson told Tammy Rosenquist that Robbie Dale was going to ask you. She's got a big crush on him, and Tammy says she's totally devastated. She's really mad at you."

"Heidi? Or do you mean Tammy?" Jami sighed. "Whatever, she'll have to get in line behind Jill Mondale. What is it with everybody going psycho all of a sudden? It wasn't like this last year. And, sure, Robbie's cute and from what everybody says, he's a nice guy and all, but it's not like he's ever even talked to me. It's not my fault if he likes me. If he really does."

Rachel nodded sympathetically, but Angie's eyes suddenly lit up.

"Ooh, ooh, ooh!" she blurted, so excited she could barely speak. "That reminds me, that reminds me what I forgot to tell you! Jill! Did you hear what happened to her at her party? It's the best thing I ever heard!"

Her voice dropped conspiratorially, and Jami guiltily looked to see who was in the vicinity, then leaned in closer so she could hear Angie's latest gossip. She knew it wasn't right, but she just couldn't help herself.

"Okay, so check this out! Dan O'Conner doesn't get to the Mondales' house until, like, almost midnight, right? And the thing is, when he gets there, no one can find Jill. So Alli Finden goes looking for her, and she hears this slow, like, total mood music coming out of Jill's bedroom. She knocks on the door, but there's no answer, so she peeks in there, and guess what? Jill's only got a T-shirt on, and she's messing around with this older guy from some other school!"

"No way!" Rachel gasped.

Well, well, well. Jami found it impossible to feel bad for Jill. Some people deserved what they got, and Jill Mondale was one of them.

"Can you believe it?" Angie was utterly gleeful. Jami knew she'd never liked Jill, either. "I hear he's from around here, but he goes to SPA. I heard he even plays at the same tennis club as Dan O'Conner!"

"So what did Dan do?" Jami asked. "He must have been pretty mad!"

"Oh, he was pissed in a big way! Alli told Jill that Dan had showed up, and she came out real quick, but he figured out something was going on before she managed to get rid of the SPA guy. John Anderson and Mike Owen had to keep Dan from going after the guy in the driveway. Jill ended up kicking Dan out of the house, too, but not before he poured beer all over the zebra-skin rug in the living room."

"I'm sure her dad will like that," Rachel commented.

"Oh, like they'll notice." Angie dismissed the notion. "She'd have to burn the place down before they get a clue there was even a party there. I thought Holli went, Jami, didn't she tell you anything?"

"Our curfew is eleven," Jami reminded her. "She was already home by then."

"That's right." Angie nodded. "I forgot your dad was, like, Amish. Eleven o'clock! That's so medieval!"

Jami wasn't offended; she could only laugh at her friend's wicked tongue. Not that she was an expert on the Dark Ages herself, but she knew Angie had about as much a clue about what was medieval as she did about the structure of the atom. In other words, nada. So how could you get mad at her for it? She pushed herself away from the table and stood up, stretching.

"Well, if you'll excuse me, Angela, I have to go get my chastity belt adjusted."

"Huh?" said Angie, puzzled, and Rachel laughed behind her hand.

"I'll come with you," she said. The tall girl stood up and Jami saw her soft brown eyes were gently envious. "I think it's nice to have a father who cares so much about you. I wish mine did."

CHAPTER 14

SHATTERED

As the garage door opened in front of him, Brien popped Sister Machine Gun out of the CD player and turned off the engine. He twirled the key ring around his finger as he contemplated whether to take his schoolbooks out of the trunk or not. He was hungry, though, and didn't really feel like doing any homework tonight since he had the Obelisk text to look into, so he locked the car door and headed toward the garage. Mom's car was there, but Dad's wasn't, which meant that there was a good chance he could talk Mom into making hamburgers tonight instead of the skinless, boneless, and tasteless chicken that Dad's low-fat diet forced on them almost every night.

"I'm home!" he yelled, slamming the door to the garage behind him. "Hey, if Dad's working late tonight, do you think we could have burgers for dinner?"

No one answered, so he shrugged off his jacket and draped it over an empty hanger. He whistled as he walked out of the coatroom and past the family room into the kitchen. But he stopped whistling when he saw his mother, sitting at the kitchen table with reddened eyes and an unopened bottle of Sam Adams in front of her.

"Hey, Mom, what's wrong?" he asked, wondering why she had a beer out. She was normally a wine drinker, if she drank at all.

His mother had never been a pretty woman. Brien had seen pictures of her when she was younger, and she'd clearly been one of those poor girls who are inevitably and cruelly described as "nice." Time had not been kind to her; an additional twenty pounds had not improved her figure, and the lines that now creased her face added character at the price of her complexion. Even so, she had a happy, ever-present smile, and normally, she carried herself with the cheerful air of woman ten years younger. But now, as her puffy red face sagged with grief and anger, she looked every one of her forty-three years.

"Oh, Brien," she said with a strangely sad tenderness as she stood up heavily and moved toward him.

The pity in her voice frightened him. The compassionate tones set off an alarm somewhere inside him that he didn't even know he had. His heart pounded. Something was wrong, terribly wrong!

She tried to embrace him, but he pushed her away.

"Mom, what is it!" He felt panic sweeping over him. "Did something happen to Dad?"

Visions of accidents, crushed cars, burning buildings, suddenly filled his mind.

"I'm so sorry. I just don't know how to tell you this, Brien. Your . . . your father left."

"Left!" Brien stared incredulously at Mom. "What do you mean, left? What are you talking about?"

He closed his eyes and swayed. The shrieking alarm exploded inside him, sending freezing slivers of ice coursing through his body. He was numb; he was frozen. He had the unmistakable impression that without warning, his ship had hit an iceberg and he'd suddenly been cast adrift in a cold and unforgiving sea.

He felt an unbearably heavy weight upon his shoulders. Then he realized it was Mom, her hands pressing down upon his shoulders. She was reaching up to him, forcing him to look at her.

Her face was still red, but it was filled with anger now, not grief, and her voice trembled with barely suppressed rage.

"What did you think I meant?" she snapped. "Your father is leaving me, he's gone! Do you understand? He wants a divorce!"

Brien shook his head, stunned by the D-word, reeling from the emotions that were threatening to hammer him down to his knees. Grief, emptiness, desperation, and rage battled within him like four pit bulls fighting to the death.

"What . . . what happened?" he whispered finally.

Mom let go of him and turned away to stare out the window that looked over their backyard.

"Your father"—she enunciated the words with a cold precision—"has been having an affair. From what I understand, it's been going on for quite some time now."

"With who?"

"Whom," she corrected him absently. "A woman at his office. You wouldn't know her. It doesn't matter. I knew about her before. . . ." She sighed and turned back to face him. "I thought it was over, but obviously, it wasn't. He called me about an hour ago to tell me that Medtronic offered him a new job in Cleveland, and he's going to take it. Then, after telling me about that, he finally got around to mentioning that he doesn't want me to go with him."

"Oh, God," Brien breathed, horror-stricken. No. No! Dad was leaving Mom? How could he even think of it?

"We've been married twenty-two years," Mom said, shaking her head. "Twenty-two years, and that . . . that. . . . He didn't even have the nerve to tell me to my face!"

It wasn't possible. Surely Dad couldn't do this to her, he wouldn't. Not to her, not to them! He wouldn't, would he? Even as Brien's mind railed violently against the unthinkable, one small voice made itself heard through his inner turmoil. He would, you know. Oh, yes, he would.

"No, there's got to be a mistake, a misunderstanding or something," Brien protested, refusing to give up hope. "Maybe you, I don't know, maybe you heard him wrong!"

His objections sounded ridiculous even to his own ears. Mom didn't reply, she only shook her head sadly. She reached out to him again, and this time he let her hold him, as if her arms could somehow take this terrible pain away. Of the four pit bulls at war, it was grief that won out at last, and he could not fight the tears that began to flow from his eyes. But even as a sob ripped itself painfully from his lips, the other three emotions, like dogs beaten but not vanquished, lurked within his heart and bided their time.

He cried against Mom's shoulder, and she cried against his. They held each other for a long time, as if their little circle of tears could somehow erase what had happened. There didn't seem to be any bottom to his sorrow, and the monstrous depth of that dark void startled him even as he felt his chest heaving with one involuntary convulsion after another.

But finally he mastered himself and he pulled himself away, wiping at his eyes. He reached into his pocket and found his keys, knowing what he had to do. Even as the tears dried on his face, Brien could feel the void inside him filling rapidly with an anger so strong it made his hands shake. It was bubbling, frothing furiously inside him, and he knew he had to leave before it spilled over and destroyed everything around him.

"Brien, where are you going?" Mom pulled at his arm. "Where are you going?"

He shook her off, gently, but with determination.

"I'm going to Dad's office," he informed her. His voice was glacial. "He's not going to do this to you!"

"I'm here to see Mr. Martin," Brien told the receptionist calmly. He was pleased with how controlled his voice sounded. The drive over had calmed him a little, and despite his utter fury, he had no desire to create a scene. "Is he in his office? I'm his son."

"Yes, he's in." Was she looking at him with pity, or with contempt? "Would you like me to tell him—"

"No, I'll just walk in on him," Brien broke in. He held up a hand. "Yes, I know where it is, thank you."

He could feel the adrenaline flowing through his veins. His

vision narrowed, and everything took on a hyper-real appearance as if he were about to go into combat. He marched down the
bland gray-carpeted hallway like an automaton, turning corners
without thinking about anything but his ultimate destination. He
reached the door he was seeking and paused for a moment with
his hand on the doorknob.

William Martin, it said on the door, in black letters engraved
onto a light gray plate. The plate was held between two pieces
of metal designed so that it could be easily removed. Just place
your fingers on it, and slide it . . . and it would be gone. Just like
that.

Did they take it down right away, he wondered, or did they
just leave it sitting there, a meaningless name attached to an
empty space, until the next guy came along? He swallowed hard
and leaned against the door, then slowly turned the doorknob.

His father was sitting at his desk, looking thoughtful and tapping his pen against his dayplanner. His office was a large one,
with two padded chairs facing toward the whiteboard that hung
on the wall behind the desk. It looked like the office of someone
who mattered to the company, but didn't matter very much. At
the sound of the door opening, Dad glanced up, then pushed his
chair back and raised his eyebrows when he realized who his
unexpected visitor was.

"Brien?" He didn't sound entirely pleased. "Well, this is a nice
surprise. What are you doing here?"

Brien clenched his teeth, trying to remember what it was that
he'd planned to say. He'd thought about a million different ways
to begin this conversation on the way over, but now, he couldn't
think of anything to say. He could feel a teary pressure building
in his eyes, and he bit his lip, desperately determined not to
break down now.

"Dad?" he started slowly, unsurely. "Dad, what is this about
you and Mom?"

He stared intently at his father, seeing Dad's eyes widen
behind his glasses, and saw understanding enter in. Dad nodded,
and looked away, then laid his pen down on the dayplanner and

stood up from his desk. He was shorter than Brien, and heavier, but he possessed a certain charisma that Brien himself had always lacked. Dad didn't have a best friend the way Brien had Derek, but he always had plenty of buddies around to go golfing or bowling with him, and everyone seemed to know him at the big picnics that the company put on from time to time during the summer.

Dad closed the door softly and pointed to one of the chairs.

"Have a seat, son. I'm sorry I didn't tell you sooner, but to be honest, I just didn't know how to do it."

He sounded genuinely sorry as he sat down in the other chair and crossed one leg across his knee. Brien didn't really feel like sitting, but he sat down anyhow.

"Brien, you're almost a man now, so let's have a man-to-man talk, okay? I know you've had all those sex-ed classes, so I don't need to tell you anything about the birds and the bees."

What did that have to do with anything? Brien was incredulous. "What?"

"Okay, well, I know you haven't really been out with too many girls, I mean, your mother and I have talked about it before." Dad waved his hands expansively. "I never did that sort of thing much myself, back in the day. I wasn't one of the popular people, I didn't play any sports, you know how it is. . . ."

"Yeah," Brien admitted grudgingly; unfortunately, he did know.

"So that's how I was when I met your mother. I didn't know anything about the world then, about how it really worked. And she was different then, you know? She was excited to see me, she'd spend hours getting ready for one of our dates, even if we were just going out for a walk in the park. She had a certain, I don't know, a spark. That's it, she had a spark."

Dad sighed and raised one hand to his forehead. He paused for a moment to massage his brow.

"That was a long time ago. Twenty-five years. One-quarter of a century. Now, when I walk into the house, she doesn't even get up from the TV. She doesn't care about her appearance, as far as I can tell, and as far as, well, other things go, man, you can just forget about it!"

Brien winced. He wasn't sure he wanted to hear any of this. He was still angry, but it was hard to deny the apparent truth of what Dad was saying. How would he feel if he were in Dad's shoes? He'd heard Mom getting on Dad's back plenty of times over one little thing or another, and he'd often wondered how Dad could just ignore it and go on as if nothing had happened. Maybe, he realized with a start, maybe Dad hadn't been ignoring it after all.

"But, Dad," he protested, "even if that's all true, you can't just walk out on her like this. You have to work with Mom, to change things for the better! And it's not right, either, I mean, what about 'till death do you part' and all that sort of thing?"

Dad shrugged. "What about it? It's just words. There's no such thing as black and white, Brien, you've learned that by now. You only get one life to live, and you've got a responsibility to get the most you can out of it. I'm not the same person I was twenty-five years ago and neither is your mother. I've changed, I've moved on. I may not be the most successful guy in the world, but this new job they're giving me, heading up all the sales for the five-state region, it isn't too bad. It's an important region for the company, Brien, and in five, ten years, who knows? I could make division manager, or maybe even VP. Not bad, huh?"

No, it wasn't bad, Brien thought, but that wasn't the point.

"That's the problem, really," Dad concluded. "I've moved on in the world, and your mother hasn't."

"So that justifies everything?" Brien asked, not seeing any holes in Dad's logic, but unable to accept it, either. "That makes it right to just, I mean, run off to Cleveland with your secretary or whoever?"

Dad's face darkened and he wagged his finger toward Brien. "Don't you presume to judge me, son. And don't you bring Gretchen into this either. You don't know what you're talking about."

"Okay, okay, Dad, maybe I don't." Brien saw that he'd stepped across a line and quickly retreated. "But isn't it wrong? I just don't see how can it be right for you to dump Mom and replace her with somebody else."

Dad sighed and rubbed at his temples. "Brien, what you have to understand is that this isn't about your mother. And what's right for one person isn't always right for someone else. This isn't about what's right or wrong for anybody else, it's just about what's right for me, okay? And if it's right for me, then it can't be wrong, can it?"

How could he argue with that? He couldn't, Brien concluded, feeling frustrated. Everybody had the right to live their life however they wanted, that was what America was all about. Could he judge Dad, or tell him what he should or shouldn't do? No, because no one had the right to do that. Dad was the only one who could decide what was right or wrong for his life.

Brien shrugged sadly, knowing there was nothing he could say. Dad smiled with relief, seeing that Brien seemed to understand where he was coming from.

"Come on, Brien, it's not like this is going to change your life. You're not a little kid anymore, and you're going to be starting a whole new chapter at the U. Boy, do I envy you! College is great, one of the best times of your life! You'll be way too busy to worry about what your old dad is up to."

"The U?" Brien exclaimed. "Dad, what are you talking about? You know I got accepted to Northwestern! Why would I go to the U?"

Dad took off his glasses and polished them uncomfortably.

"It's your decision, of course, Brien. Northwestern is a very good school, there's no doubt about it. Of course, it's also very expensive. How do you plan to pay for it?"

Pay for it? Brien lurched back in his chair, unable to believe his ears. What did he mean, pay for it?

"But . . . you said . . ." He stumbled over the words in his shock. "You said last fall that I could go there if they accepted me! We talked about it before I even applied!"

"Yes, we did," Dad agreed. He folded his hands and looked

Brien straight in the eyes. "But, as you are obviously aware, the circumstances have changed. It's very expensive to end a marriage, thanks to those money-sucking suits who call themselves divorce lawyers, and I have no doubt that your mother will find a very good one who will point out how long we were married, and what kind of style she's become accustomed to, and all that other nonsense." He rolled his eyes and scratched his head. "Highway robbery, is what it is," he concluded bitterly. "But that's neither here nor there. The point is there's no way I'm going to be able to afford Northwestern, Brien, and I don't think you can, either. And furthermore, I don't think you should. What's the matter with the University of Minnesota? It's a very good school with a very good reputation. It was good enough for me, after all."

Brien buried his face in his hands. This was not happening, he told himself. It simply couldn't be happening. It wasn't fair! For the last two years he'd been telling himself that all he had to do was make it to graduation and he'd be rid of the idiots and the bullies forever. They could go off to their stupid jock schools and drink until their brains were pickled, while he spent four years with civilized, intelligent people, getting a real education.

He suddenly had a nightmarish image of walking into one overcrowded classroom and spotting, in the middle of two hundred people, Kent Petersen. He could just see Kent pointing at him, and whispering humiliating stories to the people sitting on either side of him. He could just see them looking at him and making fun of him, the same way the kids at Mounds Park had always laughed at him, and he could feel the loser persona that he'd tried so hard to shed hardening around him as it was cemented forever in stone. He might as well get an *L* tattooed on his forehead, he realized, as go to the U. At the U there would be no escape, not in college and not ever.

"Please, Dad, you can't do this to me," he begged. "I need to go to Northwestern; otherwise, I'll just be trapped and nothing will ever change! You don't understand!"

Dad's face turned ugly and he started to raise his voice.

"I don't understand? You need to go to Northwestern? Do you hear what you're saying, Brien? You're the one who's talking about being trapped? That's exactly my point! You think you're trapped in school? Ha! Try being married for twenty years!"

"But, Dad, I can't go to the U. It's impossible!"

His father stood up and placed his hands on his hips. He was angry, more angry than Brien had ever seen him before.

"Listen to me, young man. I don't know what your problem is with the University, but from your very immature and selfish reaction, it's clear to see that your mother spoiled you far too much. I always warned her about that. You wanted a car when you were sixteen, you got a car. You wanted a computer, you got a computer. And who paid for it?"

He paused for dramatic effect.

"I did, that's who!"

Brien looked away as his father scowled at him.

"Did you ever stop to think that maybe I would have rather bought something for myself instead of working my backside off trying to give you everything you wanted? And give your mother what she wanted? Apparently not!"

Brien felt simply awful. He felt sick inside. Somehow this whole conversation had gone wrong, terribly wrong, and while he knew that it was his fault, he wasn't sure exactly what it was he'd done. All he'd meant to do was to try to keep Dad from leaving Mom, and now he'd managed to antagonize Dad, too.

"Dad . . ." he protested feebly. "I didn't mean . . . it's not that. . . ."

"I know, I know," Dad relented, and he reached out to grip Brien's shoulders firmly. "This thing with your mother is a shock, I know. But it happens. I can still remember when my parents got divorced when I was twelve, and back then, I thought it was the end of the world. But you know what, it wasn't. It won't be for you, either."

Brien nodded slowly, and surreptitiously brushed a tear away from the corner of his eye. Dad was probably right. Sometimes these things just happened, and there wasn't anything anybody could do about it. It was between Mom and Dad, and it really wasn't his business. But his future was another matter, and even if Dad couldn't afford to pay for Northwestern, there were a lot of colleges that weren't in-state.

"Dad, I understand about Northwestern, I really do." He paused, afraid to set his father off again, but even more afraid of keeping silent. "But, um, I don't think Madison costs any more than the U, and I think Stoudt is still taking applications, too."

Dad nodded and smiled sympathetically. "You're a smart kid, Brien, and I knew you'd understand." He chucked Brien on the shoulder. "Why don't you get some information on those schools, and we'll go over it before I leave for Cleveland. That's the weekend after next."

Cleveland? Two weeks? Oh, no, was everything happening so soon? Brien felt as if he had suddenly turned into a statue that had been carved out of a flawed piece of marble. He could feel the fractures snaking their way through his mind, weakening him, disintegrating him, and he hoped desperately that he could hold himself together long enough to walk out of the building without completely falling apart and breaking down in tears.

"Okay, I'll work on it, Dad."

Brien forced himself to smile pleasantly at his father. It wasn't easy, but he did it. As he closed the door of his father's office behind him, he was hoping that Derek had a serious load of weed on hand, because what he needed right now was to get as high as a freaking kite. With any luck, he'd be able to forget everything that had happened today for at least a few hours. That was his plan for this afternoon. As for what he'd do about the rest of his life, he had absolutely no idea.

CHAPTER 15

SMOKE ON THE WATERS

I JUST WANT TO FLY
LIKE A BIRDIE IN THE SKY I'M SO HIGH
HIGH, HIGH, HIGH, HIGH, HIGHER THAN HIGH
— Sugar Ray ("I Just Want To Fly")

Brien closed his eyes, feeling a smooth wave of relaxation begin to flow over him as he inhaled deeply. The water pipe gurgled noisily, then fell silent as he held his breath and felt the familiar burn heating up his lungs. He waited, counting to twenty, then to fifteen. He'd reached five for the third time when he couldn't fight the pressure inside him anymore, and he coughed explosively, hard enough to make his eyes water.

"There you go." Derek patted him on the back. "Now hit it again."

He'd barely managed to get out the news of the disasters that were ruining his life before Derek had cut him off and made for the stash of pharmaceuticals that were hidden in the bottom of his desk drawer.

"Dr. Wallace is in the howwse," Derek told him moments later, smiling sympathetically and presenting him with a packed water pipe. "Instant inner peace, just add fire."

Brien was grateful. It touched him deeply to know that Derek understood what he needed without him even having to say anything. Sometimes you really don't need to talk about your problems, you just need to forget them. And boy, did he ever need to forget today!

"How do you feel?" Derek asked him after a few minutes had passed, once they'd burned through the last of the bong's second packing.

"Better, I guess," Brien replied slowly. And he did feel better, just not better enough. "Now I feel like someone who's high, but still wants to kill his father."

Derek nodded thoughtfully. "Ah, you leave zee doktor wiz no choice," he said with a Pythonesque German accent. "Vee must bring out zee heavy artillery!"

His friend fumbled around in the lowest drawer of his desk and came out with a small ball of tin foil. Derek unfolded it carefully, and as he spread out the foil on top of an old Werewolf compendium, the loosely packed powder inside it collapsed into a little brown pyramid. It rather resembled cinnamon, except it was a good deal darker. Brien didn't know what it was. "That's hash, isn't it?"

"No, no, it's much better than that. It's dopamine. Laurence McKenzie says it's better than acid, which is high praise coming from someone who's massacred more brain cells than Timothy Leary ever did."

Brien was finding it hard to follow Derek, but he felt pretty sure this wasn't only because he was high. "It's kind of powdery. What do you do, snort it?"

"No, just hold the lighter under the foil. The heat will vaporize it and you can inhale it." Derek reached out and pushed his hand away. "Not the whole thing! Just let me shake some off here."

Brien watched with curiosity as Derek expertly shook a small pile off onto another piece of foil. His friend frowned, examined the second pile, then added a little bit more to it.

"There you go, just open your mouth over it and breathe in as it heats up. It's kind of like crack."

"Crack?" Brien cried out, alarmed. "I'm not doing that, man. No way!"

"Relax." Derek rolled his eyes. "It's not like crack in that it's a cocaine derivative, it's just got a similar delivery package. Effect-wise, it's a lot more like acid, except it only lasts, like, twenty minutes. But it's pretty doggone trippy."

"Oh, yeah?" Brien felt embarassed about his outburst. Of course there was nothing to worry about. Derek knew what he was doing. He was practically a professional. "Well, all right, then."

Derek laughed suddenly. "I read about it for the first time in *Mondo Two Thousand*. Remember that? *Mondo* was the coolest magazine back in the day. Anyhow, there was this massive drug conference or something, and McKenzie, that guy I told you about earlier, well, he's a Ph.D., and he wrote about how this stuff opens up a window for your mind to enter this alternate universe. The thing is, he says there's elves living in this other universe. Seriously, elves, no kidding. And he's going on and on about how he talks to the elves, and how they're really wise, and they just know, like, everything. I guess they were filling him in on the secrets of the universe or something like that."

"Elves?" Brien had to chuckle dubiously. "Okay, whatever, that's cool."

"Right," Derek agreed, raising an eyebrow to indicate his own skepticism. "But here's the punchline. At the conference, McKenzie's just been going on and on about the elves for, like, twenty minutes, and when he finishes, this other doctor gets up and starts telling everyone about what a great metaphor McKenzie's been making, and how massively poetic it is, you know, that kind of . . ."

Derek's voice trailed off. Brien waited expectantly for a few seconds, then realized that Derek had spaced out.

"That's the freaking punchline? Talk about killing brain cells. Stoner!"

"Shut up, let me get to it, will you?" Derek glared at him. "I was just trying to get it straight. No, so the punchline is, McKenzie totally loses it. He jumps up and starts screaming at the guy, just totally screaming at him. He's yelling 'it's not a metaphor, it's not a freaking metaphor, they're real! The elves are real! They told me themselves!' "

Brien cracked up. Derek joined him and they both laughed and laughed. Brien thought his sides were going to explode.

"You kidding me?"

"It's true, I swear, I read all about it! I mean, you've got the whole crowd thinking the guy is totally this deep-thinking philosopher-king, another genius chemical guru like Leary or whatever, and all of a sudden everyone realizes all at once that the guy is a freaking lunatic! He's just stone-cold freaking crazy!"

"That is so awesome!" Brien was amazed. His stomach almost hurt from laughing so hard. "Elves! Awesome. Geez, I can't wait to try this stuff now!"

Derek leaned toward him and handed him a translucent green lighter. With a solemn look on his face, he raised his own lighter and flicked it, summoning forth a dancing yellow flame. *Flick!* Brien answered his friend with a flaming salute of his own.

"Are you ready to meet the elves?" Derek asked him as he handed him the smaller piece of foil.

"Bring 'em on." Brien grinned, trying to hide his nervousness. His hands were shaking. He always felt this way when experimenting with something new. "But I get firsts on Galadriel!"

He watched as Derek bent over the foil in his hand. The powder disappeared rapidly, without even a trace of smoke. As his friend stopped inhaling and sat back, closing his eyes, Brien quickly imitated the process. At first it didn't seem as if he were breathing in anything but hot air, but then he felt something moving within him, pulling at his brain, and suddenly, something jerked his mind upward, sending his consciousness flying wildly toward the sky. With a surprised giggle, he closed his eyes and leaned back to enjoy the ride.

I am alone. Rocks surround me, rocks around me grayslate smashpate shattered piles of hard stone stacked up high high to the sky . . . mountains! Where? Why? And how? There is no answer there are no answers there never have been. Surrounding, abounding, black bones breaking through skin, green skin, lean skin, thin skin, stretched to the stretching point, breaking here, there, everywhere, except under my feet. I know there is grass on this knoll. I look down, I count. Carefully now . . . one foot, two foot, they must be mine. Three foot, four foot, adamantine.

I laugh aloud. How funny it is how lovely it is, all of it, everything, the sun stone sky singsong ding-a-long—celebrating and cerebrating—the stone and the stoner how come no one writes a trilogy for me? The warmheat skylove in my heart in my face and I see the sun shining down on me—Jackyl or AC/DC? I can never keep it straight. Focus, now, down, down, beyond the feet and the water runs fluidly flowedly through the greengrass of the meadow.

Below, the Valley of the Sun. Above, the Mirror of the Deep. Sky blue, the color of Zeiss Ikon eyes, the painted eyes of that Barbie doll I have never known or loved. Sky blue my blue. Cerulean blue makes you invisible if you just whisper it so I know I saw it on TV . . . cerulean . . . the fool I am . . . cerulean . . . the tool I am . . . I have been invisible since the day I was born. My mother was invisible my father smelt of elderberries and is that a foul breeze blowing in your direction?

No, not a breeze, a blast a horn long past those notes I know I told you so C-E-E-F-E spells ceefe and I am under a spell that is never going to end at the casting of a friend that will take me straight to Hell. Cry for the caribou, if you dare! But who would have thought that the old man had so much blood in him?

Horatio does not answer. He is pretty, this Hornblower, a pretty boy white-golden hair the color of the sun kissing the snow-clad peaks peeking past the fuzzy scrub scuzzy trees of these old, broken piles surrounding me on ovary side. I am waiting to be hatched, but my golden duckling will not squeak to me not speak to me he raises his horn to his lips and blows.

The sky shouts down its answer.

"Life!"

Maybe he is not so pretty. No, more than pretty, he is beautiful and his face is a skull and I knew him, Horatio. Under the thin skin, the black bones waiting, hating, contemplating a breakthrough. He is the Child of Sun and Winter, Baldur born again, a Nordic god beyond good and evil sentenced to an eternity of wandering this ageless cage of stone. He wears leather and a feather in his hat.

"Life is life!"

He sings with the sky. As one with the Choir Invisible is his voice his choice hier steh ich ich kann nicht anders and the Mermaid walks on knives. Ein Volk ein Reich ein Führer and here is the list of things that must be done the list of names and the knock-knock who's there on the door in the middle of the night. The sky is in his eyes and sun burns there too a passion flower burning yearning for something—what? Power!

One . . . two . . . three. . . . four and more and more and here in this Alpine wonderland, (this is not the Rockies, this is not my father's Oldsmobile), the Austrian's dream appears before me, a multiplication of eugenic transformation, seventy times seven Youths, four-hundred-ninety Perfect Aryans, an agglomeration, an abomination, a gaggle of gargantuan procreation.

Not geese, though. Swans, white and lovely swans, they trumpet together.

"Life!"

Am I crazy am I a freak I wonder as I watch the unspeakable confirm the irrefutable. What twisted message is my poor, tortured subconscious trying to tell me? There is truth in the dream in the vision in the sky, but what good is a dictate without the dictator?

Ah, yes, there he is. The Beast shows his face in every nightmare and here he comes for me! Wake me up before you go-go I'm not planning on dying solo—Choose Life and Screw Heisenberg, here is Horton's Uncertainty Principle: the act of self-observation changes the who you are. And without self-examination, man is nothing, which is why they should have poisoned that prick Plato instead of Socrates.

The Beast is tall, skinny, creepy, and he walks with all the confidence of the made man, a creature of the created, fabricated of dust and lust and I trust that he'll tell me the secrets of his diet.

Oh, to be so svelte, so slender, so sick-scrawny-stick thin. His eyes burn and I am not speaking metaphorically here, actually, I am, in avoiding the vertiginous versimilitude of the simile, telling nothing but the truth. His eyes are not burning like fire, they are fire and the flames scald my hands as I hold them up before him.

"When we all have the power," he tells me, in all seriousness. "We all have the best."

He glares flares stares at me, and the flames lick-flicker as they threaten to explode from his fiery eyeballs. They are suns, stars, novas, and they whisper the promise of a new birth. I listen, in equal parts fear and faith.

"Do you know what your problem is, Brien?" A voice that grinds like stone on stone. "You don't understand that power is everything. It is the only thing."

He raises one scrawny arm, and again the horn sounds from the sky. The Nazi boys below, and the world changes.

"Vee all have ze power!" the man declares triumphantly.

He is wearing leather without feather. Black leather. Nothing but leather. Leather is stylish, leather is fashionable, but most of all, leather is sexy. Got'ta give my props to my peeps—stay strong! Forty-one to freaking nothing, just throw it up there dawg, you dog, you broke my purple heart.

I stare at the object in my hands. The black metal smells of grease, of the proscribed, of porkfat, must I then bite? Unclean, unclean! The pretty boys, the Aryan toys, with their hidden black bones yearning to breathe free, have lost their hats. No feathers, no leathers, only chiseled faces in the shadow of steel helmets marked by the lightning, the mark of Odin, the black sigil of darkest death. Still they burn, these passion flowers, and they are as beautiful as they are deadly.

What is that that kneels before us in the cold snow of winter? Who is it? The Fimbul-winter is upon us, Armageddon and the End Times, and the Beast who is Surtyr who is Loki who is Shiva who is the Destroyer and the Dragon at one and the same time marches towards the Pit. It is fresh-dug, and the frozen dirt torn from the bosom of the earth is piled in a lumpy pile off to the side of forty shabby people in their ramshackle shoes and sacking-covered heads, forty peons kneeling in frightened, fearful homage.

"We all have the power," the Beast insists again, as he strides glides towards the dirt-worshippers. They gibber gabble groan, but he reaches down and with all the gentle brutality of an artist he rips away the canvas from one sack-covered head.

It is Kent. He stares at me, his lip wrinkles, and then he laughs. Ha ha ha he laughs the hyena the jackal the canine whelp. There is no fear in that weaselly ferret face, no more. Not of me. Once again there is a miracle of multiplication, an aberration of congregation, and as the Beast rips the shroud from each kneeling sacrifice, the face of hate appears. It is Kent, again Kent, once and again and always Kent. They chortle chuckle snigger, the mocking chorus of the soon-to-be-damned.

I grit my teeth. Yes I am I'm it's a fact I'm glad to be back in black, I'm ready to kill and so I shoot to thrill. I squeeze, and from my hands spits death. Rat-tat-a-tat take that! I am not the only one. The Sons of Sun and Winter howl, and their vengeance is mine. The grave is full, when the horn sounds in exultation, and this time I roar the holy words with the others.

"Life is life!"

The Beast stands before me, and the flames in his eyes die away to embers. There is nothing there but a black and formless void, but he smiles with approval. His teeth are white and perfect, like his bone-faced boy warriors.

"Perhaps there is some hope for you after all," he declares. "Every minute, every hour, you always have the power. If you remember one thing, remember that."

There are no elves. There never were any elves. I feel cheated.

"So what'ya think?"

Brien blinked several times, trying to get his brain back in focus. He felt overwhelmed trying to cope with the various noises and colors that his senses were reporting. He reached out blindly and felt something rough, but soft. Carpet, that was it!

When his mind finally managed to synchronize with his eyes and ears, he realized he was still sitting on the floor of Derek's bedroom.

"So?" Derek grinned widely, his pupils still dilated. "Pretty crazy stuff, huh!"

"Tripadelic, dude!"

Brien blinked again. Wow! He wasn't sure what he'd seen, exactly, but the bits and pieces he was recalling now were definitely strange. Things were still a little foggy. He had a vague idea that he'd managed to bruise his brain or something, if that was possible. His thoughts all seemed to have rough edges to them at the moment.

"See any elves?" he asked Derek.

"No, dude, how about you?"

"Me, neither," he confessed. "I kept seeing, like Nazis, I think. Yeah, it was like this weird fascist thing going on, with these Hitler youth types and all. Oh, and I think we shot up this whole collection of Kent Petersens, for some reason."

Derek held up the balled pieces of aluminum foil that he'd just rolled together. "Dang, that's better than elves, as far as I'm concerned. I just had this floaty kinda thing happening. It was nice, very nice, actually, but nothing too wacked out."

He tossed the metal ball into a plastic wastepaper basket and reached for the bong again. "How do you feel now? Think you need any of this?"

Brien screwed up his face. No, *nyet, nein,* a thousand times no! It was going to take him weeks to recover from this little binge, he could tell already. The first time he'd dropped acid, it was almost six months before he really, truly felt back to normal again. It took the edge off your brain, like whacking the blade of a sharp knife against concrete. Why do we do this to ourselves? he wondered, not for the first time.

"So, you're cool about your dad now?"

Oh, yeah, that was why. He remembered now. Because life sucks, and oblivion is bliss by comparison.

"I don't know about that," he answered honestly. "But at the present moment, I find myself almost utterly indifferent to anything that might happen to be happening to anyone on this planet."

Derek laughed. "Thatta boy!" He stood up and touched the bong to Brien's shoulders twice, left and right, before slipping it into a surprisingly deep desk drawer. "Then I officially pronounce you cured! Utter indifference is the only sane approach to life these days. Since nothing really matters, the only appropriate attitude is to not pay attention to anything. Or anyone."

"You just going to leave that there?" Brien ignored Derek's pontificating and pointed to the drawer. "That water is going to stink pretty bad in a day or two."

"Oh, yeah, good point. I should probably dump it out first, huh?"

"Only if you don't want the housekeeper digging through your stuff, looking for the dead mouse."

"We get those here, sometimes. Little rat bastards come in from the woods, I think. Drives my mother nuts. You ever get them at your house?"

"Just one big one, apparently," Brien answered morosely. He saw that Derek had missed his feeble attempt at black humor and explained. "My dad?"

"Oh, right." Derek fell silent and stared out the window. "I've been thinking, you know. It's our senior year, and neither one of us has ever been to a school dance before. I mean, proms are bogus, everyone knows that, but maybe there's something to it besides just a better chance to score. You ever think you were missing something?"

"No, not really," Brien lied.

He'd only sell his soul and cheerfully murder any randomly selected ten individuals if that would improve his odds on taking Tessa. A tux, a limo, a hotel room, the works, shoot, he'd be more than happy to blow his whole bank account just to set the whole thing up right, even if it was only for one night. But how was he ever going to find the nads to ask her?

"Well, there is one girl I suppose I wouldn't mind going with," he modified his earlier statement. "She's pretty hot, and since girls dig that kind of stuff, getting all dressed up and stuff, I figure taking her to the prom would up my odds, you know, of getting somewhere with her."

Derek shook his head, smiling sadly. "I don't know, man. Tessa Fenchurch?"

"Maybe, maybe not."

His friend snorted, clearly not buying his feeble attempt at misdirection.

Even if Derek did know how he felt, Brien was still extremely reluctant to discuss his secret love with him. Derek was the best, but he was always down on the girls at their school, no matter how nice or pretty any of them might be. He just seemed to hate them all indiscriminately, and for no reason at all.

"Forget her, Bry." Derek pressed his lips together. "She's no good, I can tell you that right now. She's like every other girl. She don't care who she goes with, she just wants the excuse to go buy a new dress, then get all wined and dined by anyone dumb enough to blow three hundred bucks on her on the off chance she'll put out!"

Yeah, so? Three hundred dollars? He'd happily spend twice that much just for the chance to hold her hand and see her smile! He sometimes lay awake at night, trying to think up ways he could spend more time with Tessa than their one pathetic class together. One hour a day, five times a week, left one hundred and sixty-three hours in the week he didn't get to see her. He'd even considered offering to give her a regular lift to school when he saw that she was still riding the bus, except that he lived far enough away from her that he was afraid he was being too obvious. That kind of thing might freak her out and scare her off for good, and he just couldn't take that chance.

He still remembered how warm and excited he'd felt when she'd asked to borrow his notes for biology last year. His notes! She could have asked anyone for them, but she wanted his! Forget the honor roll, that had been the crowning achievement of his junior year.

"She's not like the others," Brien insisted. "She's different. I can tell."

"You're cruising for a bruising, dude." Derek sighed. "Well, don't say I didn't warn you when she rips your heart to pieces, then stomps on them, okay?"

Fair enough. Brien felt a little irritated with his friend, but he knew that Derek was just trying to look out for him and didn't want him to get hurt. He didn't know Tessa, after all, not the way Brien did, so it wasn't his fault if he thought she was just like everybody else.

"Okay," he nodded. "And thanks. So what do you say to some Warhammer? Chaos versus Empire, four thousand points, fifty point max on items?"

Derek's eyes strayed to the old, carved chest in which he stored his minis.

"No characters?"

"No characters. Start setting up the table and I'll get my boys out of my car. Oh, and can I borrow your Hellhounds?" Brien paused a moment, pretending to be concerned that he'd said too much. "If I need them, that is."

Derek cocked a suspicious eyebrow. Would he fall for the feint? Probably not, Brien figured, but it was always worth a try.

"My demons are your demons," Derek said with a smile, and gestured grandly to the chest.

CHAPTER 16

DREAMS CAN COME TRUE

CUPID, THE BEAUTEOUS LIGHT
THAT SHINES FORTH FROM MY MISTRESS' EYNE
HAS MADE ME BOTH HER SLAVE AND THINE.
—Boccaccio, *Decameron*

The days passed quickly over the next three weeks. Mounds Park was a hotbed of rumor, gossip, and innuendo as long-time senior couples split apart almost as quickly as the new pairings were announced. Brien didn't know either Alan Cowling or Kate Porter very well, but he was shocked nevertheless when he heard that they'd broken up, and that Bill Morris was taking Kate to prom. Alan and Kate had been going together since eighth grade, and Brien, like everyone else at Mounds Park, had assumed they'd go on to get married someday. It was strange, since it really had nothing to do with him, but the news of their breakup left a surprisingly hollow feeling in his stomach.

There was excitement and uncertainty everywhere. The weather was getting warmer, and an electric feeling of energy crackled throughout the halls. Summer was coming, and another year's drudgery was coming to a close! Time to party, party, par-tay! The excitement was different in Senior Hall, though, tempered as it was by a noticeable air of melancholy. A few of the popular people seemed to sense that their long reign was coming to an end at last, that their days of being the big fish in the little pond that was Mounds Park were coming to a close. They were desperately sentimental, and Brien found it amusing how they seemed to fear the approaching future, as if graduation signaled the end of something important.

"Just think, Martin." John Monroe, one of the football captains, had somberly placed a massive hand on his shoulder. "Once we're gone, that's it. It's over. Things are never going to be the same again. I'm really going to miss you, man."

Brien had nodded in solemn agreement at the time, but he found the whole conversation a little on the bizarre side. While it was nice of John to say that, he could count the number of times the big guy had ever spoken to him on one hand, without using his thumb. Yeah, I'll miss you terribly, he thought sarcastically. And what was your name again?

There were others who felt differently, of course, like his archnemesis Petersen, who were as cocky as ever, breezily assured that no matter where they were headed next fall, they'd somehow find themselves on top of the social heap. Brien shook his head bitterly. Life was unfair enough that most of them were probably right. He just hoped none of them were going to Madison. He'd gotten his application to the University of Wisconsin in just before the deadline, and although his SATs weren't high enough to make it a sure thing, he felt pretty good about his chances.

Derek, who had test scores that were more than respectable, but abysmal grades, was now claiming that he was going to join the Marines. Brien found that very difficult to believe; for one thing, it wasn't like the Marines were going to let his friend keep his long hair or sleep in until noon, and it seemed like a pretty strange organization to join if you didn't like getting beat on. Wasn't that what Boot Camp was all about? But Derek had gone down to a recruiter's office twice, and he insisted that he really was serious about joining. He'd even taken to wearing camouflage pants and a red USMC T-shirt the recruiter had given him to school lately.

But Brien had bigger concerns than graduation and his future right now. The problem was, there were only two weeks until the prom, and he still hadn't found the right opportunity to ask

Tessa. He walked past her locker four or five times almost every day, but she usually wasn't there, or when she was, she was surrounded by her friends. Brien had enough trouble dealing with the thought of asking Tessa at all, and there was no way he'd be able to find the courage to do it with other people around.

He glanced at his watch. It was a quarter to eleven, and third hour would be ending in a little more than five minutes. The library was mostly empty, as the halls would be for another five minutes. He probably should have gone to English after all, but what the hay, it wasn't like skipping one more class was going to keep him from graduating. Hmmm, five minutes until the bell, he thought. Plenty of time to walk down to Senior Hall again and see if Tessa was going to stop by her locker in between history and gym. She didn't usually, but maybe she'd want to dump her books off before heading for the locker room today.

He pushed himself out of his favorite orange bean bag and whistled as he forced himself not to rush, to walk casually, as if he didn't have any particular destination in mind. Maybe he could walk past her locker down to the caf, get a soda, and then walk back up past her locker again just after the bell rang. That would let him pass the locker twice without making him look suspicious to anyone who happened to notice him walking back and forth through the area. Not for the first time, he wished that he'd taken Spanish; the language classroom was just around the corner from Tessa's locker, and the Spanish students had a regular hangout on the very steps he was now descending.

As he reached the landing between the second and third floors, he saw someone moving below him near the bottom of the steps, and he froze. It was Tessa! He couldn't believe it. She was even alone! She was crouched in front of her locker, pulling books out of her backpack and sliding them into the neat little wallpapered shelves she'd constructed at the start of the year. She was wearing khaki shorts, and he could see the muscles in her slim calves trembling as she finished putting her books away and stood up.

Wow! He realized that he hadn't moved or breathed since

he'd seen her, and he quickly hurried down the flight of stairs to reach her before she closed her locker. She heard him, and glanced over her shoulder to see who was there.

"Oh, hi, Brien," she said, turning back toward her locker.

"Um, ah, hi," he stammered.

He was glad she wasn't looking at him, because he could feel his face turning bright red. He closed his eyes and swallowed hard, forcing himself to relax. Don't blow it, you idiot! Be cool!

"Just get here?" he asked with only the faintest quiver in his voice.

She turned around to face him, and nodded.

"Yeah, I had a doctor's appointment this morning." She shrugged. "What about you? How come you're not in class?"

"Class? Oh, yeah." He lifted his folder. "I was just, you know, working on a paper."

"A paper?" Tessa sniffed sympathetically. "That rots, I mean, what kind of teacher assigns papers to seniors this time of year? We're, like, practically out of here already!"

"Yeah, it's a drag." He nodded hastily. "So, you know where you're going next year?"

"The U," she said. "I didn't want to go too far away, and my sister's a Kappa there."

"Kappa?" He had no idea what she was talking about. The blood pounding in his ears was making it hard to concentrate.

"Yeah, Kappa Kappa Gamma, you know, the sorority. So how about you, where are you going?"

"Northwestern," he replied without thinking. "Or, ah, Madison. I haven't made up my mind yet."

"Good for you!" she said with a smile that rocked him to his core. "That doesn't surprise me, you always were pretty smart."

Her cheerful approval echoed through Brien's whole being like a chime from the gods. It filled him with joy, and sparked a wave of hope that drowned out the anxious drumming of his heartbeat and made him reckless with courage. For just a brief moment, he felt tall, handsome, and confident.

And it was enough. All of his prepared statements, all of his painstakingly constructed invitations disappeared from his mind, and he opened his mouth with no idea of what was going to come out of it.

"So, got a date for the prom, yet?" he found himself asking her in a surprisingly assured voice.

"Nope." She shook her head, and her brown eyes met his gaze directly. "Do you?"

"Not at the moment," he admitted. "But I'd like to take you, I mean, if you'd, ah, like to go."

Augh! You idiot! Why did you do that, you jerk? I mean, um, ah . . . no! It was going so well, and then you had to go and screw it all up, you moron! I can't freaking believe you, what a complete loser you are!

"What's that?"

The furious torrent of self-recrimination caused him to miss what she was saying.

"I said, that would be nice," she repeated. "Do you have my telephone number?"

"Yes!" he answered quickly, too quickly. "I mean, it's in the school directory, isn't it?"

"Sure, but that's my home number. Here, I'll give you my cell phone."

She reached into her locker for a pen and scribbled ten digits on a piece of paper. The ink was pink, and Brien found it almost impossible to take his eyes off it. She was giving him her number, not just any number, but her cell! She said yes! She actually said yes!

He wanted to sing, to dance, to pump his fists in the air. If there had been a football handy, he would have spiked it. Maybe she'd like to have lunch today, or tomorrow maybe; after all, now they had to arrange plans. They had to arrange plans! He, Brien Martin, had actual plans with Tessa Fenchurch! No, settle down, he told himself, trying to restrain the tidal wave of happiness that was flooding through his heart and soul. Don't ask her to lunch, don't babble, just be cool. Don't act like an idiot. You got what you came for, now exit stage right with dignity, style, and grace.

He nodded slightly, and smiled at her. To his delight, she smiled back at him.

"I'll give you a call this weekend so we can arrange things." He smiled again. "I'll be looking forward to it."

"I will too," she replied.

And on that uplifting note, he turned and walked away, feeling for all the world like a conquering hero striding off into the sunset. Yes, he thought triumphantly. Yes!

There was some traffic clogging Highway 10 on the way home, but for once it didn't bother Brien in the least. He felt as if the afternoon sun was warming him all the way down to his center; for the first time in more than a month, he was happy, truly happy. Was this what it was like to be in love? He felt higher than he'd ever been before, and he found himself with the urge to giggle and laugh at the stupidest things. A silly bubblegum song came on the radio, but instead of switching it off as usual, he turned it up.

". . . your love is cand-ay!" he sang along with gusto.

A man honked his horn as an open space appeared in front of him, but Brien just grinned and waved cheerfully at him. What's the rush, dude? It was like his heart had been locked in winter for three long years, and only now was experiencing its first spring. What a wonderful thing it was! He thought about how Tessa's eyes had looked deeply into his when she'd told him she didn't have a date. How his heart had leaped into his throat at the intensity of her gaze.

Had she known, had she somehow guessed that he wanted her so much? And maybe, just maybe, she wanted him, too. "That would be nice," she'd said. Nice! And she said she'd be "looking forward to it"! It was amazing, he thought, that the love he thought he'd secretly carried for her for so long was nothing compared to the way he felt now, it was just a seed, and only now was it blooming, blossoming into full flower.

He lovingly traced in his mind the seductive curves of her white legs, and her slender ankles. He loved the way the lines of her bra showed through her T-shirt, and he itched to see and touch what it was hiding underneath. And did she have a great butt, or what! He grinned like a maniac, recalling how her khaki shorts had clung tightly to her as she'd crouched before her locker.

He was, he decided, the luckiest guy on the planet, and he was going to make her the happiest girl in the world on prom night. Already he was thinking about what kind of tux he would rent; should he stick with the classic black James Bond look or not? Maybe an elegant soft-gray coat with tails would be better, something that would be unusual, but cool and aristocratic. Hmmm. Better wait until you find out what she's going to wear, that's really the best thing to do, he finally decided.

Brien didn't bother to pull into his new space in the garage, but left his car in the driveway instead, barely remembering to turn off the engine as he ran into the house.

"Mom, Mom, guess what?" he shouted, eager to share his good news. She'd been pretty depressed lately, and he thought hearing about his upcoming prom date might cheer her up a little.

"I'm upstairs," she called back. "Be down in a second."

Brien tapped his fingers on the counter impatiently, then decided to fix himself a victory snack. But then, as his hand closed around the handle of the refrigerator door, he abruptly changed his mind. He wasn't fat, but he wasn't exactly skinny, either, and he wanted to look good for the prom pictures. He had three weeks, after all, and that was plenty of time to drop a few extra pounds.

He stared at his reflection in the dark glass of the microwave door. He looked like he needed a haircut, too. Tessa wouldn't want him showing up at her door looking all scruffy. He'd just resolved to ask Mom if he could see a dermatologist tomorrow when he heard her coming down the stairs.

"What's going on?" she asked in a falsely bright voice.

His heart went out to her. Poor Mom. She tried to be cheerful and put a brave face on things for him, but he knew she was still bleeding inside. Had she ever felt this way about Dad, or had Dad felt like this about her? No, it was different, it had to be. Otherwise, Dad never would have left. His love for Tessa was a completely different thing, it was pure, and dedicated. Three long years he'd waited for her, and now, finally, his patience had been rewarded.

"Well, I kind of asked this, ah, this girl out," he said awkwardly, and he couldn't help blushing. "To the prom, you know? Anyhow, she said yes, so I guess we're going. It's in three weeks. I should probably get a haircut."

"Oh, honey, that's wonderful," Mom said. "Is she the one you mentioned . . . ?"

She didn't finish the sentence, but looked at him inquiringly. Brien blushed again, and nodded.

Mom's answering smile was broad and happy, the first real smile he'd seen on her face since that awful afternoon three weeks ago. She threw her arms around him and enfolded him in her embrace in much the same way she had before, but this time it was a happy hug, a sharing of joy, not sorrow. He wasn't sure, but he thought he felt a suspicious wetness on his cheek that could have been a tear.

"I'm so proud of you," she whispered in his ear. "I know how hard it must have been for you, and I'm so very, very proud of you."

CHAPTER 17

THE STOLEN HEART

YOU HAVE STOLEN MY HEART WITH ONE GLANCE OF YOUR EYES, WITH
ONE JEWEL OF YOUR NECKLACE.

—Song of Songs 4:9

"So you're taking Tessa to the prom. . . ."
Derek leaned back precariously on his office-style chair
and took a big hit off his just-lit fattie. The large bay windows of
his bedroom were open, and Brien watched as his friend exhaled
and the smoke trailed outside on the strength of the warm spring
breeze.

"Well, good for you," the black-haired boy declared finally.
"I'm not saying I think it's a good idea, you know what I'm saying, but I know you've got serious wood for her, so it's cool by
me. It's definitely cool."

Derek thought it was all right? Wow, that was a relief! It wasn't
like Brien was going to cancel out on Tessa just because his friend
didn't like her, but it would have been really disappointing not to
have anyone to talk to about his plans for what he hoped would
be a magical evening.

"Why don't you ask somebody, too?" he suggested. "Then we
could double-date, wouldn't that be fun?"

Not to mention cuttting the cost of renting the limo in half.
Dang, but they were expensive! Brien had just about swallowed
the pen he'd been holding in his mouth when he learned how
much they wanted just to drive you around for a couple
of hours. Still, it would be worth it. He wasn't about to show

181

up on his first date with Tessa in his junky old beater.

"I don't think so." Derek dismissed the notion with a wave of his hand. "But I think you'll be interested to hear about a little news of my own. Remember the Obelisk text we got from that thing you said was some kind of crazy virus or whatever?"

"Sure."

Derek reached out and moved the mouse with his free hand, and clicked twice. Microsoft Word sprang to life and displayed a window full of text.

"Check it out. That professor who was looking at it e-mailed this to me today."

Brien stood up and walked over to the computer. He leaned forward and peered at the words on the computer screen. It was arranged in what appeared to be formalized stanzas, and the professor had added some kind of explanatory notes marked in parentheses. He read it aloud, slowly and softly.

[1] *In the 35th year, the terrible voice of Nergal was heard,*

[2] *the voice of the mighty (god), in the palace of the strong King;*

[3] *for the Son of Assur-natsir-pal he called. For the marcher*

[4] *over all the world he came, for the King of all the four zones of the Sun (and) of multitudes*

[5] *of men he came, astride a chariot of fire. Like the iron stone of Khapusca was his face,*

[6] *and his eyes burned like the flames that, at the walls of Zirta, the city of Udasca, once licked*

[7] *at the word of the destroyer of cities. Upon the shoulder of his mighty warrior,*

[8] *his hand he (Nergal) placed and bade him come to drink of the brilliance of heroes.*

[9] *Hea, (god) of the deep, the King of crowns, determiner of destinies, breaker*

[10] *of kings and men, has spoken; let him who hears obey.*

[11] *Great Shalmaneser no more reigns*

[12] *over (the) sea of the setting sun.*

[13] *At the right-hand of him (Nergal?) he waits,*

[14] mighty Assur-natsir-pal's Son.
[15] As he left, on clouds of blood (and) fire
[16] so Assur's hero shall return.
[17] (the) Euphrates will run red with gore;
[18] and walled cities fall and burn.
[19] He shall come to those who call,
[20] The Son of Assur-natsir-pal;
[21] To those who burn the blood and wine
[22] Upon the mighty god's great sign.

"Nergal . . . sounds kind of like Nurgle of Chaos, doesn't it? And that last part is almost like a prophecy, or something," Brien said thoughtfully when he'd finished. "Doesn't it sound like that to you?"

Derek ignored him and pointed at the screen.

"Keep reading," he ordered. "There's more at the bottom."

Brien scrolled down the document and underneath the translation he found a brief commentary by the translating professor.

Fascinating stuff! I must say, it is tremendously interesting, as this particular text does not appear in any of the compendiums published by the University of Chicago. Whether it is a small piece of an inscription which has not yet been published, or whether it is simply a clever forgery, I cannot say. At the moment, I am inclined to assert the former; at least for the first ten lines, since there are a number of terms which appear to be formulaic and are placed in a grammatical structure which is wholly consistent with the traditional Akkadian order of composition. Thematically, these lines read very much like an addendum to the Face D base of the Black Obelisk, the text of which I believe you already have. There are a few idiosyncracies, to be sure, but this is not uncommon; there is a fair amount of variance even within many of the published materials.

It is the latter twelve lines that I find especially intriguing. You may have noticed that the structure changes dramatically, indeed, I suspect that it was written some time later than the first ten lines, and by a different author. Whereas the author of the first ten lines, as with the author of the Obelisk text (and they may well be the same person), goes to great lengths to avoid mentioning Shalmaneser's name, the author of the latter twelve lines seems to feel no such concern. The latter lines also have an almost poetical ring to them which I have attempted to reproduce for you (my apologies, I've never fancied myself a poet and I'm sure the meter is disastrous), and it all has a mystical air of prophecy about it which is very un-Assyrian. A most practical people, the Assyrians, although not very neighborly.

Should this turn out to be the genuine article, I suspect these last twelve lines could shed some important light on our understanding of the Akkadian-Assyrian culture and its relation to their deities. Indeed, the references to blood and wine, as well as the prospects of a return that is closely related to some rather apocalyptic events, are very remniscent of certain aspects of the Christian mythology. Considering that the inscription would almost certainly have been carved some time before Jerusalem fell to the Babylonians in 605 BCE, the potential implications here are staggering!

Now you simply must tell me where. . . .

The rest of the letter was simply three more paragraphs asking, pleading, and finally outright begging Derek to reveal where he'd acquired the Akkadian text. Brien grinned, wondering what the good professor would say if Derek told him that it had simply printed itself out on his inkjet one random afternoon. He'd never believe it, of course, and he'd probably think Derek was lying, although what would possibly be the point? As usual, Derek had done the right thing by keeping his mouth shut, and now they had the translation. But despite that, and the additional bonus of the professor's insight, Brien still didn't know what he should think about the text. It had to be a forgery, of course, but why was it encrypted in a virus?

"What do you think?" he asked Derek.

Derek squinted his eyes almost closed, then yawned.

"I think . . . hmmm. I think that if this is a virus, it's the weirdest one I've ever heard of!" He paused and shook his head. "Naw, I don't believe it. I just don't. It's not a virus. Nobody does this sort of thing. It doesn't blow up, it doesn't screw with your files, I mean, there's not even any 'Hey, loser, you just failed the stupid test' message. It's too out there. I mean, come on, we're the weirdest people we know, and we don't even do this stuff."

That made sense, in a way. How much crossover was there between people who knew Akkadian and the kind of programmer who was skilled enough to write a virus like this one, assuming it was a virus? Brien had no way of knowing what the exact number might be, but it had to be pretty small, if not downright nonexistent.

"So what are you saying, that it's magic?" Brien imitated a scary string violin and twiddled his fingers in the air. "Whoo-oo-oo! Come on, that's ridiculous. You don't even believe in that stuff."

"Of course not," Derek said, looking disgruntled. "But wouldn't it be cool if it was? I mean, then we could have a real Nottambuli, and have this Shalmaneser guy ripping out the guts of everyone that messes with us! No more taking nothing from nobody. And when you consider how many people we owe a good stomping, I think we could keep him happy for quiet a while."

The thought did have its appeal. The King of the four sun-zones, or whatever he liked to be called, could do a lot worse than to start off with Petersen and Schumacher. Brien would love to see the panicked look on their cruel, stupid faces once they got a chance to go nose-to-nose with someone who really knew what cruelty was all about. It would serve them right!

"All right." Brien laughed. "You start figuring out what the mighty god's great sign is, and once we summon him, we'll take revenge on all our enemies. Now, if you don't mind, I've got to go to the mall and see how much dinero this tux is going to cost me."

Man, Derek hadn't been exaggerating when he said that taking someone to the prom was going to cost at least three hundred dollars. This stuff was expensive! The limo was going to run forty dollars an hour, so he was looking at least two hundred bucks right there. The tuxes ranged from fifty to a hundred, plus another twenty for the flowers, and maybe fifty bucks for dinner, so even without renting a hotel room, the evening was going to cost him between three and four hundred dollars. It was a good thing he hadn't blown his savings on that painted Orc army he was thinking about buying last month.

What a disaster that would have been. But everything was cool, he had the cash in hand, and there was no doubting that Tessa was worth it. He loved the way she said hello to him now; still just a little shy, she kept her pretty eyes downcast and usually the faintest hint of a smile dancing on her lips. Would he get to kiss those lips in just a few more weeks? The mere thought of kissing her good night sent him into transports of ecstacy. Oh, this was incredible, this was awesome.

It would be so different, having a girlfriend. He'd still hang out with Derek, of course, nothing was ever going to change that. But he looked forward to hearing Tessa's voice on the phone, making plans with her, spending the hot summer days with her lying on the beach, then going out for ice cream afterward. He dreamed of making out with her in the backseat of his car, or better yet, on the lonely bench that sat on the end of the pier at the private beach near her house. How romantic would that be? And he would be the most romantic boyfriend ever, bringing her flowers every day, candy, anything her heart desired.

Emboldened by his happy daydream, he glared at the phone. It was Saturday, and five delicious days had passed since she'd looked at him and said yes. It was time to call her, but something stayed his hand. What if she'd changed her mind? What if someone else had asked her since Monday, and she'd already decided to dump him, but just hadn't told him yet?

No, he thought, Tessa wouldn't do that. She'd been extra nice to him all week, so surely nothing had changed. Firmly holding on to that thought, he reached out for the telephone, picked up the receiver, and for the first time, dialed the number that he'd learned by heart three years ago.

Ring . . . ring . . . ring . . .

Brien was just trying to make up his mind if he dared to leave a message or not when someone picked up the phone. It was a woman, with a faint English accent. Must be her mother, he realized.

"Hello," she answered.

"Uh, hello," he said uncomfortably. He cleared his throat and gathered himself. "May I speak to Tessa, please? This is Brien Martin."

"Yes, of course. Please wait a moment, Brien."

That went pretty well. Brien nodded, satisfied with his performance so far. Not the best start, but a decent finish. Just relax, he ordered himself. His tongue felt fat and awkward. Relax!

"Hi, Brien, is that you?"

His heart leaped into his throat like a world-champion salmon heading for the sea. For one dreadful moment, he thought he was going to choke.

"Mom, hang up!" she shouted, and there was a click. "Brien?"

"Yeah, um, hey, Tessa, it's me." He forced himself to swallow. "I just wanted to call and see if you, ah, had any idea what color you were wearing. You know, your prom dress. I thought maybe if you told me, I could try to find a tie that'll match or something."

"That's so sweet," she said. "My dress is red, but it's not really red-red, it's more of a scarlet red. You know what I mean?"

"Sure," he said, not really following her.

Her dress was red. Definitely the black tux then, and no tails. James Bond was the effect he wanted, not a cocktail waiter. But would a black tie-and-cummerbund combination or a red one go better with her dress? It was hard to say.

There was a moment's silence, then Tessa spoke again.

"Tell you what, what are you doing now?"

"Me? Nothing, really."

"Well, I've got this party tonight I have to go to, but I've got a couple of hours free, so if you want, maybe I could meet you at Rosedale and we could look at the ties and vests together."

"That sounds great!" Brien answered enthusiastically. Vests, he wondered? Were you supposed to wear a vest with tuxedos? Well, whatever she wanted was fine with him. He'd go in chain mail if she liked. "We can meet at the ice-cream place, it's just around the corner from Desmond's."

"That'll work fine," Tessa confirmed. "And if there's nothing at Desmond's, Gingiss is right on the other side of the mall. See you in, say, an hour?"

"I'll be there," Brien promised her.

He had never been so certain of anything in his life.

An hour could be a very long time, Brien reflected, as he sat on one of the low, wooden benches fixed permanently in the middle of Rosedale's broad halls. He didn't want to be late, and hanging around the house just waiting for the time to pass was driving him crazy. He'd made the drive to the mall in record time, which was too bad, since now he had nothing to do for the next fifteen minutes except sit and watch the hardcore shoppers as they flowed mindlessly past the window displays like sheep with credit cards.

What were they doing in here? Was it always like this? It really was too nice to be inside. This was the first decent weekend they'd had since the spring rains had finally come to an end, and it felt just like summer outside. Summer, boy, was he looking forward to that! You could make a few extra bucks mowing lawns, that was always easy, since it stayed light out until past nine o'clock, and of course, the best part was always the girls wearing their short-shorts. He was embarrassed to realize that that last thought was no doubt inspired by a pair of cuties who were just walking past him. They probably weren't more than tenth graders, judging by their loud, conspicuous giggling, but they were worth checking out.

Everything about the two girls—their clothes, their hair, and their strange behavior—screamed: "Notice me. Notice ME! NOTICE ME!!!!" It was only polite to give them what they wanted, Brien told himself as he stared at them openly, without embarassment, until they reached the corner and turned right.

The B. Dalton's bookstore was in that direction, but somehow, Brien was pretty sure that wasn't their destination.

He glanced back toward the glass doors at the entryway, and his vision was arrested at the sight of the slim girl in white who was just entering the mall. He gulped uncomfortably, unable to take his eyes away from her. It was Tessa, but not as he'd ever seen her before. She wore white-rimmed racing-style sunglasses, which she pushed up on top of her head as her eyes adjusted to the relative darkness of the mall. Her hair was tucked back neatly behind her ears, and she walked with an easy air of confidence Brien had never seen her show at school.

As she came closer, Brien saw that her baby-doll T-shirt didn't quite make it to the top of her skirt, which was made out of a stretchy material that clung to her slender hips like a second skin. She'd apparently been out in the sun earlier today, because her normally fair skin was ever so lightly flushed. Her midriff was exposed, and he was shocked to see that her belly was pierced, with a silver stud just above her belly button and a skull-and-crossbones filling it. Too radical! He felt a hungry stirring at the sight of her; she looked like she'd just stepped out of a video or something!

He stood, feeling a little faint-headed, as she recognized him and smiled. It was a charmingly lopsided smile, and above it her eyes danced, as if she knew the effect she was having on him. He wanted to kiss her hand or make some wildly romantic gesture, but he was frozen in place, unable to move. I sure hope my mouth is closed, he thought. Open drooling wasn't generally the best way to make a good impression on your prom date.

"H-hey, how you doing," he said with only the slightest difficulty. "You look great!"

"Thanks." She beamed. "I'm going to a party tonight, so I thought I'd just get ready before I met you here. Two of my friends are supposed to show up in about half an hour, but Mandy is always late and she's the one driving, so we'll have plenty of time. My dad dropped me off."

Oh. Shoot! He'd been hoping it might be possible to stretch the tuxedo shopping into a dinner and maybe a movie, but so much for that idea. He shrugged. On the other hand, she probably wouldn't be dressed like this if she wasn't going the party afterward, so it wasn't all bad.

"Hey, no problem. Who's having the party?"

"One of the soccer players, Jason Case. You know him?"

"Yeah, I think we had a chemistry class together last year."

Geez, was she in with that crowd? He hoped not. Somehow, he'd never imagined her hanging out with the jocks. She never had at school. Well, there wasn't anything he could do about it tonight.

He concealed his disappointment and pointed to her implanted jewelry. "That's pretty cool. When did you do that?"

"Do you like it? Really?"

She seemed to appreciate his noticing it and stuck out her stomach as she fingered the skull.

"I wanted to get a tattoo that looked kind of like this, only with roses instead of the crossbones, but my Mom flipped out and said forget it. She said she'd buy me this instead, so I took her up on it. See, there's little garnets for the eyes!"

Brien obediently bent over to examine the silver skull, but he was distracted by a tiny drop of sweat trickling down the left side of her stomach. This close to her, he couldn't help noticing the sweet scent of her body, and it was delicious. She smelled of honey and almonds, and he could almost feel the sun's warmth radiating from her body.

"Isn't it cool?" Tessa declared happily, when he finally managed to force himself upright and away from her.

"Yeah, it's . . . it's cool. Really cool. Garnets, huh?"

Oh, how he wanted to pull her close to him and bury his face in her neck, and inhale that wonderful fragrance forever! Honey and almonds, almonds and honey. . . . This was turning out to be the best day of his life!

"So come on," she commanded as she pulled at the short sleeve of his shirt in the direction of the formalwear store. "We don't have all day."

Forty-five minutes later, after trying on more combinations than he could count, Brien, with Tessa's approval, decided on a black Pierre Cardin tuxedo with a black tie and a black-and-red vest. Tessa doubted that the red of the vest precisely would match her dress, but she was sure the shade was close enough that the two of them would look really good together.

Brien stood in the three-way mirror, admiring the way that the jacket made him look slimmer, and more sophisticated. He ran a hand through his hair, imagining what it would look like slicked wetly back. Not James Bond, exactly, but not all that bad, either. Better than he'd hoped, really. He shot a sidelong glance at Tessa, and was heartened to see her nodding approvingly at his ensemble. Maybe he could talk her into bagging the party tonight, and they could—

"What's up, girlfriend!" he heard a girl's high-pitched voice shriek from the front of the store.

Or not. Oh, well, her stupid friends were bound to show eventually. The three girls babbled excitedly, and although Brien caught a few random words—*prom*, *beer*, and *party*—they were speaking too quickly for him to follow what they were saying.

"Sir, will that be all?"

The sales assistant was a nice, chubby old lady. Brien checked to see if Tessa wanted him to rent anything else, but she was too busy talking with her friends for him to catch her attention. He reluctantly removed the jacket, slipped off the vest, and handed both articles to the saleslady.

"Yeah, I think that's it."

"I think you've made a very good choice, if you don't mind my saying so. So then, you can pay twenty percent down, and give us the rest when you come pick it up. I believe you said the date of your school's prom was May first?"

She rapidly punched the numbers into an old green-screen computer.

"Your total will be eighty-nine seventy-four. So we'll need seventeen ninety-five to reserve everything."

He gave her the money and tucked the receipt into his wallet, then turned back to Tessa. She was practically glowing with enthusiasm, and her excitement lifted his spirits again. So what if she was going out with her friends tonight? She'd been doing that for the last three years, and it had never bothered him before. Why should it bug him now?

She clutched at his shoulder, and her touch sent tingles through his body.

"You know Mandy and Jennifer, right?"

He nodded to both girls, and shook Mandy's proffered hand.

"Yeah, I've never met you guys personally, but I know who you are. Nice to meet you."

"Nice to meet you, Brien," Mandy cooed.

Mandy was kind of cute, Brien thought; in fact, she'd be pretty hot if she dropped about fifteen pounds. Jennifer, on the other hand, was a big girl, almost as tall as he was, and she easily outweighed him. She looked like a linebacker wearing a wig.

"It's very nice to meet you," she said flirtatiously.

She had a grip like a linebacker, too. Brien tried not to wince, or wring his hand once she released it. It wasn't easy.

"Well, we'd better get going," Tessa told him. "I like what we picked out, don't you? Well, I guess I'll see you Monday in econ."

Brien couldn't believe it when she leaned in toward him and kissed him on the cheek. He caught the scent of honey and almonds, and then it was gone as she turned and flounced cheerfully away, an angel in white lacking only wings to complete her perfection. He stood there in the front of the cash register like a statue, stunned, holding his right hand to his face.

He swallowed once. He blinked once. He swallowed again. He blinked once more, and finally the spell that rendered him mute released him. Tessa had already left the store.

"Bye," he said softly, full of joy, and unable to comprehend his good fortune.

CHAPTER 18

BLOOD MAGIC

LET NO ONE BE FOUND AMONG YOU WHO SACRIFICES HIS SON OR DAUGHTER IN THE FIRE, WHO PRACTICES DIVINATION OR SORCERY, INTERPRETS OMENS, ENGAGES IN WITCHCRAFT, OR CASTS SPELLS, OR WHO IS A MEDIUM OR SPIRITIST OR WHO CONSULTS THE DEAD. ANYONE WHO DOES THESE THINGS IS DETESTABLE TO THE LORD. . . .

—Deuteronomy 18:10–12

Brien was whistling happily and there was a spring in his step as he walked up the steps to Derek's front door. It opened just as he was about to ring the doorbell, and he was surprised to see Derek standing there with a wickedly sharp knife in his hand.

"Whoa," Brien said, placing his hands up. "Don't shoot!"

"Are you whistling what I think you're whistling?" Derek asked suspiciously. "Because if you are, I just might have to gut you with this thing."

"What was I whistling? How should I know? It's not like you whistle something on purpose, you just do it!"

Brien tried to think what song the little melody had come from, but when he couldn't, he licked his lips and whistled a few bars again. A moment later both he and Derek burst out laughing.

"Spice Girls?" his friend said dubiously. He turned the knife around and offered it to Brien, hilt-first. "Here, I think you'll be wanting this."

"No, suicide's too good for me!"

Brien ran his finger across the edge of the blade. It was a military-style knife with a black rubber handle. It was a big, evil-looking thing that made you want to strap it to your leg.

"What's up with this? Couldn't find the pizza cutter?"

"No, not at all," Derek had an eager look of anticipation on his face. "But I'm glad you came over. I was hoping you'd make it before dark."

He pushed Brien backward, and then stepped out of the house himself, closing the door behind him. He led Brien toward the backyard, where the Wallaces had their swimming pool, patio, and stone fire circle. It was an excellent setup for summer barbecues; unfortunately, he and Derek weren't popular enough to throw a party, although Derek's parents were known to throw a massive shindig every now and then. But maybe all that would change now that he was seeing Tessa. Certainly Mandy and Jennifer had been nicer to him than they'd ever been before. He grinned at the thought of seeing Tessa all tan and oiled up with sunscreen, lounging next to him by the pool.

"What are you so giddy about?" Derek asked suddenly as they walked around the side of the big house.

"Tessa met me at the mall to pick out my tux," he said, and then he blushed. "She, well, she kissed me afterward."

"And you are happy," Derek said mockingly with his fake German accent. "Like a little girl!"

But he slapped Brien on the shoulder to congratulate him all the same. He knew what a big deal it was to Brien, and it wasn't necessary for either of them to say anything more. Brien was glad he didn't; it would have embarrassed him.

As they walked onto the tiled patio by the shallow end of the swimming pool, Brien realized that Derek had set up a bunch of white candles inside the circle of stones. They were actually set up in the shape of a pentagram, he realized, with a small pile of kindling in the middle. There were also two circles of white stuff surrounding the rocks. Sitting on top of one of the big, flat-topped stones that made up the circle was a bottle of cheap Australian Merlot that Brien recognized as coming from Mr. Wallace's wine cellar.

"Are you trying to play magician?"

"Sort of," Derek confessed. "I got kind of bored when I was messing around on the Web today, so I started digging through that Necronomicon site I told you about before. They actually had a page all about this Shalmaneser guy. There wasn't anything about the stuff the professor translated for us, but it turns out that his sign is this!"

Derek pulled a dollar bill out of his pocket and pointed to the eye in the pyramid.

"The all-seeing eye, the eye of Horus, whatever. Anyhow, I figured, let's burn the blood and the wine like it says, and see what happens. I mean, we don't believe in any of this stuff for real, but it would be so cool if it was, I just thought we should try it for kicks, you know?"

Don't even think about it, a small voice protested from somewhere deep inside him, but Brien paid it no attention. Why not give it a whirl? Brien knew better than to believe in black magic, or any other kind of supernatural hoodoo-voodoo, but he had to admit that the idea of it did hold a certain fascination for him. He was like Mulder, in a way. He wanted to believe. He wanted to believe in something beyond this everyday life in the suburbs, something better, or at least different. In a way, he wanted the Nottambuli to be real. He wished he could strike fear, not into imaginary vampires, but all the jerks in the real world who got off on treating everyone like carpet.

"Sure, it can't do any harm," he concluded aloud. "Except, didn't you say something about blood?"

Derek chuckled. "Yep."

"Whose?"

"Ours."

Brien nodded, and sighed as he glanced at the knife's wicked edge again.

"I knew you were going to say that. So, what do we do, just set the stuff on fire?"

Derek shook his head. "No, I think the thing to do is to combine the instructions from the translation with this Conjuration of the Beholder deal." He pulled a piece of paper from his pocket and unfolded it. "See, it says the Beholder comes from a race that isn't human, but he doesn't seem to be a god, either. I'm figuring if it works for this Beholder, it should work for our Assyrian dude, as long as we put the right stuff in the bowl."

"What bowl?

"Oh, shoot, I left it in the kitchen. Here!"

He handed the creased piece of paper to Brien. "Why don't you take a look at this while I'm getting the bowl."

Brien shrugged and looked at the paper in his hand as Derek ran back around the house. The sky was red, and the sun was starting to go down, so he had to squint a little bit to make out the words properly. Sure enough, it was a spell, although it was a lot less complicated than he'd feared it would be. There was no non-sense about digging up graveyard bones or slicing up a poor lit-tle black kitty, thank goodness. There were limits to even his idle curiosity. But this particular exercise didn't look like it would do anyone any harm.

When thou wilt summon the Beholder, thy heart must be pure and thy faith strong. Thou shalt have no altar save the Wooden Bowl carved with the sacred sign. And thou shalt conjure fire, and when the green flames dance, thou shalt know the time is ripe for the consum-mation of the sacrifice. And the name of the Bowl shall be GRAKH USSRU MAL.

Thou shalt place GRAKH USSRU MAL inside circles three.
The first circle shall be stone, for BUL, the supreme, father of the gods.
The second circle shall be flour, for BALTES, the great queen, mother of the spirits of the earth.
The third circle shall be salt, for INCU, the prince of the sky, lord of the heavens.

And the Sword shall be placed in the fire.
And the Conjuration of the Beholder must be made, so:

*EHIQ EUST ASCA RPAH AUNB UONS APOR EIOS CAVO
PIAN OSEN ZARU MORE
ADES SOLO SOLO VOLI OIOM ACHI LHAD ETTO QUES
TOSO EMIO*

*When thou speakest the words QUES TOSO EMIO, thou shalt
take the Sword from the flame and thrust it into the flesh of the great
queen before the GRAKH USSRU MAL. And so the Beholder shall
appear.*

All right then, Brien thought as he finished reading. Bake ten
minutes and serve when cool. Derek's army knife was obviously
the Sword, and the circles were already prepared. He licked a finger, reached down and touched the third line, then gingerly
tasted it. *Blech!* It was definitely salt.

He folded his arms and watched as Derek came jogging
around the side of the house, carrying a largish salad bowl. He
couldn't repress a snigger. Somehow, it was hard to picture the
Son of Assur-natsir-pal as a vegetarian.

Melusine sighed as another of Kaym's messenger imps
appeared in front of her as she relaxed on the rooftop of the
Lewis house, enjoying the approach of darkness. It wasn't that
she thought that he was wasting her time, but not knowing what
the Fallen lord was so busy arranging was starting to get on her
nerves. She'd done as he'd commanded and labored hard on convincing the kiddies that there was nothing else in the works, and
it really hadn't been too hard.

Boghorael had taken to his new Tempter's duties like a tiger
released into a petting zoo. He was clumsy, and his inexperi-
enced methods were easily countered by Aliel, but his energetic
enthusiasm kept Holli's Divine Guardian far too busy to notice
what else was going on in the household. As for Holli herself, she
appeared to be so preoccupied with her boyfriend and prepara-
tions for the prom that Aliel's concerns for her charge's chastity
were starting to show on her thin face.

Maligor, on the other hand, had been forced to take a more restrained approach. Paulus was a worthy foe, less unpredictable than Mariel, perhaps, but every bit as wary. But Maligor was strong, too, and despite the big Guardian's best efforts, he had managed to keep Jami's attention focused more on the material world than other, more dangerous matters.

"The Baron expressed a desire that you leave at once, Mistress. . . ."

At least this imp was more courteous than the last. He didn't even try to look at her, but kept his eyes averted even as he pestered her again. He must have heard about what she'd done to Balazel's last messenger.

"I heard you the first time," she barked imperiously, and the frightened imp leaped back a good ten feet. "Be patient!"

He quivered, silent and motionless, as she glared at him. Then Boghorael appeared, and bowed down low before her. He was looking very well, she thought proudly, and in another year or two, might even make a worthy opponent for Paulus.

"Great Mistress, I am at your service."

The new Tempter sounded servile enough, but she saw his bark-brown lips twitch and knew he was simply playing the fool in front of the imp. That was fine with her; she needed an ally she could rely upon, not a boy-toy, after all.

"I'm being summoned by an archangel, so I have to leave here. I don't know how long it will take, but I don't think I'll be away for more than a few hours. Can you handle keeping an eye on both Christopher and Jami?"

"Your humble servant is honored by your faith in him, Great Mistress."

Melusine laughed shortly. He was a wiseacre. She liked that, but who would have known?

"Don't push it, Boghorael. I smoked Pandaema because she couldn't keep her eye on the ball, and I'll do the same to you if I have to."

The handsome demon's green eyes grew serious, and he straightened out his shoulders as he abandoned his pretense at meekness. "I know, Melusine. Don't worry about it, I'll stay on top of things."

"Good," she said, and she brushed her lips lightly against his ear as she moved past him. "Because I wouldn't want to have to," she told him softly, then took the waiting imp's hand.

The world boiled away in a melange of color, then reformed itself into a remarkably similar landscape. She was standing on another rooftop, which, judging by the clouds smeared thinly across the reddening sky, wasn't too far away from where she'd just been. Lord Kaym was there in his guise as Balazel, accompanied by four other fallen angels. Two of them were large, and radiated great power, but she didn't recognize any of them immediately, not until one turned around and looked at her.

"Verchiel," she gasped at the broad, arrogant face of the Zodiac Lord. "L-Lord Verchiel, is that you?"

She hadn't seen him in thousands of years, but it would have been impossible for her to have forgotten him, the conceited Archon her once-beloved charge had defeated in the Circle of Fire. She was desperately curious to know what it had been like for him, beyond the Beyond, but this didn't seem like the right time to be asking him about the experience.

"Do I know you?" he asked contemptuously.

"Her name is Melusine, and you wouldn't know her," Kaym answered him impatiently. "But she knows you. Melusine, my dear, you've obviously recognized Lord Verchiel, and this"—he indicated the other powerful angel—"is the Archon Rahdar."

He said nothing about the other two angels, who seemed content to lurk quietly in the background as she genuflected before the two archons. The other two looked like tempters, if she wasn't mistaken, most likely of the two young mortals below them in the backyard who seemed to be building a bonfire. As to the Archon Rahdar . . . yes, she recognized the name. He was a Zodiac Lord as well, of the sign of the Crab, if her memory served her correctly. Two Zodiac Lords, here in the Cities! It was unheard of. What were they doing in this poor excuse for a backwater?

"Why do you honor us with your company, Great Lords?" she bowed again, a little deeper this time.

"I have a score—" Verchiel started to say, but Lord Kaym cut him off with an upraised fist.

"Quiet!" Kaym snapped at the Archon before inclining his massive head to the two nameless angels. "You may leave now. You have done well, it will be noted."

Both angels bowed respectfully.

"Thank you, Baron," one said.

"When shall we return, Ar-Balazel?" the other asked.

Lord Kaym shook his head, and a twisted smile creased his bestial face.

"You will not be needed again," he informed them. "There will be no further tempting required. Return to your captain and tell him that you are available for new assignments."

The Tempters bowed again and disappeared immediately.

The disguised angel lord nodded with approval at the Tempters' unhesitating obedience, then the air shimmered as Kaym returned to his customary Aspect. He swirled his cloak of stars dramatically, and a cold wind began to blow from the north as he turned his shrouded gaze toward Melusine and the two Zodiac Lords. He grinned faintly, and Melusine wondered what he had in mind for the two boys. They seemed utterly unremarkable, from what she could see.

"They are, they are," Kaym agreed aloud with her unarticulated thoughts. "Almost completely beyond notice, even by their own kind."

Don't do that! She dared to glare peevishly at him, but he didn't deign to notice.

"Unlovely and unloved, and for the most part, uninteresting," the fallen angel continued. "Which is why they are integral to my plan. You see, I have chosen them to be my warriors, warriors of destruction, these two, who can pass unnoticed in places where even Archons might rightly fear to tread."

Melusine glanced at Verchiel and Rahdar. Neither of them appeared to be paying much attention to Kaym's words, although Verchiel rolled his eyes at that last remark. Then the implications of what Kaym was saying struck her, and she clapped her hands.

"You're setting them up for a blood offering," she guessed, but with conviction. "You'll take out the Lewis children after they've consecrated a Temple of Blood!"

She didn't mind it, really. The decision was obviously coming from a very high level, perhaps even the Prince himself, and no blame for Christopher's soul would attach to her in these circumstances. His death wouldn't be accidental; in fact, it would be quite the opposite!

Kaym stroked her cheek affectionately. "Perhaps you would be so bold, my little crimson wildcat, but my designs are a little less lofty. No, that may well be an unexpected benefit, but the elimination of the former Baal Phaoton is not the center of my intentions. No, I would rather seek the death of his heart. My main purpose is to simply let him know that I am still his master, and I am one with whom he dare not trifle! Slaying a few dozen of his friends and acquaintances before his eyes and in his very backyard should underline my point most eloquently, I should think."

"Not exactly subtle, is it?" Lord Rahdar said dryly. "As long as you're out to butcher children, Chemosh, why not simply wipe out that kindergarten down the street? It seems that would be more your style."

Melusine held her breath as Kaym's dark glasses were aimed at the Zodiac Lord for an uncomfortably long time. But then the dark-haired angel shrugged indifferently, and the momentary tension evaporated as he tapped a finger against the white skin of his temple.

"Perhaps you are mistaking me for my good friend Baal Moloch, Archon Rahdar, and in this place you will call me Balazel. You will never name me as anyone else, not even amongst ourselves!"

Kaym sounded coldly furious. Melusine wondered if he was really concerned that the Divine might learn of his presence here through Rahdar, or if he was simply taking the opportunity to remind the Crab of his place.

Kaym wasn't finished. Glaring at the Archon, he continued:

"In answer to your foolish question, it is extremely difficult to instruct a five-year-old to intentionally mow down a room full of his classmates. Such action is contrary to the child's fundamental instincts. Take that same child, throw him to the lions for ten years, and he'll willingly pull the trigger without requiring much in the way of guidance at all. The child still knows how to love; the teenager knows only hate."

"Your soliloquy grows tiresome," Lord Verchiel complained, yawning.

Melusine closed her eyes and reached out into the hearts of the two boys, who were now busy placing different objects into their fire. Neither seemed to be carrying an unusually heavy load of sin, and although both were clearly sensitive souls, she didn't detect any spectacular capacity for violence or rage. There was a fair amount of hate and pain scarring the hearts of both youths, but it was nothing remarkable. She'd certainly seen far worse. Had Kaym made a mistake, perhaps?

"Are you sure these are the two you want?" She raised a skeptical eyebrow. "Unless you take them over completely, I don't see them following through on what you're contemplating."

"That's because you lack the vision. Their minds may look healthy enough now, but they are both like the tree which has rotted from the interior, its heart devoured by insects. One well-struck blow, and the tree will fall at once."

He cracked his knuckles, and she could just see the red tongue of one of his tattoos snaking its way out of his silvery robe sleeve and up the back of his hand. He held his hand up before her, and as the sleeve fell away, the whole of the serpentine tattoo was revealed in all of its beautiful, venomous glory.

"The blow will be well-struck. I have gone to some lengths to prepare these two particular trees, Melusine. And I assure you, when I strike, the boys will fall!"

Kaym inclined his head for a moment, and magically

exchanged his cloak and robes for the Ray-Bans, leather and black jeans of his Dark Biker Aspect.

"If you'll excuse me, I'm feeling this inexorable compulsion to appear before my dread summoners." He grinned sardonically as his form began to shimmer, and Melusine knew the angel lord was mocking the boys' feeble attempt at a conjuration. "Alas, but I must once more tread upon this mortal coil. . . ."

CHAPTER 19

SOMETHING WICKED THIS WAY COMES

DISASTER! AN UNHEARD-OF DISASTER IS COMING. THE END HAS COME!
THE END HAS COME! IT HAS ROUSED ITSELF AGAINST YOU. IT HAS COME!
—Ezekiel 7:5–6

The flames in the stone fire pit were crackling hotly as they consumed the wooden bowl and its contents. Brien could see that the wine, its purity adulterated with Derek and Brien's blood, was bubbling already. Another small bead of blood swelled from the small wound on his wrist, and he licked at his thumb and rubbed at the wound, smearing the blood in a half-hearted attempt to make the bleeding stop. He would have preferred for Derek to cut his finger instead, but Derek had insisted on slashing their wrists. Fortunately, the cuts weren't deep.

Derek was on his knees chanting the spell now, and Brien watched his friend reach out carefully for the knife, which was precariously balanced between one of the stones of the pit and a burning piece of wood. The fire was burning fairly high, and he wondered if the rubber blade might start to melt.

"ONIL DIAV OLOM!" Derek shouted skyward at the last, disappearing vestiges of the sun, and he withdrew the heated blade from the fire, then stabbed it violently into the ground before him. At just that very moment, the bottom of the sacrificial bowl burned through, and there was a loud hissing sound as the boiling wine inside it flowed down onto the heart of the fire. Steam

mingled with smoke, and to Brien's surprise, the fire abruptly went out. The wine had completely doused the flames somehow, and not a single glowing cinder remained alight.

"What happened?" he asked Derek.

"Son of a freaking gun! That handle was hot! I should have worn gloves."

"The fire went out," Brien pointed out. "We didn't put that much wine in the bowl, did we? Did we?"

Derek ignored him, and looked around the backyard. "I guess it didn't work," he said, sounding disappointed.

"Why would you say that?" someone asked from the direction of the swimming pool.

Brien whipped his head around, and he took an inadvertent step backward when he saw a tall man dressed in black, standing in the middle of the swimming pool. He was just standing there casually, *but he was standing on top of the water*! Brien shook his head and looked more closely to make sure he wasn't imagining things. He wasn't. The guy's leather motorcycle boots were firmly planted on the smooth, glassy surface as if the water was asphalt instead of highly chlorinated H_2O.

"Are you Shalmaneser or what?" he heard Derek ask disbelievingly.

The man grinned and exposed a perfect set of teeth. He was actually very good-looking in a neo-Gothic way, as in the rising moonlight his white skin and teeth stood out from his black hair and clothes to create a coolly monochromatic image. He looked reasonably normal, except for the lame sunglasses-at-night deal. Well, there was also the walk-on-water thing, too; that wasn't all that normal, either, come to think of it.

Brien didn't think the guy was Shalmaneser, though, unless the *Encyclopedia Brittanica*'s pictorial conception of Assyrian dress was seriously off base. He steeled himself and fought the urge to run as the man walked toward them, stepping off the water onto the surrounding tile without seeming to notice any difference between the two surfaces.

"No, I'm not the son of Assur-natsir-pal," he said in a friendly voice that sounded surprisingly normal. "He was a good servant of mine, in his day. Your exploits, I fear, will not live on through the ages as his have done, but I shall cherish them all the same."

"Who are you?" Brien demanded fearfully, as Derek took offense at the man-who-wasn't-Shalmaneser's words.

"Our exploits? What exploits? What are you talking about, cherishing them? Who are you? What are you?"

"Derek." Brien elbowed his idiot friend in the side. Hard. "Shut up!"

This was a new situation, but Brien was pretty sure that if it was stupid to mouth off to the jocks, then you'd have to be a complete freaking moron to get in this dude's face.

The monochromatic man nodded politely toward him.

"My name does not matter in the least," he told them. "You will never see me again, nor, when I am finished here, will you remember me. But you are sealed to me, now and forever, consecrated with the blood."

Brien and Derek looked at each other, and each of them saw dawning fear and horror in the other's eyes. This wasn't a virus, obviously, but it sure felt a lot like failing the stupid test.

But then the man laughed cheerfully, and he smiled in an amused manner that seemed to suggest he'd just been messing with their heads.

"There's no need to be afraid," he said soothingly. "Don't fear me. I'm not going to harm you in the least. In fact, I've gone to a great deal of trouble to keep both of you from harm. You are my warriors, and what I once did for Shalmaneser, I shall do for you. I will give you what you most desire—power, raw power, and freedom from the chains of those you hate! No one shall restrain you, and you shall walk like gods over the lifeless bodies of your enemies!"

Derek nodded, impressed, but Brien was just confused. This wasn't making any sense to him. "What are you talking about? I don't get it."

The tall man shook his head, and his thin lips twisted to the left. "Whether you understand me or not doesn't matter in the

least, Brien Martin. What must be, will be. Life is life. I have chosen you, and you have called me, and I am here. That is enough,
not one iota of the Law has been broken."

Brien started when the man mentioned life. Life, and power,
and lifeless bodies. He was reminded of that bizarre dream-
vision he had when they were tripping a few weeks ago. But this
tall man, radiating self-confidence and power, looked nothing
like the scrawny Nazi dude with the eyes of fire. Unless, of
course, they were hidden behind the dark glasses.

"Show me your wounds," the man ordered them unexpectedly.

Wounds? Brien didn't get it at first, but then he saw Derek,
seemingly mesmerized, was extending his arm, palm-upward.
Oh, the knife cuts. But Brien decided he didn't want to go along
with the program and folded his arms instead.

"Take your shades off first," he insisted.

The man slowly raised his right hand, and Brien saw he had
either a tattoo or a bad scar marking the back of it. He watched,
holding his breath, as the man's fingers closed around the plastic
frame of the sunglasses and gracefully drew them away from his
face, revealing a perfectly ordinary pair of black eyes. They were
a little on the cold side, perhaps, and pale, but otherwise ordinary. Brien didn't know if he was relieved or disappointed.
Either way, the man's eyes were unreadable, and told him nothing more than had the dark glasses that hid them.

"All right, then," he said, and he held out his left wrist for the
man to examine.

He was taken aback when the man then leaned forward and
placed his lips against the little scratch, kissing it lightly.

Derek looked alarmed as the man did the same to him, and
Brien could understand why. Whatever the guy was, there was a
wrongness about him.

The man ignored them and raised his hands above his head.
He held them in a strange position, not straight up, but almost as
if he was using his hands to hold up the sky.

"Come, lords of the sky wheel, come gods of light and night.

Come Lion, come Crab, I call thee hence, enter these, the vessels which I have prepared for thee!"

Then, without warning, his hands reached out for them again. Brien leaped backwards as soon as he realized the man was going to grab him, but he didn't move fast enough. The man caught his arm and held him fast. He pried at the long, white fingers, trying to escape, but the man's grip was unbreakable.

"Let me go!" Brien screamed, panic-stricken. "Let me go!"

Above him, the stars were glowing red, and he could feel something hot burning his wrist, as if the scratch had somehow caught fire. He felt, rather than saw, the presence of a second figure appearing behind the man holding his arm, and then the stars began to spiral in front of him. His stomach dropped sickeningly away as they rushed toward him, and he fainted.

Melusine was vaguely intrigued by Kaym's vengeful plans, but she didn't find watching Verchiel and Rahdar taking possession of the two boys to be particularly interesting as a spectator sport. It made her wonder, though, what in the world Lord Kaym was thinking to be using Zodiac Lords for such a simple task. Surely the boys' Tempters would have sufficed; after all, they'd clearly done an excellent job in the time leading up to this point.

Kaym winked at her from the ground and, a moment later, was standing next to her on the rooftop. He seemed pleased with himself and was in an unusually talkative mood.

"Not the most interesting show tonight, my dear, but it was necessary, and I promise you, the headline attraction will be well worth it. Think of this as the casting call, perhaps."

Melusine stared evenly at the angel lord. She had serious doubts about his enterprise, and although she would have been happy to keep them to herself, she knew he would see them anyhow if he took the trouble to look.

"I don't mean to be disrespectful, Lord Kaym, but if you remember, you chose Christopher to take part in your schemes three months ago, and he was much like these two when you took him then. And when he returned two hours later he was already lost—sixteen years wasted! Are you sure that won't happen again?"

"I will not permit that to happen." Kaym waved away her concerns. "We are in a different time, in a different place, under the rule of a different King. The two situations do not bear comparison. And remember, I demanded a great deal of Christopher, much more than I require of these two. I gave him too much power, and it went to his head. Perhaps he's truly serious about serving the Enemy, or perhaps he isn't; it may well be that he is simply trying to use the Enemy as a way to protect himself from me. He surely knows I'm coming for him sooner or later."

Melusine shook her head, irritated. Kaym hadn't been around Christopher lately, and she had. He simply didn't understand the situation, she was sure. Christopher wasn't concerned about his former mentor; indeed, on the few occasions he did think of Kaym, there was almost a regretful, wistful tone to his thoughts. Whatever his true motivations might be, hatred or fear of Kaym didn't appear to be among them.

"I think he's serious, Lord Kaym. He believes, he has true faith. I see his thoughts, I watch his dreams, and he's one of them now."

The angel lord shrugged indifferently.

"That is unfortunate. A sad loss. But that's also why I chose the two Archons to take the place of the Tempters you might have used in my place. They are strong, and they can withstand scores, even centuries of lesser Divine."

That was true, although Melusine didn't see why they would need to. The Divine weren't going to start a major war over two young good-for-nothings who were already in the palm of the Prince.

"It just seems like a waste to me, to use Archons in this way. They are strong, but are they skilled in the art of temptation? Tempting is a skill, you know, it takes time. And practice."

"I didn't expect professional jealousy from you!" Kaym smiled faintly. "But perhaps you'll be relieved to know I've given both of them strict orders not to do any tempting at all. They are simply to watch and wait, until the proper time. Then, they will be needed to protect my intrepid young warriors from the inevitable Divine interference."

Melusine had always been attracted to Kaym's great power, and he did have a certain distant charm, but she was starting to think that his casual contempt for all of his lessers might be a weakness. Perhaps it was even one of the factors that had caused Christopher to switch sides on her. The Enemy was hard and inflexible, but he at least made a pretense of caring for what he called his sheep.

"Oh, I do care, my dear. But not that much."

The angel lord reached out and took her hand. Just as he'd done with the boys, he raised it to his lips, and she felt an electric surge of power rush through her body as he kissed her fingertips. It was delicious, but it reminded her that while she might be a favorite of Kaym's, she was not his equal.

She lowered her eyes in penitence. It was not her place to question a Great Lord, and she was fortunate he had not simply blotted her from existence for daring to do so. Familiarity is a trap, she reminded herself. There is no friendship among the Fallen, she knew that. How could she have forgotten it, even for a moment?

Melusine bowed as humbly as she could. "Forgive me, Great Lord. It is not my place to question you, and I look forward to witnessing the full revelation of your will."

Kaym laughed and she shivered. In his voice she could hear the pride of the fallen angel, the surety of the demon lord, and the hungry anticipation of the god of blood and fire. One thing she knew. Whatever Kaym intended was going to create an ungodly mess.

Chapter 20

The Dog That Gets Beat

I'm the dog that gets beat
—Alice In Chains ("Dirt")

Monday mornings always blew, Brien thought, and groaned as he saw a hand shoot up in the second row of his fourth-hour history class. He used to like history all right, but listening to Mr. Olson's meandering lectures was a massively boring waste of time. The only thing worse than Olson's pointless droning was having to stomach the stupid, self-serving questions of the honor rollers, who were either angling for extra-credit or simply harbored a desperate craving for attention. Getting an A for them wasn't so much about intelligence or study habits; it was the sign of a psychological problem.

The hand waving so urgently belonged to Amy Bellows. She was one of the worst of the bed wetters, as Derek had contemptuously labled the more conspicuous members of the A Honor Roll.

"Bed wetters?" Brien asked him once. "Why do you call them that?"

"Because that's what those sorry losers do when they have their recurring nightmares about waking up and finding out their name isn't listed in the local paper with the other brainless suck-ups. They wet the freaking bed!"

And sure enough, Amy managed to come up with a question that was outrageously stupid, even by her usual moronic standards.

"Since we're talking about atomic bombs and stuff, Mr. Olson, well, I was reading *The New York Times* this morning, and they said that NASA is going to put nuclear waste on the next space shuttle. So my question is, if it exploded, you know, the nuclear waste, wouldn't that be bad, and how big would the explosion be compared to, like, the one in Hiroshima?"

Brien smiled derisively as the teacher stared at the brainless wonder with a carefully blank look on his face. The poor dude didn't even know where to start with that one! Amy was really firing on all three cylinders today. He wondered if he'd get kicked out of class if he stood up and applauded. Probably.

"Well, let's just say it would be best if we didn't ever find out, Amy." The brown-bearded teacher adroitly managed to avoid addressing the lame question. "But back to President Truman's decision to use the bomb on Hiroshima as opposed to . . ."

Let's just say it's nuclear waste, not a nuclear bomb, dimwit! Brien directed a savage telepathic message in Amy's direction. It clearly didn't get through, though, because the valedictorian candidate sat there just as smug and proper and as clueless as ever. Brien shook his head. It was amazing how so many people managed to mistake rote memorization for brains. At least he only had to suffer through a few more months of this; Madison, he felt sure, would be different.

He rubbed at the tattoo he'd gotten two days ago with Derek. It was still a little sore. He'd gone over to the Wallace house after his triumphant almost-a-date with Tessa at the mall, and for some reason that wasn't quite clear to him now but had seemed vitally important at the time, they'd wound up cruising Grand Avenue in search of a needle shop. Brien stared admiringly at the lion on his wrist. It was kind of medieval-looking, raising up on its two hind legs and exposing its claws while at the same time baring a nasty set of fangs.

Don't mess with me, you could almost hear it say. Don't even think about it! It was cool, and totally appropriate, too, since Brien was a Leo. He'd wanted to get something he wouldn't regret when he got older, and the tattoo guy had suggested their names, but Brien thought that was ridiculous. It just made you look like you were too stupid to remember your own name. Then Derek thought of using their birthsigns, and Tattoo Guy redeemed himself in Brien's eyes by producing the designs for this wicked-cool lion and the most vicious-looking crab he'd ever seen. Just having the tattoo made him feel tougher, and more ready to stand up for himself.

At long last the bell released him from the purgatory that was Modern American History, and after dropping off his books at his locker, he headed down to the cafeteria to meet Derek. They'd arranged their schedules in such a way that they both had fifth and sixth hour free, allowing them a full hour-and-a-half for lunch. Sometimes they'd drive off campus and eat at McDonald's, other times they'd skip eating altogether and spend the whole time playing Magic in the library.

He was hoping Derek didn't want to game today; his stomach was rumbling and the strange-smelling aromas drifting up to Senior Hall from the kitchen were actually kind of appetizing. He checked his pocket to make sure he had the change to pay for a hot lunch, then walked down the west staircase. Progress was slow, though, as a cluster of students had gathered halfway down the stairs, peering out a large window set into the exit door that led out toward the soccer field.

"What's going on out there?" he heard somebody asking.

"There's gonna be a fight." The high-pitched boy's voice cracked in mid-sentence. "It's that senior, Petersen. The little dude."

Brien raised his eyebrows. Kent getting in a fight? It seemed too good to be true, since he usually picked on people who couldn't, or wouldn't, fight back. People like I used to be, he thought bitterly, glancing at his wrist. Although he always loathed the crowds of people who gathered like a flock of vultures every time it looked as if a fight was breaking out, he couldn't keep himself from following the crush of underclassmen as they rushed outside, sensing blood. He justified his actions with the thought that if somebody did beat up Kent, he'd hate himself for missing it.

But by the time the crowd got to the large oak tree that spread its branches over the mesh fence that protected the soccer fields, Brien knew there wasn't going to be a fight. Not much of one, anyway. Kent Petersen was there, surrounded by a small circle of girls and boys, most of whom were eagerly egging him on, although a few girls, less avid for bloodshed, were averting their eyes, and one or two brave souls even dared to urge restraint. What froze Brien's heart, though, was the desperate, hunted look in the familiar eyes of Petersen's victim, a slender boy nearly six inches taller than the curly-haired soccer player.

It was Derek. He held his fists up awkwardly, almost reluctantly, as if he knew they weren't going to do him any good. His posture was defensive, shrinking away from Petersen's arrogant chin, which Kent held up pugnaciously, as if it were a weapon. Already heavy with fear for his friend, Brien's heart sank when he saw how Derek looked wildly around the savage circle, looking for an avenue of escape that just did not exist. He knew the encircling students would interpret his friend's fear as cowardice, and whatever sympathy they might have held for him was irretrievably lost.

Then Derek's eyes met his, and for just a moment, the look of panic was replaced by a flash of recognition. Brien nodded at his friend, then gritted his teeth and started to step forward. But Derek, correctly reading his intentions, shook his head. His fate was already sealed; there was no point in sacrificing both of them to the crowd's bloodlust and the scorn that would inevitably follow.

"So you wanna fight, huh." Petersen stuck his chest out and pushed forward, his hands at his sides. "Go ahead and hit me, fairy boy. What's the matter, you scared now?"

"I don't want to fight you, Kent." Derek's voice was low, and Brien had to strain to hear him.

"You were talking pretty big before, Wallace." Petersen's beady-eyed glare was withering in its scorn, and his words dripped with contempt. "Put your money where your mouth is, come on, take a swing at me! Go ahead, I'll even give you the first shot. Do it!"

Derek didn't say anything, he simply refused even to open his mouth. The crowd murmured angrily at his lack of reaction, disappointed that the fight appeared to be fizzling out. Petersen clearly sensed their mounting irritation, and, always the showman, raised his hands above his head and turned in a circle.

"First he wants to fight, and now he doesn't. You know why that is?" He shouted as he played to the crowd. "He's all talk and no show, he's too chicken to even put his fists up like a man! Come on, freakshow!"

With impeccable precision, Petersen spat a monstrous gobbet of gooey green spit into Derek's face just as he finished his theatrical turn. It was the disgusting spittle, not the silly taunt, that pushed Derek over the edge.

"Derek, no!" Brien shouted, seeing that it was a trap, but he was too late. Derek's fist had already shot out, seemingly of its own volition, and struck Petersen just below his right eye.

It was not the hardest punch Brien had ever seen anyone throw, but there were years of repressed hate behind it, and the blow staggered Petersen. The watching students roared with excitement and approval, and for a second, Brien thought Derek might actually have a chance. But Derek, for all of his years of heroic role-playing, had no instinct for real fist-to-fist fighting. He did not step in to hit Petersen again and finish him off as the little brown-haired bully reeled; instead, he stood motionless, staring at his fist as if it had taken him by surprise.

It was a bad mistake. Petersen was a bully, but unlike most bullies, he was also a born fighter and there was not a cowardly bone in his body. In seconds he had recovered himself, and with an audible snarl, he launched himself at the taller boy.

It was hard to see exactly what was happening in the crush of the crowd, but Brien thought he saw Derek land a single, awkward blow on the top of Petersen's head before being knocked off his feet as Petersen slammed into him. The two combatants rolled over several times, grappling desperately, before Kent managed to get on top of Derek and throw four or five hard punches at his face. All of them landed squarely, and when Petersen drew back his fist after the last blow, his hand was red, covered with blood.

Several girls screamed with fear and disgust, but the sight of blood only served to inflame the rest of the crowd.

"Get him, Kent!" they were yelling. Hit him, kill him, smash his face in, hundreds of variants of the same barbaric theme. Hit him, hurt him, beat the smack out of him! It was like a feeding frenzy, and the mob's shining, eager faces made Brien want to throw up.

"Hit him again!" a freshman girl shrieked, her voice squeaking with excitement. "Hit him again!"

Petersen, his own face flushed with excitement, obliged her by throwing one more punch that crashed into Derek's face with a sickening thud that sounded like a baseball bat hitting a steak. The terrible sound made Brien reel, shocked with horror, and it must have distressed some of the other students, too, because a black-haired senior quickly stepped into the circle and grabbed Petersen's arm, which was already drawn back to deliver another blow.

"Come on, Kent, that's enough," he said as he pulled Petersen off Derek's unmoving body. "Leave him alone, it's over. You won, that's enough."

"Let go of me, Case!" Petersen struggled furiously with the taller boy until the boy let him go. "You saw it, he hit me first!"

"Yeah, I saw," the taller boy said. "And you kicked his butt. But it's over, Kent. It's enough."

"No it isn't," Petersen spat venomously, his handsome face still twisted with fury.

Before the black-haired boy or anyone else could stop him, Petersen turned and kicked Derek savagely in the ribs. Derek, apparently still conscious, grunted sharply, then curled up on his side and began to moan with pain. His nose was bloodied and his bruised left eye was already starting to swell, but worst of all, Brien could see tears starting to run down his beaten friend's cheeks, trickling through the spattered blood to fall silently on the ground.

Silently, but not unnoticed.

"Look at him," someone jeered. "He's crying like a baby."

Petersen nodded with satisfaction, satiated at last. There was a slight swelling under his own right eye, and Brien hoped desperately that it would eventually blacken on him. It wasn't enough, but at least it might be a mild consolation for Derek.

"Now it's over," Kent pronounced, and he smiled cruelly before turning his back on his victim and walking back into the school.

The crowd began to disperse as well, and Brien waited a little while before going to Derek, giving him some time to compose himself. By the time he kneeled down next to him, Derek was already sitting up, his face a smeared mess of bruises, tears, and blood. One hand rested gingerly on the side that Petersen had kicked; the other shielded his eyes from Brien's view.

Brien thought at first that Derek was still crying, but he should have known better. There were no tears left in Derek's eyes, no pain or humiliation, just an empty hatred that burned with all the furious fires of Hell. He searched for words of sympathy or consolation, but there was nothing to say. Wordlessly he extended a hand to his friend, and just as silently Derek took it. With Brien's help he got to his feet, and together, they walked slowly toward the school.

It wasn't over, Brien thought, as his sense of sick helplessness began to transform into anger. Petersen was wrong. It wasn't over yet. Quite the contrary. Things were just getting started.

CHAPTER 21

GET DOWN ON IT

IF CULTURE IS AN ARISTOCRATIC PHENOMENON—THE ASSIDUOUS, SOLITARY AND JEALOUS CULTIVATION OF AN INNER LIFE THAT TEMPERS AND OPPOSES THE VULGARITY OF THE CROWD—THEN TO EVEN CONCEIVE OF A CULTURE THAT IS SHARED BY EVERYONE, PRODUCED TO SUIT EVERYONE AND TAILORED ACCORDINGLY IS A MONSTROUS CONTRADICTION.

—Umberto Eco, *Apocalyptic and Integrated Intellectuals: Mass Communications and Theories of Mass Culture*

Jami sneered at her brother, who was watching her closely with an expression of mixed concern and grudging approval. She'd cleared the third blue screen and she could see he was sweating now! Exhaling slowly, she rolled her tense, aching shoulders and rubbed her wrist as the music of "The Chase" bleeped cheerfully from the oversize speakers of Christopher's new stereo. Do-do-dee-do-dee-do. . . . Fifty-five hundred more to beat Christopher *and* her personal high score, and all she needed was one yellow banana to do the trick.

Oops. The board was pink, but unfortunately, this wasn't the banana board. This was the first time she'd gotten this far, and she'd forgotten about the pear. Darn it!

"Down to your last guy, sis," Christopher taunted her. "You're gonna choke."

No, I'm not! She ignored his feeble attempt to psych her out and focused all of her attention on the glowing screen in front of her. Her fingers barely touched the keyboard, pressing left, down, and right as Ms. Pac-Man chomped her beribboned way through the pink maze, sweeping through the dangerous box of death at the bottom before Blinky and his little friends could zoom down to block the only exit. The ghosts were moving fast now, much faster than pokey Ms. Pac, and Jami had to be careful not to get caught on one of the straightaways.

Thump . . . thump . . . thump . . .

She heard the bouncing fruit sound she'd been waiting for just before catching sight of the green pear moving slowly down the left side of the maze. The orange ghost, what was her name, Sue? She was over there too, but she was zooming towards the ghost pen in the middle of the maze. So instead of heading immediately toward the left, Jami sent Ms. Pac zigzagging right, drawing the eager ghosts toward her like a round yellow magnet.

As they rushed toward her en masse, the thought of going down for a power pill occurred to her, but she dismissed it. That wasn't going to work on this board. The ghosts changed too fast, and it wasn't until the next screen that their blue state would hold long enough for you to rack up serious points on them. Playing it safe, she quickly ducked through the exit and appeared on the other side. *Gulp!* The pear disappeared and she was two thousand points closer to her goal. Yes!

"You're losing it," Christopher intoned sorrowfully. "Should've gone for the corner."

"As if," she muttered grimly.

She juked left to evade the light blue ghost, then held her breath as Blinky whizzed past the corner she was momentarily trapped in. That was lucky! Now for the power pills . . . She scooped up two without once attempting to chase a blinking ghost. No time for that now. Ms. Pac chomped furiously, desperately trying to summon the second pear. The maze was three-quarters cleared when she heard the noise again.

Thump . . . thump . . . thump . . .

She heard Christopher muttering something under his breath and grinned as she dodged Blinky again, cut around one more corner, and nearly broke a fingernail as she excitedly jammed her middle finger hard against the up arrow. The pedal was to the metal, and the pear was hers! *Gulp!* She raised her free hand in the air and pumped her fist, but her shout of triumph died in her throat. Pinky had cut stealthily through the exit, and she ran smack into the folds of the wretched little ghost's pink bedsheet.

Whee-oo-whee-oo-woo . . .

Ms. Pac-man disappeared with a sad little *pop!* and Jami slumped in her brother's comfortable chair, burying her head in her hands. No! She was close, so very close to winning. She felt drained, as if this one game had been her one chance at arcade glory, and she had burned up a year's worth of luck and skill.

Behind her, Christopher sighed deeply.

"Nice job, James," he reluctantly praised her. "You win."

What? She raised her head and looked at the screen. There it was, in beautiful pulsating white text at the top of the screen: 53380. Fifty-three thousand, three hundred eighty points, sixty more than she needed to beat the fifty-three thousand, three hundred twenty that her brother had racked up with his one guy.

"Yes!" She leaped out of the chair, raising her fists to the sky. "I win! I win, I win, I win!"

She did an impromptu dance, excitedly beating her heels against the thick blue carpet before breaking smoothly into her formal victory dance, strutting back-and-forth as she shook her hips and shoulders like an electrocuted chicken. All the while she jabbed her finger triumphantly at Christopher.

"I am the winner," she sang happily. "The only winner! You are the loser. . . ."

Christopher just snorted and folded his arms as he waited for her to finish her in-your-face celebration. The best part was watching the conflicting emotions flashing across his face. Irritation, annoyance, chagrin, and amusement, they were all there, as always, until the latter finally won out and she saw him start to smile. They burst out laughing together, and when he held up a congratulatory hand, she high-fived him enthusiastically.

"Say it," she demanded. "You have to say it now!"

Christopher grinned and made a grandly theatrical bow. "All hail Jami, Princess Pooyan and Everqueen of the Arcade!"

Jami raised her hand imperiously and made a half-turn accompanied by a Barbie-doll wave, graciously accepting the plaudits of her imaginary subjects. Then she stopped and frowned at her brother. "Hey, you left out the part about my beauty and total perfectness!"

"Perfection," he corrected her. "And I never agreed to that. Forget it, you'll have to beat me even up to make me say that."

She eyed him, calculating. "I'll spot you ten thousand," she offered.

"No, forget the points," he responded. "That's boring. Give me three guys and you're on."

"Two!" she demanded. He didn't need three and they both knew it. He was just negotiating.

When Christopher nodded his agreement, she quickly added: "And you have to say it at school. Out loud, and in front of people."

Christopher rolled his eyes and shook his head. But he wasn't telling her no, he just didn't think she could really pull it off. Which was pretty unlikely, she had to admit. Of course, it didn't cost her anything to lose, so it was pretty much a win-win situation as far as she was concerned.

"Oh, why not." He shrugged his shoulders. "It's never going to happen. Deal."

She couldn't resist one last push as he offered his hand. "And Rachel Jensen has to be there, too."

"No way!" He jerked his hand back as if he'd just been burned. But his emphatic rejection was fast, way too fast, and he blushed as he realized she'd just caught him out.

Before she could rag him on it, though, the door opened behind him, and Holli, in her usual pre-date state of near-complete undress, stuck her head in the room. Her hair was done, but her cheeks were red with that freshly scrubbed look that Jami knew preceded either bedtime or a twenty-minute session in the bathroom, and she was wearing nothing but a big yellow towel. Good thing she didn't have to go, Jami thought. At least she didn't think she had to. . . . Doggone it, now she had to.

"What are you doing, Jami?" Holli complained. "We're supposed to leave in half an hour, in case you forgot, and you haven't even started getting ready yet. Oh, and Christopher, I forgot to tell you. Paul told me you can come, too."

"Really?" Jami said in near-perfect stereo with her brother.

"Cool," Christopher said, looking pleasantly surprised, until Jami poked him in the chest.

"Rachel's going to be there, stud puppy."

"So?" Holli said, puzzled.

"So he's in luuuv!"

Jami mockingly drew out the last word, and Christopher punched her in the shoulder. Not hard, of course, but that didn't stop Jami from shrieking and dropping to the carpet as if she'd been struck by a sledgehammer. She was a good diver; if the five-meter field dive ever became an Olympic sport, she'd give the Italians a run for the gold. Facial expression was big, but the real trick was letting your whole body go limp. It was lame, of course, but it was a skill you needed if you wanted to play center-mid.

"Penalty!" she shouted. "Red card! Vicious and totally unprovoked, ref, make the call!"

Despite her impatience, Holli laughed and raised both hands, holding up two imaginary cards and nearly losing her towel in the process. "I say you both get yellow. Now, hurry up, Christopher, because I told Paul you were driving us to Jason's and he's meeting me there."

Holli tightened the towel and disappeared from the bedroom, and moments later Jami heard the bathroom door slam. Darn, darn, darn, there goes your chance, Jami thought as she grabbed the nearest post of Christopher's bed and pulled herself to her feet.

"Can I use your bathroom?" she asked Christopher hopefully. "Please?"

"Why can't you just get ready with Holli?" he asked, not catching her drift. Then he raised his eyebrows as she scowled at him. "Oh, sure, go ahead. I think I'm out of T.P., though—"

"Never mind." She waved him off. What was she thinking? Boys were so gross. It was safer to sneak quietly down to the guest bathroom and hope Mom didn't hear anything. The downstairs bathroom was supposed to be off-limits to all three of them, and to Dad as well, but Jami figured she'd rather take the chance of getting yelled at than risk entering her brother's biohazard zone. Right from where she was standing now, she could see a tattered towel covering the blue-and-white tile, white toothpaste spots dotting the mirror, and a crumpled pair of boxers on the counter.

She shuddered. High-school boys might be past the whole cooties-and-girl-germs thing, but they were still barely ahead of chimpanzees on the civilization scale. They were just disgusting, that's all there was to it. How could they be so nasty, but so cute, too, at the very same time? It was a mystery, but Jami wasn't sure it was one she really wanted to solve.

"That's what you're wearing?" Holli asked, raising her slender eyebrows as Jami joined her in their two-sink bathroom. She herself had on a little black skirt and a sleeveless cotton babydoll top that Mom would say was at least one size too small. Her eyes were done, and she was just starting to apply her lip liner.

Jami glanced at herself in the mirror and shrugged. What was the matter with khaki shorts and an Abercrombie T-shirt? She eased her ponytail out of her scrunchie and shook her hair free. Okay, maybe tonight she'd wear it down, for once.

"Yeah, so?"

Holli shrugged herself as she picked a stray blond strand from her tight black shirt. Jami shook her head. Between the two of them, you'd think someone was hiding a golden retriever in the house.

"Well, Jason is going to be there, obviously, since it's his house, and so is Robbie Dale. I just thought you might want to make a good impression, that's all. One of them is probably going to ask you to the prom, you know, so maybe you want to show them what's up?"

Jami glanced at her sister's reflection in the mirror, then back at her own. Her sister had a good three inches on her now thanks to her chunky-heeled sandals, and she couldn't deny that Holli had a definite look going on that she herself was missing. That was nothing new, of course, and Jami didn't usually mind since she knew how much time and effort her twin put into putting herself together. But tonight, for once, she didn't feel like being overshadowed, and she certainly wasn't in the mood to see the boys' eyes resting on her for just a moment before flicking dismissively past her.

Of course, she couldn't care less if she went to the stupid prom or not, but it was hard to resist the tempting thought that she'd score a ton of points if one of the seniors really did ask her. And Holli had been so busy running around with Paul and his friends lately that every once in a while Jami found herself feeling left out of things. A boyfriend might not be such a bad thing, especially if she went out with one of the soccer players, like Jason. Or, for that matter, Paul. It was a bit of a shock when she realized that maybe some of her recent irritation with Holli was rooted in jealousy. She had so much more in common with Paul than Holli did; why hadn't she been the one he'd wanted?

She reached down and opened her drawer. It was mostly empty, with two barely used tubes of lipstick, three eyeliner pencils, and an unopened compact rattling around with two big bottles of sunscreen and scrunchies of many different colors and sizes. The contrast with Holli's overstuffed drawer could hardly have been greater; it was a sad, but accurate image of their love lives, too.

"Want me to do your makeup?" Holli asked her kindly, seemingly reading her mind as she anticipated her request. "You can wear my new pink skirt, too. It'll look really good on you!"

Jami ran her hands through her straw-colored hair and lifted it up, away from her head. She narrowed her eyes and stuck her lips out, imitating the bored attitude projected by the models in Holli's fashion mags. Okay, the sunburn around her eyes sort of ruined the effect, but at least the mirror reassured her that she wasn't a hopeless case.

"You don't mind?" she asked Holli. "Won't that make us late?"

Her twin shrugged. "Oh, it's all right. It's in a good cause, and besides, it'll be fun to see the look on Jase's face when you walk in. If he's liking you already, then this'll make his jaw drop!"

Holli smiled confidently as she stepped back and pointed to the counter. "Sid'down, girl. Just close your eyes and think pretty thoughts. I'll take care of the rest."

You could hear the *thump-thumping* of the music from the end of the block, which was where Christopher had to park the Explorer, since there were cars parked bumper-to-bumper on both sides of the street. Jami felt horribly self-conscious as she slid carefully out of the high seat, and once out of the truck, she tugged anxiously at her borrowed skirt.

"Are you sure I look all right?" she asked Holli. "It's not too short?"

"You look awesome," Holli reassured her. "Don't worry about it!"

Christopher walked around the front of the Explorer and cocked his head as he examined her. "If you weren't my sister, I'd say you look pretty hot. But is this one untied shoe some kind of, like, Michael Jackson thing or what?"

"Hrrrahh." Jami started to make a face at him, until she realized he wasn't just ragging on her. Sighing, she placed her foot carefully on the running board and tied her almost new ankle boots for the third time. She'd bought them a while ago, mostly because Angie had encouraged her to, but she never wore them. She hadn't remembered why until now—they were cute, but they had those round shoelaces which were sadistically designed to come untied every ten minutes. She quickly double-knotted the laces. You couldn't be too careful, especially not if you were wearing a miniskirt.

Jason's house was in the middle of the block, with a brick-and-stucco exterior and a pointed roof that reminded Jami of the ski chalets at Powderhorn. The sidewalk leading up to the house were littered with plastic pop bottles, along with a solitary beer can, and as they walked past a red Honda Accord, Jami was surprised to hear faint murmurs coming from inside the parked car. She glanced down, and was surprised to see a couple making out in the front seat. Embarrassed, she quickly looked away.

"Dang, get a room," she said.

"Who was it?" Holli asked distractedly. She was checking out the group of boys sitting on the front step, looking to see if Paul was there waiting for her.

"I don't know. She was blonde, is all I saw."

"Nothing like getting an early start on things, I guess," Christopher remarked philosophically. He seemed pretty relaxed considering it was his first senior party.

Jami took a deep breath. Even though it wasn't her first party, and Paul had told her that Jason really wanted her there, she still felt a little nervous about walking into a place where she didn't really belong. The boys on the steps had noticed them now, and from the way that a familiar-looking redhead sat back and pushed up his baseball cap, it appeared that Holli's magic had done the trick after all.

"Hey, what's up, Holli?" Dan Larson was a junior at their school, and Jami's appearance seemed to have taken him off guard. "Jami, wow, you look, like, older."

Holli snorted disdainfully, and Jami had to keep from cracking up when Christopher whispered in her ear.

"Watch out for Dan, he's pretty smooth."

"She's too old for you, anyway, Larson," one of the other boys said with a knowing smile, and the rest of the juniors burst out laughing. Jami remembered there had been a story going around last year about Dan asking out a seventh grader from Chippewa. Apparently, it had been true, judging by the guy's face, which was now redder than his hair.

Holli opened the door without knocking, and the volume of the music hit them so hard it nearly made Jami retreat. The bass was so loud that she could feel it penetrating through her chest, like an out-of-sync second heartbeat.

"Why does it always have to be rap?" she shouted in Holli's ear.

"Because they have to show off how cool they are!" her twin yelled back. "Don't worry, somebody's girlfriend will complain pretty soon, and they'll put on some dance music."

"You're the one going out with Paul! Do something!"

Holli looked surprised. "Oh, I suppose that's true," she said. "Well, let's go find Jason and make him turn it down, at least."

Jami turned back and grabbed Christopher's arm. He was glancing around uncertainly, and she remembered that he probably didn't know anyone here except for a few of the soccer players.

"Just follow us," she instructed him. "We're looking for Paul."

Her brother nodded quickly, pleased that they weren't abandoning him. Jami gave Holli a little push to let her know it was okay to move on, and the three of them made their way through the crowded front room. They were encountered by more than a few unfriendly glares from some of the snobbier senior girls, but Jami took her cue from Holli and blew them off as they made their way to the kitchen.

Jason was there, as was Paul and four or five other guys. Jason was sitting on the counter, popping the cap off of a bottle of beer, and while Jami wasn't surprised, she couldn't help being a little dismayed. She'd never heard he was a drinker, but then again, she'd only been to three or four upper-class parties before.

"Hey, it's the twins!" Aaron Chau was the varsity left midfielder. He was one of the nicer players on the team and was ridiculously smart. He was supposed to be going to Stanford next year, from what Jami had heard.

"And my man," Paul said cheerfully, locking thumbs with her brother in that weird guy handshake. "What's up, Christopher? Want a beer?"

Jami knew Paul meant well and was including Christopher in on things, but she was still glad to see that her brother wasn't afraid to shake his head. "Thanks, but I'm driver man tonight."

"Good for you, Christopher," Jason said, handing the beer

he'd just opened to Aaron. "Paul and I have track regionals next weekend, so we'll just be the Dry Musketeers tonight!" He laughed, and both Christopher and Aaron grinned at him as if he had said something amusing, but Jami didn't see anything funny about it. Neither did anyone else, apparently, but only Holli was brave enough to ask.

"Was that, like, a joke?"

Aaron and Christopher looked at each other for a moment, then Aaron shrugged and explained.

"In German, the word for three is *D—R—E—I*, but it sounds like 'dry.' So he was making a play on words about how the three of them weren't drinking tonight. Kind of a pun, you see."

"Don't you mean a palindrome?" Christopher interjected quickly.

"Oh . . ." Holli said reflectively, after giving everything a moment's thought. "But that's not funny!"

That set all the guys off laughing, except Paul, who slipped his arm protectively around Holli and guided her out of the room.

"I say we forget these losers," he said with a smile. "We'll go dance and have a good time while they sit around making dumb jokes to show off how smart they are. Jason, put something else in the CD player, will you?"

"All right," Jason answered. He glanced at Jami. "Want to help?"

He really was good-looking, Jami decided suddenly. Maybe he wasn't quite as magazine-boy pretty as Robbie Dale, but he had an easy aura of casual confidence that was really very attractive.

"You going to be all right?" she asked Christopher. "Rachel should be here soon."

"Don't worry about me," he assured her. "I just want Aaron to tell me who he had to bribe to get into Stanford."

"No, no, blackmail works better. . . ." Jami heard Aaron telling him as she followed Jason out of the kitchen. She wasn't sure, though. In fact, she wasn't sure about anything at the moment except for the fact that Jason had just taken her hand in his.

It was strange. She'd been fine just a moment ago, and now she felt that the whole world had closed in on her. She was suddenly conscious of her heart beating, and was amazed how loudly her breathing sounded. Surely he could hear it! His hand was cool and dry, and she worried that this must mean hers was warm and sweaty. She tried to see his face. Was she grossing him out?

But if Jason was bothered by her clammy hands, he didn't show it. Smiling easily, he led her into what looked like his dad's office, and offered her a seat in a big, comfy-looking leather chair. He opened a tall wooden door that revealed shelves full of high-tech stereo equipment that was all made of matching silver and looked very expensive.

"I think there's enough engine in this bad boy to launch the space shuttle," he joked as he extracted a monster-sized remote, then pulled out the high-backed chair that was set in front of the big wooden desk and sat down next to her. "It's, like, nuclear powered or something."

"How many CDs does it hold?" A lot obviously.

"That big piece there is a one-hundred CD changer, which is about ninety more than any reasonable human being needs."

"I don't know about that," Jami heard herself replying. "My brother could sure use it. Then maybe he could listen to more than the same three Metallica CDs."

"Metallica? He doesn't look like a metal head. I would have figured him for, oh, I don't know, maybe an alternative guy?"

"No, not him. He likes the hard stuff, some of the electronic stuff, too, Nine Inch Nails, Disturbed, and all that."

Jason nodded absently as he pressed a button on the remote. "There, that'll keep them for a while. Picked it up last summer in London. A little happy dance music never killed anybody." He returned his attention to her. "So how about you? I take it you don't so much dig the Metallica?"

Jami was feeling more comfortable with the idea of talking about her brother at the moment, or London, or pretty much anything else right now, and the direct question about herself flustered her.

"Oh, I like all kinds of music."

"No way," Jason argued, shaking his head. "People say that, but they can't really mean it. It just means you listen to the radio, and you don't particularly care what it is as long as there's a beat and a decent melody."

"Fair enough," Jami admitted. But what was up with him? she wondered. It was like he was showing off, in kind of a weird way. "So you really like music?" she asked.

"Yeah," he admitted. "I always wanted to be in a band, but I never really had time for it, what with soccer and all. My dad bought me this little Casio keyboard when I was in junior high, but I never really learned how to play it. I can't read music or anything, you know? I write songs sometimes, but I guess they're really poems since there isn't any music to go with them. Except it's not really poetry, even though it rhymes."

What? His babbling story was pathetic, but for some reason Jami found it charming, too. Before tonight, she'd never thought of Jason Case as being anything but a cute older guy who played sports and was really good at them. To hear that an All-State superjock whose sleeves were lined with letter bars could have his own frustrated dreams was a revelation to her. With a start, she realized that even though he was three years older than she, he was just as nervous here as she was. Maybe even more so.

To put him a little more at ease, she decided to compliment him. But she didn't want to be too obvious, or give him any wrong ideas, so she casually looked him over for something that would be safe to talk about.

"I like your pants," she told him. No, no, no! she mentally shouted at herself. I like your pants? What are you thinking?

He looked down at them. They were a fairly nondescript pair of khakis.

"They're missing some buttons," he told her seriously. "I keep forgetting to have my mom sew them back on."

They looked at each other, and as their eyes met, they both started laughing.

"This is ridiculous," he said, shaking his head. "I can't

believe . . . why can't I talk to you like a normal human being?"

"Well, why am I talking about your pants?" she replied, equally embarrassed.

He laughed out loud, and a playful spark lit up his dark eyes.

"Don't even go there!" she warned him. "I mean it!"

"Okay, okay." He raised his hands in mock innocence. "Forget the pants. But the thing is . . . I mean, what I wanted to talk about was . . ."

He looked away, and his face flushed slightly.

"Yeah . . . ?"

So he was going to ask her to the prom! She was sure of it! Now that she had a handle on where things were going, Jami found she could almost enjoy the situation, despite all the awkwardness. She was surprised to feel a sudden rush as she realized how much power a girl had over a guy at a time like this. She could play dumb and pretend not to understand what he was getting at; she could make him suffer by making it dificult. She could even destroy his cool-guy reputation at school by dropping a word or two in the right ear later. It would be so easy!

But she didn't want to. She actually found his vulnerability more appealing than his customary nonchalance, and hurting his feelings was the very last thing she wanted to do.

"Okay." Jami mentally applauded him as he cleared his throat and worked up his nerve again. "Here's the deal. I know you're only a freshman and all, but I think you're really pretty, and I was wondering if maybe you'd, ah, like to go to the prom."

This time he didn't look away, but stared at her with an intensity that suddenly made it hard for her to swallow.

"With me," he added unneccessarily.

"That would be fun!" Jami managed to say as a giddy sense of excitement flowed over her. "Maybe we can even go double with Paul and Holli."

Jason nodded. He was smiling, but more than anything, he looked tremendously relieved. "Yeah, the thought had crossed my mind. About us going with them, I mean. So let's go tell them what's up, hey?"

He leaned forward, and for just a second, Jami froze, thinking he was going to kiss her. She wasn't sure if she wanted him to or not, at least not yet. But he was only reaching out to pick up the remote for the CD player, and a moment later she was filled with a strange mix of relief and disappointment as he led her out of the study and back downstairs to the party.

CHAPTER 22

FORKED TONGUES, BITTER MOUTHS

I'VE SEEN THE WICKED FRUIT OF YOUR VINE
DESTROY THE MAN WHO LACKS A STRONG MIND
HUMAN PRIDE SINGS A VENGEFUL SONG
INSPIRED BY THE TIMES YOU'VE BEEN WALKED ON
—Creed ("What If")

I hate you. I just thought you should know that."
Distracted by her own thoughts, Jami shook her head and found herself staring into Angie's freckled face. "Huh?"

"I said, I hate you. What's the matter with you, girl? If you say you were just thinking about what kind of dress you're going to wear, I swear I'll kill you."

Angie was jealous about her date to the prom, of course, but at least she was honest enough to admit it. And after Jami told her about Jason, her normally sarcastic friend hadn't even said anything nasty about him, but had instead screamed and given her a big hug. Of course, it hadn't taken long for her personality to return to normal.

"The thing is, I expect this kind of thing from Holli. You know, getting all dressed up, going out with the older guys, getting asked to the prom. But I expected more from you! I mean, what happened to your ponytail? I didn't have you getting interested in the boys until at least eleventh grade!"

"Sorry," Jami mumbled.

She was too distracted to pay attention to Angie's monologue. So she half-listened to her friend's extensive catalog of complaints as she entertained herself by watching the intricate, flow-ing patterns of social interaction as various little groups of boys and girls swirled together, coalesced, then dissolved into new gatherings. She watched as one girl in a red T-shirt flowed from a conversation with two other girls into a larger group that included three guys, which was then divided and divided again, three times in all, finally leaving the girl with her arms around the shoulders of a skinny guy with braces, dancing closely to the slow, romantic music that was now coming out of the speakers. Was it that late already?

But the song came to an end and was replaced by an up-tempo song from a boy band. Renewed energy seemed to fill the room as the slow-dancing couples split apart and began dancing separately. Whew! Apparently the one song was just an aberration.

She spotted Christopher talking to someone over on the far side of the room. He looked deeply involved in his conversa-tion, and it wasn't until she leaned out and peeked around a football player's pumped-up arms that she could see Rachel was the girl sitting in front of him. She smiled, pleased. They seemed to be getting along all right without her help, so Jami decided to leave them alone. Of Holli, there was no sign, although Paul wasn't around, either, so it wasn't hard to figure out that they were probably off somewhere together. Jami was a little disappointed that she hadn't been able to tell her twin about Jason yet, but then again, considering the effort Holli had put into dressing her up before the party, she probably already knew.

"Yuck, check out who just got here." Angie's lip curled with disgust.

Jami followed the line of her friend's gaze and saw that a small group of seniors had just arrived, led by Kent Petersen, the little bully who was always picking on people. His beady eyes scanned the room, searching the crowd like a vicious weasel in search of defenseless prey. Jami's heart skipped a beat as he appeared to be heading toward her brother, but Kent stopped before reaching the far end of the room and exchanged high fives with his friend Jim, who'd been clumsily putting moves on a girl in a tight white dress.

Still concerned about Christopher, who was the only sophomore guy there, and therefore Kent's most promising target, Jami abandoned Angie and started to force her way through the crowded living room, hoping to warn him. But before she reached the other side, she saw that Jim had already pointed out her brother to his friend, and the undersized senior's ferretlike face was lit up at the prospect of making a scene.

"What're you doing here, dorkface?" Kent stuck his chin out, trying to make himself taller. "You don't belong here, stupid tenth-grader!"

Heads began to turn, and electricity filled the air as the room's atmosphere grew tense. Jami froze in place, all too aware that if she tried to jump in and protect her brother, she'd only make him look like a loser who couldn't handle himself. She should find Jason, she thought, but she was reluctant to leave her brother alone with no one to back him up.

"Leave him alone," Rachel muttered softly.

Kent gave her an incredulous look. "Was I talking to you? I don't think so!"

Rachel flinched at the senior's harsh tone, and a spasm of anger crossed Christopher's face.

"Don't talk to her like that, Petersen!"

Now Jami felt like flinching. This could get ugly.

"Did you just call me Petersen, jerkwad?" Kent's voice was low and threatening. "Don't you dare call me that!"

Her brother rolled his eyes, but managed to force a fake smile. "Look, Kent, I'm not going anywhere, and I'm not looking for trouble, okay? So why don't you just leave us alone?"

He started to turn his back on the bully, and the little senior's face grew ugly with fury. He reached out and grabbed Christopher's shoulder, twisting him around so that her brother was forced to face him.

"Don't freaking turn your back on me! Do you really think

I'm afraid to kick your butt, beanpole? Why don't you tell your little girlfriend here how we used to whitewash your stupid crack?"

Some of the guys with him laughed, and Kent exchanged a blind high five with one of his followers, his eyes never leaving Christopher's face.

"It was my face you used to rub in the snow," Christopher said, pleasantly enough, but his eyes were hard. "And I haven't forgotten, Kent, but I have decided to forgive you."

"Forgive me? What's that supposed to mean? What are you, one of those church losers or something?"

"I'm a Christian, yes."

The two boys stared at each other, and Kent finally made a disgusted face.

"Whatever. Guess you're even more of a loser than I thought." He glanced at Rachel and smirked. "I guess you won't be getting any action from the choir boy here tonight. Stick around, and maybe we'll see what's up, huh?"

Jami didn't see what exactly Christopher did, but there was a flash of movement and Kent was instantly doubled over. Her brother's face was filled with cold fury as he threw a sharp left cross that smashed into the side of Kent's head and sent him crashing helplessly to the floor. Jami started forward, not sure whether to cheer or restrain her brother, when he surprised everyone in the room, including her, by dropping to his knees in front of the other boy.

"Oh, no!" he cried out. "Kent, I'm so sorry. I shouldn't have done that, I shouldn't have. I'm really sorry!"

The look of utter dismay on his face left no doubt that his apology was sincere. Jami heard someone snigger behind her, and saw that it was a tall junior who was bursting out with laughter. Nor was he the only one amused by the sight of Kent dazedly pushing himself up from the carpet, clutching at his stomach and gasping for breath. Kent was clearly stunned, not only by the blow but by the sudden violence of the attack, and he seemed more bewildered than angry. His face was a hilarious picture of disbelief and wounded astonishment, and it was obvious that he had no desire to continue the fight.

"What, does that kid do karate?" Jami heard someone saying. "Holy smokes, did you see how fast he moved?"

"I wouldn't mess with him," another guy commented.

That seemed to be the general consensus in the room, and one apparently shared by Kent, who was waving off Christopher's abject attempts to apologize with some degree of alarm. He pushed himself away and self-consciously brushed at the white-patched green leather of his letter jacket without meeting her brother's eyes. He still seemed a little freaked out as he retreated back into the crowd, followed by his friends.

Well, good. The little jerk could use a lesson or two; maybe then he'd stop making everybody else's lives miserable. Jami never understood how some guys got off on pushing people around.

She reached Christopher and tugged at his arm. She was proud of him for standing up to Kent, even if he didn't seem to feel that way about himself.

"I should not have done that," he repeated. "Why did I do that?"

"Are you okay? What happened?"

Her brother grimaced and shook his head. "Oh, I just lost it, that's all. I mean, it was bad enough that he was bugging me, but when he started, you know, hitting on Rachel, I just reacted. I wasn't even thinking. One minute I'm trying to tell him I forgive him, and then the next thing I know, he's going down! I really didn't mean to hit him."

Jami laughed. "You're such a nut! Look, if you didn't mean to hit him, then it was an accident. No big deal, I mean, it's obviously not the first time anyone's ever punched him, right? It serves him right."

"Besides, if you didn't, I was going to smack him one," murmured Rachel.

That snapped Christopher out of his guilty reaction, and Jami had to smile at the dumbfounded look he gave her friend.

"So maybe it was wrong to hit him." The pretty brown-haired girl shrugged indifferently. "But it was nice of you to defend me like that. Not everybody would, especially not against a senior."

Her brother's expression brightened. He clearly hadn't considered that aspect. The way the two of them looked at each other then. . . .

Well, it's clearly time for me to vacate, Jami thought wryly. One thing puzzled her, though. Where had her brother learned to fight like that . . . ? Oh, right, like the kissing thing, it must have been a skill he'd picked up somewhere along their fantastic adventure last winter. That experience had sure changed a lot of things, not only for him, but for her as well.

In fact, once you were aware of the whole angelic dimension, it changed almost everything. As she thought that, she happened to catch a glimpse of Kent moving across the other side of the room, and for just a moment, she was able to see him differently, not as a bully, but as a wounded spirit badly in need of love and affection. Then the moment passed, and she was glad that it did. Maybe he needed some things, but who didn't? Kent would just have to find them somewhere else. Christopher could forgive him, and that was good, but Jami wasn't going to. He didn't deserve it, the jerk.

Then, out of nowhere, a powerful sense of nearby evil smashed into her, and she reeled, stumbling into her brother. Christopher must have felt it, too, because he almost went down as she clutched at his arm, and only Rachel's support kept them both upright. As quickly as it appeared, it was gone, and Jami glanced wildly around the room in a desperate attempt to catch a glimpse of whatever it was. She saw nothing that hadn't been there before, just the packed room full of half-drunken boys and girls, any number of whom were certainly bent on violating at least one of the Ten Commandments at their first opportunity, but there was nothing that appeared likely to account for this feeling of active evil lurking somewhere amongst them.

"Hey, are you okay?" Angie had made her way over to them and was holding her wrist. "You look all pale!"

"Yeah, I'm fine," Jami said. "Hey, did you see anything strange tonight?"

Angie snorted. "Besides your brother beating up Kent?" she asked. "I guess it depends what you mean by that. It's not like Kent being a complete jerk is out of the ordinary or anything. Tim Griffin's throwing up in the backyard, but that isn't exactly new either. Rena Thompson disappeared with some guy from SPA a while ago, and Ginny told me Robbie heard Jason got to you first and he's all mad about it."

"Hmmm. He is?"

That was certainly interesting news, Jami thought. So Robbie really did like her after all. Well, too bad. He was cute, but Jason was the more intriguing prospect. By far.

"Yeah. Hey, check that out!" Angie pointed. "Now, that's weird!"

Jami turned around and saw Jim Schumacher dancing closely with the girl to whom he'd been talking earlier. When she looked more closely, she saw they weren't actually dancing, they were making out to the music, swaying around a little, but not really moving.

"Who's she?"

"I think she's a junior. Gross, can you imagine kissing him?" Angie shuddered. "I'd rather lick my cat's litter box!"

Jami winced at the image, but Angie was right. That would be a hard call. She was repulsed, but she found it hard to look away from the couple. For some reason, the memory of Jason leaning toward her suddenly flickered across her mind.

"Ewww, now he's taking her upstairs. Do you think they're going to do it?"

"Angie!"

Still, she couldn't help wondering the same thing herself.

"Rachel and I are going for a walk," Christopher announced unexpectedly from behind her. Jami noticed that he was all-too-casually holding her friend's hand. Good for him! "I'm supposed to have you guys home by eleven, so why don't we meet at the truck in forty-five minutes. Can you tell Holli?"

"Sure," Jami told him, and when she glanced at Rachel, she was pleased to see that her friend's cheeks were coloring nicely. She's digging him, all right, Jami thought to herself. They didn't make a bad-looking couple, either. "I'll see if I can find her."

Christopher nodded and Rachel waved shyly, leaving her alone with Angie. Which would be fine if she could only shake this sick feeling at the pit of her stomach. It wasn't just Jim Shumacher. Something was wrong, something was very wrong, and she didn't know what it was. But she wasn't going to think about it now, she decided firmly. Tonight was all about having fun, not good and evil. It would just have to wait for tomorrow. She checked her lipstick in the reflection of a nearby picture, took a deep breath, and went off to find Jason.

Chapter 23

Blue Monday

How does it feel?
How should I feel?
Tell me how does it feel,
To treat me like you do?
—Orgy ("Blue Monday")

Brien couldn't help being in a good mood, even though it was a Monday morning. He whistled as he pulled into the parking lot and smartly eased his car in between two pickups, one of which was brand-new and bore the unmistakable mark of an early graduation present. Brien wasn't envious, though. A new truck was one thing, but he was looking forward to the prom with Tessa, which after last Saturday's almost-but-not-quite-a-date was looking pretty promising, much to his delight.

As he walked up the gentle hill toward the front door of the school, the thought crossed his mind that perhaps going to the U wouldn't be so bad after all, since Tessa was going to be there herself. With her at his side, he knew he could survive the worst that a thousand Kent Petersens could throw at him, and do it with a smile.

It was strange how confident he found himself feeling. He grinned at himself and checked out his hair in the glass door's reflection. Not too bad, not too bad. No one was ever going to pick him to play the next James Bond and the glasses didn't help, but now that he'd lost some weight and his skin was clearing up, he was almost starting to resemble someone that dated girls on a regular basis. And with any luck at all, the girl he'd be dating over the summer would be Tessa.

He made his way through the crowded staircase and waited patiently, as it took a while for the bottleneck at the top of the stairs to sort itself out. Senior Hall was buzzing with the usual post-weekend chatter, as the inevitable stories about who got drunk, who got stoned, who hooked up with whom, and who threw up where, were passed on from ear to eager ear, with most of the factual details being rendered totally unrecognizable in the process. The approach of graduation tended to lead to an increase in both the frequency and intensity of senior partying, which was good since there was a chance that people would find something else to talk about besides the beating poor Derek had taken at Kent Petersen's hands.

"Hey, Brien."

He was surprised when Mandy, Tessa's cute friend, touched him on the shoulder as he passed her locker. She smiled at him, but seemed to be a little uncomfortable for some reason. Probably just not used to talking to me here, Brien thought, and he smiled back at her.

"Hi, Mandy, right? How are you? How was the party?"

"Oh, it was all right, I guess." She looked away, and he wondered if she felt bad about not inviting him. It's no big deal, he wanted to reassure her. It's not like he ever went to those kind of parties anyhow. "Say, I think Tessa's looking for you. She wanted to, like, talk to you about something."

"Really? Okay, thanks." Brien barely managed to keep an idiot smile off his face. "I, um, I guess I better go find her, then."

"Right," Mandy agreed, nodding her head. "Well, see you later."

"Sure, thanks a lot, Mandy!"

Although he was only a few rows down from his own locker, Brien didn't bother dropping his books off but instead turned around and headed directly for Tessa's locker. He glanced at the clock on the far end of the hall, and saw he still had three minutes before the bell rang for first hour. Plenty of time. People were starting to slam their lockers and wander off toward their class-rooms, so he had to jostle his way past a few slower-moving peo-ple, leaving only a mumbled apology in his wake.

"Tessa!" he called happily when he finally saw her, crouched down as she withdrew an English grammar book from her lower shelf. "Hi. Mandy said you wanted to see me?"

"Oh, Brien," Tessa said, looking a little startled. "Mandy? Oh, yeah, that's right."

She looked tired, and her whole demeanor seemed to be some-what withdrawn. When she stood up, she sighed, and she only glanced at him briefly. Their eyes met, for just a moment, and then she flicked her soft brown gaze away from him. He cocked his head, trying to read her expression more clearly, but she hid behind her long bangs and refused to let him clearly see her face.

Obviously, something was wrong. Brien's heart started to beat faster. But what was it? Had he said something wrong? Had he done something? Oh, no, had Derek been spreading around a bogus story about the two of them that had gotten back to her? No, that was impossible! Derek wasn't even coming to school this week, at least not until the bruises on his face were healed.

"Tessa, what is it?" He forced himself to remain calm, to keep his voice steady. "Is something wrong?"

"I'm a horrible, awful, person," Tessa burst out unexpectedly, shaking her head. "I can't believe this, I really can't, but there's nothing I can do about it."

"What . . . no, you're not! What are you talking about?"

She was wearing a man's blue pinstripe oxford shirt, he sud-denly noticed, that was far too large for her. It hung loosely open over a white scoop-neck T-shirt, and the sleeves were rolled up to her elbows. It looked pretty worn—probably her dad's shirt, he surmised. And she wasn't wearing a bra either, he saw as she took a deep breath. It was weird. He felt as if time had slowed, that he had stepped outside of his body and was watching her from somewhere far away.

"Brien, I'm really sorry, but I just started seeing somebody this weekend." He watched her lips move, and heard the words she spoke, but they seemed to rattle around uselessly inside his head, making it impossible to understand their meaning. "I mean, I know it's really, really bad timing and all, but it's like, I guess I'm kind of involved with him now, so I don't think it would be right for us to, you know, go to the prom now."

"You're saying you don't want to go with me?" Brien said, stunned. "Is that it?"

"It's not that I don't want to, it's just that I can't. I . . . I can't. I'm really sorry."

She couldn't look at him. She looked at her shoes, the floor, the stairs, anywhere but at him.

"The party," Brien said dully, shaking his head. "It was the party, wasn't it."

Her head snapped up, and her eyes blazed indignantly at him. He took an inadvertent step backward, surprised.

"That has nothing to do with it, Brien, all right? Look, I'm really sorry about everything, because you're a nice guy and you deserve better than this. But what am I supposed to do? You tell me! I can't exactly blow off my new boyfriend, can I!"

The anger faded from her eyes now as they pleaded wordlessly with him, begging for, if not understanding, at least a degree of sympathy. And to a certain extent he did understand. As much as he didn't want to, he did. Girls like her weren't for guys like him, it was as simple as that. It was the one certain law of the universe. What had happened two days ago was just an aberration, that one magical afternoon was the exception that proved the rule.

Who is he? he wanted to scream at her. Is he so much better than me? Will he love you the way I wanted to love you? Will he hold you up on a pedestal and worship you like the goddess I thought you were? He won't. He can't. But who is he? Who is he!

The bell rang, interrupting the desperate flow of thoughts through his mind. Although for a moment he'd been conscious of nothing but Tessa, the rush of bodies and the slamming of lockers abruptly brought him back to reality.

"I should probably go," Tessa said, clearly relieved by the

excuse offered to her. "Look, it's not like you won't be able to find a date. I mean, Jennifer said she thinks you're cute, and Mandy's boyfriend is in college, so there's no way he's going. If you want to take either of them . . ."

Brien folded his arms, and her eyes widened as he frowned scornfully at her. He glared at her as if his eyes could throw flames, and she was a figure made of wax. She melted in stature, becoming petty and small, shrinking even as he looked at her.

"I never, ever, wanted to go with anyone but you, Tessa," he told her with bitter truthfulness, before turning his back on her.

Fortunately for his dignity, he managed to stalk angrily around the corner before the full impact of her careless rejection struck him and he went weak at the knees. As he leaned on a nearby locker for support, he could feel a titanic wave of hatred and shame and self-loathing crashing over him, smashing to bits the delicate castle of self-confidence that he had built within him over the last two weeks.

As the last shards of his ego were flayed painfully away, some-thing stirred inside him, a whisper that was new to him and yet ancient. *You will have your day*, it promised. *Soon, your day will come.* Without realizing it, he caressed his new tattoo. The mark of the beast was hot to the touch, and its red eyes gleamed with anticipation.

Considering that it was a Monday, Jami was surprised at how swiftly the first four hours of the day flew past. Clearly word about her upcoming date with Jason had gotten around, because she had quickly become the subject of more than a few whis-pered conversations and admiring looks. That was all right, but she couldn't believe some of the nasty comments some of the would-be popular girls were making about her, right in front of her.

Actually, right behind her would be a more accurate way of putting it. Just after social studies had ended, she'd been cutting through the library on her way to the lunchroom, and happened to see Stephanie Redman and Brittany Williams talking near the water fountain. She smiled and said hello, and they both said a friendly hello back to her, but just as she passed them, she clearly heard Stephanie say:

"I heard she puts out even faster than her sister. That's why the seniors like them so much."

Jami could feel the blood rushing to her face. She wanted to turn around and confront Stephanie, but she couldn't think of anything to say, and she didn't want to risk the chance of losing her temper completely and socking the lying skank. She hadn't done anything at the party, anything at all! She glared furiously at her feet, refusing to look up at anyone, knowing that half of the faces smiling at her would be sticking their knives into her as soon as her back was turned. It was so unfair!

She reached the cafeteria and slammed her books down onto the table where Rachel and Angie were sitting. The loud report made both of them jump, and almost brought a smile to her face. Almost, but not quite.

"Do you know what they're saying about me? Do you?"

"What's the matter, sweetie?" Rachel was sympathetic, but Angie only grinned like a madwoman.

"So did you hear the one about you and Holli getting it on with Jason, Paul, and Jeff Elstrom? That's my favorite so far. Although the story about you messing around with Jim Thorne in his car right in front of Jason's house was pretty good, too."

"Doesn't anyone at this stupid school have anything better to do than talk about me?" Jami wailed. "I didn't do anything! Jason asked me to the prom and I didn't even kiss him!"

"I'll bet that's 'cos he didn't try," Angie guessed shrewdly, with a wicked smile on her face.

Jami made a face at her as Rachel patted her hand softly. "They're just jealous of you, girlfriend. It's bad enough that Holli attracts so much attention, but everybody's used to that. I remember when Brian Falardeau kept trying to kiss her on the playground in first grade. Remember him? He was always chasing her, and we'd all run away screaming, and then he'd catch her and kiss her on the top of the head."

"What a weirdo," Angie commented. "Who are you talking about? He must have left before I got here."

"His family moved to Colorado or something in seventh grade." Jami shrugged. "Okay, Rache, you say they're all used to Holli, so she's all right. But I'm not?"

"Oh, come on, Jami. It's not like Holli always has it easy. She just takes it better than you, because she knows you can't be popular without everybody hating you. It's just no big deal for her, it's like, she'd probably think something was wrong if people like Sue Morelli and Bridget Richter started being nice all of a sudden. I mean, really nice, not that fakey-fake stuff."

"Not to mention Stephanie Redman," Jami muttered bitterly.

"Steph? Oh, who cares what she says anyway." Angie waved her hand dismissively. "What-ever. The thing is, I heard some really interesting stuff about this one girl who was seen disappearing with the only sophomore at the party. . . ."

Rachel blushed, and Jami couldn't help laughing as Angie grinned at her with an unrepentantly mischievous smile.

"Can I get a whoo-whoo?" Angie sang happily as Rachel made a halfhearted attempt to slide under the table. "Can I get a wha-wha? So tell us what happened, lovergirl."

"Nothing!"

Rachel was insistent in her protests, but Jami didn't believe her for a second. Her face was far too red, and she was way too reluctant to look directly at either of them for her to be telling the truth. Angie clearly didn't believe her, either, and she cross-examined their embarrassed friend as relentlessly as if they were in a courtroom and she was the prosecuting attorney.

"You might as well admit it, Rachel. Christopher already told Jami everything, didn't he, Jami?"

"Actually, he didn't say anything."

Jami was tempted to go along with the gag, but it was more important to reassure her friend that her brother wasn't a kiss-and-teller.

"Could you be more useless, Jami?" Angie complained. "So you're saying the two of you had to leave a perfectly good party for forty-five minutes, just because you felt the need for a little stroll? I don't think so, babe! Just tell us, was there some quality smooching going on or did he chicken out?"

"I'm not telling you anything," Rachel said defiantly. "So there!"

Angie's eyebrows rose as her friend's face turned an even deeper shade of red, and she glanced at Jami.

"Well, what do you know?" She laughed, but not cruelly. "Oh, come on, you have to at least tell us if he's a good kisser or not."

"Actually, you don't," Jami said, shuddering theatrically and putting her hands over her ears. Secretly, though, she was pleased that Rachel had hit it off so well with her brother. They were such a cute couple.

"All right, all right." Angie waved off her inquisition. "Anyhow, Rachel, you know I'll get it out of you sooner or later. But guess what? Remember that girl in the white? The one we saw with Jim Schumacher? I found out who she is! Molly Nelson knows her and she's a senior, her name's Theresa, no wait, it's something else. Tessa, that's it. Tessa Fenchurch! She's the one who was getting all hot and heavy with Schumacher at the party!"

"I liked her dress," Jami said. "Too bad she doesn't have better taste in guys."

"That wasn't a dress, ditz, it was a skirt. Didn't you see her belly was pierced? Boy, are you having a blonde day or what?"

The three of them were too intent on their conversation to notice as the heavyset boy eating lunch by himself at the next table turned as white as a ghost. Jami did hear a loud scraping noise as a nearby chair was pushed away from a table, but she paid it no attention. A moment later she had completely forgotten it, just one of the ten thousand unremarkable little things that happen all around you every day.

Brien was in pain. Actual physical pain. He wanted to throw up, burst into tears, collapse screaming on the ground, and kill himself, all at the same time. Filling his mind like a bad horror movie was the indelible image of Tessa, with her velvety, sweet-smelling, barely tanned skin, locked in a passionate embrace with Jim Schumacher. Jim freaking Schumacher! How could she go for him, of all people, the slag! Was it his pointless sadism that she particularly got off on? Or was it the cruel look of bestial emptiness that filled his eyes like a junkyard dog looking for something to lift its leg on?

Even Kent Petersen would have been more tolerable. Petersen was an evil bully, a nasty, twisted jerk with a Napoleon complex, and in a just universe, there was no question that he would have been struck dead by lightning years ago. But at least Petersen was his own guy, whereas Schumacher was just a follower, a mindless loser who couldn't even think up his own acts of senseless malice. The thought that Tessa had chosen someone like Jim Schumacher over him was unbearable.

The worst thing was that it wasn't even as if Tessa didn't know that he wanted her. For three years he'd waited for the right moment to let her know his secret, and then she'd trashed everything in thirty seconds. He could still see how she wouldn't meet his eyes, how her feet were fidgeting the whole time they were talking there in front of her locker. And telling him to take her fat friend—the girl would look like an overstuffed hippopotamus in a prom dress! All this just so she'd be free to get busy with Jim in a hotel room somewhere! The mental picture of the two of them together filled him with agony.

It was at that moment that Brien decided he didn't want to live anymore. If this was all that life had to offer, nothing but humiliation, failure, rejection, and pain, then he didn't want any part of it. No matter what lay waiting on the other side, it had to be better than this. It certainly couldn't get any worse. Exactly how and when he'd bag the whole stinking mess, he didn't know. But he didn't want to be here anymore, of that he was sure. Not in school, and not on this planet. Shaken to the very core of his being, Brien made his way through the parking lot to his car with all the shambling grace of a recently unearthed zombie. Another visit to the good doctor was in order.

CHAPTER 24

CTRL-ALT-DELETE

EVERYTHING YOU SAY TO ME
TAKES ME ONE STEP CLOSER TO THE EDGE
AND I'M ABOUT TO BREAK
  —Linkin Park ("One Step Closer")

The *rat-tat-tat* of machine-gun fire was the first thing he heard as he approached Derek's door. There was another burst, then a moment's pause broken only by the garish pounding of Skinny Puppy, followed by a massive explosion.

"Take that, punk monkey!" he heard Derek shrieking. "Who's your daddy! Who's your freaking daddy!"

"Hey!"

Brien had to shout. Derek had his massive speakers cranked up to full volume, with the sound effects set up to overpower the crunching evil that was emanating from the CD player.

Derek hit Escape to pause the game, and the sudden onrush of relative quiet made Brien feel like he'd lost his balance. It was like having a rug jerked out from under your feet.

"Whoa, dude, don't bring me down like that," he said, extending his arms and pretending to stagger. He'd come to his senses on the way over, and although he was still determined to hit the bong hard enough to approach exit velocity, he didn't seriously feel like steering his car into the path of a semi anymore. The thought had crossed his mind, of course, but now the idea of steering it right over Jim Schumacher held even more appeal.

250

"What are you doing here?" Derek asked, turning around carefully. "It's not even sixth hour."

Brien winced at the sight of his friend's face. The whole right side was puffy and swollen, and his right eye was a grotesque mass of purple and black tissue. It was barely open; there was just the merest slit through which he could see. There was a thin crusting of blood around one of his nostrils, and his lips were split in several places. He looked as if he'd been playing football without wearing a helmet.

"How're the ribs?"

Derek shrugged. "They don't hurt so bad now. The doctor taped them, but I took it off yesterday. That sticky stuff started to get pretty gnarly when I took a shower and got it wet. It's mainly my nose that hurts. Dr. McElfresh straightened it out okay, but man, it hurt like a mother when he popped it back in place. Everything looks bad now, but he says I'll heal all right. No scars."

"That's good."

Derek squinted with his one good eye. "You still haven't answered my question, dude. What's going on?"

When Brien told him, it was Derek's turn to wince.

"She did *what!* Schumacher? You kidding me?"

"I wish I was." Brien shook his head miserably. "She told me herself. Man, I don't know who I want to kill more—him or her."

Derek shook his head. "Him, dude, definitely him. That jerk's pretty close to the top of my list. Hey, you don't think he knew, do you, and did it on purpose?"

"Knew what?"

"About you and Tessa?"

Brien stepped back, unable to imagine how purely evil you would have to be just to think up such a petty, malicious act. Was it possible that Shumacher had somehow heard about him taking Tessa to the prom and had decided to step in for the sheer sadistic pleasure of screwing things up? No, he decided finally, Schumacher was a disgusting lowlife, several steps down on the evolutionary ladder, but he was no doubt innocent by reason of stupidity. Kent Petersen might possibly be capable of coming up with such a monstrous plan, but if he had, there was no way he would have foregone the pleasure of seducing Tessa himself.

After all, if the dumb slag was willing to put out for Schumacher, then she'd do it for anybody. Except him, of course, darn the luck! No, the more he thought about it, the more he realized that the whole idiotic thing was simply accidental. It was the worst freaking luck in the history of human existence, of course, but it was still nothing but bad luck.

"Here, this'll make you feel better."

Derek had gotten out of his chair and was offering it to him.

"What is it?" Brien asked as he sat down in front of the computer. "Looks like a new Quake mod . . . hey, it's that one of the school you were working on!"

Derek rubbed his hands together. With a mad grin on his beaten, discolored face, he looked like some kind of crazed fiend just escaped from one of Dante's lower circles.

"This morning I scanned in some of the pictures from last year's yearbook. Check out who you're blowing away!"

Brien studied the frozen screen. It was hard to recognize at first, as the bitmap stretched over the 3-D model distorted the image somewhat, but as he looked closer, he saw that the figure in the foreground which was about to be eviscerated by the flechette blast from Derek's upraised needlegun had the face of Kent Petersen.

"All right!" he said, raising a fist. "Please tell me you've got Schumacher in there, too."

"Go down to the cafeteria," his friend instructed him. "There's a kitchen crawling with them. This is your mission should you choose to accept it. Show no mercy!"

Brien nodded, hit the Escape key, and at the same time, held down the left mouse button. Amidst the cacaphony of battle exploding from the speakers, there was a whirring burst of high tech gunfire punctuated by a howling scream. Brien glanced up at his friend and nodded with satisfaction as on the screen in front of him, the image of Kent Petersen was blown to pixels in a magnificent eruption of simulated blood and gore.

It was two hours, three beers, and several repackings of the giant water pipe that had been christened Big Ben, when Derek, staring at the ceiling with an unlit joint in his hand, announced his intentions.

"This is all bogus. I tell you what. You know how they say all morals are relative? That's bogus, too. There is still one moral imperative, and that's to kill yourself as soon as you wake up to what this whole bogus world is really like."

"Totally," Brien agreed absently. He was too stoned, and too mired in his pain and self-pity, to pay much attention to Derek's philosophic babbling.

"No, I'm serious. Once you realize that there isn't any point to things, then what is the purpose in putting up with it anymore? Only an idiot keeps banging his head against a wall once he discovers there's a wall in front of him. I mean, even a freaking lab rat is smarter than that!"

"So go around the stupid wall."

"Oh, okay," Derek said sarcastically. "You do that. You think that'll work? Look at you, have you ever made it around the wall in four stinking years of high school? No, because it's never going to happen. Four years, and all you get for your trouble is seeing a jerk like Jim Schumacher score with the girl of your dreams?"

Brien was quiet for a moment.

"That was low," he said finally.

"No, it's called reality!" insisted Derek. "You've got to face it, that's what I'm saying. You know the wall is there now, so you've got no excuse. You either bang your head on it, or you just say, forget it, I quit!"

"I suppose there is some truth to that," Brien admitted. "It's kind of a death before dishonor thing, just giving them all the finger, once and for all."

"Right. It's not like anyone really cares what happens to us anyhow."

Brien laughed shortly. That was sure true.

With the back of his hand, Derek felt around the floor for a lighter. Brien spotted one on the desk next to the keyboard, flicked it, and leaned back in the chair. Derek lit the joint, inhaled deeply, and handed it over to Brien.

"So you ever think about how you'd control-alt-delete?" he asked, pretending to hit three imaginary keys in the air.

"Sure," Brien admitted. "I always thought that the best way to do it would be to go down to the river right before sunset, with a bag of really good weed, a liter of vodka, and some downers. I'd smoke the whole bag, then, right when the sun has dropped just below the horizon, you know, when all the light in the sky just fades into night all of a sudden and the stars start to come out, I'd pop the pills and drain the whole bottle in one smooth chug. It'd just be one sweet, smooth ride into sleep. . . ."

Brien made a sliding gesture with his left hand, and closed his eyes.

"No, that's too selfish," Derek judged critically. "Me, I say those two guys out in Denver did it right. That was freaking heroic, what they did. Remember how all the jocks were being really nice to everybody for about a week? That was because they were terrified that somebody was going to go atomic and do the same thing to them here! They got over it, of course, but the thing is, if all the losers and rejects could just get organized and pull a Columbine, like, every two weeks, this world would be a better place. For everybody, I mean, even the beautiful people might start learning to behave like human beings for a change!"

"The ones who weren't dead, you mean," said Brien dryly.

"Well, yeah."

Brien sat there, the stoned languor making his arms and legs feel three times heavier than normal, thinking about the unthinkable. Derek did have a good point. If you were going to die anyhow, why not do it in a way that would leave the world a better place after you were gone? There certainly wasn't any question that there were certain people whose absence would significantly improve the planet.

"You're not really serious about this, are you?"

Brien was shocked to discover that the ghastly idea filled him with excitement, for a reason that he couldn't, and didn't want to, understand. To his surprise, he found he could easily picture the two of them stalking through the familiar, cursed halls like a pair of ruthless Grim Reapers, mercilessly blowing away every single person who'd ever laughed at them, made fun of them, or messed with them in any way. The thought of his tormentors' panicked faces, screaming in fear and horror, was delicious, and he found himself trembling with a tingling anticipation. It would be like that Quake mod, only in real 3-D, brought to life with a true 360 degrees of freedom. But they couldn't ever do it, there was no way. Was there?

"I'm stone-cold serious," Derek said coolly.

Brien saw that beneath his bruises, his friend's face was an iron mask of pitiless determination. There was a purity to his hate; it was clean, almost holy. His expression was the sort of thing you could imagine on an Aztec priest, or on a medieval noble crying havoc over a fallen city. Brien shivered, but whether it was with pleasure or with fear, he couldn't say.

CHAPTER 25

CONFRONTATION

BUT THE WICKED WILL PERISH:
THE LORD'S ENEMIES WILL BE LIKE THE BEAUTY OF THE FIELDS,
THEY WILL VANISH—VANISH LIKE SMOKE.

—Psalms 37:20

Jami shared an uneasy look with Holli as they sat quietly together at the breakfast table. They'd gotten up early, but her plate was already clean and she sipped slowly at her half-empty glass of orange juice as Holli toyed with the remnants of her scrambled eggs. The moment of truth was nearing, and they were just waiting for Christopher to appear in order to present a united front against Mom and Dad. The three of them had organized their strategy last night, and although Jami was pretty sure her parents would cave before their united lobby, there was just no way to be certain of that.

"Hey." Christopher yawned as he shambled down the stairs. "Any coffee left, Dad?"

Dad glanced up from his twice-folded newspaper and arched his eyebrows.

"Well, this is a pleasant surprise. It's not often we get the whole clan assembled this early in the morning."

Jami saw Holli glance at her, and nodded her approval. Might as well get it over with.

"Actually, Daddy, there was something we wanted to talk to you and Mom about."

"Uh-oh," Dad said, with mock suspicion. But he was smiling,

and he laid his newspaper on the floor next to his chair. "What is it, sunshine?"

"Well . . ." Jami started to say, but Christopher broke in on her.

"Paul and Jason asked them to the prom, that's what."

"The prom?" Mom quickly joined them. "Jami, someone asked you, too?"

"Yeah, can you believe it?" Christopher said quickly, stifling Jami's instinctive protest with a warning glare.

"Of course I can believe it," said Dad, who reached out to squeeze Jami's hand. "Who wouldn't want to take a beautiful girl like her?"

"Mom, please, we really want to go," begged Holli. "This will be my only chance to go with Paul, he's graduating this year, you know that."

"I don't know." Mom shook her head disapprovingly. "Paul is a very nice young man, of course. But who is this other boy? Is he an older boy, too?"

"Mom, it's the prom," Jami said, unable to contain her exasperation. "Of course Jason's older than me. Only juniors and seniors can go, underclassmen can't unless somebody who's older takes them."

"So he is a senior?" Mom didn't look pleased.

"It's just a school dance, really, Elaine. Senior, junior, who can tell these days?"

Jami shot Daddy a grateful look, but Mom was frowning. She was still wearing her red bathrobe, and Jami wondered if dropping this particular bomb on her first thing in the morning had been such a good idea.

"It's very different now than when we were in high school, Ronald. Don't you remember that article in *The Pioneer Press* last year? There's an awful lot of drinking that goes on, and apparently some of the parents are even renting hotel rooms for their children! Now, you can't tell me that there's nothing going on in those rooms that shouldn't be, and maybe I do sound like my mother when I say this, but that's just wrong!"

She looked surprised when Holli agreed with her.

"You're totally right, Mom, which is why we're not asking if we can stay out all night or anything like that. We're not asking to go to any of the parties or whatever, we just want to go to the prom, and then have the guys bring us back here. We can be back by, like two, if you want."

"That's three hours past your curfew," Dad pointed out. "Seems pretty late to me."

"But, Daddy!" Holli joined Jami in an urgent chorus of protest.

"I think the dance runs from nine until midnight, Dad," Christopher said. "I don't think it's fair to make them run out before it ends, do you?"

"We haven't even decided if they're going at all!" Mom interjected. "Everybody just hold their horses. Holli, Jami, you haven't even told us when it is, or where it's being held!"

"It's at the Hilton," Jami told them. "On May first."

"How very apropos," Daddy said, chuckling to himself. "Some things never change. I don't suppose there will be a Maypole?"

"What's that, Ronald?" Mom asked, looking suspiciously at Daddy.

"Oh, never mind, never mind. It's just that one can hardly ignore the fertility-rite aspects of . . . seriously, though, I don't see any reason why the girls shouldn't go. We decided it was okay for them to start dating once they were in high school, and as far as I'm concerned, this is just another date. It's probably safer than most, actually, since it will be chaperoned."

"That is true." Mom nodded. "Perhaps we could even volunteer to—"

"Mom!"

"No!" Holli's protest wasn't as quite as quick as Jami's, but it was louder. "You wouldn't do that to us, would you?"

Christopher was laughing. "I don't think that's the best idea, Mom. Did you want your parents at your prom?"

Daddy chuckled. "No, I don't believe she did, did you, Elaine?"

"Things were different then," Mom insisted, but there was a

faint smile on her face, and Jami could tell she was weakening. "All right, since no one else seems to have any objections, I have to admit that I don't see why the two of you shouldn't go, either. But I want to meet this Jason character first, Jami, and both of you are to be back here by twelve-thirty sharp."

"One-thirty," Jami countered immediately. "Come on, Mom. . . ."

"One o'clock, then," Daddy said, and there was the ring of finality in his voice.

Jami knew better than to argue any further, although she was wondering how she was supposed to tell Jason that he had to make such an early night of it. Daddy was always the easier one, but once he took a stand, that was that.

"Thanks, Mom, thanks, Daddy," Holli was saying. "We won't get in any trouble, I promise."

"And we'll be back on time, too," Jami added. "We really appreciate it."

But both of them were apprehensive when Mom unexpectedly raised a warning finger.

"There's just one more thing," she said, raising an eyebrow in a way that usually entailed an incoming lecture.

"Yeah?" asked Jami uneasily. Shoot! And everything was going so well, too. . . .

"When are we going shopping? For your dresses?" Mom's eyes sparkled mischievously. She obviously knew they'd been thinking down entirely different lines. Well, Jami thought, you could say a lot of things about Mom, but you couldn't say she was a bad loser.

"All right!" Jami cheered happily as Holli got up from the table and gave Mom an enthusiastic hug.

"Hey, what about me?" Daddy said, and Jami was quick to get up and hug him, too. "That's better."

Christopher got up, too, and checked his watch. "Sorry to put the kye-bosh on this very touching display of family unity, but unless you guys want to be late, we've got to get a move on. We're supposed to meet the gang in ten minutes."

* * *

The gang was just the Bible study, actually, the kids in the Bible study who were morning people or at least capable of getting to school fifteen minutes early. They met at the flagpole every other week, where they would join hands to form a prayer circle and pray briefly for their school, its students and teachers. Mr. Maples had suggested the idea to the group not long after the night Christopher had stormed out of the Bible study; Meet You At The Flagpole was a movement of sorts that had apparently started a few years ago, although Jami had never heard of it before.

She'd felt kind of funny the first time they'd gotten together, but once they'd met a few times, she got used to it and now she even felt good about what they were doing. Everybody needed prayer, and maybe it wasn't doing much, but it was something. It was a start. Some of the other kids made fun of them from time to time, but it wasn't a big deal, and one or two kids she didn't know had even come up to her and asked her to pray for them.

And why not? Even if you didn't believe in God, or in the lordship of his Son, how could it possibly hurt? School was tough enough, and most people could use all the help they could get. Holli had some last-minute homework to finish before first hour, so she headed off for the library while Jami and Christopher went to meet the others.

"Hey!" Asako waved to them as they approached the little gathering. "Glad you could make it."

"Of course." Jami smiled as the Asian girl warmly hugged her brother. Asako never had been the sort to hold a grudge, and she and Christopher had gotten to be pals over the last few weeks.

"How you doing?" Blaine, the big linebacker, put an arm around her shoulder.

"I'm doing good." She grinned up at him. "Our parents said we could go to prom."

Blaine nodded. He'd been dating Karin Eliason, the football cheerleader, for years. "That's awesome. Jason's a good guy. I don't know him as well as Paul, but he's all right. I think he was in one of my history classes last year."

"All right, everybody!" Scott, the other senior guy, was kind of their unofficial leader. He grabbed the hands of the two kids nearest to him and lifted them up in the air. "Let's get started. Does anybody have any specific prayer needs?"

No one did, apparently, so Scott led them in a simple prayer, asking God to bless Mounds Park, to give all of them a productive day of learning, and to help them behave as good, Christian role models for the nonbelievers they would encounter that day. He was just about to close, when a nearby voice intruded on their devotions.

"What do you think you're doing, you retarded losers! Your freaking god is dead! He's dead, and he's not coming back!"

Startled, Jami raised her head and looked for the source of the profane interruption. It was a tall boy, and though his eyes were hidden by black sunglasses, his face was twisted with rage. He wore a T-shirt decorated with an ugly cartoon figure, and Jami found herself inadvertently curling her lip at the vulgar image. She felt threatened, even though he was as skinny as a scarecrow and she was standing safely between Blaine and her brother. His white arms were scrawny, and they protruded from his T-shirt like fleshless bones.

"Amen," Scott said firmly, before turning deliberately toward the intruder. "Can I help you?" he asked politely.

The boy responded by hurling obscenity after obscenity at him, some of which was almost remarkably inventive. "I hate you freaking Jesus freaks!" he concluded savagely, apparently concerned that someone might have somehow managed to miss the point.

Jami was impressed by Scott's forbearance; he didn't retort in kind, but only nodded his head.

"I'm sorry to hear that," he said, stepping to one side as he dodged a wad of spit directed at him by the boy.

Blaine's grip was growing tighter, and it was starting to hurt, but Jami held on to his hand, worried that he might hit the boy.

That would certainly set a great example! She couldn't blame him, though. She certainly wouldn't mind smacking him one right in his foul mouth herself.

"Losers, you're all losers!" The boy made rock concert devil-signs with both his hands and stuck out his tongue. He was practically frothing at the mouth, Jami saw to her disgust. "Satan rules!"

That was too much for Blaine, and he pulled his hand away from Jami as he started to step forward. Fortunately, the first bell rang, and psycho-boy abruptly whirled around and ran off toward the safety of the school.

"Let him go, Blaine," Scott ordered his friend, and reluctantly the football player nodded.

"I will, I will. But, man, was he asking for one or what?"

"Yeah, he was!" Jami agreed enthusiastically. But when she glanced over at her brother, expecting support, she was surprised to see that he was sitting on the flagpole's concrete base, staring off in the direction of the tall boy's retreat with a thoughtful look on his face.

"Christopher? Are you all right?"

He looked up at her as if she'd surprised him.

"Yeah, of course, I'm fine." He scratched at his head. "I just thought that was kind of weird, didn't you?"

Jami nodded. Yeah, it was weird, and she sort of wished that Blaine had gone ahead and punched out the scrawny creep. But that would be wrong, and she was glad he hadn't. She shrugged and helped Christopher up from his seat. Maybe the guy had just forgotten to take his Ritalin today or something. She had more important things to think about now. For instance, was Jason going to be at his locker before second hour? She hoped so. She didn't want to have to wait until lunchtime to see him again.

CHAPTER 26

STEAL, KILL, AND DESTROY

I FEEL FORCES ALL AROUND ME
COME ON RAISE YOUR HEAD
THOSE WHO HIDE BEHIND THE SHADOWS
LIVE WITH ALL THAT'S DEAD
                    —Creed ("Bullets")

It was as if he were living in two different worlds, Brien thought as he slowly turned over a twelve-gauge shotgun shell in his fingers. It was kind of like *The Matrix*, where the day-to-day world in which he got up, ate breakfast, went to school, and then came back again didn't even exist, it was just a superficial layer that only served to hide the real world. The real world was a more exciting place, where important things happened, and where decisions of life and death were being made all the time.

Sometimes it was hard to keep up the pretense, and he felt like he would burst open at any second if he couldn't tell the terrible secret he was keeping tucked away inside him, and at other times the whole situation struck him as just being horribly funny. He walked through the halls during the day lost in a mystic haze, like a god of death hiding in disguise in the very midst of his unknowing worshippers. Perhaps that one would die, struck down by his fateful hand of vengeance, or maybe that one. They didn't know, they were such idiots that they had no clue at all that their doom was already walking among them.

At such moments he could barely repress the urge to giggle

with delight, and he found that he could barely force himself to wait the two long weeks until the first. One day, as he found himself caught within the post-sixth hour press on the stairs leading up from the cafeteria, he suddenly realized that this was exactly what undeath must feel like for the vampire. To experience the fullness of that which sets you apart, that which makes you superior to the crowd, is to become something fundamentally different from what you were before. He and Derek had somehow become the legendary daystalkers, those who did not have to hunt by night. The Nottambuli were just a silly, juvenile conception of that which lay at the true heart of all power, the ability to destroy.

"You ready?" Derek asked him. "Remember, if we get caught, you've got to stick to the whole high-school-prank thing. Since the end of the year's coming up, they'll find it easy to buy the idea that this is just some kind of stupid dare."

"Yep." Brien nodded. "I still think I should be the one driving, though. You can run faster than I can."

His friend shook his head. "If it comes down to running, we're screwed, dude. The whole point is to not get noticed. Besides, I've got a record and you don't, so if we did get busted, they'd be more likely to believe that kind of story from you."

That was true. Derek had also changed since they'd made their momentous decision. He was quieter and more thoughtful now, almost to the point of being philosophical. He reminded Brien of a character in a Herman Hesse novel, an initiate filled with a calm tranquility that was tangibly serene. Derek didn't even smoke much anymore; it was as if he was beyond the drugs now, as if getting high would actually be bringing him down, or something like that. Brien shrugged. It was hard to articulate, exactly, except that his friend was starting more and more to resemble a holy man, or a priest.

Only a holy man was unlikely to come up with a plan for taking down twenty-six people. That was their target number, which would set a new record and was also two times thirteen, which was Derek's lucky number. In truth, Brien didn't really care, as long as Jim Schumacher was among the twenty-six.

They had decided on shotguns as their weapons of choice, not only because of the obvious Doom-based coolness factor, but also because a careful Internet study of various mass shootings had revealed that unless they could get their hands on a fifty-caliber heavy machine gun, there simply weren't very many weapons that were all that effective for their purposes. Brien had argued for assault rifles, until Derek pointed out that in one California incident, the shooter had fired about a million rounds with an AK-47, and still had only managed to kill five people.

"How lame is that? There's not much point in wasting your time with something that can't even knock down a kindergartner. All that high-speed military junk is useless, it just makes tiny holes, it doesn't have any stopping power."

"Well, if assault weapons are so lame, how come everybody's always trying to ban them?"

"Beats me. But check it out. This police report says that even though they had nine millimeters at Columbine, most of the fatalities were caused by the shotguns. That's why twelve-gauge is the ticket."

"What about explosives? Should we make some pipe bombs?"

"No, I thought it was weak how Klebold and Harris got themselves caught on tape shooting at that stupid propane tank, trying to make it explode. They looked like amateurs, you know? Pipe bombs are good for noise, but not much else. Unless we're going to go car bomb, which means a ton of ammonium nitrate, a lot more than we can afford, there's not much point. It's just a waste of time."

Derek had decided that they weren't going to buy the guns, either. Instead, they invested in four hundred rounds of twelve-gauge, one hundred rifle slugs, and four bandoliers that made them look like a pair of freaking Mexican revolutionaries. In a moment of sheer brilliance, Derek had come up with what would be their ultimate rebel gesture; they would steal the guns from the police.

"Just think about it." He smiled evilly. "They start the whole tracing procedure, and what do they come up with? It's their own freaking guns! I just wish I could see the face on the guy who figures it out first. Can you imagine the press conference? 'Uh, ladies and gentlemen, we have learned that the alleged killers obtained their weapons from, uh, us.' Awesome!"

Now that the moment of truth was nearly upon them, though, Brien was starting to wish they'd just settled for buying a pair of cheap Winchesters at a sporting goods store. He'd checked out a place in Roseville, and for a few hundred bucks he could have spared himself this whole nerve-racking business. Derek was driving, and they were only two blocks away from the Taco Bell, where several cops usually got together for lunch. They were as prepared as they could be, having made two previous dry runs and with license plates they'd stolen the night before screwed onto the Honda in the place of its real plates, but Brien still didn't feel ready.

"Gloves?" Derek asked as his eyes scanned the vicinity. The Burger King parking lot was three-quarters full with the lunch rush. A lot of business types came to this particular string of fast-food restaurants, which were almost always crowded at this time of day.

"Check," Brien said, pulling his Minnesota Wild baseball cap down low over his shades and pushing his glasses back. He tugged on the transparent plastic gloves he had obtained from the school nurse. He didn't want to leave any fingerprints, but he couldn't be seen wearing a pair of black leather gloves this close to summer, either. "Ready to rock."

His pulse throbbed uncomfortably, and his throat felt tight as Derek smoothly turned through the last corner. The familiar white stucco of the Taco Bell building came into view, and as they'd expected, there were three police cars parked toward the far end of the lot, which was only half full. Brien felt a sudden rush of adrenaline, as if he was at the top of a roller-coaster just about to plunge down a steep track.

"I love it when a plan comes together," he muttered grimly.

"Thank you, Hannibal," Derek said, his eyes never ceasing their constant movement. "Okay, see that green Audi? I'll slow down and you get out as soon as we're behind it. Use that and the rusty Oldsmobile as cover. Stay low, keep moving, and if the driver's-side door is locked, don't screw around, just move on to the next car. The whole thing should take fifteen seconds, tops. I'll loop around toward the building, then pick you up just behind the third car."

"Right." Brien nodded, taking a deep breath. Here goes. . . .

The car slowed to a crawl.

"Go, go, go!" Derek urged harshly, but Brien had already shouldered his door open.

Ooof! He slipped and fell to his hands and knees, and the rough sting of gravel on his left palm told him that his glove had torn open. Doggone it! What now? Keep moving, you clumsy dork, he cursed himself as he crawled rapidly toward the first car.

Click-click-click. The door handle moved impotently upward.

No! It was locked. He rose to a crouch and ran as fast as he could around the nose of the white vehicle. Ignoring Derek's instructions, he tried the passenger side, but that door, too, was locked. Stinking conscientious pig! What, did he think some idiot was going to try to steal his stupid car or something?

He spun around, still in his crouch, and tried the next car. It was also locked. Cursing furiously, Brien quickly rushed around to the third and last police car and tugged at the door handle. There was a loud *chunk,* and the sudden lack of resistance indicated that the door was unlocked. Yeah, baby! But when he pulled the heavy door open, he looked around the car's interior and saw nothing resembling a weapon of any kind, much less a shotgun.

Brien swore like a madman as he eased himself backward and shut the door as quietly as possible. He didn't think anyone had seen him, but in an exposed area like the parking lot, it was impossible to be sure. As the low roar of an engine approaching from somewhere to his right grew louder, Brien fell to one knee and pretended to be tying a loose shoelace. It was probably

Derek, but he couldn't see from where he was kneeling behind the police car.

Rubber crunched on gravel as the onrushing car swung in behind him and quickly braked. It was Derek after all.

"It's cool!" his friend shouted through the window, looking past him toward the restaurant. "Nobody's seen anything."

Brien nodded and stood up slowly, dusting himself off and casually strolling the short distance that separated him from the vehicle. Just pretend nothing's going on, and no one will pay any attention, he reminded himself, although the three seconds it took him to reach the Honda seemed to take about five minutes. He opened the door without hurrying and slid into the passenger seat.

"We got jack," he announced as Derek turned the car around deliberately and headed toward the frontage road. "The third one was open, but it didn't have anything in it."

Derek nodded. "Plan B, I guess. Dang!" He pounded the gearshift. "That was going to be so cool!"

"We could always try again, like, next week," Brien suggested.

"Too risky. We've already been through here three times, and eventually someone's going to notice something's up." He blew his long bangs out of his eyes. "No, let's just buy the stupid guns."

"Okay, but remember, there's a waiting period, so we'll have to do it soon."

"You'll have to do it," Derek told him. "I've got a record now, so I don't think I'll pass the background check."

"Then we've got a problem," Brien answered slowly.

Derek looked surprised. "Why?" he wanted to know. "We can get the money."

"That's not the problem," Brien replied. "You forgot something, dude. I'm not eighteen."

Brien wasn't surprised that following their disappointing failure to acquire the required armaments at Taco Bell, Derek opted not to go to school that afternoon. But Brien didn't have anything better to do, so after dropping Derek off at his house and sharing a consolation post-op tokage, he found himself pulling into the school parking lot. What am I doing here? he wondered. Even if we can't get our act together, it's not like I need to be here.

There was a certain clarity to this presuicidal state that he found absolutely invigorating. Even if he chickened out in the end and didn't decide to off himself or anyone else, he had realized that he didn't have to accept life on its own terms any longer. He made the rules now, nobody else, and if he chose to continue to play the game for another month or another year, that was just fine. The important thing was that he didn't have to play anymore; everything was optional. It was a liberating feeling.

There seemed to be somewhat of a commotion in the halls, and small groups of students were clustered here and there, gossiping intensely about something. Brien craned his neck around, but didn't see anything out of the ordinary.

He grabbed the arm of a passing freshman. "What's going on?"

"Huh?" the kid said, alarmed. When Brien repeated his question, the smaller boy relaxed and pushed back his glasses, which had been coming perilously close to falling off the end of his nose. "Dude, there was, like, this total locker search and a whole bunch of juniors got busted for having weed and stuff. There's about fifty cops here, and they've got dogs and everything. I hear they're doing Senior Hall next."

"Thanks." Brien patted the boy on the shoulder, and couldn't help grinning when he saw the kid looking around to see if anyone had noticed him talking to a senior. It was a good thing he'd never been dumb enough to keep his stash in his locker; anyone who thought that the school would hesitate to search its own property was an idiot who deserved to get busted.

A thought struck him. If there were so many cops here, then where were all their cars? He walked quickly up the stairs and past the gym to the back parking lot, and saw there were eight or nine police cars parked in the reserved spots and up on the sidewalks. Fifty cops? Yeah, sure, whatever. More like ten.

He knew it was probably a bad idea, but he couldn't keep him-self from pushing the door open, and checking out the cars. Much to his surprise, several policemen had left the doors to their vehicles ajar, and one car even had its trunk lid sticking up in the air. To his utter delight, he could see something made of dark blue metal lying partially exposed under a coil of rope and a pair of black-and-yellow jumper cables. Wrapping his sleeve over his left hand, he carefully pushed aside the rope, and saw that the metal belonged to two automatic shotguns. Twelve-gauge, from the looks of it.

Jackpot! But how was he going to get the guns out of there and over to his car without anyone noticing? He wasn't wearing a trenchcoat, and it wasn't like he could pretend he was out hunt-ing pheasants or something. A bag, that was what he needed. A big long bag, like the kind they used for skis. Or hockey!

He punched his fist into his palm excitedly. This was a sign! It had to be! He rushed back into the school building and hurled himself headlong down the basement stairs leading to the boys' locker room. It was a dark and dingy place, its brick walls slathered with crudely applied paint that had long ago faded from its original bright red to an ominous shade that looked more like blood. The old equipment cage was on the right, with rust flaking from the poles that supported the thin metal mesh. It was supposed to be locked, but it never was, since the ancient sports gear stored there was too old and worn out to be of inter-est to anyone. Since you could lock it from the inside, couples often used it to mash during the day. Not that he ever had, of course.

Brien frantically dug his way through ancient shoulder pads, decaying reversible T-shirts, and football jerseys that had been out of style since the eighties. Much to his amusement, he also found several empty condom wrappers. Finally he uncovered something that wasn't exactly what he was looking for, but would manage to serve his purpose. It was an old canvas football bag, designed to hold shoes, shoulder pads, and helmets. It was worn, and there were holes in it, but the main thing was that it was long enough to hold the guns.

He stretched it out. Mounds Park Indians? Geez, how old was this thing? On the side of the bag was a large logo of an Indian chief wearing a full headdress of feathers. Nice mascot. No wonder they chucked it, he thought disapprovingly, clutching the heavy canvas in both hands as he raced back up the stairs, breathing hard.

Pshew! Brien had to pause at the top of the stairs to catch his breath. Sweat was starting to trickle down from his forehead, and he wiped it away irritably with an untucked shirttail. This was hard work! He froze as he heard a group of people coming down the stairs that led to the freshmen lockers, but fortunately it wasn't, as he feared, policemen escorting the busted juniors out to the waiting squad cars, it was only a gaggle of excited underclassmen who'd been excused early from class.

That meant the bell was going to ring soon. He had to work fast, before the parking lot was covered with gawking students. He rushed outside and strode straight for the car with the open trunk. If anyone stops you, then you just saw the weapons lying out in the open and you thought they might be dangerous, he told himself. You're taking them to the principal's office.

It was hard to avoid looking surreptitiously around, or otherwise acting guilty, but Brien managed to keep a purposeful demeanor about himself as he reached into the trunk and gently slid the two weapons out from under the jumper cables, then rolled the unzipped opening around each gun, one at a time. At every moment he was half-expecting an unfriendly hand to clap him on the shoulder and demand to know what he was doing, but he gritted his jaw nonetheless and zipped the bag shut, then carefully withdrew it from the police car. It only took a moment to readjust the rope and cables to cover the absence of the guns, and then he was walking away from the car, hoping desperately that no one had noticed what he had just done.

Every fiber of his being screamed to take the shortest route to his car by walking around the outside of the building, but he forced himself to stick to his cover story. As long as he was in the building, he could claim to be heading for the principal's office, or, if he was caught heading in the wrong direction, he could say he was looking for the policemen. Not the best excuse, maybe, but since he wasn't known as a troublemaker, it would probably hold up well enough. Plausible deniability.

The bell rang, seemingly right in his ears, and he jumped. Calm down, he urged himself. Come on, dude, relax! One more corner, here it is, the last stretch and then you're clear, just take it one step at a time. The guns were heavier than he'd expected, though, and his right arm was getting sore. As he rounded the corner, he stopped for a moment and slid the straps of the bag over his left shoulder. There, that was better!

But as the once-empty front hallway was filled with the crush of bodies in a matter of seconds, Brien found he had to hurriedly press himself against to the left wall in order to avoid smacking into someone with the guns. Dumb, dumb, dumb! He should have stuck to the other side, he realized, as he now had no choice but to go against the flow of traffic. I sure hope they're not loaded; he winced as the thought crossed his mind for the first time.

But as a girl who might have been Tessa walked past him on the other side of the hall, Brien made the mistake of looking over his shoulder. He couldn't quite see if it was actually her or not through the blur of moving heads that were blocking his view—uff da! The straps on his shoulder tightened painfully as the guns swung across his body and he was forced to a sudden and unexpected halt.

"Ow!" a young girl cried, doubling over and clutching at her stomach. "Watch where you're going, dillweed! You just hit me!"

"Are you all right, Ang?" A cute blonde girl bent over her friend with a concerned look on her face.

It was two of the frosh he'd overheard talking about Tessa and Jim Schumacher, Brien realized as he tried to step back and swing the bag as far behind his body as he could. A third girl, another blonde who must have been the other one's sister judging by their similar features, jabbed her finger at him.

"You know, you could at least say you're sorry!"

Um, sure, whatever.

"Yeah, I'm really sorry," Brien mumbled. He just wanted to get out of there now. "I didn't see you."

"What the heck do you have in there anyhow," spat the first girl, glaring at him. She was a thin-nosed girl with dishwater blonde hair and a shrill voice. "Lead pipes? You almost knocked the wind out of me!"

"I have to go," Brien muttered as he pushed his way past the girls, who were still staring angrily at him.

"What an idiot," he heard the first girl declaring loudly as he hurried toward the front door. "You'd think he'd know not to walk on the wrong side of the hall!"

Too bad you're just a freshman, Brien thought murderously as he walked down the cement spiral staircase and made his way through the crowded student lot. His nervousness was gone, replaced by clean, cold anger. As he reached his car, he dug into his baggy shorts for his keys, unlocked the trunk of his Taurus, then, with relief, lay the heavy bag into the felt-lined interior. Otherwise, girlfriend, you'd be on the list!

CHAPTER 27

THE POWER OF TWO

CONSIDER HOW THE LILIES GROW. THEY DO NOT LABOR OR SPIN. YET I TELL YOU, NOT EVEN SOLOMON IN ALL HIS SPLENDOR WAS DRESSED LIKE ONE OF THESE. IF THAT IS HOW GOD CLOTHES THE GRASS OF THE FIELD, WHICH IS HERE TODAY, AND TOMORROW IS THROWN INTO THE FIRE, HOW MUCH MORE WILL HE CLOTHE YOU, O YOU OF LITTLE FAITH!

—Luke 12:27–28

Jami sat in front of the television, restlessly clicking the remote without even seeing what was on the channels that she was flashing by so quickly. *Click*-MTV-*click*-ESPN-*click*-CNN-*click*-somebody cooking something-*click*-talk-show nutcases . . . hmm, My Lover Has a Secret . . . like I care . . . *click*-VH1 . . .

"The amazing thing is that we actually think we're busy, most of the time," her brother commented as he sat down on the arm on the other side of the couch.

"Go away," she told him, not taking her eyes off the screen. *Click-click-click.* "And Mom says don't sit there, it's bad for the couch. Anyhow, I'm bored."

Christopher shifted his weight and slid down onto the cushions next to her. "Yeah, me, too. Everything seems to slow down in the afternoon. I guess that's why they invented cartoons."

"True," she agreed absently. Jason, who'd qualified for state, was still running track or she'd be with him now. "So, how's things with Rachel?"

"Pretty good, I think." He bobbed his head. "She's really nice, I mean, she's easy to talk to. And she's so pretty. . . . She didn't say anything about me, did she?"

Jami eyed him out of the corner of her eye. He was trying to act all indifferent, but now he was leaning toward her and paying close attention. She couldn't resist the temptation.

"Well, she says you're nice, but you're a lousy kisser."

Christopher blanched. "She didn't say that, did she?"

"Yeah, she was really disappointed, since she thought you were cute and all. She said it was kind of like being licked by one of those, oh, I can't remember what they're called. The big dogs . . . Weimer-something, maybe? No, Rottweiler, that was it. She said it was like being licked by a Rottweiler."

Her brother suddenly looked like Angie had when that fat senior hit her in the stomach the other day. His expression was a wonderful cross between total shock and utter horror.

"I . . . I didn't know. . . . It was that bad? I had no idea!"

Jami tried to keep a straight face. She fought off the urge to smile as long as she could, until finally she couldn't contain herself any longer. "Ha!" She leaped from the couch, pointing accusingly at him. "You did kiss her, then! I knew it!"

"Huh?" Christopher's expression looked exactly like the way she imagined a fish's would look at the very moment it bites into a nice, juicy worm and discovers a sharp, not-so-nice hook. For the smart one in the family, he was pretty slow sometimes. "But you said she—"

"She didn't say anything, you dork! Even Angie couldn't get anything out of her. Except I can tell she likes you a lot, because she keeps blushing whenever we ask about you. Holli and I, we had a bet about whether you kissed her or not on Saturday, and I just won, baby!"

"Well, good for you," her brother said sourly. "Wait, you said she likes me?"

"Of course she does." Jami rolled her eyes. When it came to girls, *Clueless* was still his middle name. She batted her eyelashes, then pretended to look shyly away from him. "What do you think that is? That's all she ever does around you!"

"Cool," Christopher said, and his eyes grew distant. "Very cool. . . . You know, I wonder if she'd like Warhammer? I was going to play with Don this weekend, so maybe—"

Jami shook her head. You could clean them up, polish them off, and shine a spotlight on them, but it didn't do any good. Once a geek, always a geek.

"How about taking her to a movie instead," she suggested kindly as she tried to keep from laughing. It was hysterical, though, to imagine Rachel's face if Christopher had dragged her along to one of his little game thingies. "I think she might like that better."

"You think so?"

Her idiot brother actually sounded surprised.

"Ah, yes, I do. I really, really, do."

"All right, then." Christopher nodded, apparently understanding. "I wanted to see that new Van Damme movie anyhow."

Jami buried her head in her hands. She didn't know if she should laugh or cry. Poor Rachel. She was doomed.

The phone rang, and Jami leaped off the couch to answer it. "Hello?"

"Hi, is Jami there?"

Jami grinned happily, and waved off Christopher, then pointed to herself. It was Jason.

"Yes, this is she. And this is?"

"It's Jason."

"Jason . . . Jason who?"

There was a deliciously uncomfortable moment of silence.

"Um, Jason Case. I'm taking you to the prom, I think?"

Jami laughed. "I'm just teasing, Jase! I knew it was you. I recognized your voice right away. Is practice over already?"

"Oh, good." Jason sounded relieved, and a little confused. He didn't have any sisters, Jami remembered. Well, that just made things that much easier. "Yeah, we just did some stretching today. Say, I was thinking, if you weren't doing anything, maybe we could go and check out some tuxedos or whatever. You know, for the prom?"

"What a great idea!" Jami made a face and flipped off Christopher, who was silently mimicking her gestures and responses. She was really looking forward to seeing Jason outside of school, and was impressed by his thoughtfulness, too. This would be her first prom, of course, but she'd heard horror stories about guys showing up at the door with pink tie-and-cummerbund combos, plaid tuxedos, or worst of all, the Abe Lincoln thing with the goofy top hat. "I'd love to help you look around. I don't have my dress yet, but at least we can pick out a basic style or something."

"All right," Jason told her. "Pick you up in ten minutes?"

"Sure . . . but actually, why don't you make it fifteen," Jami suggested.

"Fifteen, then. See you in a little bit."

"Bye," Jami told him, and she hung up. "I am out of here!" she announced as she ran for the stairs. It wasn't a date or anything like that, but she wanted to look good all the same. "If Mom calls, tell her I'll be at the mall with Jason, but I'll be back in time for dinner."

"Okay," Christopher called after her. "But if you're going to Rosedale, you'll probably see her. That's where she took Holli."

And here Jami had thought that Holli was out with Paul. Apparently not. Well, in that case, she should probably call Mom on her cell and let her know what was up. She didn't want Jason to get off on the wrong foot with her parents. Jami reached the bathroom, stopped, and stared into the mirror. Fifteen minutes. And no Holli, either. She pursed her lips and pulled open Holli's drawer. It was a cosmetic jungle, full of traps and pitfalls for the unwary. She tapped her fingernails thoughtfully against the ceramic counter, then settled for withdrawing only a single tube of pink lipstick and a navy eyeliner pencil. In makeup, as in war, discretion was usually the better part of valor.

Melusine was finding it difficult not to laugh at Boghorael this evening, as the increasingly confident demon strutted his way through the hordes of other spirits following their charges around the busy shopping center. He was a quick student, she'd learned to her delight, but he'd also started to develop an attitude and although he was always carefully subservient around her, almost to the point of toadying, she knew she would have to keep her eye on him in the future. Clearly, he was one of those spirits who found power very much to his liking.

It wasn't that being the sole assistant to a Temptress who was far from being in the favor of the local prince was anything to brag about, but it was a huge step up for a nonentity stuck to a tree and saddled with a name like Bogspittle. How awful it must be, reflected Melusine, to be trapped against your will into the smallness of the physical world, to be unable to take a part, however small, in the great war against the Enemy.

Thus, she empathized, and found to hard to hold her protégé's annoying new habits against him. Nevertheless, it was her job to keep them from getting out of hand, before his conceit angered the wrong spirit and he was crushed like young Philip at Crècy. She sighed, thinking longingly of the days when her own power had flowered like a white rose of destruction, its frosty beauty and dangerous perfume spreading massive devastation wherever it touched.

"Pay attention, now," she ordered him. "And forget those Succubi, you don't want to mess with them."

The would-be Tempter shot one last, wistful glance at a pair of tall, exotic demonesses who were pretending not to notice that he'd been staring hungrily at them. They were nakedly gorgeous, with pure silver skin and featherless black wings, long white hair that fell past their waists, and eerie blue eyes that lacked whites or pupils. They were also dangerous and wouldn't hesitate to prey upon any lesser demon foolish enough to fall into their claws.

"Remember what you did to Pandaema?" she asked him, arching an eyebrow.

"Yes, of course," he said, sounding curious. "Why?"

She indicated the two Succubi who were walking away from them now, apparently having lost interest.

"Because that's what they'll do to you, if you give them the chance."

"Oh. . . . I didn't know!"

Melusine was tempted to slap him, but she refrained. Fabulous, she thought. He's got that lovely bark covering his brain as well as his skin. Was just a small spark of intelligence too much to ask for?

"Let's try to concentrate, shall we? Here's the situation. A Great One has something in the works, and we're supposed to make sure that these two don't interfere with it." She pointed toward the two Lewis twins, who were chatting enthusiastically with their mother and the tall, attractive boy who had been creeping so often into Jami's thoughts lately. "Now, take Jami, here. She's your responsibility, right? So what do you suggest that we should do next, how should we try to influence her?"

Boghorael thought hard. He wrinkled his green brows and concentrated intensely on his new charge. He glanced back and forth between the girl and the tall boy, and his thoughts were so apparent that Melusine could almost see the gears turning in his head.

"It's got something to do with the school, right?" he asked, looking for confirmation.

"Yes," she answered patiently.

"Okay, well, I think that one night we should encourage her to go off alone with him. And see, what we'll do before that is we'll work with his Tempter and petition the Prince for one of the Pazzidrim to possess him. And then, when he's alone with her and is fully possessed, he kills her!"

Melusine stared at him incredulously. "Doesn't that seem a bit heavy-handed?"

"Do you think so?"

Patience, Melusine reminded herself, is not a virtue for a demoness, it is an absolute necessity. At times like this she almost wished she'd left the dryad in his cursed tree.

"There's at least three problems with that approach, Boghorael, my dear. First, she belongs to the Enemy, which means she has a Guardian who isn't going to sit by and watch that happen. Second, there are limits to the power of even the greatest Pazzidri. The boy's soul may be unguarded, but it hasn't been corrupted to the point where he can be influenced to such an extent.

Perhaps if his mind was torn apart by a very powerful influence, but if you look at his habits, you can see he's not likely to expose himself to the drugs or esoteric practices required for that."

"I thought you said three things?" Boghorael said, sulking, and Melusine could see that he was more than a little offended. What a touchy little brute he'd turned out to be!

"I did," she admitted. "The third thing is that Prince Bloodwinter would never grant you your petition. The Enemy protects his own, and even watches over those close to them. Just the presence of a Pazzidri might bring a cohort of archangels down upon us, and the Prince knows that. Subtlety, and then isolation, that is the better way. You must never strike to kill until you have first separated your target from her protectors—you understand?"

"All right, I get it, I get it," Boghorael said ruefully, and he flashed her a charmingly self-deprecating smile that didn't fool her in the least. "The first thing is to be subtle. I'll remember next time. I promise."

Melusine doubted that, but she didn't see any point in starting an argument. At least he was paying some attention to the task at hand, unlike his predecessor. Subtlety was the key, although it was unsatisfying at times. She was pleased that she'd managed to keep the Lewis children so fully occupied with their day-to-day lives at school, but even so, she hadn't seen them falling away from the Enemy's influence in any significant detail, either. Christopher's and Jami's increased interest in the opposite sex offered some promise, naturally, but that was inevitable no matter what she did.

She shrugged. Sometimes all you could do was watch and try to take advantage of the inevitable opportunities when they came your way. Mortals were only human after all, and if you could count on anything, it was that they'd eventually do something stupidly self-destructive. Tempting was a serious responsibility, but sometimes you almost felt redundant.

"Great Mistress, Great Mistress!"

The high-pitched voice of a nearby imp attracted her attention, and she turned around. She saw that the misshapen little minion was addressing her, and she was surprised to note that he was wearing the purple-and-white livery of Prince Bloodwinter's court.

"Great Mistress, the Prince has commanded that I escort you to his Presence. With your permission, we will leave at once."

Melusine nodded coolly, but her mind was frantically investigating the possibilities. She hadn't done anything out of the ordinary lately . . . unless, of course, Bloodwinter had discovered Balazel's true identity. She shivered, and hoped that Kaym had thought to keep her knowledge of his presence here in the Cities to himself.

"Can I come, too?" asked Boghorael in a low voice. Despite her warning, he was preening conspicuously for the Succubi, acting as if the summons had included him as well. Her slow-witted protégé didn't realize that there was every chance that this summoning meant nothing but trouble.

"Fine." Melusine sighed. "If you want."

She glanced back at the Lewis girls and shrugged. She probably should have seen if she could tempt them into buying dresses that were more seductive than they might have otherwise have selected, but considering the present circumstances, she'd have to put her trust in teenage hormones. Which, when you thought about it, was really all that any decent Temptress should ever need. Very well. She nodded her acquiescence to the Prince's imp, spread her wings, and leaped into the air.

CHAPTER 28

THE COURT OF WINTER

FOR I KNOW HOW MANY ARE YOUR OFFENSES AND HOW GREAT YOUR SINS. YOU OPPRESS THE RIGHTEOUS AND TAKE BRIBES AND YOU DEPRIVE THE POOR OF JUSTICE IN THE COURTS. THEREFORE THE PRUDENT MAN KEEPS QUIET IN SUCH TIMES, FOR THE TIMES ARE EVIL.

—Amos 5:12–13

Prince Bloodwinter's court was held, unsurprisingly, at the locus of three major lines of power. The building was a towering mass of white marble that was planted atop a hill like a monumental tomb. Occult symbols were engraved in many places, and Melusine noted approvingly that it had obviously been constructed by masons adept in the dark art of mystic magnification. There was even a pagan statue of a gilded Apollyon driving four snorting steeds mounted at the base of the grand cupola, such a blatant symbol of Luceric authority that even Melusine was shocked at its boldness.

The great building radiated a strong sense of dominion and power, and it was not hard to see where all of this awesome power had been derived. Most of the surrounding city was lifeless and dead, its inherent vitality drained to the dregs by the Prince, and even the great river which flowed past the city only a few miles away seemed to lose a small part of its mighty vigor simply due to its proximity.

The guards at the entrance were unlovely, grim-faced spirits of warding. They were giant, muscular figures with dead eyes, ashy gray skin marked with sigilistic patterns, and they wore crimson cloaks which obscured the fact that they had no wings. As Melusine approached, followed by Boghorael and the messenger imp, two of them stepped forward, and short blades of black fire appeared, seemingly out of nowhere, in their hands.

"What is your business here, Temptress?" the one on her right asked.

Melusine gestured toward the imp.

"It is my fortune to have been summoned by the Prince of the Cities."

The spirit to her left reached past her, and sank his fingers into the messenger imp's temple. His lifeless eyes did not even blink as the imp let out an agonized screech. A moment later he released the imp, who collapsed, sobbing, on the ground, ignored by everyone.

"She speaks the truth." The guard bowed to her, very slightly, and moved aside. "You may enter," he told her. "And the other with you."

Melusine was glad to put the cruel red-cloaked ones behind her as she passed through the great wooden doors that opened directly into the great hall. Bloodwinter's court, like his guards, was dark and dreary, built on a scale that made the observer feel small, and Melusine wondered if this was a reflection of the harsh winters here in this northern land, or if it was simply a side effect of the Prince's dour personality. Most likely a bit of both, she decided.

The hall was not crowded; there were at most thirty or forty spirits present, including one who wore a white cloak rimmed with gold, and a circlet of purple flames which indicated his status as the Prince of the Cities. Prince Bloodwinter was speaking quietly with a small group of archdemons at the far end of the hall. I've seen him before, Melusine realized to her surprise, as she recognized his tall, regal form. He was at the Lewis house last winter! But what was he doing there?

As she drew closer, she saw that one of the archdemons involved in the conversation, which was really more of an intense argument, wasn't even an archdemon. It was Kaym, in his guise as Balazel, and he was occupied with defending himself against the angry accusations of the others.

"No, Vulkan, I'm not going to create any new problems for you. No, it won't make the Divine target this city. Don't you remember that Crusade you were so worked up about? What was it, three years ago?"

"Four," the archdemon snapped back. "Stop trying to change the point, Balazel. You came into this city without permission, killed three of the Enemy's preachers, openly attacked one of their churches, and now you're telling us to sit back and let you try to massacre an entire school? Your Highness, how can you even listen to this lunatic? The Enemy will drop ten legions on our heads if you allow him to go on like this!"

Kaym-Balazel shrugged. "Ten legions, what is that? There were fifty thousand Divine on a Heavenly rampage here during that Crusade a few years back, and what did they steal from you, something like thirty thousand souls? And can you even detect any signs of that today, only four years later? No, I didn't think so. So there you go, what is there to fear?"

The dark-faced archdemon folded his arms, refusing to concede the point despite Kaym's reasoning, but Prince Bloodwinter raised his hand, cutting off any objections. He nodded to Melusine, and although his cold, hawk-like eyes betrayed no signs of friendliness, his voice was smoothly courteous as he drew the others' attention toward her.

"Since this difference of opinion will most likely last until our friends with the notorious equestrian enthusiasm mount their steeds and usher in the unveiled reign of our Great Prince, I see no reason to continue the discussion. Ar-Balazel, I believe this is the temptress whose presence you requested?"

The Prince's politeness did not put Melusine at her ease. He hid it well, but underneath that icy expression was a volcanic temper just waiting to explode. *Kaym, what are you doing to me, you arrogant charlatan?*

She eyed him, hoping for a hint, but he gave her no clues.

"I am here, Great Lords, as you have commanded."

"As the Prince of these Cities has commanded," Kaym corrected her. "I have no authority here, it was merely my suggestion that you should join us, a suggestion which the Prince kindly accepted in his wisdom."

Melusine kept a straight face, but it was hard. Since when was Kaym a world-class brown-noser? No, he wasn't kissing up after all, Melusine decided, he was allowing Prince Bloodwinter save face before his court. Bloodwinter must already know that it was Kaym, but he could not dare to let every ambitious archdemon in the Cities know that he wasn't calling the shots in his own town.

The Prince didn't respond, except to nod slightly, and his face did not change expression. No doubt he was throwing up inside.

"Melusine," Kaym addressed her. "You alone have been permitted to know I am not the archdemon Balazel. I ask you now to reveal my true identity, that these loyal servants of the Great Prince we all serve may know me as I am."

He was laying it on pretty heavily, Melusine thought, but she obediently reached out with her mind and stripped the obscuring image of the large, ugly archdemon away from Kaym's slim and handsome figure. More than one monstrous jaw dropped open with dismay and surprise as the gathered archdemons took in the fallen angel's haughty black eyes, his silver robes, and above all, his starry cape which, impossibly, seemed to contain within its dark folds all the vast depth of the night sky. Although the Fallen warriors towered over him, he radiated so much power that he stood out like a god among men, or, perhaps more accurately, a hero amidst monsters. He stood there calmly, unafraid and overtly aware of his mastery.

Vulkan was the first to acknowledge Kaym, and the other demons were quick to follow. Prince Bloodwinter, as was his right, was the last. The Prince of the Cities was reluctantly beginning to kneel before the revealed demonlord when Melusine heard Boghorael speaking unexpectedly.

"I know you!" he hissed. "I remember you!"

Melusine turned around, alarmed by the hate-filled tone in her protégé's voice. The apprentice tempter's green eyes were blazing with anger, and glowed with an intensity that took her by surprise. Boghorael's malevolent stare was directed at Kaym, and Melusine felt her stomach turning over when she saw that the former dryad's incautious words had caught the fallen angel's attention.

"You remember me?" Kaym smiled contemptuously, and then, as he looked closer, he raised his haughty eyebrows, not in disdain, but in surprise. "Don't tell me. . . ."

Melusine stuck out her arm as Boghorael moved forward, but the demon shoved her roughly aside and pushed past her to confront Kaym, face to face.

"How long has it been?" he imperiously demanded of the fallen angel. "Tell me how long it has been? I remember nothing since you sent me on that fool's mission, you lying, back-stabbing traitor!"

Vulkan reacted before Kaym could respond, grabbing Boghorael's throat in one great, black-nailed hand and effortlessly lifting him off his feet. Melusine winced as her protégé scrabbled frantically at the archdemon's scaled fist, but Vulkan's powerful grip was unbreakable, much stronger than iron. What was the matter with Boggie? He couldn't hope to stand up to an archdemon, much less a Great Lord like Kaym!

"Respect!" Vulkan roared, his yellowed teeth only inches from Boghorael's bulging eyes. "You will fear your masters!"

"My, my," Melusine heard the Prince comment idly to no one in particular. "When did he become such a stickler for propriety?"

"Put him down, Vulkan." Kaym's smile was even broader now. "No, I mean it, put him down!"

The big archdemon was reluctant to obey the fallen angel's order, but after one last, vicious squeeze of his hand that almost caused Boghorael's eyes to pop out of his head, he released his victim. Boghorael immediately dropped to the marble floor, and only an outstretched hand kept him from sprawling completely flat on the floor.

"Where did you pick up this one," Kaym asked, and Melusine started when she realized he was talking to her.

"Him? Oh, well, he was a petty spirit of the woods, he possessed a tree not far from where my mortal charge lives. I needed help with the other mortals after you . . . after Shaeloba was destroyed, and Pandaema was worse than useless. He seemed promising, and so I allowed him to take Pandaema's place."

"Possessed a tree?" Kaym was staring at Boghorael, looking vastly amused despite the other's furious glare. "That is about all you are suited to rule, you know."

Prince Bloodwinter raised his hand. He seemed to realize that there was something happening here about which he knew nothing, and he obviously wanted to change the situation into one that was under his control.

"Under whose authority did you replace this Pandaema, Melusine? Why was I not informed?"

Melusine might have laughed had she not been surrounded by powerful spirits on every side of her, any of whom could easily blast her beyond the Beyond with the merest word or gesture. Not informed? In fifty years as a Temptress in these Cities, she'd never once so much as spoken to their Prince. She tried to imagine his reaction if she'd come to him with tales of her fellow temptresses' malfeasance—he'd probably have blasted her simply for wasting his time.

"She did it under my authority," Kaym lied, obviously uninterested in the minor politics. "But, my dear Prince, perhaps it might interest you to know that this disrespectful little tree demon was once known as the Lord of the Sword."

Kaym smiled cruelly and nodded to Boghorael.

"Did you enjoy the last six millennia, old friend? That's how long it has been, in answer to your question. Quite a few things have changed, naturally, but our great crusade continues. Some would even have it that we are winning, but then again, that is a thought which has been wrongly thought before."

Melusine stared at her protégé, who had eyes only for Kaym. Now it made sense, both his dawning arrogance and his strangely fearless hatred for Kaym. Her little Boggie was truly Jehuel, the princely angel who had once been Prince Lucere's viceroy and Leviathan's keeper. She shivered, remembering how strong Jehuel had been that day, effortlessly hurling her across that vast, fiery chamber during his desperate struggle with Phaoton fought leagues below the surface of Rahab, that accursed, shattered planet. And to think that he had shrunken so, that whatever lay Beyond had reduced him to the puny state in which she'd first encountered him, without memory and almost without mind!

"Give me my power back and meet me in the Circle." Boghorael's voice was low, and his emerald eyes never left Kaym's as he pleaded for an opportunity to seek his vengeance. "Would you deny me the chance to repay you this debt?"

"How the mighty have fallen." Kaym sighed theatrically. "Of course I will, and I'll deny you more than that if you happen to stick your leafy head anywhere it doesn't belong over the next several days. Unless you want to return to the dark fire of Sinyata, obey your mistress and stay out of my way!"

The fallen angel's tone was cold and inflexible, so that even Boghorael recognized the futility of protest. He bowed, meekly enough, and retreated, although Melusine saw that his shoulders were still shaking with repressed rage.

Kaym nodded, apparently satisfied that his old enemy had backed down. Melusine watched as he spread his hands and turned to address Prince Bloodwinter and the archdemons, most of whom had backed well away from him. They had not achieved their positions of power by carelessly rushing into dangerous situations, and the appearance here of a Great Lord of the Fallen, combined with the return of a legendary name from the Beyond, promised nothing but peril. The Lord of the Sword! What could his presence, even in this much-reduced form, possibly mean? Was he an omen of good fortune, or was he an untimely reminder of how their triumphs were so often rendered empty by the Enemy?

The shattered gates of Heaven turned into impenetrable opalescent walls. The criminal's grave transformed into the empty tomb. The weapon treacherously turning on its wielder.

Melusine shook her head. There had been so many disappointments. But then, she reminded herself, there had been successes, too. Surely in this particular instant, events had progressed too far to be stopped. The chosen ones were prepared and ready, and the ravenous spirits were in their place, awaiting only the proper time.

"So, my Lords, Prince Bloodwinter," Kaym addressed the spirits of the court. "I stand revealed before you, a Knight of the Golden Sefiroth and the Master of the Star Wheel. Is there any who wish to dispute my right to take the actions I have taken? If there are, I command you to speak now."

He glanced significantly at Boghorael. The wretched spirit was compelling testimony, and the sight of what had befallen this former member of the Sarim intimidated the great demons of the court into silence; it was obvious that not a single one would dare to openly disagree.

Prince Bloodwinter readjusted his flaming coronet, as if to remind himself that he still ruled in this place, and raised his hand to convey a blessing on Kaym. Melusine had no doubt that the proud prince would far rather be laying a curse on the noble fallen angel, but he nevertheless managed to feign a convincing air of dignity as he declaimed before his court.

"Go then, Lord Chemosh, with the full approval of this assembly, in the company of angels and archangels, to serve our great cause and our Great Prince."

"Hail, Chemosh!" the assembled spirits cried, some with less enthusiasm than others.

Kaym pretended not to notice, though, and with an elegant flourish of his starry cape, he made a stately exit. Melusine was quick to follow him, although Boghorael was slow to react, and she was forced to grab his arm and drag him along with her. But she could feel that his feeble spirit was still engorged with malice, and as she hurried him quickly through the large wooden doors and out into the night, Melusine had the uneasy feeling that another fiasco might be looming.

* * *

Jami sat on her bed, dubiously eyeing her prom dress, which was hanging down over the front of her closet door. She had been ecstatic when Mom agreed to buy it for her last week, but now, looking at it under the unflattering lights of her bedroom only one night before she was to wear it, she wondered if maybe she'd made the wrong choice after all. There were so many dresses out there; how in the world did anyone possibly expect you to pick the right one?

Hers was a colorful dress, mostly pale pink, but shot through with various blue and yellow pastels. It was one hundred percent silk, and it felt so very wonderful next to her skin, almost as if she were wearing nothing at all. The silk was so delicate that it was almost translucent, and Holli had warned her, once safely out of range of Mom's hearing, of course, that she'd have to be careful about standing where she'd be backlit. Then again, that was part of the appeal, of course, and she smiled mischievously as she thought about the look on Jason's face when he saw her in this dress. And if he really behaved himself, he just might catch a glimpse of her standing accidentally-on-purpose in front of a spotlight.

Her dress was beautiful, of that there was no doubt. Considering what it had cost, it had better be. But it wasn't really a prom dress; at least, it wasn't what Jami had always pictured when she'd thought about the prom when she was younger. For her, the whole idea had always conjured up images of big poofy dresses, with bows and chiffon and all those silly things, crinkly satin dresses with crisp folds that hinted at magical things from the past like cotillions and handsome southern men with slicked-back hair and cigarette lighters.

Of course, she lived in Minnesota, the guys wore their hair too short to slick it back, smoking was bad for you, and she wasn't exactly sure what a cotillion was. Some kind of ball, she supposed. The thing was, her dress, for all that it was pretty and sexy and cool, lacked magic. That was what was wrong with it. It had no romance.

Her door opened, and Holli stuck her head inside.

"What's the matter?" her twin asked, closing the door behind her. "Thinking about Jason?"

"No, it's my dress."

"What's wrong with it?" Holli looked genuinely surprised. She'd been delighted when Jami had decided upon the pink silk. "You don't like it now?"

"It has no magic," Jami said sadly. "It's nice, but it's just a dress."

Holli nodded sympathetically. She understood, of course, although her dress was even simpler than Jami's, just a plain red spaghetti-strap gown with clean lines and an understated elegance.

"Sometimes, growing up is a drag," she said with a shrug. "It would be fun to go there wearing one of those gorgeous old-fashioned *Gone With the Wind*-style dresses, but then everyone would think you were some kind of fashion victim and they'd never let you hear the end of it."

"Or your grandmother dressed you," Jami agreed wryly. "I guess it just seems like we always do things because we have to, not because we want to, you know what I mean?"

"Welcome to the real world." Holli made a face, and then she smiled curiously. "So, what's up with Jason? Are you excited about him? Is there anything I should know about?"

"Um, no," Jami said pointedly. "And I should be asking you that. You guys had the music up pretty loud in there last time Paul was over."

Holli's blue eyes grew distant and dreamy. She smiled happily.

"He's so nice, and his lips are so soft. . . . I didn't expect that from him, somehow. He's so, like, big and tall, you know, around everybody. But inside, he's really very sweet, and very gentle."

Jami sat up and folded her arms disapprovingly. She'd been a little bit nervous about Holli's relationship with Paul for some time now, and although she wasn't feeling jealous anymore, she was concerned that her sister might be letting things go farther than they should.

"You're not, I mean, you don't . . . you haven't—"

"No!" Holli protested, shocked by her insinuation. "I mean, that's none of your business, but still . . . of course not!"

Jami raised her hands. "Sorry," she apologized. "But you don't tell me about Paul all that much. Well, you talk about him, but not like you used to, when you were going out with other guys. It's like, you've got this line or something, that I'm not allowed to cross. You're keeping stuff to yourself!"

"Am I?" Holli seemed genuinely surprised. "Really? I'm sorry, I had no idea I was doing that."

"It's okay." Jami bit her lower lip thoughtfully. "I guess it's just part of that growing-up stuff. But it feels funny, you know, when I don't always know what's going on with you, and I know you're too busy to know what's going on with me."

Holli's eyes misted over for a second, and she looked sad. Then she raised a finger and rushed out of the room, returning less than a minute later carrying an armload of small bottles. She dumped them haphazardly on the bed, then flopped down next to Jami with a cheerful smile on her face.

"Well, if we're stuck with growing up now, that just means we have to do more grown-up things together!" She raised a small object in her left hand, and gestured towards Jami with her right. "Give me your foot," she demanded.

"Why?" Jami asked suspiciously, as she extended one bare foot to her sister.

"We're painting our toenails—it's a very bonding activity," Holli said. "And besides, they need to be done for prom."

Jami watched, bemused, as her sister lifted a bottle and raised it toward the dress on the other end of the room, then shook her head and selected another polish. This one seemed to meet her favor.

"It is?"

"Oh, totally," Holli said, seriously as far as Jami could tell. "That's what we were doing in here on Tuesday, you know."

"Paul painted your toenails?" Jami asked incredulously. It seemed a little far-fetched to her, the star athlete dabbing away at her sister's feet with Maybelline number thirty-six.

"Oh, no," Holli said, grinning as she unscrewed the top off the second bottle and sniffed delicately at the opening. "I painted his. I told him it would be really sexy. I can't believe he fell for that one again."

Jami threw back her head and laughed, delighted at the picture in her mind of Mr. I'm-Going-to-North-Carolina-Soccer-Stud wearing toe separators.

"You didn't!"

"Wanna bet?"

They laughed together, and Jami felt a happy sense of joy filling her with a familiar warmth that she'd been missing for weeks. Maybe they had to grow up sometime, and maybe things wouldn't always be exactly the way they had been. But she was glad to know that the walls she'd imagined between her and Holli weren't really there, they were only walls of air, as momentary and insubstantial as a bad dream.

She leaned forward suddenly and hugged her sister. It was so good to be a twin, and know that no matter what, someone was always there for you.

CHAPTER 29

PLAYGROUND OF ILLUSION

THERE IS ONLY DEATH AND DANGER
IN THE SOCKETS OF MY EYES
A PLAYGROUND OF ILLUSION
NO ONE PLAYS THEY ONLY DIE
—Megadeth ("99 Ways To Die")

Crrhk-crrck! The shotgun cracked with the sound of metal sliding on metal as Brien tugged on the lever that ejected the last shell from his weapon. The Winchester automatic held six shells at a time, and he'd practiced his reloading technique to the point that he could now slip six of the bulky yellow beasties from his ammo belt and slide them into the shotgun in less than ten seconds. The practice had cost him a few skinned fingers and pinched fingertips, but so what? A warrior of the Apocalypse was beyond pain.

He felt grimly satisfied, and imagined that this was what a Viking warrior must have felt like going into his last battle. Die well, and take as many of the bastards with you as you can, that's really what it's all about. Murder, after all, was just an extroverted form of suicide. He'd read that somewhere, and it didn't sound so bad when you put it that way. He'd been an introvert for too long, way too freaking long; it was long past time for him to do the dealing for a change and share a little of the pain he'd been keeping locked inside.

"So you wanna do the tape?" Derek asked him, nodding toward his little Sony digital camera. He was wearing his rented tuxedo jacket over a KMFDM T-shirt which said, simply and appropriately, BLOOD. After some discussion, Brien had finally convinced Derek that if they were going to go out, then they should do it in serious style. Not only would the tuxedos make getting into the prom a lot easier, but aesthetically, the image was just very cool. James Bond with a twist. Trenchcoats were so 1999, what with both Columbine and *American Psycho*, so it was time for a new fashion statement.

Ladies and gentlemen, Brien imagined the VH-1 commentator commentating. *This spring, the well-dressed executioner will be wearing Pierre Cardin. Accompanied by the latest model from Winchester, our models will be looking sharp as they blow your freaking heads off!*

"Sure," he answered Derek, glancing in the mirror and running his hands through his hair. "You might want to lose the jacket now, though. Strap on the bowtie and you'd look like a doggone Chippendale."

"Y-M-C-A . . ." Derek pranced about the room and they both laughed. "Maybe that's how we should do it," he suggested as he stripped off the jacket and placed it carefully over a chair back. "You be the cop, and I'll be the construction worker."

"Nah, I'd rather be the Indian. That monster headdress is the bomb. But we'd need, what, three more people? Or is it four? I can never remember."

"Three, I think. But you know, I don't think we'd be able to talk anyone into it. Not even Rob, that chicken! Say, remember that freshman we played Vampyre with a few months ago? The one who got all flipped out over the pipe bomb? Wouldn't he just freak if he had any idea what we were up to?"

Brien snorted. "Yeah, him and like everybody else, I imagine." He gestured to the camera. "All right, so turn that thing on already. I have some very important last words to record."

Derek flipped off the lens cap with both hands and shouted an obscenity.

"I was actually hoping for something a little more, I don't know, articulate," Brien said with a grin. "But I suppose that will do for the abridged version."

He propped the shotgun up against the bed and moved over

to the camera. He unplugged one of the cables attaching it to Derek's computer and held it up. "Say, are you sure this is a good idea? If we upload this stuff too soon, somebody might see it and call the cops on us or something."

Derek sighed. "Dude, the revolution must be televised. You know what'll happen if we don't upload it. The cops will find it and sit on it for a year and by the time they get around to releasing it to the public, no one will even notice. And they'll edit it, too, you know they will. This is the only way we can be sure that our message gets out exactly the way we want it to."

"All right," Brien said, but he still didn't like it.

"It's just too bad we can't do some kind of Web cam action, you know, stream everything live to the Net while we're shooting up the place. Man, that would set the world on freaking fire! We'd be bigger than O.J.'s Bronco!"

Brien shrugged. "We wouldn't need that much stuff, just a laptop and a cellphone with an adapter, but hauling it around with us would be a major pain. Still, we might as well bring the camera along, it's small enough and there'll be plenty of memory once we dump this stuff into the PC. They'll never put out any of the good stuff, but at least we can blow the minds of a few cops, you know."

"Hey, you know what?" Derek looked delighted. "If a bootleg gets out, we could even make the next Faces of Death video!"

"Oh, good." Brien wrinkled his lip. "I don't see how you can stand that junk. It's sick!"

"It's educational," Derek insisted defensively. Brien was just handing him the video camera when there was a knock on the bedroom door.

"Guys?" It was Mrs. Wallace. "Are you hungry? I was just going to pick up some sandwiches from Panino's. Can I get you anything?"

Brien froze, but Derek stayed calm. He quickly slid his shotgun under the bed, then grabbed the one Brien had been holding and slipped it behind his back just as his mother opened the door. There were five or six shells lying around loose on the floor, as well as a shell belt which was fully loaded, but there wasn't anything either one of them could do about that now.

Brien's heart was in his mouth as he studiously tried to avoid glancing at the floor, but he needn't have worried, he realized a second later. Mrs. Wallace was as hot as ever, but she was in a hurry, and her pretty face was completely distracted.

"Hello, Brien," she said kindly, smiling rather absently at him. "Derek, if you don't mind, I'm just going to run out to the mall and get you boys some sandwiches. I've got book club tonight, and I'm running a bit late. I haven't even looked at the book we're supposed to be reading, can you believe that? Well, I suppose I can always just skim the back cover."

Derek quickly shook his head. "No, no, we're all right, Mom. Don't worry about us, we're fine. Panino's sounds pretty good, though, so maybe we'll just drive over there later."

"Oh, that would be such a big help!" his mother enthused gratefully. She leaned forward and kissed Derek on the cheek. "You have a good evening, then. Nice to see you again, Brien."

"You too, Mrs. Wallace," Brien said politely, feeling as if his fake smile had frozen on his face.

She stepped backward and closed the door, and Brien sighed. Even in her business clothes, Derek's Mom was something else. Those white blouses she wore were like half-transparent, and she filled them out all right. . . . He shook his head. Stay on target, young Jedi.

"That was too close!" Derek said, shaking his head. "I thought you were going to wet your pants!"

"I think I did. You were pretty cool, though." Brien nudged a yellow shell with his foot. "I can't believe she didn't see these."

For just a second Derek's face was wistful, as he remembered bygone times. Then he laughed, bitterly, and reached out to pick up one of the loose shells.

"I don't think she's really noticed anything I've done since I was ten years old." He picked up two more shells and began to juggle them, and the bright twirling cylinders tumbled over one another in a hypnotizing pattern. "I have a feeling everyone will be paying attention tomorrow night, though."

CHAPTER 30

AN EVENING OF DESTINY

NO DIALECTICAL ARTIFICE CAN SPIRIT AWAY THE FACT THAT MAN IS DRIVEN BY THE AIM TO ATTAIN CERTAIN ENDS. . . . WE CANNOT APPROACH OUR SUBJECT IF WE DISREGARD THE MEANING WHICH ACTING MAN ATTACHES TO THE SITUATION, I.E., THE GIVEN STATE OF AFFAIRS AND TO HIS OWN BEHAVIOR WITH REGARD TO THIS SITUATION.

—Ludwig von Mises, *Human Action* (1949)

Jami was almost wild with impatience, but she tried to keep smiling as Dad snapped what had to be the five millionth picture of the four of them. The boys, wearing identical black tuxedos with black ties, had shown up five minutes early in their rented limo, a big white Cadillac that had a CD player and a VCR in the back, but not, thank goodness, a PlayStation. Paul wore a vest and cummerbund that was the same vivid shade of red as Holli's dress, while Jason wore an off-white tie and matching vest. They both looked great, but although Jami would never have said it out loud, she was secretly of the opinion that Jason looked much more sophisticated.

And he's so cute! She snuggled a little closer into his side, and squeezed his arm. He had, as she'd gently suggested last week, slicked his dark hair back, and the tan he'd picked up during the recent sunny weather made his white teeth stand out so that he looked more like somebody going to the Oscars than a high school guy. She couldn't wait to walk into the ballroom on his arm; even though she didn't usually like it when people paid too much attention to her, tonight she sort of hoped they would.

Bzzzzt-click! She blinked as the flash went off again. Okay, that's got to be it!

"Let's get one now with Christopher and the girls," Mom suggested, pushing her brother forward. He tried to resist, but Holli was already reaching out for him.

"Great idea, Mom! Jami, get on his other side."

Grrrr.

Jami sighed, but she dutifully grabbed Christopher's left arm and tried to dredge up yet another smile. Then she jumped and had to stifle a scream as he tickled her unexpectedly.

"Hey," he said in a low voice. "You're supposed to be having fun!"

"Maybe I would, if Mom and Dad would let us get out of here!"

"Take it easy," he said behind lips that weren't moving, but were locked into a cheesy smile. "A couple more minutes and you're out of here."

"That's it!" Dad announced, and Jami wanted to cheer. She'd always hated having her picture taken, but it was even worse having to do it in front of Jason. Fortunately, Dad was finally through playing photographer, and Jason was walking toward her with a big grin on his face.

"Hey, get your arm off my date," he told Christopher in a mock-threatening manner.

"All right, all right." Christopher stepped away from her and raised his hands. "Just take good care of my baby sister."

"I'm not your baby sister!" Jami protested, but everyone ignored her.

"Yeah, yeah." Jason grinned at Christopher. "I've heard that from my parents, and your parents, too, but I don't think I have to take it from you, dude."

"Well, I had to say it, you know. I'm the big brother after all."

"I know." The two boys shook hands firmly. "Don't worry,

she's in good hands. I'll even see what I can do to keep Romeo over there under control."

Jason pointed at Paul, who was holding both of Holli's hands and laughing at something Mom was saying.

"You can't stop him, you can only hope to contain him!"

"Sport-center!" Jami cried, and both the guys cracked up. "All right, Mr. Case, let's get going or we'll be late for dinner. So are you going out with Rachel tonight, Christopher?"

"No," her brother answered as he walked her and Jason to the limo. "I'm getting together with Bob Maples and Pastor Mark. I guess we're going to do a Bible study or something."

"Whoo, don't live so fast, Big C," Paul said as he and Holli passed them, but he said it in a way that showed he didn't mean anything by it. "Seriously, have a good one, my man."

"You, too," her brother answered cheerfully. But when Jami started to follow Paul into the back of car, Christopher grabbed her hand and stopped her for a second.

"Keep your eyes open," he whispered urgently. "Pastor Mark didn't say anything, but I think he's worried. It's really a prayer meeting."

Jami glanced at Jason, who was smiling unconcernedly as he held the door for her, waiting for her to get in. What was there to be worried about? It was the prom, for Pete's sake, and she was going with a nice guy who didn't drink or expect her to put out for him. What was there to go wrong?"

"Sure," she said to humor him. "I'll do that."

But by the time the door had closed, and the driver pulled out of their driveway, Jami had forgotten Christopher's whispered warning. Holli was already snuggling up close to Paul when she looked down and saw Jason's open hand stretched out before her. She looked up, and felt something melt inside her at the sight of Jason's intense brown eyes. She took his hand, and felt a little chill of pleasure run down her spine. Tonight was going to be awesome, she thought with an excited shudder. There was nothing in the whole world that could possibly spoil it!

* * *

"Ready to rock?"

Brien nodded and checked his watch. It was half-past eight, and the first couples should have started showing up at the Hilton about twenty minutes ago. The prom officially started at eight, but they didn't want to get there too soon, because some of the self-anointed beautiful people who were at the top of their list were bound to be arriving late. They had another fifteen minutes before they needed to get a move on. It was only a ten- or fifteen-minute drive to the hotel, and then the fireworks would start at precisely nine o'clock.

"How long you think it'll take for the cops to get there?" he asked Derek. They'd gone over this again and again, but the truth was, there was just no way to tell. With any luck, the police would do something stupid like they did in Colorado, and stay outside waiting for a SWAT team. Under the cover of darkness they might have hours before going down in their final blaze of glory.

"Can't really say, but I'm thinking we'll have at least twenty minutes. The first guys won't go in right away, they'll be busy helping people get away outside."

Derek was calm, frighteningly calm, as he stood up and examined himself in the mirror. Then he reached into one of his dresser drawers and withdrew a razor blade. Not the safety kind you shaved with, but the sharp old kind you used for scraping paint off glass.

"What are you doing, man?" Brien asked him nervously.

"Putting on my war paint," Derek answered in a nonchalant voice.

Brien winced as he watched his friend close his eyes and cut a shallow circle into his forehead. It had to hurt pretty badly, but Derek didn't seem to feel a thing. Derek didn't make a sound as he added five more quick strokes, then opened his eyes and stared into the mirror with satisfaction as small trickles of blood ran down over the bridge of his nose. It was a pentagram, an unholy mark of evil protection.

"Dude!" Brien protested, unsure if he was more appalled by

the symbol, the blood, or the creepy smile on Derek's face. Derek's eyes were cold and dead, as if he wasn't all there anymore.

"Why are you looking at me like that? Can't you feel it? Don't you know that it's time to die?"

And Brien could feel something inside him, pushing him off to the side, but although it felt kind of weird it was pleasant, too, and impossible to resist. It was easier, so much easier, to relax and go with the flow. As he gave way, his empty soul seemed to fill again with hatred. His doubts and misgivings about their plan seemed to disappear as if by magic, replaced instead by a savage sense of violent purpose. He was there, and yet he wasn't there. Everything looked the same, and yet he had the strangest feeling that his vision had shifted and he was looking out of two cameras instead of his own eyes.

"Give me that," he heard himself say as his hand reached out for the dripping razor blade.

The inside of the hotel was a blur of ribbons, lights, and noise, and Jami felt exhilarated as she followed the cardboard arrows through the high-ceilinged glass lobby of the Hilton. The arrows led toward a bunch of green-and-white ribbons decorating the huge, wooden doors that opened onto Ballroom B. She found herself wishing they'd gone to the Grand March earlier, but the guys insisted it was totally hokey, so they'd skipped it. Still, the Italian restaurant where they'd had dinner was really nice, and now it was finally time for the main event. Outside the doors there was already a long line waiting for the official photographer who was set up outside in the hallway, and she was glad when neither Jason nor Paul showed any signs of wanting to get another set of pictures taken.

"Whas'sup!" shouted a pair of senior guys that she didn't recognize as they stumbled out of the ballroom, dragging their giggling girlfriends along behind them. They appeared to be pretty drunk, and Jami's guess was confirmed a second later when they got close enough for her to smell them. The shorter guy's hair was wet, and he reeked so badly of beer she wondered if he'd dumped an entire bottle over his head.

"Hey, it's Mary-Kate and Ashley," one of the girls said, pointing at her and Holli. She had a round face and was wearing a huge, puffy, peach-colored gown that made her look like a pumpkin. "Buy one, get one free!"

Jami and Holli shared a disgusted look. Whatever.

"Dudes, Jenny's got a room up in two twenty-one," the taller guy was proudly telling the guys. "Come up and party with us, ayight?"

"Yeah, right on, Tommy," Jason assured him, patting him on the back. "You go on ahead, we'll be right there . . . not," he added for Jami's benefit as they watched the two couples lurch off on their unsteady way. "Well, he's still walking and it's almost nine o'clock, so that's an improvement over last year."

Jami made a face. "You'd think they might like to remember some of this."

"You'd think." Jason squeezed her hand. "I know I do. You look . . . so beautiful tonight. You really do."

Jami blushed, and she found that she suddenly needed to avoid his embarrassing gaze. Fortunately the deejay was loudly pumping Britney Spears out of the speakers.

"Let's go dance," she suggested as her cheeks continued to burn. "I like this song!"

"All right," he agreed easily. "Hey, guys, we're going to go dance."

"We'll follow you!" Holli yelled back.

Her sister's red dress was striking amidst all the dark tuxedos, and Jami was glad to see that she looked like she was having a great time. Jami took Jason's hand and followed him through the crowd, but unfortunately, by the time they managed to push their way through everybody and reach the dance floor, the deejay had faded the song into a slow Janet Jackson number.

"Well, so much for that," Jason said, although he didn't look too disappointed. "Still want to dance?"

Jami looked up at him. He was smiling confidently, but she knew that was just an act. He'd already allowed her to see how sensitive he truly was inside. A warm feeling of happiness spilled over her, and she smiled back at him.

"I'd love to," she said, as she slipped her arm around his shoulders and pressed her cheek against his chest. They fit perfectly together, as if they'd been designed for each other. The rest of the world seemed to fade into nothingness, leaving only the two of them as she closed her eyes and let him hold her close. They swayed together, softly, slowly, to the gentle, romantic rhythm of the music.

This limo dude is annoyingly loquacious, Brien thought murderously as they rode through the night toward their final destination. He was half-tempted to open up his guitar case and give the guy a round of buckshot right in the back of the head, except the poor guy was just trying to do his job, and what else could you expect from a guy who drove a car for a living? Also, a big, blood-spattered hole in the freaking windshield just might attract a bit of unwanted attention when they pulled up at the front of the hotel.

"So no dates, huh?" the driver said, completely unaware of how close he was to death. "Just going stag, then, that's cool, nothing wrong with that."

"No," Brien agreed shortly.

"Bet there's some big parties going on upstairs, though. That's where the real action is, ya know." The driver laughed knowingly. "I used to deliver pizzas until about six months ago, see, and I tell you what, I seen some things, ya know, delivering pizzas."

Brien glanced at Derek and saw his friend was shaking with silent laughter.

"What a dork!" Derek mouthed silently.

"I imagine people will see a few things tonight," Brien told the driver.

"Yeah, I bet they will." The guy chortled.

It seemed like an eternity, but it was only twelve minutes later that they were pulling up in front of the brightly lit front of the hotel. There were a few kids from school scattered around the entrance, most of them smoking cigarettes or barely concealed joints, but for them and the big green-and-white banner over the entrance, there were no signs of a prom in progress. Brien nodded approvingly. That means everybody must be exactly where we want them. I just hope that jerk Schumacher is there.

"So, are you guys with the band, or what?" the driver asked, looking at their guitar cases as he held the door open for them.

Derek pushed a fistful of money into the guy's hand without bothering to count it.

"Do yourself a favor, and get out of here, dude," he said, almost kindly. Brien laughed as the guy stared at them, open-mouthed, apparently noticing their bloody foreheads for the first time.

"Uh, yeah, sure," the guy stammered. He didn't hesitate to get right back in the car, and the engine revved pretty hard as he pulled away from the curb, his tires squealing.

Derek turned and held out his hand, brother-style. Brien took it, and clasped it firmly.

"You were the only friend I ever had," he told Derek sincerely. "I just wanted to say thanks."

Derek smiled, but his eyes were bitter. He stared at Brien for a long moment, and then he nodded.

"I'll see you in Hell," he answered quietly. Then he turned and walked off, holding his hand to his head as if he had a headache. Brien followed at a more leisurely pace.

They'd gone over their plan so many times on Derek's PC, he could have done it in his sleep. Derek would infiltrate to the back of the ballroom, while he waited in the hallway just outside. Once Derek got things started, the panicked crowd would stampede right toward him, where his deadly ambush would take them completely by surprise. Then after the ballroom had been cleared, they'd go up and sweep the upper levels room-to-room, bringing all the private room parties to an early and unexpected end.

The police would arrive at some point, of course, and then the curtains would come down to end the show. That would be their ultimate finale, the big shoot-out with the law. Brien had no fear of dying now because he knew it would be quick and painless, just a hailstorm of lead and then the screen going red. How many times did they shoot that guy in New York, something like forty times? And he hadn't just shot up a bunch of kids, the only crime he'd committed was carrying a wallet. No, the cops would do their best to take him out fast, no doubt about that. They'd better, too . . . or he'd take them down first. There would be no surrender!

He smiled grimly as he reached the hallway, crowded with sweaty, overdressed couples and infested with all kinds of ridiculous ribbons and whatnot in the school colors. It was all so stupid! The cheesy dresses, the dorky penguin suits, what was it all for? There was nothing elegant here, it was just another night to party, more sex and beer for the pretty people.

Brien found a big, comfortable chair and pulled it to a position directly facing the large doorway. No one paid him the slightest attention as he lifted his guitar case to his lap and unlatched it. He balanced it there with his right hand inside the case, gripping the loaded shotgun's stock. With his other hand he reached around under his tuxedo jacket for the buckle of his cummerbund, which was no longer needed to cover his twenty-four shell ammo belt. Pulling it off, he dropped it to the side of the chair, then withdrew his prescription shades from his breast pocket. All he really needed now was a joint, he thought regretfully as he slipped off his regular glasses and replaced them with the shades.

The deejay was spinning an old Janet Jackson song, which, Brien realized with amusement, was "Let's Wait a While." Sure, let's do that, Janet. No problem. No problem at all. He sat back and watched patiently as the fat, tuxedo-wearing photographer snapped picture after picture of happy, unsuspecting couples. It was kind of too bad that Derek had the video camera, he thought absently. The light was better out here.

He waited calmly. The photographer's flashes didn't disturb him in the least as they flared harmlessly against his lens-shrouded eyes.

CHAPTER 31

EXIT LIGHT, ENTER NIGHT

IT'S LIKE A WHIRLWHIND INSIDE OF MY HEAD
IT'S LIKE I CAN'T STOP WHAT I'M HEARING WITHIN
IT'S LIKE THE FACE INSIDE IS RIGHT BENEATH MY SKIN
—Linkin Park ("Papercut")

Jami's first hint that something was wrong was not anything that she could put into words, exactly. Despite Jason holding her close, she felt as if the world had suddenly gone cold. The lights seemed to darken, and she could almost feel a wintry breeze blowing cruelly on the exposed skin of her back, giving her goose bumps. Where is that coming from? She shivered, and pushed herself back from Jason.

"What's the matter?"

"That wind, is there a window open somewhere? I didn't think it was that cold out!"

"There's no wind, Jami." Jason still held her, but at arm's length now. "Are you all right?"

She pulled away from him and hugged herself. It was freezing! And the lights . . . they weren't glowing the way they should. . . .

"Jami!" Holli was reaching out for her. "Can you feel that?"

"Do you have any idea what they're talking about?" Paul asked Jason.

"No, I don't know. All of a sudden she just started freaking out about the wind, or something."

"This is bad, Jami," Holli insisted urgently. Her eyes were huge. "I can see . . . I think we should get out of here!"

"I don't know. . . ."

Jami was alarmed herself, but she didn't like the way Jason and Paul were looking at them. The guys had been pretty tolerant of all their little conditions, well, most of them were Mom and Dad's, to be honest, but still, they'd been very cool about everything. Maybe there was something strange going on, and maybe there wasn't. She didn't want to leave Jason with a bad impression, and she didn't think that running off screaming into the night for no reason would score the right kind of points with him.

Then the music stopped. Jami glanced up at the stage where the deejay was set up and saw that the man bending over the sound equipment didn't look much like a deejay. He was too young, for one thing, and was dressed for the prom in a black tuxedo, black tie, and a ruffled black-and-yellow cummberbund. He was messing with the equipment for a second, and then he stood up, looked out over the crowd, and smiled. It was a scary smile, full of cruelty and evil, on a face that Jami had seen before. It was psycho-boy, from that morning at the flagpole, and she suddenly knew that Holli was absolutely right.

"Let's go," she hissed at Holli as she grabbed Jason's hand. "Now!"

People were grumbling about the interrupted music as they pushed past them, but then the sound system came back to life. A heavy drum began to beat, and then a metallic voice came thundering over the big speakers.

"The beautiful people, the beautiful people!"

As a distorted electric guitar roared at earsplitting volume, she heard a loud explosion behind her. A second explosion followed, and then a third, but it wasn't until someone started screaming in high-pitched terror that she realized the explosions were actually gunshots.

"No!" Jason yelled at something she couldn't see. He pulled at her as she kicked off her high heels. "Jami, come on, we've got to get out of here, now!"

She couldn't help looking back, though. It was a terrible

sight. The tall boy in the deejay booth was standing on top of the platform now, holding a long gun, and pointing it down into the crowd. His face was a white mask of terrible joy. There was a flash of light and another roar, and two boys appeared to leap backward into a small group of girls, sending the whole group sprawling.

"No!" she shouted in horror, but Jason yanked at her arm so hard that pain went shooting through her armpit.

"Run!" he commanded savagely. Thanks to her mysterious early warning, they were one of the first to reach the doors at the far end of the ballroom. But where's Holli? Jami started to panic, thinking her sister might have fallen, but then, she glanced back and saw her sister's red dress immediately behind her. Paul was running with her, too—Jami could have wept with relief.

Thank you, Jesus, keep her safe, she prayed fearfully. *And get me out of here!*

Behind them, the ballroom echoed with piercing screams and booming gunshots as they burst out of the dark room into the relative light of the hallway. But to her horror, she saw a man wearing sunglasses was rising from a chair, holding a rifle that was pointed right at her.

"No!" she screamed, holding up her hands in feeble self-defense.

BOOM! The sound was deafening, and she found herself twisting sideways through the air as something smashed into her from the left and knocked her facefirst into the carpeted floor. BOOM! BOOM! BOOM!

She looked up and saw the gunman moving forward, past her, stepping over three or four people who were on the ground in front of him, although she couldn't tell if he had shot them, or if they had only fallen down, like her.

"Holli!" she screamed, not seeing her anywhere. Someone pulled at the back of her dress, and she tried to bat their hands away. "Holli!" she screamed again frantically.

"Get up, Jami!" Holli shouted in her ear. "I'm right here! Come on, we've got to get out of here."

Oh, thank God, thank God, thank God!

"What happened?" Jami asked, relieved, but confused. She thought . . . no, maybe she hadn't seen . . . it was impossible to think, with the screams and the gunshots, and the sharp stink of the gunsmoke.

Jason suddenly loomed before her, his face white with fear. He pushed her away from the ballroom, where the firing still continued.

"Run, run, you guys! Now!"

"But where's Paul?"

"I don't know! I don't see him!"

Holli tried to resist, but Jason was too strong for her. He grabbed her wrist in one hand and Jami's in the other, and forced them to run with him. They ran through the lobby and out into the parking lot, and Jami was so scared that she barely noticed the rough asphalt on her bare feet. There were kids milling aimlessly, and some were still running, crossing the street in order to put as much distance between themselves and danger as possible. Several people were shouting into mobile phones, and Jami wondered what they were supposed to do.

She heard the sound of an onrushing car, and in her state of panic, leaped backward in an attempt to get away from it. She tripped, and as she fell, she saw it was actually a big sport-utility vehicle. The brakes squealed as it came to a sudden halt, and Christopher leaped out of the driver's seat. He didn't bother to shut the door, he just ran around the front of the car and pulled her to her feet as if he'd been looking for her and knew exactly where she'd be.

"Holli!" he demanded.

"I'm right here," Jami heard her say. "Christopher, what are you doing here?"

"Who cares, just get in the car!" Jason ordered.

He pushed Jami toward the Explorer, but Christopher shook his head. He pointed to the hotel entrance, which was still crowded, as terrified teenagers and frightened hotel staff continued to pour out of it.

"No. Come on, guys, we have to go in there."

Jami stared at her brother. Was he crazy?

"Christopher, you have no idea—"

"Yes, I do," he answered. "They're killing people, and they're going to kill a lot more if we don't go stop them, now. So come on!"

Jami didn't move. Neither did Holli. They both just stood there, looking at Christopher in disbelief, and paralyzed by fear.

"It's a Warriors thing," he explained. "Mariel showed up during the meeting and told me all about it. So let's go!"

Jami's heart sank. Going back into that hotel was the last thing in the world she wanted to do. But she had no doubt whatsoever that Christopher was telling the truth. She could see it in the hard set of his face.

She took a deep breath, and grabbed Holli's hand. She could feel her sister shaking, but when Holli looked up, her eyes were hard. She was ready.

"Okay, then, let's do it," Jami heard herself saying. "Anyways, Paul might still be in there."

"What!" Jason was beside himself. "Are you nuts! Jami, what do you think you're doing?"

She ignored him, and held on tightly to Holli's hand as her sister prayed.

"Lord Most High, Heavenly Father, give us the strength and courage to face this evil. We trust in your power, and ask that your will be done, but nobody and nothing else's, in the name of your Son, Jesus Christ of Nazareth!"

Jason, seeing that she wasn't paying him any attention, finally stepped in front of Christopher.

"Look, kid, you have no idea what you're dealing with. I don't know how you got here now, or who Mary is, but there's people with guns in there, all right? I can't let you do this!"

Jami held her breath as her brother placed his hand on her date's chest.

"There's a lot worse things than guns in there, Jase, and that's why we have to do it." Christopher slipped his keys into Jason's hand, then pushed him gently out of his way. "I don't know how long it will take for the ambulances to get here, so you'll probably have to drive people to the hospital. Stay in the car, and keep the engine running."

Jason glanced from Christopher to Jami, and back again. He looked like they'd suddenly turned into aliens or something, but at least he didn't seem inclined to stand in their way again.

"Dude, at least let the girls stay out here." Her date shook his head. "Look, just let them stay and I'll go in with you, okay?"

Jami's heart melted. It was the bravest thing she'd ever heard anyone say. And to think that he would do that for her. . . .

"Jason, it's okay," Jami reassured him, and she stood up on her tiptoes to kiss him lightly on the cheek. "Please, listen to Christopher and stay here. He's right, people are going to need you! Trust me, we know what we're doing. Think of it, like, I don't know, a Buffy thing, okay? It's kind of like that."

Jason shook his head, but he finally stayed out of their way.

"Be careful, you idiots!" he finally yelled after them, and Jami waved to him in what she hoped was a confident manner. Then she swallowed hard and gritted her teeth. She wasn't ready for this. God, please, please, please, be with us and protect us, she prayed fervently. And send every angel you can spare!

The three of them held hands, with Christopher leading the way and her in the middle, as they pushed in through the surge of fleeing people. It was slow going at first, and it was tough to hang on to Christopher because they were going against the flow. But this was apparently the final wave, because the crowd was a lot thinner once they fought their way in past the lobby and began to walk cautiously toward the ballroom.

A sobbing girl ran by, her yellow dress stained with blood, and Jami was shocked when she recognized Jill Mondale.

"Not that way!" Jill shouted at her as she ran past them. "They're still in there. . . ."

Another gun blast punctuated her cries, and Jami winced. As they drew closer, she could hear moans and pleading cries nearly drowned out by the loud music roaring out of the ballroom. There was another loud blast.

"Sounds like a shotgun," Christopher commented. He squeezed her hand. "It's nothing. Don't be afraid."

"Who, me?" Jami tried to remind herself that she'd confronted demons before. No big thing, really . . . oh, come on, girl. Admit it. If you manage not to wet your pants, you're doing good.

The thing was, the demons they'd run into before weren't possessing kids armed with shotguns, and come to think of it, most of those confrontations had ended with her and Holli running away. Which, to her mind, was starting to look like a really good strategy.

"Oh, no," Holli said softly as they turned the last corner. Christopher breathed in sharply, and Jami herself was forced to close her eyes. She felt Holli drop her hand, and she didn't have the strength to hold on herself.

It was hard to open her eyes again and take in the awful sight. The entrance to the ballroom was filled with guys in tuxes and girls in dresses, all lying sprawled in impossible poses. But she could see that some of them were still alive, because they were still moving. One dark-haired girl even lifted up a hand to Jami, her anguished eyes begging for help, but Jami couldn't do anything for her because Christopher was pulling her forward again, into the darkness of the ballroom.

They stopped just inside the doorway. The grinding music was so loud it made her ears hurt, but Jami barely noticed. She was focused on the two tall, shadowy figures stalking about the other side of the large hall, searching for signs of life. As her eyes adjusted to the gloom, she saw that there were some thirty or forty kids still in the room, and although most were lying wounded or worse on the floor, a small group of eight or ten kids were huddled fearfully in a corner. It was toward this last group that the killers were gradually making their way.

They didn't seem to be in a hurry, though. One of them, the

shorter one wearing sunglasses, paused as he stepped over one injured boy, then pointed the gun downward and fired with the barrel less than two feet away from his target. The boy below him convulsed violently, and then lay still, as the killer pumped his fist. He waved the other killer over, and after pointing out his latest victim, the two of them exchanged a high five. Jami felt herself swaying, and wondered if she was going to faint or throw up first.

The lights came on without warning, and the two killers alertly spun around toward her. The taller one had to shield his eyes against the sudden brightness, but the one with shades on was already raising his shotgun to his shoulder. Jami started to shout a warning, but then the music stopped abruptly, freezing the killer where he stood.

"I always hated Marilyn Manson," Christopher announced with false bravado as he stood up next to her with an orange extension cord in his hand. He was standing next to the light switch that she had somehow missed seeing in the darkness.

"Who are you?" the taller killer snarled. He walked slowly toward them, full of hatred and menace, followed by his partner.

It was definately psycho-boy. Jami felt sick as she recognized him from school. She'd never seen the other killer, the one with the shades, but she could not mistake the taller boy. His face was deathly pale, and his eyes had something weird going on with them, but even more disturbing, she saw he'd painted a pentagram on his forehead. No, she realized as he came closer and she saw the ragged shape of the occult symbol. The crazy killer had actually carved it into his skin. In fact, both of them had.

Strangely enough, the horrid marks made her feel more confident. This wasn't insanity. It was total in-your-face Fallen evil, no question about it, and that was something she knew how to deal with.

"We are servants of the Most High God," Christopher answered the possessed boy.

"Who, by the way, beats your masters every time," Jami added.

The two killers looked at each other. The taller one's face twisted with rage.

"What are you talking about? I don't have any masters, I'm my own freaking master! You think your pathetic god can protect you here?"

He raised his gun and pressed the blue metal barrel against Jami's temple. It was warm, almost hot.

Jami swallowed, but she refused to look away from the killer's eyes. This close, she could see what was wrong with them. They weren't so much cold as dead, as if the demons inside him had somehow drained all the life out of him. There was no mercy, no compassion, nothing but pure hate and rage. Out of the corner of her eye, she saw movement, and she realized Holli was quietly helping those who could still walk to leave the ballroom through a service exit on the side. They needed time, though, and then, Jami knew what she was supposed to do. It was simple, really. But did she have the faith?

I believe, Lord, but help my unbelief! The killer didn't matter; she had to deal with the demons inside him first.

"Tell me who you are, in Jesus' name," she commanded the evil spirit she knew had to be lurking somewhere inside the boy.

"Jesus who?" The killer's voice was different now, more mature and bitingly sarcastic. "Maybe I am Jesus!"

"Jesus Christ of Nazareth," she answered firmly. The killer snarled, and his eyes rolled back in his head so that only the whites were showing.

"Just blow her freaking head off already!" the other killer shouted with irritation.

He raised his weapon and pointed it at her, but Christopher raised his hand. "No!"

It was a command, not a plea.

Click! The guy with the shades pulled the trigger, but nothing happened. He cursed, and as he tugged at the ejection lever, Christopher grabbed the weapon. Yellow shells went flying everywhere.

"I don't think so," he said as he wrenched it out of the killer's hands and spun it around to point it back at him. With the ease of an expert, he slammed the gun back into place. "Don't even think of moving, because it'll work this time, I guarantee it."

Jami found herself smiling, despite the shotgun that was still pressed against her head.

"I said name yourself," she demanded again. "Now!"

The tall boy growled, and he lowered his weapon.

"I am Verchiel," the demon admitted reluctantly.

Christopher wrinkled his lip. "Come back for another round, loser?"

"You haven't won anything yet!" the boy spat back.

Jami scowled at her brother and made a knock-it-off gesture. What was he doing? Okay, the demon wasn't pointing the gun at her head anymore, but wasting time with smack-talk didn't strike her as their best option here.

"You, what is your name?" she demanded of the other boy, who was holding his hands up in the air.

"I am Rahdar."

Jami caught Christopher's eye, and they exchanged a meaningful glance. He made a "yer-outta-here" sign with his thumb, and she nodded. All authority on Heaven and Earth, that was what the Bible said. Maybe it wasn't hers, but it was hers to use, for sure.

"All right, then, Verchiel, Rahdar, I bet you know what comes next. In the name of the only Son of the Most High God, Jesus Christ of Nazareth, I command you to leave these boys!"

Jami wasn't sure exactly what she was expecting, but she was both relieved and surprised when the boys' heads didn't spin around and they didn't scream or anything, they both just suddenly slumped to the ground, unconscious.

"Whew!" She wiped cold sweat away from her brow. She could still feel that shotgun barrel pressed against it. "Thank you, God, thank you, God, thank you, God! That was so not fun!"

"I guess I always thought an exorcism would be a little more dramatic than that," confessed Christopher as he laid the shot-gun carefully on the ground. "But, man, that was too close. I'm glad that's over! Now we'd better see what we can do for these—"

"It's not over until I say it's over, my dear friend," an arrogant voice smoothly interrupted.

Chapter 32

Decisions

"THERE IS NO SPOON."
—Neo ("The Matrix")

At the sound of the voice behind them, Jami snapped her head around so quickly that she almost sprained her neck. Hovering in the air only ten feet away from them was a beautiful demonlord with black wings. He looked familiar, and with a start, Jami recognized him as the one they'd confronted last winter at the grade school. But this time, he had lot more than just two or three demon babes with him; now he'd brought along what looked like a small army of evil spirits. There were forty or fifty of them, and they were the most random mix of big, ugly, creepy, scary beings that Jami had ever seen.

"Kaym!" Christopher breathed. "You did this. . . ."

Floating on either side of Kaym were two big, scary-looking angels. One had a man's body and a lion's head, while the other had a human head, but two massive red-shelled pincers in the place of his arms. The demonlord smiled coolly at her.

"Your brother is already acquainted with my colleagues, of course, but I don't suppose you have been properly introduced. Allow me to present the archons Lord Verchiel and Lord Rahdar."

Jami backed warily away from the looming horde of evil spirits. She looked around and was glad to see Holli had left the room. *I just hope she stays the heck out of here!* Fear gripped her insides as her mind grasped frantically for something she remembered reading some time ago in one of their Bible studies. One of us can put a thousand to flight, two of us can send the legions fleeing—wasn't it something like that? A legion, that was a lot more than fifty. And there were two of them!

The handsome demonlord laughed. "Don't believe everything you read, you stupid girl."

So they could read minds? How was that fair? Well, take this, then! She taunted the evil spirit by deliberately recalling the image she had seen of him last winter, shrinking before the silver fire of the Holy Spirit.

The arrogant smile disappeared from the angel's face. "We'll see about that!" he snapped.

"You can't touch us, Kaym, you know that!" Christopher insisted, and the demonic army roared with laughter. "We are protected by the blood of the Lamb!"

The demons laughed even louder.

"Shut up, Verchiel," he snapped angrily. "Remember the Circle!"

The lionheaded angel stopped laughing, and he bared his long fangs menacingly. "Oh, I remember it, assuredly. How could I possibly forget?"

The demonlord impatiently stilled Verchiel and the rest of his followers with a gesture, and indicated the fallen bodies strewn about the giant room. There was blood everywhere, and the smell was terrible.

"This place has been consecrated, dedicated to the Great Prince. Blood, you say? This is a Temple of Blood, ah, and the incense is sweet, indeed! Your prayers will not be heard by the Enemy here—nor would his angels dare to enter this place."

"Oh, yes, they would, forsaken one! Others have prayed and the mandate given!"

Jami jerked her head up as she heard a familiar voice behind her, and she recognized Paulus, her guardian angel, as he zoomed over her head. His flaming sword crackled as he slashed at the demonlord's face, and Kaym, taken off-guard, barely managed to evade the blow. Paulus didn't slow down, and he chopped down the demon with the crab claws on his backswing. A blizzard of white flashed past her eyes as a flight of Divine angels crashed into the crowd of Fallen, and Jami raised both her fists into the air.

"Get 'em, Paulus," she cheered wildly as her Guardian sliced apart two freaky-looking things with hairless gray heads.

The demons were clearly taken off-guard by the fury of this unexpected attack, and they began to fall back in some disarray. But then a red-skinned demoness evaded the thrust of an angelic sword and leaped toward her with a spiked club raised high over her horned head. Yikes!

"Help!" she screamed.

A huge white-robed form stepped in front of her, and intercepted her attacker with the point of his fiery sword. There was a blinding flare of red light, and the demoness was gone.

"Here!" Her savior was a huge angel with midnight skin and a deep, rumbling voice, and he gently placed his sword in her much smaller hands. "Take this!"

As her fingers closed around the hilt, he patted her reassuringly on the shoulder and then launched himself at a scorpion-tailed demon with red wings. A moment later he disappeared into the fray, his bare hands locked around its throat.

Jami stared stupidly at the sword. It was lighter than it looked, but the flames were crackling and hissing, and she could feel the heat coming off it. And what exactly am I supposed to do with this?

Something growled in front of her, and she looked up to see a huge, purple demon with a goat's head rushing at her, its great jaws dripping with disgusting flecks of yellowish foam. She shrieked and slashed the sword wildly in the general direction of this new attacker, and was lucky enough to score a hit on the left side of its giant, beastly head. The big demon screamed and dropped its weapon as it clutched at its ruined eye. Jami whooped, and brought the sword back like a softball bat, then swung as if she were going for the fences.

The goat's head went flying, and the demon's purple body dropped to the floor before exploding into nothingness with a bang. She looked around, and saw that Christopher had acquired a sword now, too, and was battling one-on-one with Kaym. Wow, he really knew what he was doing with that thing, she thought, impressed with her brother, as he parried the demonlord's black-flamed sword with his own golden blade and almost managed to spear the malignant spirit with a fast, two-handed thrust at his midsection.

"You've lost, Kaym, you've lost again!" she heard him shout triumphantly as his adversary leaped back. "Don't you know you'll never win?"

But the demonlord smiled contemptuously and, surprisingly, sheathed his dark sword once he was out of reach.

"You think you've won, simply because you survived? You always lacked vision, Christopher. And imagination. Not everything will be as it is written."

The evil spirit gestured around the room. "Behold, the work of my hand. We shall dine well in Hell tonight, don't you agree?"

The demonlord raised his arm imperiously and swept his starry cloak over his head in a broad, all-embracing gesture.

Jami blinked, and he was somehow gone, along with his whole demonic crew.

Christopher met her eyes, and his face was full of suspicion.

"Where'd they go?" she asked him, looking around the room, half expecting the small Fallen army to pop up again momentarily. "How'd he do that?"

"It's not important," Paulus answered her. Her Guardian put his arm around her shoulder and sighed heavily. "Come, my dear. There is work yet to do."

Jami forced herself to look around the ballroom, still festively decorated, but in addition to the balloons, ribbons, and flowers, now strewn with bodies as well. Now that her adrenaline wasn't pumped up to face demons and her own immediate danger, she was forced to see the victims as people for the first time, and the sight shocked her to the very core of her being.

"Thirty-two in here," Christopher counted rapidly as he tore a strip of fabric off one wounded girl's dress and pressed it against her bleeding side. He'd been a Boy Scout, Jami remembered. Did they have a merit badge for trauma? Either way, he seemed to know where to start. He glanced up from what he was doing. "Where's Holli, James?"

"I think she's outside," Jami said, pointing to the door. "What should I do?"

Her brother pointed with his chin toward a small black object lying on the floor nearby.

"See if you can call 911 with that cell phone and tell them it's safe for the paramedics to come in. Then find Holli and see how many people are hurt in the hallway."

"Okay," she said as Christopher bowed his head and began praying for the wounded girl. The phone was still on, fortunately, and it only took a moment to get connected with the emergency operator.

"Tell the paramedics they have to hurry, there's, um, about thirty people shot at the hotel. Yes, the one with the prom." She glanced over to where the killers were still lying unconscious. "No, I guess you could say they're kind of out of commission. You want me to stay on the line?"

She looked over at Christopher, but Paulus shook his head.

"No, I have to help somebody here. Look, I'll call you back in a few minutes, okay. But I think you're going to need a lot of ambulances, so tell them to hurry!"

She flipped the little phone shut, hanging up on the operator.

"Why didn't you want me to stay on the line?" she asked Paulus.

Her angel didn't say anything, but took her by the hand and led her back toward the double doors. The first thing she saw was another angel, Aliel, standing in the hallway. And there, at Aliel's feet, she saw Holli sitting on the floor, cradling Paul's head in her lap. His eyes were closed, and the front of his shirt was covered with blood, so much so that it was impossible to tell it had once been white. He wasn't the only victim, but Holli didn't even seem to notice that there were others.

She looked up at Jami, tears streaking her face. "He's dead."

Jami nodded slowly, as her memory flashed back to the vision of a boy rising slowly from a chair and pointing a gun at her midsection. And she remembered that sudden blow from behind that had saved her, that feeling of something powerful striking her, hurling her down to the floor and out of danger. Not something, but someone. Paul.

"I think he saved my life," she told her weeping sister. "He pushed me aside, and so he got shot instead."

Holli didn't say anything, but she nodded as she stroked Paul's peaceful face, and her bloodstained hand left a thin red trail on his too-white skin.

Jami looked pleadingly at Paulus. "Can't you guys do something?"

The angel shook his head. "No, we cannot."

"Come on, you can, too!" Jami insisted. "What about Pastor Walters? He was, like, basically dead from that heart attack, and he was all right after we prayed for him. . . ."

Her voice trailed off. Paulus was staring at her intensely, as if he wanted to tell her something, but couldn't. Did angels know how to play charades? Sounds like . . . oh, okay, that's what he was getting at. Jesus said four things. Feed the poor, heal the sick, cast out demons, and *raise the dead*.

"It's up to us, isn't it? We have to do it. Okay, well, fine, if God can raise one person from the dead, then I don't see why he can't raise thirty!"

She kneeled down and grabbed Holli's hand, and placed her other hand on Paul's mangled chest, ignoring the blood. But as she started praying, a strong hand grabbed her wrist.

"Wait," Paulus interrupted her. "You are correct, and you have done well here tonight, but there are things beyond your understanding, rules and laws of which we may not speak."

"For every action there is a consequence, and for every refusal to act there is a cost," Aliel added. "The Lord sought one who would stand in the gap to prevent this evil; three times, you were given a chance to intervene and each time you declined, not out of malice, but because you would not see. Even so, the Lord Most High has blessed your actions here tonight. So now you must choose."

Three times? What was she talking about? But then an image filled her mind. A boy on the floor, sprawled in front of a ransacked locker. Then that same boy, sitting alone at a table, listening intently as she gossiped with her friends. A girl in white, dancing closely with another. A collision in the halls. And finally that same boy, rising slowly, gun in hand, like the vengeful dead.

God, God, God, you can't tell me this is all my fault! It can't be!

"There is fault to be found, but the blame for these deaths is not yours," Paulus assured her. "It lies with the two who lay fallen within."

"What is done is done." Aliel's voice was firm, but her brown eyes were sympathetic. "But here is another fork in the road."

"How?" Jami asked. "Paulus, you said I can choose, so what am I choosing?"

"Who will live and who will die," Paulus answered her. He waved his hand, and suddenly there were a bunch of silvery figures standing in front of her, beings that looked like people made of a shimmering light. Jami realized that she knew some of them; there was Jim Schumacher, and Kara Hammel, and Kjirsti Tornquist, and there, standing off to the left, was Paul. He was the only one who appeared to be able to see her, and his soft puppy-dog eyes glittered with what seemed to be both amusement and concern. He was even smiling.

"Holli," she whispered urgently.

"What?" her sister replied, not looking up, lost in her sorrow.

"Never mind." Jami shook her head. Last time, at the Tower, it was her sister with the sight. Now it was her turn, apparently, and she wished it wasn't.

"The Lord Most High has heard your prayers, and the prayers of others as well. Because he is merciful, he has decreed that fourteen of these shall rise again and live."

Jami was horrified. Paulus couldn't be serious. How could he stick her with this?

She couldn't believe it, but her angel actually smiled at her!

"One day you will judge us, my dear. This is but a prelude."

He had to be kidding. Who was she to play God?

"This is not of his doing, Jami. Paulus is only the messenger." Aliel went on to confirm her fears. "Go to each of those you would choose, and place your hand above their heart. Tell them to awake, in the name of the one you serve."

Jami shook her head, not in refusal, but in shame. How could she send fourteen people to their deaths, when it was partly her fault that they were dead already? That didn't make sense, she knew, but nothing else did tonight, so there. Jim Schumacher was a jerk, but did that mean he deserved to die? Of course, Paul had to live, there was no question about that, but still, the whole thing didn't seem fair.

"The time grows short," Paulus told her. "If you would act, you must do it now."

But . . . but . . . but . . . well, that didn't leave her much of a choice, then. She kneeled down again, and started to place her hand on Paul's bloody chest.

Then she stopped. Something about the glowing spirits of the dead was bothering her. Considering that he was dead, Paul looked pretty happy. Joyful, even. So did some of the others, while the rest appeared to be screaming, as if they were scared out of their minds.

She glanced inquisitively at Paulus, but he shook his head. Clearly, he couldn't tell her anything more.

"Jami, hurry up," Holli urged her. She had heard the whole conversation, although she couldn't see the dead people. "What are you waiting for?"

A thought struck her. Even after she'd gotten over the jealousy thing with Paul, she'd still been a little bit concerned about his taking advantage of Holli. Her sister, though, had always dismissed her concerns out of hand, despite Mr. Maple's advice against dating non-Christians. But she'd never actually asked Paul about what he believed, she realized. She'd just assumed he wasn't because of Jason; she didn't really know.

"Holli, was Paul a Christian?"

Her sister looked up at her suspiciously. "Yeah, he was. Why?"

Jami counted quickly. Fourteen smiling, fourteen screaming. It was possible that she was wrong, but she didn't think so. It added up, certainly, and besides, what else did she have to go on? Now she knew what she had to do, and she even understood why the choosing had been left to her.

"That's great," she said, even as she stood and turned away from Paul's body. "Paulus, is it okay for you to point out who is, you know, who?"

Her angel slipped his arm around her shoulder, holding her tight. She was grateful; she needed his support badly.

"That, I can do for you, my dear."

"No!" Holli cried, tugging at her dress. "Jami, please, you can't leave him! You can't just let him die!"

But Jami looked at Paul, the real Paul, not the empty shell being cradled by her sister. He was nodding approvingly, and when he saw that she was looking at him, he gave her the same cheerful two thumbs-up he used to give her on the field. She could feel tears start to build in her eyes, but she fought them off and grinned back at him.

Thank you, she mouthed at him silently. *I'm sorry.*

Don't be, James, she heard his voice in her head. He sounded lighthearted, almost giddy. *Don't worry about it. And you know what? It's amazing! It's awesome!*

Jami nodded, swallowing hard. *I'll tell Holli that*, she promised him.

Oh, and James?

Yeah?

Tell her I love her.

He waved to her as a giant angel appeared behind him. The angel, a massive Guardian, smiled reassuringly at her as he placed his big hands on Paul's broad shoulders and then Paul disappeared from sight, along with the other silvery forms. Jami couldn't fight her tears any longer, and she began to cry even as she knelt down at the side of a boy with a grievous head wound.

He was an obvious goner, and Jami found it hard to imagine how even an all-powerful God could heal someone this messed up. But she was too full of too many conflicting emotions to doubt, or even think. This was the time to act; there would be plenty of time to figure things out later.

"This one?"

Paulus nodded.

Jami sniffed and wiped at her nose, which had started to run, then she did as she'd been told. Her hand was on the boy's heart as she ordered him to live again.

"Get up, in the name of Jesus Christ . . . of Nazareth!"

Okay, probably God wasn't picky like the demons were, but she figured it was best to be on the safe side. She was watching closely, staring at the boy's head and wondering how the terrible wound would be healed, when it simply vanished. There was nothing to see, one moment it was there and the next it was gone. Holy cats and hallelujah! The boy's eyes opened a second later, and Jami was unsettled to see how alert he was. His eyes were full of fear.

"I was watching you," he said suspiciously. "But I was over there . . . how did I get here? What happened?" He shuddered. "And what were those things? They were awful, howling and grabbing at me. . . ."

Jami shuddered herself. She knew what it was like to have demons grabbing at you, and she couldn't imagine that it felt any better once you were dead. At least this was one soul they wouldn't be dragging off to Hell, not yet, anyhow. She met his eyes and shrugged. What could she say that wouldn't sound completely nuts? Besides, she couldn't wait—there were still thirteen more kids to save. She patted the resurrected boy on the shoulder and quickly stood to follow Paulus. All the while she could feel Holli's angry, grief-stricken eyes boring a fiery hole into her back.

Outside she could hear sirens. She had to hurry. There wasn't much time.

CHAPTER 33

RED SCREEN TILT

I know her, Jami thought, as she stared down at the bloodless face of the dead girl at her feet. It was the girl in white from Jason's party, the one who had somehow been involved in this whole deal. Her mouth was open, as were her sightless eyes, and it was clear from her horrified expression that she had seen her death coming. Jami swallowed hard. Of all the terrible, awful, very bad things she'd seen tonight, the look on this girl's face was quite possibly the worst.

She glanced at Paulus. The angel's attention seemed to be elsewhere, and his face was stern.

"Her, too?" she asked uncertainly. Thirteen of the fourteen lives she'd been promised had already been restored. But why should this girl live at Paul's expense, if she was responsible for everything?

"The choice is yours," Paulus told her again. "Paul is beyond concern, as you know. She, on the other hand, is being tormented by the Eaters of Souls even as we speak."

"Right, right, and who am I to judge anybody." Jami shook her head and wearily pushed her hair out of her eyes, trying to ignore the sticky blood already matting it together. "Doggone it! Okay, then, if you want to get out of there, girl, wake up in Jesus' name."

There wasn't any reaction at first, and Jami looked uncertainly to Paulus. The angel smiled briefly and shook his head. Then Jami realized that the chest under her hand was heaving, and that tears were leaking out from under the girl's now-closed eyes. Emotionally drained, and still in shock from the evening's terror, Jami cried, too, and pulled the girl up to a sitting position and held her close. That was how the black-armored police discovered them as they rushed into the room only seconds later, followed by two teams of paramedics.

The cops were swearing furiously, shocked by the sight of so many dead and wounded kids. Even the paramedics, used to seeing all kinds of awful car accidents, seemed to be stunned by the mass carnage. They were almost silent as they went to work, moving quickly from victim to victim as they determined who might yet be saved and who was beyond help.

"No sign of the shooters!" the first armored SWAT cop to enter the room shouted. "Reports said two, I got nothing but casualties and one-two-three unarmed kids."

"Where's the little punk who did this?" Another cop, a tall, muscular man who was carrying a wicked Army-style machine gun, jabbed his finger at Jami. "I can't believe this. Not here, not in this town, things like this don't happen here!

"They're over there," Christopher called as he pointed out the two unconscious killers on the floor. "The two guns are over there. They must have dropped them."

Jami could only see the big cop's eyes, since the rest of his face was covered by a black mask, but she could see they were studying her brother suspiciously. Christopher was the only kid there who wasn't all dressed up, which did look kind of strange in the circumstances. How did the cops know who were the bad guys, and who weren't?

"Those two? What happened to them? Are they dead?"

"I don't think so, but I wasn't here when they were shooting everybody," Christopher answered honestly, if incompletely. "I came in looking for my sisters when everyone else was running outside. That's my sister there, the blond girl . . . my other sister got out already."

"That true?" The cop was looking at her now.

"Yeah, he was just trying to help us."

Well, it was true, in a way.

The cop lowered his weapon and shook his head slowly.

"Man, kid, are you crazy or just stupid? No, don't move, stay right here." The cop moved cautiously over to her brother and patted him down quickly.

Christopher submitted to the search without complaint.

"Okay, you're clean. Move over there—"

"Sure," Christopher said obediently. "But, um, I think one of them just moved."

"What!" The SWAT cop whirled around, and there was a click as he thumbed his weapon off safety. "Hold it right there!" he roared as one boy rolled over to his stomach and the other one sat up, blinking at the overhead lights.

"Don't even think of moving, hold it right there, right there! You, put your hands on your head, and you, put your hands out in front of you! On the ground! Get on the ground!"

The girl in Jami's arms screamed, frightened by the sudden shouting, and Jami hugged her even tighter as she tried to shush her. Within seconds the police team had formed a deadly semicircle around the two boys, and were training their weapons on them. Jami winced, half-expecting another explosion of gunfire, and although she wanted to close her eyes, she found that she couldn't bear to look away, either.

One of the boys obeyed the shouted orders, but the other one, the chubbier one, didn't seem to understand them. Ignoring the five guns pointed at him, he pushed himself to his feet with a dazed expression on his face. He'd lost his shades, and it was almost as if he had just woken up, as if he had gone to sleep in some other place and awoken to discover himself in the midst of this nightmarish scene. He looked around the room and shook his head in disbelief.

"What the . . ." He mouthed the words silently, but Jami had no problem reading his lips.

"I told you not to move, kid!" The cop's commanding voice was furious, but to Jami, his anger sounded almost desperate. He must not want to shoot the boy, she thought.

"Oh, my . . . Brien? That's Brien," whispered the girl in her arms. "I can't believe . . . how could he do this? He couldn't, it's just not possible!"

"Oh, Derek, what did we do?" the boy said, closing his eyes and swallowing hard. He looked like he was about to be sick. "What did we do! I didn't want this! I didn't want anything like this! I didn't!"

He looked desperately toward the other boy, the one still on the carpet. The other killer's face was hard, and showed no sign of the remorse that was shattering his friend. His hands were still on his head, but he ignored the guns threatening him, and Jami was shocked to see that he was even smiling.

"Like it ever matters what anybody wants, dude. They got what they deserved."

"Shut up!" the big cop cut in. "And you, get your hands on your head like your big-mouthed friend there and nobody has to get hurt. Do it!"

The sitting boy rolled his eyes and rebelliously extended one finger on each hand, but kept his mouth shut nevertheless. The standing boy, though, shook his head and started to reach inside his jacket.

"Don't make me shoot you, kid!"

The boy's hand stopped, and he stared at the policeman with eyes that were darker and more lost than anything Jami had ever seen. They had been blank before, when the demons were possessing him, but now they were filled with a deep sadness that was emptier than any void. Then he shrugged indifferently.

"Go ahead," he answered without pretense. "What difference would it make now?"

The policeman didn't take his finger away from the trigger,

but something in his rigid posture seemed to relax, and his voice softened, just a little.

"It's not worth it, kid. I don't want to shoot you. Nobody wants you dead."

Jami's vision blurred, and suddenly she could see Kaym's arrogant figure, standing with his arms folded just behind the boy. He smiled at her, an arrogant, twisted smile that made her want to hit him. A vortex of darkness emanated from his form, engulfing the boy in a black and pulsating fog. She looked around desperately for the Divine angels, but Paulus was the only one in sight.

"*Do something,*" she thought at him.

"*He has had those two in his grasp for far too long,*" the angel replied in her mind, shaking his head sadly. "*It is up to the boy . . . the choice is his alone.*"

As she looked back at the demonlord, he faded into nothingness, but not before cocking a smugly irritating eyebrow at her.

"Brien!" The girl she had been comforting pushed herself up, using Jami's shoulder as a prop. "Listen to them! Just do what they say!"

Jami saw the chubby killer's eyes widen as he looked over toward the girl. He squinted owlishly and leaned forward to peer uncertainly at her.

"Tessa? But . . . I shot you! Twice! You can't be alive!"

The entire front of the girl's white dress was dark, still wet with blood, and her face was smeared with the marks of Jami's stained hands, but she stood fearlessly in front of her would-be killer and pleaded with him. Not for her life, this time, but his.

"Brien, I'm so, so sorry that I hurt you, that I treated you like I did. It was wrong, I know it. But it wasn't you, it was me, it was my fault. And the thing is, I know you, and a nice guy like you could never do something like this, not by yourself. You're a good guy, inside, you really are! So it wasn't you that did it, it couldn't be. It had to be something else, something wrong inside you. But don't hurt yourself, please, just put the gun down and we can talk about it. They'll get someone to help you!"

Tears began to appear in the killer's eyes as she spoke, and Jami, listening breathlessly, clenched her fists. You go, girl! She didn't know much about her, but she couldn't help being impressed with the girl's courage and her willingness to help the guy who'd shot her. Maybe it was a good thing Paulus had urged her to save the girl after all, because without her intervention, Jami had little doubt that the guy was going anywhere but straight to the eternal fires of Hell.

"Dude—" the other boy started to say, but the cop immediately quieted him.

"You, shut your trap!"

The sitting killer grumbled, but subsided. The standing boy, the one called Brien, was now breathing hard, his chest was heaving, and tears were starting to leak out from behind his closed eyes and run down his face. He had lowered his head and looked close to collapsing. Thank God, Jami thought. There had already been too many deaths here tonight; one more wouldn't solve anything. An armored cop was already moving cautiously toward the boy, a pair of handcuffs in hand.

But then the killer's eyes opened again, and beneath his tears Jami could see a broken spirit of self-loathing and despair. His eyes were only for the girl, Tessa.

"I'm sorry, Tess. I was really looking forward to tonight. This wasn't how I wanted it to end."

His hand dropped quickly inside the fold of his tuxedo, obviously reaching for a weapon, and Jami looked away.

There was a short burst of gunfire, followed by a brief groan and a muffled thump. Still keeping her eyes averted, Jami stood up and reached out for the girl beside her, thinking to comfort her again. But the bloodstained girl was numb with an overload of horror now, and she did not cry out, she only covered her mouth with her hands as she stared at the floor.

"Shooter down," one of the cops muttered into his microphone as two officers rushed toward the boy who'd just been shot, and two others handcuffed the boy on the ground. "Other shooter is in custody. Area clear."

"I'm sorry too, Brien," the girl said quietly. "I'm sorry, too."

The first policeman, the one who'd fired, dropped his weapon as he felt about the fallen boy's throat for a pulse. Then he felt inside the boy's jacket. But he found nothing there, apparently, because when he stood up again, he pulled his helmet and mask from his face, and hurled them to the floor. His face was flushed with helpless anger and frustration as he turned away and shouted for the paramedics.

Jami glanced over at Paulus, and then at Christopher. The angel's face was sad, but he smiled at her and nodded slightly as he, too, faded into invisibility. Her brother looked like he'd just been slapped in the face, and his brown eyes were wide and filled with helpless anger. Jami went to him as two policemen escorted the surviving killer roughly from the ballroom, and she put her arms around him. She pressed her cheek against his shoulder and felt him shaking his head.

"Do you know, I used to want to be like Kaym?" he confessed suddenly. "But there's nothing there, there's just nothing there but evil! And I hate him, I just hate him now, so much!"

"I know what you mean." Jami pushed herself away from him. "He was there, you know, the whole time, the jerk. Just watching and smiling, enjoying it all. Enjoying the pain. And some day, you know what? God is going to wipe that smirk off his face once and for all, and we're going to be there to see it."

"And so is Paul." Christopher smiled fleetingly. "One of the angels told me what happened, that they stuck you with the decision. But you did good, sis, you did the right thing. I know you did."

"Yeah, well, tell Holli that," Jami said sadly as the implications of her decision came rushing back to her with a vengeance. "Let's find Holli and go home, big brother. I've got some serious crying to do."

CHAPTER 34

RESTORATION

BUT IF ALL ARE ALIKE BOTH WRONG AND RIGHT, ONE WHO IS IN THIS
CONDITION WILL NOT BE ABLE EITHER TO SPEAK OR TO SAY ANYTHING
INTELLIGIBLE; FOR HE SAYS AT THE SAME TIME BOTH "YES" AND "NO."
AND IF HE MAKES NO JUDGMENT BUT "THINKS" AND "DOES NOT THINK",
INDIFFERENTLY, WHAT DIFFERENCE WILL THERE BE BETWEEN HIM AND A
VEGETABLE?

—Aristotle, *Metaphysics*

Six weeks later summer had officially arrived, but Jami still wasn't feeling any of that awesome wild-and-free, let's-go-crazy summertime spirit that she normally felt about ten seconds after the final schoolbell buzzed an end to another school year. Maybe it was because that bell never actually rang; following the prom shootings, the school administration decided to cancel all classes for the rest of the year. More likely, though, it was the shadow of those fourteen deaths, fifteen, if you counted Brien Martin as she did, still hanging over the minds of everyone who had anything to do with Mounds Park.

It was hard to feel young and immortal and invincible when so many familiar faces were now just pictures in a fading newspaper clipping. Jami wasn't sure if losing the sense that nothing bad could ever happen to you was part of growing up, but if it was, then she was practically an adult now. And she had also learned that she didn't like it, not one little bit. She longed to remember what it felt like to really be a kid again, to be only vaguely aware that sometimes bad things happened, somewhere out there in the world, in a place that belonged to somebody else.

Why was I in such a hurry to grow up? she thought wonderingly to herself. Why doesn't anybody ever tell you that it sucks? It sucks rocks in the biggest possible way! She half wished she could give up on the whole idea and turn herself into Peter Pan or something.

Summer soccer had finally started, which was cool because it kept her busy even though it reminded her of Paul now and then. Coach Simmons had finally managed to put together a decent Nike girls' team this year, and even if they weren't good enough to beat the Blackhawks' 'A' team in state, Jami thought they had a reasonable shot at the North Suburban championship. She probably should have played with the KPAC traveling team instead, she thought regretfully for the umpteenth time, but she just didn't seem to have the heart for it. KPAC had left for a week-long trip to California only four days after the funerals, and it was just too soon for Jami to deal with everything, so she'd given up her spot on the team. But there was always next year, and if she had a good sophomore season, she knew they'd want her back.

They held the joint funeral service on the football field, and more than three thousand people showed up for it. The camera crews from the TV news were there, along with students, parents, teachers, and a lot of people who just wanted to be there. Seeing Paul's parents, and watching them as they tried, and failed, to hold it together, was about the saddest and most painful thing Jami had ever seen. The whole ceremony was too awful for words, and yet somehow there was something timeless and beautiful about it, too. With the exception of Brien Martin, who'd been buried separately, of course, most of the murdered kids came from Christian families, and Jami felt both touched and inspired by their unshakable certainty that they would someday see their children again.

"You will, you will," she whispered softly to no one in particular. "I know you will!"

Things were good with Jason, although it seemed weird to start having her first boyfriend in the middle of all this sadness. He was taking Paul's death pretty hard, she was sure, but he tried not to let it affect their relationship too much. He came over every evening he didn't have a game, and they'd spend hours in the backyard together, kicking her old ball back and forth until it started to get dark. Sometimes they talked, and sometimes they didn't—it was enough just to spend time with him and know that he was there. He never left without kissing her good night, though, and her heart always started beating a little bit faster when he would glance up at the setting sun, flip the ball up into his hands, and smile at her.

From time to time she still found herself blaming herself for not doing something, anything, that might have averted the catastrophe, but mostly she had managed to accept whatever portion of responsibility was hers and tried to learn from that while letting the rest go. It was still hard to talk to Holli—not that they didn't get along or anything, but everything seemed different. For the first time, Jami found them being *nice* to each other, which just felt totally wrong. It was weird. It was fake, superficial. It wasn't *real*. They didn't talk much now, and when they did, Holli always avoided her eyes. They never talked about the important stuff, either, about feelings and relationships and stuff like that. And every time she tried to bring up Paul, or prom night, Holli turned away.

It was hard, and in some ways it felt like a part of her was missing, but Jami figured it was just going to take a while before Holli would be able to forgive her. Every now and then she was tempted to lose her temper—after all, it wasn't her fault that she'd been the one stuck with making the call, and she knew that Paul himself had agreed with her decision, not that Holli had ever given her the chance to tell her about him—but she'd never given in to the temptation. Instead, she prayed for her twin, every night before going to bed, asking God to take away her sister's pain, to heal her wounded heart, and remove this rift between them.

She sighed and looked out the window at the backyard. The sun was just starting to set, and the light spilling over the treetops was glowing with a rich, golden hue that always made her imagine

God turning up the brightness on his TV. It never lasted long, but it was Jami's favorite time of the day. It was a thick sort of light, dripping down from the green leaves in a way that made you think you could almost feel it and taste it—if you could, she just knew it would taste like butterscotch, or maybe maple syrup. It was so very beautiful, and she wished Jason wasn't playing tonight.

"Knock-knock," someone said.

"Hey," Jami replied, pushing herself up to a sitting position on her bed. It was her sister, and she was leaning nonchalantly against Jami's open door. "What's up?"

Holli looked down at her feet for a second, then up again. She seemed to be forcing herself to hold Jami's gaze.

"I just wanted to say I'm sorry, you know, for, like, everything. None of it was your fault, I know, but I still wanted to blame you anyhow. It was, like, easier or something. I don't know why, but I did, and I'm sorry I've been so awful to you."

She started to cry, but Jami couldn't help laughing even as she leaped up from the bed and rushed to throw her arms around her sister. She squeezed her hard, and then laughed again. She couldn't help it.

"What's so funny?" Holli asked even as tears continued to flow from her eyes.

"Holli, you wouldn't know how to be awful even if Angie gave you private lessons!" She hugged her sister again, and she started to cry, too. "Oh, Holli, I am so, so sorry. I know you loved him. And you know what? He loved you, too."

An hour later, both their faces were stained with tears, Holli's hair was hopelessly messed up, and Jami's nose was red, but she felt that a tremendous burden had been lifted from her heart. She told Holli of how Paul's last thoughts were of her, and though Holli's eyes were wet, her expression was one of remembered happiness, not sorrow. As the tear tracks dried tightly on their faces, Holli suddenly blinked and tapped her urgently on the knee.

"Oh, I almost forgot, I actually came to talk to you about something else. Do me a favor?"

Jami nodded. "Sure."

"Christopher and I were talking the other night. I mean, there was obviously a big spiritual thing going on with this whole thing, right? So, I think maybe the people who lived, lived for a reason, you know, so they could be given another chance."

"All right." Jami thought she knew where this was going. "So you think we should go talk to the kids who didn't die?"

"No." Holli shook her head. "I want you to go with Christopher and talk to the guy who shot everybody. The one who didn't kill himself."

Jami stared at her. She remembered the guy, tall, white, and skinny, sitting on the ground and flipping off the cops without the slightest sign of remorse.

"Are you sure? I mean, I was there when he got arrested, and I don't think it's going to do any good, seriously. I don't know if he's under treatment or what, but he's a total psychopath."

Holli shook her head firmly. "I don't care. Everyone deserves a chance. Even him. You're probably right, but, if we don't offer it to him, we'll never know. So I really think it's important, it's, like, our job, you know." She looked down. "It's just I don't think I can face him, though, not yet, which is why I'm asking you to go."

"Why can't Christopher go by himself?"

Holli didn't respond, she just stared back at Jami with a skeptical look on her face. Jami laughed and gave in.

"Okay, good point. I'll go. Even if it won't do any good. When am I going?"

Holli glanced at her alarm clock. A floor below them, the sound of a car starting could be heard from the driveway. "Like, now, I think. Christopher called the lawyer yesterday, and I guess he set up the appointment."

Jami kissed her sister on the forehead and reached for her shoes. She really didn't want to do this, but she was just so happy to have Holli back again that she didn't mind at all.

"Well, thanks for the warning. I'll let you know how it goes."

* * *

The jail wasn't anywhere as grim as she'd been led to expect by the movies. For one thing, all the bars and gates and locks and stuff weren't gray metal, but instead had been painted yellow. Not a bright yellow, but a pale, gentle yellow. Even the concrete had been painted the same color, making her feel like she was in some kind of strange Teletubby world. The visiting room was just a plain old room, with faded orange carpeting, six-month-old magazines, and a large glass window on one side. A telephone was attached to the wall, and the uniformed guard who'd brought them here explained that they'd be talking to Derek Wallace over the phone.

"It's a new system," he told them. "Keeps visitors from passing contraband to the prisoners."

"People do that?" Jami was surprised.

"You wouldn't believe some of the things they try to pull." The guard shook his head with disgust. "You've got fifteen minutes, kids. I'll be back in a little while, just press that button there if you finish up before I get back."

He walked out of the room, and Jami and Christopher stared at each other, wondering what to do. Jami finally picked up an old *Sports Illustrated* and idly flipped through the much-creased pages as Christopher examined the communications system. A few minutes later the boy they'd come to see entered the room on the other side of the window, accompanied by a tough-looking woman guard. He was wearing a baggy orange jumpsuit, which made him look even thinner, and the acne on his cheeks stood out starkly against his pale skin.

He seemed to recognize them as he picked up the phone and pointed at them.

Christopher picked up the receiver on their end, and held it so that both of them could hear.

"What are you doing here?" the killer demanded. "You wanted to see me?"

His face was scornful, and his eyes were full of contempt for everything they took in, including them. His black hair was uncut since his arrest, and he had a habit of pushing it impatiently out of his eyes, to no avail.

Jami looked at Christopher. Her brother smiled thinly at the boy and shook his head.

"I could give you a number of reasons. How do you like this one? 'Remember those in prison as if you were their fellow prisoners, and those who are mistreated as if you yourselves were suffering.' "

The killer sneered. "A Bible verse. That's right, now I know who you are, you guys are the Jesus freaks. Don't tell me you take that stuff seriously?"

"Don't you?" Christopher leaned forward, and his voice grew sarcastic. "No, of course not. You're far too smart for all that, right? It's all bogus because everybody knows that there's no such thing as absolute morality, right? I mean, that's what your teacher says, that's what MTV says, so of course, they must know, right? And that means you're not a criminal, not really, you're the hero instead."

Jami raised her eyebrows, but something in the killer's face prevented her from trying to intervene. The edge to Christopher's voice was so dismissive that Jami was sure that his words would infuriate the other boy. Somehow, though, they had the opposite effect. The contemptuous look abruptly disappeared and was replaced by a wary, guarded expression, although the sneer on his lips remained.

"What do you mean by that?"

"I mean that you're right. You're absolutely right, and I respect that. You're the only one who plays by the rules they taught us; the rest of them are just total hypocrites."

Huh? Jami was flabbergasted! She stared at her brother, wondering what had gotten into him. She started to open her mouth, but he elbowed her sharply before she could get a word in.

"I'm not kidding," Christopher continued. "Who's to say your thing is any more or any less wrong than anybody else's? They reject God, you reject God, it's all the same. The only difference is the body count."

"Okay, I get it." The killer grinned mockingly. "And you're not telling me anything new, not really. I mean, you're right, you've at least got something to stand on, even if it's nothing but two-thousand-year-old fairy tales. So good for you. Logical consistency. I give you respect for that. But it's still fairy tales, and so your morality is just as full of it as theirs."

Christopher smiled slowly, and Jami felt like she was witnessing an elaborate contest, a duel of some kind, for which she didn't know the rules. It was harsh, like watching two mountain goats bashing heads on the Discovery Channel.

"I have no doubt that you believe that," her brother stated confidently. "It's what I'd expect of you."

The killer jerked his chin at her, and his cold blue eyes scanned her indifferently. She tried not to let her disgust for him show, but all the same, his stare was almost as bad as being groped.

"Don't try to condescend to me. I didn't ask you to be here. Why doesn't she talk? What's she doing here?"

Jami forced herself to hold his gaze. He's human, not a monster, she told herself firmly, even if he doesn't act like it. Judge not, lest ye be judged. . . . It was impossible! It wasn't just that he was a murderer, he was such a total jerk!

"I came because I didn't want him to offend you by getting in your face too much." She leaned over and tried to talk into the receiver. "But I guess I shouldn't have worried about that."

The boy laughed, not unpleasantly, and shook his head. Despite the fact that he made her sick, he almost had a certain charm, if you could manage to look past the breathtaking pride, the monstrous superiority complex, and, of course, the psychotic mass-murderer thing. She remembered reading somewhere that serial killers tended to be more intelligent than the average person, and after listening to this guy, she had no doubts that it was true. He was like Ted Bundy with acne.

"You can't offend me, Blondie, because you don't exist for me, all right? You're nothing. And while I suppose I should appreciate your concern for my nonexistent soul, you're just wasting your time. There is no God, it's a fact! The concepts of good and evil are only man-made inventions, and the only Hell that exists is the one we make, got it? 'Do what thou wilt' is the whole of the law—"

"—judging by your present situation, you seem to have forgotten the bit about 'due regard for the policeman around the corner,'" Christopher interrupted.

"Oh, I'll take Crowley over Maugham any day," Derek said derisively, but his eyes glittered and Jami had the impression he was starting to enjoy the conversation. "You really think we were concerned about getting caught? The whole point was to take as many of those losers to Hell with us as we could."

"I thought you didn't believe in Hell."

The killer rolled his eyes. "It's an expression, girlfriend."

Jami growled under her breath. He was so infuriating, and the stupid smirk on his face reminded her of the demonlord Kaym. Every time Derek looked at her, he acted like he was looking at a bug or something. Finally she lost her temper, and grabbed the phone away from Christopher.

"Don't you even feel sorry for any of the people you shot?" she shouted at him. "Don't you realize how much pain you caused their families? Doesn't that mean anything to you at all?"

The boy only chuckled at her little rant. "It means nothing to me. Not a thing! That's what you will never understand. And what you say doesn't mean anything—it's just words! Those families couldn't have cared less about me when their poor babies were torturing people like me and Brien and every other idiot dumb enough to let on they had half a brain, so why should I pay any attention to their stupid pain?"

Christopher reached out and grabbed her arm, putting his other hand over the receiver before she could respond. She tried to pull it away from him, but he tightened his grip on her arm until she realized that she was the one out of control. Still glaring at Derek, she let go of the phone and and clamped her mouth firmly shut. She looked up at the clock. Ten more minutes could not pass soon enough for her!

"So . . . I don't suppose you'd like a Gospel tract?" Christopher said lightly. "We have blue ones and red ones."

The killer burst out laughing. "You two are the strangest freaking missionaries I've ever seen," he told them. "I mean, you want to talk philosophy and English lit, and I think she wants to, like, beat my head in or something."

"I think she does." Christopher glanced sidelong at her. "But it'll pass."

The boy nodded, but his smile faded quickly. "All right, whatever. It's been fun, but this is getting old." He waved his hand, and the guard on his side started to walk toward him.

"Fair enough," Christopher nodded his head. "But I've got two words for you. Body count."

The killer's eyes narrowed, and he held up his hand. The guard stopped and looked down at her watch, then shrugged.

"What do you mean by that?" he asked Christopher.

"I read that you guys fired sixty-seven rounds of twelve-gauge, but only fourteen people died. I'll bet you can't figure out how that happened. I'll bet it bothers you that guys you really wanted to take down, guys you *knew* you took down, guys like Schumacher and Petersen, survived. So I'll make you a deal. Let me come visit you again, and I'll tell you how."

Jami watched closely as the killer folded his arms behind his head and leaned back, staring at her brother's face. She couldn't tell what he was trying to read there, but he was looking for something.

"All right, then," he said finally. "You can come back and explain that one to me. I've been chewing it over for weeks, and I've got nothing. But it better be good!"

Then Derek glanced over at her, but the cold smile that flickered across his lips didn't touch his eyes.

"You, Blondie, I don't so much want to see, unless you're going to, like, put on a show. You know what I'm talking about?"

She did, and it took every ounce of her self-control not to flip him off. She smiled sweetly instead. "God bless you, too," she told him, feeling like the biggest hypocrite in the history of the world. Oh, well, at least she didn't cuss him out. Not that he didn't deserve it, the creepy loser!

The guard took him away, and it was with a great feeling of relief that Jami reached out to summon the visitor's guard. She couldn't wait to get out of this place and get home; after five minutes in Derek Wallace's presence, she felt like she needed a shower. His arrogant evil was like an aura radiating outward from him, tainting everything around it.

Christopher thanked the guard as he showed them out, and he took Jami's hand as they walked through the parking lot together. Their ride home was long and silent; it wasn't until they were pulling into the driveway that Jami felt like saying anything.

"Christopher?"

"Yeah?"

"Do you really think there's any hope for that guy? I mean, otherwise, what's the point of going back there and talking to him again? He seems like a total waste case."

Her brother turned the truck off, and she sat there next to him in the warm summer darkness, staring up at the star-filled night sky as she waited for him to answer. He made a thoughtful clucking noise with his tongue and shifted in his seat a few times before finally turning to face her. His face gleamed palely in the light shining down from above the garage door.

"Look," he said finally. "David was a murderer, and God used him. The apostle Paul was a murderer, basically, but God still used him in a big way. And don't forget, I'm not necessarily innocent of that sort of thing myself."

Jami grimaced. The golden face, the black blades, the predatory glide. . . . She hadn't forgotten. Although it would be nice if she could.

"The thing is, every time, God sent someone to tell that person to turn away from their evil, and when they finally did, God found a way to use them. Now, maybe God has a way to use Derek somehow, or maybe he doesn't, but all I know is that I'm probably the only one who knows what he's thinking and understands what he's going through right now."

Jami nodded. She certainly didn't, and everyone else she knew thought that the electric chair was far too good for him.

"Do you think he'll believe anything you tell him? I mean, you have to admit, if you hadn't seen it yourself, you wouldn't believe it."

Her brother shrugged. "That was true once. I don't know if it would be now. Once you eliminate the improbable, all that's left is the impossible."

Okay, whatever you say. Jami had about as much interest in philosophy as she did in algebra, so she opened her door and hopped out of the truck. She'd already slammed her door shut and was walking toward the front door when she realized Christopher wasn't behind her. Frowning, she returned to the truck and knocked on his window.

"Hey, aren't you coming in?"

"In a second. I just want to sit here and think for a while."

All right. She walked up to the front of the house and unlocked the door. When she turned back to look at him, she saw he had placed his hands over his eyes, and he was leaning forward on the steering wheel. Her heart swelled with a warm surge of affection for him. That's right, you pray for him, big brother, she cheered him on silently. And I'll pray for you, and Holli'll pray for me, and together we'll survive everything those Fallen jerks throw at us. They may be big and scary, but they're not bigger than our God.

She raised a fist to the night sky. You rule, God! Whatever it is, let your will be done!

CHAPTER 35

A VERDICT IS IN

EVEN NOW MY WITNESS IS IN HEAVEN; MY ADVOCATE IS ON HIGH. MY
INTERCESSOR IS MY FRIEND AS MY EYES POUR OUT TEARS TO GOD; ON
BEHALF OF A MAN HE PLEADS WITH GOD AS A MAN PLEADS FOR HIS
FRIEND.

—Job 16:19–21

Jami sat two rows back from Derek Wallace and his lawyer,
immediately behind Derek's parents and some other people
who looked like they might be his relatives. It was a glorious day
outside, but the mood in the courtroom was dark and angry.
Emotions had been running high all morning, since today
marked the start of the long-awaited trial for what the national
media had labled the Mounds Park Massacre, and the courthouse was surrounded by television journalists, policemen,
demonstrators, and the sort of people who were simply drawn to
the presence of a crowd.

Inside the courtroom the animated chatter of nearly two hundred people echoed loudly off the wooden floors. Some people
were crying, some were arguing, and almost everyone was talking. Most of the people who'd been allowed inside the trial had a
direct connection with the killings; many were members of the
victims' families, and there were a few juniors and seniors Jami
recognized from school. Some of them still bore scars from the
attack, and one boy was in a wheelchair, which, according to the
newspaper reports, he was unlikely ever to leave.

How awful is that? She was thinking not only of the poor crippled guy, but also of Derek Wallace, who, despite his posturing, had to be feeling some guilt today. How could you not? It was his fault, too, that she was here today, as he had specifically asked for Christopher to attend. Her brother had been visiting Derek regularly since their first visit, although he went without her now. He had been there almost every week since, in fact, although he refused to discuss their conversations. So her brother's invitation made sense, but she didn't understand why Derek had asked for Holli to be there as well. Since her sister agreed to go, Jami had to go along, too, to provide moral support. She loved her brother, but despite the many wonderful changes in his life, he still wasn't the consoling type.

Derek, sitting in the defendant's seat, was wearing an expensive blue suit. His hair was cut much shorter than when she'd last seen him at the prison, and he didn't seem to be nervous, although it was hard to see his face from where she was sitting. Two people had already been dragged out of the courtroom by the huge-armed security guards for shouting at him, but Derek hadn't even blinked, and Jami wondered if any of the commotion had even gotten through to him. He didn't look around at all, he simply stared straight ahead at the high, imposing desk where the judge would soon be sitting. Of course, he had a lot to think about. Minnesota didn't have the death penalty, but life in prison would be an eternity for someone who was only eighteen years old.

The jury entered, and several of them glanced curiously at Derek, who ignored them completely. He didn't look up, and Jami had the idea that his mind was off somewhere else altogether. What could he be thinking about? She glanced at Christopher, who was tapping his fingers impatiently on the polished wooden bench. Her brother had been angered earlier by a homemade sign he'd seen a demonstrator carrying on their way into the courthouse, calling for an appallingly medieval form of execution, and he still seemed pretty worked up about it.

"What's wrong?" she whispered, leaning across Holli.

"Nothing, really," he said, shaking his head. "I was just thinking that, when you see those angry faces outside, you can understand why the Lord says vengeance belongs to him."

Holli was listening, too. "They only hate like that because they hurt, Christopher. Because of what he did. Because of what they lost."

"I know, I know," he agreed quietly. "And maybe that's the reason we can't be trusted with revenge, Holli. Those aren't bad people, and normally, they wouldn't act like that. But when we hurt, and our hurt turns into hate, then evil like Kaym can take advantage of us. And then you end up with something like this again. It's like this horrible vicious circle that never ends."

"I don't hate anybody," Holli said, her eyes filling up with tears. "I'd probably even forgive him if he asked me. But it still hurts, it hurts so bad."

"I know," Christopher told her, patting her knee as Jami slipped an arm around her and hugged her tightly. "I know that."

It wasn't long before a man made them all stand up, and then the judge walked into the courtroom. He was a big black man with a squashed nose and a hard, inflexible expression. He didn't seem fazed by all the activity outside the building, not in the least. He banged on his gavel so hard that it made her jump, and informed everyone that he wasn't going to put up with any nonsense, or as he actually put it, "behavior inappropriate to the dignity of the proceedings." Everyone in the courtroom quieted down pretty quickly after that.

No one made a peep when he started reading off the list of charges against Derek in his deep Darth Vader voice. But it was a long list, and it took him a while to get through it. She could feel Holli's body getting tense when he mentioned Paul's name, and she had to grind her teeth pretty hard to keep from crying herself. As the judge continued, there were muffled sobs scattered throughout the crowd, and one woman wailed when Gina Schmidt's name was read. But Derek still just sat there in his seat next to his lawyer, refusing to react to anything.

"Derek Wallace, how do you plead?"

The room was silent, but there was a brief murmur when Derek's lawyer started to stand up and Derek glared angrily at the man. He made a slashing gesture with his hand and whispered something in a harsh tone of voice. The lawyer shook his head, and Jami could see the man wanted to argue, but nevertheless, he stayed in his seat when Derek repeated the gesture again. Then the murmuring grew even louder as Derek rose slowly to his feet, clasped his hands before him, and stared directly at the judge.

"I plead guilty, to every charge, your honor," he said clearly and distinctly. He looked sure of himself, as proud as any fallen angel, and his self-controlled tone of voice made Jami shake her head and wonder if she'd heard him correctly.

The tall boy paused for a moment as the courtroom immediately fell silent. He glanced down at the floor, then looked up and spoke again, more humbly now.

"I know no one will believe me, but I am really very, very sorry for shooting those people. I'm sorry for the people I shot, for those who died, for their families, and those who loved them. I'm sorry for Brien, too. . . . You probably can't believe it, but he was a good person down deep inside. The thing is, we should never have done it. . . . It was just stupid, it was a stupid and pointless waste of everything. Of life. I can see that now, and I just wish I could have seen it before. . . ."

He paused briefly, then took a deep breath and went on:

"But don't think I'm saying this because I'm asking you to take it easy on me, because I'm not. Just sentence me to whatever you think is right, to whatever you think I deserve, and that will be fine with me."

Jami held her breath, completely surprised by his confession. She realized that she'd totally misjudged his intentions. It wasn't arrogance or pride that she'd first heard in his voice, but steely determination. It was strange that he'd decided to plead guilty, though, because his parents were rich and his lawyer was an expensive defense attorney they'd hired to come in and defend him. Pleading guilty just didn't make any sense.

The big-shot defense lawyer raised his hand, but Derek warned him off with another glare.

"I'm not crazy, your honor, and I know exactly what I'm doing. I have nothing more to say, except that, again, I am truly sorry."

He sat down, and Jami shot a questioning look at Christopher, who answered with a raised eyebrow. Holli's eyes were closed, and tears were running down her cheeks, but her lips were moving silently in prayer. Jami shook her head, wondering if what she was starting to suspect could possibly be true. It was impossible, but then again, with God, anything was possible. Anything at all.

Lord Jesus, I don't know what you've done here, but if you can change a heart full of hate and pride like his, then I really believe you can do anything. You really are Lord!

Somehow, in the noisy disturbance of the crowd's reaction to Derek's plea, she missed what the judge was saying, but it wasn't long before he struck his gavel and ended the session. Jami watched intently as Derek rose to his feet. His lawyer, with a furious look on his face, was trying to tell him something, but Derek only shook his head and patted the man reassuringly on the shoulder. Then the policemen came for him and he was escorted out, flanked on either side by muscular, stone-faced officers. But for the first time since Jami had seen him that strange morning at the flagpole, Derek himself looked relaxed, and at peace.

As he walked up the center aisle toward the exit, his eyes met hers for a second, and he nodded in recognition. A faint smile flashed across his thin lips, and then he was gone, impervious to the shouts and jeers now being directed at him from all sides. People were talking loudly all around her, but Jami just sat in her seat, unable to move, biting her lip as the full extent of God's amazing grace became clear to her.

Around Derek's neck, over his tie, she had seen a gold chain supporting a small gold cross marked with engravings that were suspiciously familiar. She glanced over at Christopher, and her suspicions were confirmed when she saw that her brother's own neck was bare. A life in prison was a long time, but it wasn't an eternity, and eternity, in the end, was all that really mattered. God is everywhere, she found herself reflecting, even in a prison cell.

Her brother stood slowly, with one hand still resting on Holli's shoulder, and although his face was somber, she could see the satisfaction in his eyes as he extended his other hand to her. She took it and held it, squeezing it tight. Despite her sorrow for those who had been slain so wrongly, and so unfairly, she suddenly found that she could smile, because somewhere, in a place that was both very near and very far away, angels were singing songs of thanksgiving for a lonely soul that was lost no more.

SELAH